The Professional

The Professional

W. C. Heinz

Foreword by Elmore Leonard

DA CAPO PRESS

HEINZ

Design by Jane Raese
Set in 10.5 point ITC Century Book

Cataloging-in-Publication data for this book is available from the Library of
Congress.

First Da Capo Press edition 2001
Reprinted by arrangement with the author
ISBN 0-306-81058-1

Published by Da Capo Press
A Member of the Perseus Books Group
http://www.dacapopress.com

Da Capo Press books are available at special discounts for bulk purchases in the
U.S. by corporations, institutions, and other organizations. For more information,
please contact the Special Markets Department at the Perseus Books Group,
11 Cambridge Center, Cambridge, MA 02142, or call (617) 252-5298.

1 2 3 4 5 6 7 8 9—05 04 03 02 01

To George Hicks

Also by W.C. Heinz

The Professional (1958)

The Fireside Book of Boxing (1961)
editor

The Surgeon (1963)

Run to Daylight! (1963)
with Vince Lombardi

MASH (1968)
with H. Richard Hornberger, MD

Emergency (1974)

Once They Heard Cheers (1979)

American Mirror (1982)

The Book of Boxing (1999)
coeditor with Nathan Ward

What a Time It Was (2001)

Foreword

Elmore Leonard

The way I remember it, I read *The Professional* when it came out in January 1958, and for the first and only time in my life wrote to the author to tell him how much I liked his book.

I must have taken months to work up the nerve, because the reply from Bill Heinz, which came within a few days, was dated October 11, 1958, my birthday. He wrote:

> You are only the second person, outside my circle of friends and acquaintances, who has felt impelled to comment to me or the publisher about *The Professional*. The first was Ernest Hemingway, who cabled his compliments to Harper's about six days after the book came out. You are a writer, however, and understand, as does, of course, Papa, and that is what gives your letter added importance to me.

In my letter I told Bill that I'd bought the book or got it from the library—I'm not sure now which it was—after reading a review in *Time*. In his letter, Bill said it must have been *Newsweek*, because "*Time* blasted it and me."

But I'm positive it was the *Time* review and still recall it being extremely unkind to both the work and Bill's style.

I got hold of the review again recently to see why it prompted me to read the book. It appeared in the magazine's February 13, 1958, issue and it was brutal: an opinion laden with showoff references—the British critic Cyril Connolly, for God's sake—the reviewer pontificating on his belief that sportswriters should stick to sportswriting and not "tangle with the elusive opponent, literature." It was acceptable, though, to wax literary in writing the review, despairing that "you cannot write novels about boxers with boxing gloves." Read that again. I think he meant wearing the gloves when writing, but who knows? It belongs in that filler *The New Yorker* used to run called "Block That Metaphor."

Reading the review I must have been thinking, The man doesn't get it. He admits the story is a wonderful example of tough prose, but still doesn't get it. He says, "It's about the fight game, see." Which is what reviewers do, end sentences with the word "see" to indicate that anyone can write tough prose. All you do is imagine Cagney, or Edward G. Robinson, talking out the side of his mouth.

Since there was no byline, I asked Bill recently if he knew who wrote the review. He said "No, they used to shoot from the woods in those days."

Perhaps the review irritated me to the point where I had to read the book. I did, I ate it up, and told Bill as well as I could why I liked it.

In his letter in '58 he said,

It pleases me that you observed how I employed dialogue in character development. I have long felt that most writers get between the reader and the characters. Characters, to live, must be permitted to think for themselves, each with his own manner of speech and level of thought. The writer should be kept out of there. He should not tell, but show.

If I was praising his work for the right reasons, I must have been on the right track at an early stage of learning to write fiction, developing a style I might be able to handle. At least I knew the difference between showing and telling, allowing the characters and their voices to carry the story.

But it was Bill Heinz who brought it home in his letters, and showed exactly how to do it in his book.

He said in that first letter, "Also I'm happy that you admired the restraint. The best fighters I have known have all had that—the ability to keep the fight moving at their distance and always directly in front of them, pursuing their aim with a quiet purpose with all kinds of hell breaking loose on all sides from the throats of amateurs."

Perhaps that will always be true, the showy writer, novelist, or critic, getting more attention than the pro.

Shortly after our exchange of those first letters, Bill arrived in Detroit to interview Gordie Howe, then the backbone of the Red Wings, for *The Saturday Evening Post*. Bill came to our home for dinner on a Sunday and missed his ride with Howe to Olympia, where the Wings played their games at that time. Howe lived only a few blocks from us, but I got Bill to his house a few minutes late. The outcome, we drove down to Olympia together, I got to meet the Wings and watch the hockey game from the press box. After he returned home to Connecticut, Bill sent a copy of *The Professional* inscribed to my wife and me: "Two fine people who, one Sunday in Lathrup Village, saved my life."

But the highest point of Bill's visit, for me, was spending a couple of evenings with him, listening to his stories about boxers and ballplayers and talking about writing and Ernest Hemingway.

He told me that he met Hemingway during the war in Germany, when he was covering the Allied advance for the *New York Sun* and Hemingway was sending his dispatches to *Collier's*. Hemingway had taken over a house in the Hurtgen Forest that became a meeting place for the correspondents. Bill presented Hemingway with a bottle of Scotch in appreciation of the man's work. Hemingway was so moved he urged Bill to use his bedroom, rather than sleep on a cot in the attic, for as long as Bill was there—an invitation to a stranger that Bill found touching but that he turned down.

It was Toots Shor, the New York restaurateur, who sent a copy of *The Professional* to Hemingway in Cuba. Hemingway cabled the publisher his reaction to the book. Bill's editor called to relay the quote, and as soon as they'd hung up Bill told his wife, Betty.

Quote: *The Professional* is the only good novel I've ever read about a fighter and an excellent first novel in its own right. Hemingway. Unquote.

"Well," Betty said, "I think we should have a drink."

They sat, late that afternoon, before the fire in the house in Connecticut, sipping their drinks, silent at first, and then she said, "You know, I remember when you were first starting to write your short stories. After working all day you'd come out looking depressed and you'd go over to the bookcase and take something of Hemingway's down and read it. This must be the greatest day in your life."

"If you don't stop," he said, "I'll start to cry."

"A tear," she said, "just dropped in my drink."

Bill wrote and thanked Hemingway, telling him what Betty had said and mentioned the panning he had taken from *Time*. Hemingway wrote back:

> What I cabled was straight, and you believe it. Critics, mostly, don't know much about it. They can't tell the players without a scorecard.

It was Betty who had prompted Bill to write the book he had been thinking about for several years. He had sold a piece on Eddie Arcaro to *Look* magazine for a lot of money and Betty said, "Now you can afford to write your book, so write it."

Nine months later *The Professional* went to Harper, and they grabbed it.

By the time I had turned to the second page of the book, I was aware of Hemingway's influence. It was Bill's use of the word *and*.

"She was sitting there with another woman, and they were in their late thirties and their coats and accessories were obviously new and selected with too much care and not much taste."

The sentence is simple, an observation that shows an attention to details; but notice how the words are put in motion, given almost a feeling of drama, by the repeated use of "and."

Newsweek said in its review that "Heinz writes with spare, Hemingway force." The *Saturday Review*: "A novel as good as *The Professional* is in no way a mere derivative of 'Fifty Grand'. It would have been written exactly as it was, and just as effectively, even if Hemingway's story had never been published."

Forty-three years ago reading *The Professional*, I began to see ways Bill Heinz stripped his prose of unnecessary words. I realized that *said* is the only verb you need to carry dialogue.

"What time is it?" Doc said, as we were finishing.

"One-twenty," I said.

"That's right," Eddie said. "We better get to the studio."

"You know why I'm doing this?" Doc said to me.

"No."

"I'm a kindly old man. I feel sorry for that dame."

"Ethel Morse?"

"Whatever her name is."

The verb *said* nails it, gives it a beat. You don't need answered, replied, suggested, averred, any of those. I learned also that you don't need an adverb to explain *how* the line of dialogue is said. "Adverbs get in the way," I now state authoritatively. They can destroy the rhythm of the sentence, distract, stop the flow of words cold. An adverb modifier is the author's word, not the character's; and if he is to remain invisible, his words must be kept out of the prose.

If there is even one adverb modifying the verb *said* in *The Professional* a copy editor slipped it in when Bill wasn't looking.

You cannot imagine how important it was for me to learn these unwritten rules of writing. I had been writing fiction, Westerns, for only the past seven years. I knew I didn't want to write in the classic style of the omniscient author, I didn't have the voice for it, the language. Studying Hemingway I felt I was getting close to the style I wanted to develop. I began reading *The Professional* and there it was on every page.

In May 1959, I sent Bill a copy of one of my Westerns and told him I was working on another. In his reply he said, "I would like you to work at developing character through conversation— each person talks differently and so defines himself. You must be able to see and hear each character as he talks. You've got to try for a cleaner cleavage between the various manners of speech and of thought development."

The review of *The Professional* in *The New Yorker* said:

This precise, poignant, and absolutely honest book examines, almost day by day, the month of training a middleweight prize-
fighter, Eddie Brown, undergoes at an upstate New York summer
resort before his first crack at the world championship after nine
years in the ring. It ends just after the fight, and the outcome, if
devastating, is not in the least pitiless.

That's what the book is about.

But to me it's so much more. Over the years I've spoken end-
lessly of Hemingway being a major influence, failing to mention
W. C. Heinz as the all-important link, the next step. It has taken
a rereading of *The Professional* for me to see clearly where I
came from.

Thanks, Bill.

Elmore Leonard

1

The subway is elevated there. There is something wrong about that, but there are long sections of the subway in the Bronx where it comes up out of the ground and runs along high above the street like the El. I suppose that some day they will put that under the ground, too, and that will be unfortunate because you can see a lot of New York from there, the way it is now.

I mean that often, as long as three or four days after a rain, you can still see puddles of water glistening on the flat, tarred roofs and reflecting the sky. On a windy day you can see the gray metal ventilators, some of them spinning and the others, with vanes like manes, snapping their heads in the gusts, sensitive and nervous the way you sometimes see a thoroughbred going to the post and trying to ease the bit with the boy standing on him and first hoping to soothe him and then swearing at him, if you could just hear it.

You can see the flower pots, too, on the fire escapes. Most of them have geraniums in them, but sometimes you will even see a rosebush, and always, a long time after they shouldn't be there any longer, you'll see the long, yellow leaves of Easter lilies, and the pink foil still around the pots.

1

"So why don't you tell him?" a woman was saying.

There was an empty seat between us, and I was turned toward her so that I could look out of the window. She was sitting with another woman, and they were in their late thirties and their coats and their accessories were too obviously new and selected with too much care and not enough taste. I wanted to bet someone that they were going shopping and then to a movie.

"Tell him?" the other woman said. "Tell him what?"

When I got off at the station and carried my bag down the long flight of steps there was a cab parked under the structure and just back from the corner. The driver was reading a tabloid, folded and resting on the wheel in front of him. I opened the back door and lifted my bag in and got in and shut the door.

The driver was reading the *Daily Mirror*. He had it folded to that column called "Only Human" and written by a fellow named Sidney Fields, and I had time to see that at the top of the column there was a two-column cut of a cabbie, his elbow sticking out of the window of his cab and the cabbie smiling out over his elbow.

"Where to?" the driver said finally, putting the paper down on the seat beside him.

When I told him he started the motor and then he flipped the flag and shoved the shift in and made the right turn at the corner almost in one motion. I had to put my left hand out flat on the seat, but my bag fell over on the floor.

"Sorry," the driver said.

"That's all right," I said.

"Guy's got a story on a hackie in the *Mirror*," he said.

"Oh?"

"He wants a story on hacking, I'll give him one. I mean, I could give him plenty of stories."

"I'll bet," I said.

It was a broad, black avenue. It was just 9:30 of a gray morning, with the signs of early spring in the dampness of the litter in the gutters and in the mud tracked onto the oil-stained concrete aprons of the filling stations and of the garages where they do welding and auto-body repair. After a block or two the garages and the used-car lots gave way to old clapboard houses, all of them built high and square with porches on the front, here and there a porch enclosed with small panes of glass.

About a mile up the avenue we turned right and then made a left and another right. We started down a street of narrow duplex brick houses, each two houses pushed together and looking like one, except for the two concrete walks leading up to the separate entrances.

"You know the house?" the driver said.

"No, I don't."

The street itself was potholed, where the blacktop had given way, and now the holes held muddy water. Taking it slowly, the driver tried to skirt the holes, and then he settled for playing them as best he could.

"Got to be in the next block," he said, "but these are good houses. They put them up about thirty years ago. They built good in them days. A guy owns one of these has got something, a nice home for himself and his family."

The houses were not of really good brick, and some time ago the lime had weathered out of the mortar and left white stains. Between each pair of houses there was just room enough for a driveway, and in front of each house there was a small plot, about ten feet square. The plots afforded the only evidences of individuality. Some of them had low hedges around them and some were just grassed over with a shrub or two against the house. One of them had been concreted, so that it was of one piece with the sidewalk and the entrance walk and the driveway, except that the plot area had been painted light green.

"A guy's doing all right, lives in one of these houses," the driver said.

"But he should never come home with a load on," I said. "He'd never find his own house."

"You think you're kiddin'?" the driver said. "One night I picked up a drunk at the subway lived on one of these blocks. He says he can't think of his number, but he knows the house. It's about three o'clock in the morning, and he tells me to stop at one of these places and he's got no dough. He says his old lady will pay me. He goes up the steps and starts ringing the doorbell. A dame comes to the door and slams it in his face. Then he gets real mad. He starts kickin' on the door. I get out and try to pull him off, and he rips two buttons off my shirt. Then the cops come. It ain't the guy's house. They find out he lives in the next block.

"So they take him down there and I tail them. Well, finally his old lady has to pay my meter. The cop says it's legal, but she looks at me like I'm the guy got her husband drunk, and she stiffs me for a tip."

"That's what I mean," I said.

"That's what *I* mean," the driver said. He had pulled over to the curb and he stopped the cab. "People always talking about how hackies roll drunks. This is your place, the left side."

"Keep the change," I said.

"Thanks," he said, "but if a guy wants to write a real article about a hackie in the paper, let him come see me."

Well, I thought, he certainly worked me for the big tip, if that was what he was doing. Do you suppose he did roll the souse and then wait it out through all that rumpus and the cops for the fare? That would take a real brigand, but then he wouldn't be a talker.

"Yes?"

"Oh," I said. "Mrs. Brown?"

After I had pushed the doorbell I had been thinking again about that cabbie, and now she was standing here with the door half open. She had one of those round, even, pretty faces and big brown eyes with the white very white around them and dark brown hair drawn back and held by I couldn't tell what.

"Yes?"

"I'm Frank Hughes," I said. "Eddie said I could meet him here about 9:30."

She was in her late twenties. She had on a white-and-red-flowered quilted housecoat and red mules, and her fingernails were painted the same red.

"Oh," she said. "I think he mentioned something about it."

She said this, pushing the door back and motioning me in. There was a small, gray-carpeted hall with carpeted stairs running up and the rest of the hall leading back to a kitchen. Off to the left was a rather small, square living room, carpeted the same as the hall and, after I had put my bag down, she led me in there.

"You might as well sit down," she said. "Eddie just got up."

"I'm sorry I'm early."

"It doesn't make any difference."

She had her hair pulled back in one of those pony tails, and it was held by a small ribbon of the same red as the housecoat and the mules. She took a cigarette out of one of the pockets of the housecoat and had a lighter out of the other before I could get mine out. Then she sat down on the sofa and pulled the housecoat around her, and I sat down in a chair opposite.

"You're the one who's going to write the magazine article about Eddie."

Her face never moved. I knew it had to open for her to say this, but it never moved and she didn't look either at me or through me. It seemed as if she didn't look quite as far as me, as if she were looking at a pane of glass between us.

"Yes. I'm the one."

"What kind of an article are you going to write?"

"Oh, I never know. It'll be a nice one."

"Let's hope."

"If it's about Eddie it will have to be a nice one. He's a nice guy."

"Said he, before he pulled the trigger."

"I'm not a trigger man."

"Let's hope."

What a placid face for all of that, I thought. Now it was turning slowly about the room. The room looked quite new, with the gray carpeting and the modern furniture and the precise folds of the drapes and with the woodwork and ceiling a flat, clean white.

"You have a nice home here. It's very pleasant."

"I do the best I can."

"Look," I said, "if it'll put your mind at ease, all I'm going to do is spend a month in camp with Eddie and write a piece about how a fighter comes up to and goes into a championship fight."

"Oh?"

"I mean, I'm just going to watch Eddie and the people around him and see what he does and listen to what he says. I want to write a piece that will give the reader an understanding, or anyway a feeling, of what a fighter goes through."

"Do you think anybody cares about that?"

"All I know is that there's a magazine editor who cares. It was his idea, not mine, although I like it."

"Hello," Eddie said.

I had heard him coming down the stairs. He had on light gray flannel slacks and tan loafers and a light woolen maroon sports shirt, buttoned at the neck. He always had good taste in clothes, and he always fitted into them perfectly. I put it that way because Eddie had a good neck and shoulders and chest and a narrow waist and small hips. Without knowing him you would know that he was an athlete, and only the slight heaviness of his brows and one small scar across the bridge of his nose gave him away as a fighter. His light brown hair was cropped in a crew cut and he had light blue eyes, and when he smiled he seemed to mean it.

"I see you and Helen met," he said, after we had shaken hands.

"Yes," I said.

"I'm sorry I'm late."

"It's all right with me."

"But I told you I'd be ready at 9:30."

"Look, I'm not going to get into a fight with you about it. You might be able to lick me."

"How about some breakfast with me?"

"No, thanks. I've eaten."

"Have a cup of coffee while I'm eating. Helen will make coffee."

"It's made," she said.

There was a small breakfast nook with a window at the end of the table and you could see a garage and a small back yard enclosed with galvanized wire fencing. There was a sandbox and a swing-and-slide combination in the yard, and a small boy was playing in the yard. He had on blue jeans and red rubber boots and a brown hooded jacket, and he was standing by the fence, trying to push a stick through one of the openings between the wires. He appeared to be about five years old.

"I judge that's Eddie, Jr.?"

"That's him," Eddie said.

"And no trouble at all?"

"Yeah," Eddie said, looking up from his cereal with a sliced banana on the top. "This morning he woke me at seven-thirty."

"He woke me at seven," his wife said.

She was standing by the gas range. She had a flame under the coffeepot and was boiling a couple of eggs over another.

"So I chased him out," Eddie said. "At eight o'clock he was back. I chased him again. When he came back I hollered to Helen. I said: 'Get him out of here. I want to sleep.'"

"You slept plenty," Helen said.

"I wanted to sleep some more."

"You slept enough."

Eddie let it pass then, but I thought about it. The big thing he has to sell, I thought, is his body. It is one of the wonders of the world, this body of a good fighter. Think of the things it must do when the mind orders it, and because it can do these things it bought this house and the furnishings in it and the clothes you all wear and the food you eat. A month from now this man is going in there with that body against another man. There will be much written and read about this, and there will be many thousands of dollars involved. Throughout this country people will watch it in their homes and in bars, and after it is over they will read about it and, if it is a good fight, think about it and talk about it. All of this, I thought, depends upon this body, so if he wants to pamper it now, let him pamper it.

"You take sugar and cream?" Eddie said.

I couldn't buy that Helen.

2

We drove over to the Bronx River Parkway and then north on that, the sun starting to come brassy through the gray and the day getting a little warmer. Eddie had a Chevrolet convertible, dark green and two years old, and he drove it as if it were his living.

"You ever had an accident?" I said.

"What's the matter?" he said, laughing at it. "I make you nervous?"

"Just the opposite. I drive so much myself that I can't sit still with most people, but I've never known a good athlete who wasn't a good driver."

"I guess some of them have accidents."

"Sure. Art Houtteman, the Cleveland pitcher, was almost killed in a crash down in Florida when he was with Detroit. First they didn't think he'd live and then they didn't think he'd pitch again, but I rode with him after that through heavy traffic in Detroit and I relaxed. Maybe it's in my mind, but good athletes have such great reflexes that I believe in them."

"I had one small brush a couple of years ago," Eddie said. "One Sunday another guy and I scraped fenders. I had Helen and the kid with me, out for a little ride, and the guy wanted to make a big thing of it."

"What happened?"

"Well, he wanted to swing on me. He was kind of a big guy, but in no shape."

"That's a laugh. What did you do?"

"I conned him out of it."

"Did he find out who you are?"

"When I gave him my license. He looked at it and he looked at me and he said: 'What business you in?' I said: 'Boxing,' and he said: 'Are you Eddie Brown, the fighter?' I said: 'That's right.'"

"Then what?"

"He cooled out."

"I'd still like to see a fighter handle one of those SOBs someday."

"You never will."

"Probably not. The law says a fighter's fists are lethal weapons."

"Besides, what are you going to prove?"

"Nothing. The rest of us have to prove our manliness, or something, by standing up to some guy. A fighter never has that urge because he gets rid of it in his work. That's why I say that, when everything else is equal, fighters are the best adjusted males in the world."

"I don't know. You mention that ballplayer. I wish I coulda been a ballplayer."

"You win this, and you're middleweight champion of the world."

"Where I came from, on the West Side, you couldn't play much ball. We played stickball on the street, but what's that? I envy those ballplayers."

"And Ted Williams looks up to fighters."

"I don't know," he said.

Eddie drove from the Bronx River Parkway into the Taconic State. Then he cut over toward the Bear Mountain Bridge and we went up that narrow, winding blacktop road, first climbing among the trees and then coming out on those turns where they have the low, thick stone walls across the roadway on your left with the rock rising straight up on your right and the view of the Hudson all down there beyond and below the walls.

"This is something, isn't it?" Eddie said.

The sun had been eating at the haze, and you could see perhaps three or four miles. Down the river, where it widens, a small freighter was moving slowly toward New York, and up the river, where it narrows and turns, you could see, beyond the gray, looping span of the bridge, the hills, so green and so tumbled and so intimate with the river.

"It's a great view," I said.

"I always like it," Eddie said.

"If it were somewhere in Europe, Americans would come back raving about it. I'm not running for President on the See America First ticket, but here we take it for granted, and no one ever mentions it."

"That's right."

"I think that if they passed a law that all the inhabitants of the Highlands of the Hudson must speak only some foreign language—say German or Dutch—and dress only in native costumes, this view would become number one on the postcard parade."

"You ever in Germany?"

"Only during the war, but when the bridge across the Rhine at Remagen was captured and we finally got a look at the river around there I said to myself: 'This is the Highlands of the Hudson, between Bear Mountain and West Point, and, because it's here, the writers and the poets have been singing about it for centuries.'"

"I often wished I was in the war, especially when some of the older guys on my block got in, but I was only seventeen when it ended."

"I've realized that."

"My old man came from Germany."

"Then your name isn't Brown?"

"No. Doc changed it."

Doc Carroll was his manager.

"What was your name?"

"Braun. B-r-a-u-n. The same as that basketball player."

"Why did Doc change it?"

"When I first turned pro, it was right after the war. When Doc took me over he said he remembered how it was with the Germans here in the First World War, so he changed it."

"What did your old man say?"

"He was dead then almost four years."

"What did he do for a living?"

"He was a plasterer."

"That's a tough racket."

"I know. My old man wasn't well, and I used to try to help him, Saturdays and sometimes Sundays and during vacation, when I was about fourteen and fifteen. You stand up on a scaffold and you plaster a ceiling all day long, and gotta be strong. It's all holding that stuff over your head and my old man had terrific shoulders and arms, but he had hardening of the arteries. He used to get dizzy."

"That can be bad enough in itself."

"He'd get so dizzy he'd have to grab out for the wall to keep from falling. Then he'd sit down and hold his head in his hands. I'd say: 'Look, Pop, let me do it. I can do a ceiling coat.' He used to let me do the rough coat on the walls, but he'd shake his head and get up and steady himself and say: 'More schtuff.' That's what he called it—'schtuff.' Once I had to catch him, he was falling, and he sat down and put his head in his hands and I had to turn away. I was crying. I mean, I was fourteen or fifteen and I was crying like a baby, and I didn't want him to see me crying."

"He must have been a man of great courage, Eddie."

"I hear some guys say some fighter's got guts. Sometimes after a fight I read in the papers that some fighter has a lot of guts. Sometimes they've even written that about me."

"They should."

"I'm not knocking the newspapermen. I appreciate it."

"I know you do."

"But no one seems to understand, and it makes me—I don't know—kinda sad. You know what I mean? What does a fighter do that's so great? It's your business. You don't even think of those punches. You don't even feel them."

I know, I know, I was thinking, but please don't say it. You are balancing the equation between fear and courage, telling me that you don't know the one, and so don't need the other. As I try to climb up to you, I find always that it is to me instead that you are climbing down.

"What does a fighter do, like my old man?" he said. "My old man, nobody ever told him he had guts. Nobody ever paid any attention to him, and he was standing up there every day, fighting that dizziness, and all the time he was dying."

He stopped talking, but I said nothing. I could think of nothing to say.

"When I think of my old man, I think of his temper, too. He used to holler sometimes so bad at my mother that she used to cry. He used to holler at me and belt me, when I was a kid. Sometimes, after he'd blow his top, nobody'd talk around our house for a couple of days. I probably shouldn't say it now, but a lot of the time I used to hate him. We never really got along. Now I'm ashamed to say it."

"You shouldn't be. It's all very understandable."

"They write about guts," he said. "My old man had the guts."

After we crossed the bridge we came to that traffic circle where the road to the right leads north to West Point and the road straight ahead leads west through the state park. I was thinking of the time, a few years ago, when Fordham had a good football team and they were playing Army at Michie Stadium.

The Army announced that anyone driving to the game who hoped to see the kickoff should plan to reach the traffic circle no later than 1:15. All the New York sports pages ran the announcement in a box or in their stories before the game, and consequently everyone tried to reach the circle at just 1:15. They were backed up for miles, and it took the cops a couple of hours to clear the jam.

"Sometimes I think I'd like to live up here somewhere," Eddie said. "I think about it quite a bit."

"You have a nice home," I said, "and what would you do up here?"

"I don't know. I'd like it, but Helen wouldn't want to leave New York. She likes New York."

"Where does she come from?"

"My old neighborhood. We knew each other as kids. Her old man still runs a bar over there."

"How long have you been married?"

"Oh, seven years."

"Having been in your home, I'd say she does a good job of it."

"I'm not complaining. I've got it so much better than so many guys, but it's tough on her."

"It must be. What does she do while you're away, like this, for a month?"

"Her mother comes and stays at our place for a few days at a time. She takes care of the kid, and that gives Helen a chance to get out. She sees some of her old girl friends, and I guess they go to a show or go out shopping or go out for a meal. It's a break that she can get away from the kid."

"All kids are problems."

"Our kid is a problem, because we're not supposed to let him get too excited. He's a smart little kid and he's got a temper, too, but we're not supposed to hit him or even discipline him too much."

"Who says so?"

"The doctor."

"Oh? Has he had some trouble?"

"He has epilepsy."

"I'm sorry. I'm very sorry."

"About a year ago, we found it out. I came home from the gym one afternoon and Helen was crying. The kid had had kind of a tantrum, or something, and then he passed out right on the kitchen floor. Helen called the doctor and he came and gave the kid something. Then they made some tests and he said the kid has epilepsy, so we've got to go very easy with him."

"I'm sure he'll be all right," I said, trying to think of how to say it. "You can live a pretty normal life with that."

"That's what the doctor said."

"Do you remember Tony Lazzeri, the old Yankee second base-man?"

"Sure. The Italians in my neighborhood were all crazy about him. Poosh-em up, Tony!"

"He was an epileptic."

"He was?"

"Sure."

"He really was?"

"Certainly. I don't think many people knew it, but when Paul Krichell, the Yankee scout, was scouting Lazzeri out west he called Ed Barrow, the general manager of the Yankees, one night. I think Lazzeri was Cubs' property, and they wanted $50,000 for him. Krichell told Barrow on the phone what a terrific ballplayer Lazzeri was, and Barrow said: 'What else?' Krichell said: 'Well, he's got epilepsy.' Barrow screamed: 'What? You want me to pay $50,000 for an epileptic?' And Krichell said: 'He's an epileptic, but he never throws fits between one and four o'clock in the afternoon, and that's when you play ball.' So they bought him."

"He was a great ballplayer."

"Sure, and he never had an attack during a game. Once he had one down in Florida during spring training, and I think he might have had one in the clubhouse at Yankee Stadium once, but that's all. He played great ball for years."

"And the people never knew there was anything wrong with him."

"Of course not."

"Is he still alive?"

"No, he died a few years ago."

"That's right. I think I remember now."

I can never figure out how the mind works. I was thinking of Lazzeri and the stories in the papers at the time, telling how they found him in his house on the West Coast, dead at the foot of the stairs. Then, I don't know why, I got to thinking back to that traffic circle, and that Army-Fordham game.

Eddie was not saying anything now, and I was seeing that mist falling on that raw November day and hearing the noise that hung over the stadium from the start to the end and the players in the middle of it. Fordham was undefeated and Army was, too, and had maybe the best team in the country. They were both so high for this, and with the crowd never letting up, that at first they couldn't do anything but rock one another, and then, finally, Army broke it up with passes at the end of the first half. Army went on to win it, 35 to 0, but the second half was the roughest football you ever saw because one Army player came off the field with the lower half of his face all blood and another staggered to the bench like a fighter at the end of a bad round and some from both sides were thrown off for fighting and there were Fordhams mud-caked and lying on their backs with the wind knocked out of them.

After the game there were colonels walking around behind the press box trying to get somebody's ear and complaining about Fordham, and there were old Fordhams cussing the Army, and finally we all went down to the Bear Mountain Inn and we stood around that bar there in that pine-paneled room and we had a wonderful time.

"After that first half, Fordham couldn't have won except by a knockout," somebody, maybe Tom Meany, said.

"If Tim Cohane made this match, he's the new Mike Jacobs," I said.

"If you didn't see the first Dempsey-Firpo fight it's all right, because you just saw the second one," perhaps Tom said.

"They should have swapped the electric clock operator for a knockdown timekeeper," Jimmy Cannon said. "How about that?"

"I don't care for outdoor fights this late in the season," Wilbur Wood said, and that stopped it.

Then we went into the dining room and had another round of drinks and ate some of Jack Martin's steaks and told stories and finally we broke up and went out and got our cars and drove back through the mist to New York. The next day I was probably depressed again, writing the column for Monday and trying to place myself in the middle of what had happened down there on the field. It is always that way. It was that way in the war. Only the ones who did what they did could understand it, and the rest of us who wrote about it never really belonged.

"So Tony Lazzeri had that, too," Eddie said.

"Yes," I said. "He did."

3

Eddie felt better as soon as we got to camp. The camp is on the west shore of the lake, where you miss the sunsets, but the railroad did that when it took the east shore. There are a few summer cottages on the east shore, in the places where the railroad is back a hundred yards or so, but they always have those two trains a day shoo-wooing and sooting at them, and it spoils it for them.

Even without the sunsets, though, it is quite nice where the camp is. The lake is three miles long and about a mile across at its widest, and there is a lot of pine and hemlock in the hills. The hills appear to roll right down to the lake, so that from a distance you are quite unaware that the railroad runs along one side or that a narrow blacktop road winds between the hills and the lake on the other.

Because of the railroad, almost all of the building has taken place on the west shore, and you can trace the eras in the architecture. First, around the turn of the century, there were only the two small summer hotels, the one at the foot of the lake and the other halfway up this west shore, steep-roofed, clapboarded, gingerbreaded and the progenitors of the line. Their issue, after the First World War, were the summer homes, heavy-set on a wooded acre or two, fieldstoned and brown-stained shingled with large open porches facing the lake and screened sleeping porches above them. After the Second World War the summer homes spawned the cottages and camps spotted among the trees and between the summer homes, some cement-blocked and square, some synthetic log cabins, some prefabricated Cape Cods with rose arbors and pottery gnomes. About ten years ago the fighters started using the hotel halfway up the lake, and now during the autumn and winter and spring they share it with the bar trade and occasional diners, and in July and August, when boxing slows down, it becomes again a summer hotel.

"Well, it looks the same," Eddie said as he drove down the incline of the driveway and turned to the right to put the car in the empty parking space by the lake. "I really like it here."

"Yes, it's fine," I said, but I was thinking that you had better like it here because you are going to have it for a whole solid month.

"We can take our stuff in later," he said.

The hotel is painted white now, with the windows and door trim and those gingerbread cornices painted red. I suppose this is excusable, because the owner's name is Jean Girot and he is from Lausanne and calls the place Chalet Swiss. He wanted to call it Chalet Suisse, but his wife, being Irish, wouldn't stand for that, so it says Chalet Swiss on the neon sign at the head of the driveway and on the small, red rectangular sign with white letters that hangs by a chain over the two steps leading up to the porch.

"Hey! What's going on around here, my bon ami?" Eddie said.

He pronounced it the way you pronounce the household cleanser, because it was a pleasantry he and Girot had between them. The last time I had been out to the camp Eddie had been there and Girot had been trying to get him to pronounce it correctly, and then, finally, he had shrugged his shoulders and quit on it.

"Hello, Eddie," Girot said. "And Mr. Hughes."

It is a small square lobby with speckled linoleum on the floor and three plastic-covered occasional chairs, a blond coffee table and an artificial palm tree. At the back there is the small hotel desk, with the key rack behind it, and against the wall on the left, near the door to the bar and dining room, are two phone booths. When we came in, Girot, wearing his butcher's apron, was leaning against one of the booths and watching a telephone repairman, who was on his knees by the open door of the other booth, putting some tools into his metal tool box.

"So what's new, bon ami?" Eddie said.

"He's fixing the phone," Girot said, nodding at the repairman.

"It's fixed," the repairman said, looking up, "but I'm telling you, Girot, the next time it happens, out it goes."

"What's the matter with it?" Eddie said.

"I'll tell you what's the matter with it," the telephone man said, looking up at Eddie. "Some wise guy's been trying to rig it again, banging on it."

He got up and turned to Girot.

"I'm not kidding. I'm telling the office. This is the third time. These things ain't made to be banged around. Out it comes."

"It's the last time," Girot said, nodding.

"Who did it?" Eddie said, when the telephone man had gone out and shut the door behind him.

"You know," Girot said, shaking his head. He is short and thin and in his late fifties and, since he stopped drinking, he always seems to me to be in perpetual mourning.

"I know?" Eddie said. "Who?"

"Your friend," Girot said. "Al Penna."

"*My* friend?" Eddie said, smiling. "He's not *my* friend."

"That's a fighter?" Girot said, shaking his head again. "He found some way, the last time he was here, to hit the box of the phone with something—I don't know what it was—and it makes a sound like a quarter is dropped in. I heard him telling some of the other fighters one time, and I told him to stop it."

"He's crazy," Eddie said, smiling.

"What kind of a fighter can he be?" Girot said, sadly. "All the time he is fooling around. Always he is kidding. How can that be a fighter?"

At least when Girot drank he was a champ in his own league. For a little man he was astounding, and then nothing, not even fighters like Al Penna, bothered him. I was thinking how some doctor must have scared the life out of him and how it was too bad. Now he is just sad.

"So you got the bridal suite for me?" Eddie was saying.

"For a nice fellow like you, anything I have," Girot said. "I mean that, Eddie."

"Thanks."

"And you, too, Mr. Hughes."

"Thank you, Girot."

"Who's up here?" Eddie said. "I mean, besides Penna."

"That heavyweight from Buffalo who eats all the time. That Paul Schaeffer. All he does is eat."

"He's building up his strength," I said, smiling, because for some strange reason there is something amusing about the excessively doleful people like Girot. I often have the urge to egg them on.

"Yes, strength," Girot said. "Soon he will be so strong that when he gets knocked out it will take a team of horses to pull him back to his corner."

"Who else is here?" Eddie said.

"Strength," Girot said, still thinking about it and shaking his head.

"Is Cardone here?"

"Yes, he is here."

"That's right. He fights the week before I do."

"And Booker Boyd. That is all."

"Let's go out to the gym," Eddie said to me.

"You do not want to bring your things in now?" Girot said.

"We'll bring them in later."

"You have the corner room over there, on the lake," Girot said, pointing up. "And you are across the hall, Mr. Hughes."

"Thank you."

"When Johnny Jay comes, he will use the other bed in your room, Eddie. Is that right?"

"Yes."

Johnny Jay was Eddie's trainer. That was his title, but actually Doc Carroll trained Eddie as well as managed him, and Johnny Jay was just the conditioner and rubber and the pail man in the corner.

"That Girot isn't a bad guy," Eddie said, when we walked into the sitting room. "I like him."

"He has his troubles," I said.

At the back of the sitting room a stairway leads to the second floor. There was an old tan, rattan summer rug on the floor, and a mahogany console television set stood looking out from the far corner opposite the stairs. Most of the furniture in the room—an old maroon plush sofa and two or three overstuffed chairs with soiled slip covers on them and a couple of wooden folding chairs—was grouped in a sort of semicircle, facing the television. With the room deserted, I had the impression that the sofa and chairs had finally cornered the TV set and were about to spring upon it and crush it in repayment for all the indignities it had visited upon them in a long, long chain of nights past.

The gym is beyond the sitting room. It was added to the original hotel about thirty years ago as a flat-roofed dance hall, and it is still a dance hall on Saturday nights during the summer. During the other seasons, however, it makes a quite excellent gym, even with the bar there and the tired and dusty but red, white and blue paper streamers still looped from the ceiling.

As you come through the door, the bar is on the left, stripped now of bottles and glassware but used by the trainers to fill their water bottles. The ring sets toward the back of the room, with three rows of folding chairs in front of it, and there is a punching bag platform between two of the windows on the left and a heavy bag is chained about ten feet from that. In the far left corner two plywood partitions have been bolted to the ceiling and the floor to make a dressing room about fifteen feet long by about ten feet wide.

"From Brooklyn, New York!" Eddie said, raising his voice as he walked past the rows of chairs to the ring. "Al Penna!"

Penna was in the ring with Booker Boyd. They were moving around during a break between rounds, just circulating and shadowboxing, and when Penna heard Eddie he stopped and turned around and smiled, and with the thumb of his right glove he hooked his white rubber mouthpiece out.

"Thankew! Thankew!" he said, raising his two gloves above his head in the prize fighter's salute. "How are you, Eddie?"

"Time!" someone said, calling it.

It was Barnum, standing on the ring apron. Barnum was an old Negro. I don't know how old he was or his straight name, because everyone just called him Barnum, but he had been around forever. I know he was around Joe Gans, because in any argument about fighters and fighting he would go back to Gans. Gans was his big saver, the way Gans did this or did that or what Gans said, but no one resented it in the arguments, the way you get to resent old-timers, because he didn't play it like a record, over and over, and because he knew as much about pure boxing as any man alive. He really did, and for years he had been bringing colored kids up out of the amateurs and then losing them. I could name a half-dozen good fighters he made, in the sense that he was the one who put the best that they had into them, but someone was always moving him out. Someone would always get to the kid, and the kid would listen to the white salesman and look at the white salesman's clothes and then look at old Barnum and be gone. They would pay Barnum a thousand dollars maybe, and some of those kids made money after that, but they were never what they should have been because after they left Barnum they never got much better, and I often wondered how good they might have been.

I used to get sore about this, and one night I watched one of those kids go for the featherweight title and get a good clobbering. Walking out of the Garden I saw Barnum standing in the crowd in the lobby, standing against the wall and wearing the dark blue beret that some of those old Negroes affected after Jack Johnson.

"It's too bad, Barnum," I said.

He just shook his head and I walked away and then, the first thing I knew, he had another one. Now he had Booker Boyd.

Booker Boyd was a light welterweight and one of those dead-pan Negroes, more like Ike Williams than Joe Louis. Joe was dead-pan, all right, especially in the ring, but outside the ring you could see, every once in a while, a quick, small smile playing behind it. With Ike Williams you could see nothing, and Booker Boyd was just like him.

Boyd was stalking Penna now, always walking forward, feinting, jetting out that left, that face never changing, trying to corner Penna. Penna was moving, awkward, too tall and gangling for a lightweight, too loose and without purpose, except to protect himself and punch when he saw the chance. They both had up good sweats and Penna's had spotted through his T-shirt and Boyd's had soaked his tight against that mahogany torso, and we watched them for a couple of minutes, Boyd stalking and Penna skating and then stopping to try to punch Boyd off and then skating again.

"I might as well bring my foot locker in," Eddie said.

"I'll give you a hand," I said.

We walked out to the car and Eddie opened the trunk compartment. He hauled the heavy black foot locker out and put it down on the gravel and reached in and put his hand on the handle of my suitcase.

"We can take our bags in now, or we can get them later."

"Why don't we get rid of the foot locker first?" I said.

"All right."

"What ever made that Al Penna want to be a fighter?"

"I don't know."

"He looks more like a basketball player."

"He's a little better fighter than he looks."

"But he's got no chance."

"I know."

He slammed the trunk compartment shut and turned the handle. We picked up the foot locker, he at one end and I holding the strap handle at the other, and we walked it that way across the driveway and jockeyed with the door and walked it through and across the gym and into that dressing room.

Vic Cardone was in there alone, and he was just finishing dressing. He was a good-looking kid, handsome, dark-eyed and dark-haired and almost classic features, and the first time I saw him fight I knew that was going to be his trouble.

"Hello, Vic," Eddie said.

"Hello," Cardone said, looking at us.

"You know Frank Hughes."

"I've seen him," he said, nodding to me, and then he picked a towel up off one of the benches and put it around his neck and went out.

"Some talker," I said.

"He never says much," Eddie said, looking out of the window at the lake. "Penna calls him Silent. He used to call him Tyrone Cardone, but now he calls him Silent Cardone."

"His face is his problem."

"You're not kidding. You ever notice how he's always pulling his head away from in close?"

"I know. He should make up his mind whether he wants to be a fighter or look like a movie actor."

"I suppose."

There is space enough in that dressing room for the rubbing table and a couple of benches and a couple of those folding wooden chairs. There are hooks on the partitions for clothes and equipment, and there is a door leading into the men's room. This dressing room was improvised after the men's room, of course, so over that door there is one of those rectangular frosted-glass lights with the silhouette on it of a man in top hat and tails and looking like he might be a brother of that Johnnie Walker in the whiskey ads. When this became a fight camp, and that dressing room went up, the men's room was enlarged just enough to hold a shower.

"Hey there!" somebody said, and it was Polo. His right name was Tony Poli, but everyone called him Polo and he was a helpless, little sallow-skinned mouse of a man who managed Paul Schaeffer. I had seen the two of them, Schaeffer punching the big bag and Polo watching, when we first came into the gym and when we carried the foot locker through, and now he was holding the door open for big Schaeffer, who came through, red-faced and too fleshy and sweating inside a white terrycloth robe.

"Hey, Polo, Paul," Eddie said. "You know Frank Hughes?"

"I know Polo," I said, shaking hands with him, "but I've never met Paul."

"Hello," Schaeffer said, giving me that big paw with the bandages and tape still on, and then sitting down on one of the chairs, sweating and spreading his legs. "I'm tired."

"That's what I tell you," Polo said, working with the scissors to cut the tape on Schaeffer's right hand to unwind the dirty gym bandages. "You stay in shape, you don't get so tired."

Schaeffer looked up at Eddie, his face red and wet from the exertion, and winked.

"He thinks I'm kidding," Polo said, turning and protesting to me, as if I were the one who was going to solve it for him.

"When you fighting?" Eddie said.

"A couple of weeks," Schaeffer said.

"He's fighting that Irish Jimmy Locke, in Holyoke," Polo said.

"Are you a manager, or something?" Schaeffer said, looking up puzzled at me.

"No," I said, smiling. "I'm a magazine writer."

"Oh," he said and then, after a pause: "That's a good job, ain't it?"

"At times."

"What you gonna write about up here?"

"Eddie."

"Yeah?" he said, and then he looked at Eddie. "That's good."

"You're going to write a magazine article about Eddie?" Polo said.

"That's right."

"What are you gonna write?" Schaeffer said.

"I don't know. I just got here, Paul."

"How would he know what he's gonna write?" Polo said to Schaeffer. "How would he know that when he just come up here? Why don't you get undressed and take your shower?"

"Just let me sit a while, will you, Polo?" Schaeffer said.

What a pair, I thought.

4

The fighters and their handlers eat together at one long table. It is just inside the doorway from the bar and also close to the kitchen. There are about a dozen smaller tables spaced around the room, several of them under the windows that look onto the lake. In each of the two far corners of the room there is another of those artificial palm trees, light-faded and dust grayed, standing in a dirt-filled dark wooden cask.

"The steak is good, Eddie?" Katie said.

Katie is Girot's wife. She is a red-faced, gray-haired, smiling woman who is about the same height as Girot but about twice his size. She does the cooking and, with a couple of women who live on the hill across the road from the hotel, just about everything else in the place. Girot does the ordering and keeps the books and tends bar.

"It's good," Schaeffer said. "I could eat another one."

"You could eat anything," Penna said. "Besides, who's asking you?"

"I don't know," Schaeffer said, eating.

"It's a good steak, Katie," Eddie said, smiling at her. "Very good."

"For the new champion, Eddie," Katie said, and smiled on him again and went back to the kitchen.

Eddie was sitting at the head of the table and Penna was sitting at his left and I was at his right. Next sat Schaeffer and Polo, opposite each other, and then Booker Boyd and Cardone, with Barnum between them, at the other end.

"Boy, what a steak we had in Providence that afternoon, hey, Polo?" Schaeffer said.

"Who'd you ever fight in Providence?" Penna said.

"I don't know," Schaeffer said, and he looked at Polo. "Who'd I fight?"

"Ain't that something?" Polo said, putting his knife and fork down and talking to me. "He don't remember the guy he fought, but he remembers the steak he ate."

"Well, it was a good steak," Schaeffer said.

"Whatta you want, Tyrone?" Penna said.

"Throw me some toast, will you?" Cardone said.

"Hey!" Penna said, tossing the slice of toast. "He talks. The silent one has spoke. Noisy Cardone."

Barnum and Booker Boyd had not been saying much, either. Once in a while Barnum would say something in a low voice to Boyd and Boyd would seem to answer in a word or two and then they would go back to eating.

"Well," I said. "Dumb Dan Morgan used to say that a heavyweight has to have only four moves. He has to be able to walk to the table, sit down, pull up his chair and go with both hands."

"He's right," Penna said. "Look at Schaeffer and you're seein' the new heavyweight champion of the world."

"Yeah," Polo said, looking at me again. "Morgan thought that was funny, but he didn't have this guy. This fat slob's eaten into me for eleven hundred bucks by now."

"Tell him about the great hotel fire, too," Penna said, laughing it.

"Yeah, you think that's funny, too," Polo said, looking at him. "Some comic. Some Milton Berle."

"What happened?" Eddie said. "What fire?"

"This wise guy almost burned this place down," Polo said.

"Who? Me?" Penna said, dropping his jaw. "I was the hero."

"You're a jerk," Polo said. "You know what he did?"

"Not me," Penna said.

"Will somebody tell us what happened?" Eddie said, enjoying it.

"Well, this guy," Polo said, nodding at Penna, "he started a fire in a wastebasket in our room—one of them metal waste-baskets."

"Me?" Penna said.

"Paul is up there taking a sleep before his workout yesterday."

"That's a workout?" Penna said.

"So this guy gets a lot of paper and junk in the wastebasket and he sets fire to it. Then he bangs on the door and hollers: 'Fire! Fire!'"

"I'm a hero."

"Then when Paul wakes up and tries to get up, this guy has tied his shoelaces together. He can't move his feet."

"And then, gentlemen of the press," Penna said, "I heard these horrible screams so, not even thinking of my own safety, I rushed into the flames and picked up the burning basket and I ran out with it and I put it in the shower and I came back and I rescued the baby and I returned it to its mother's loving arms."

"Remind me to sleep with my clothes on tonight," I said.

"That's right," Eddie said, laughing though.

"This place is all wood," Polo said. "It would go up in a minute."

"Relax, relax," Penna said. "Now I got that practice I'll save all you dopes."

"Yeah," Schaeffer said, eating. "You did it all right."

"I did it? Here's a guy tryin' to take my medals away. Why, I'm the guy saved your appetite for the world. If I don't save you, Schaeffer, you never eat again. Just think of that."

"You did it," Schaeffer said, still eating.

"And they bury you six feet under, and the worms eat you. What a feast! Boy, what a feast them worms got to look forward to."

"This kid is insane," Polo said, nodding toward Penna again but talking to me once more. "Believe me, he's absolutely insane."

"Our room still smells from that smoke," Schaeffer said.

"Girot gave him hell," Polo said. "What'd he tell you?"

"He told me I'm a hero for saving his place," Penna said. "He told me I'll always be first with him around here, from now on."

After dinner Barnum and Booker Boyd went for a walk and Polo and Schaeffer and Cardone went into the sitting room and, when I looked in, they were sitting in front of the television set, watching a news program. Eddie and Penna were in the bar, playing the pinball machine, one of those electrified quadrupeds with lights that flash on and off and a buzzer that sounds and then a bell that rings if you reach a certain total approximating Louis B. Mayer's annual income. There seems to be an endless variety of these things, and at first glance they appear so complicated that I never play them because it would be like learning another foreign language and hardly worth it.

"Now hit for here," Penna was saying while Eddie was playing it, the lights blinking and the buzzer sounding. "Come down here."

"What do you get if you beat this monster?" I said.

"A big hello from Conrad Hilton," Penna said, nodding toward Girot, who was standing behind the bar.

"If you're drinking," Eddie said, shooting, "you get a free shot of whatever you're having. Us, we get two bits."

"So that proves Girot serves two-bit whiskey," Penna said. "Don't it prove that?"

I looked at Girot. He just shook his head.

"Let's go to the movies," Eddie said, watching the last ball roll down until it disappeared and the noise within the machine stopped. "What's playin'?"

"I seen it," Penna said. "A good picture. *Flight to Our Years.* The broad in it is terrific."

"That's where that song came from, isn't it?" Eddie said.

"'Our love is forever,'" Penna said, raising his voice to a tenor and throwing his arms out, "'no flighty, transient thing.'"

"You want to go?" Eddie said to me.

"Anything you want. I'm with you."

"You want to see it again, Penna?"

"I got nothing else to do. I'll give you a break."

"Be my guest," Eddie said. "We'll walk."

"The man said walk?"

"It's only a mile and a half," Eddie said. "I always walk."

"Not me. I'm sorry," Penna said.

"All right," Eddie said. "Tonight I drive, but after this we walk."

It was what the motion-picture critics call a Technicolor triumph, and with swelling sound. When we came in, she was emitting beauty and elegance, and he good looks and character, and they were standing in a bedroom with small-flowered white wallpaper and fluffy, snow-white curtains. It evolved that the room was in a white colonial inn, with a tall-pillared portico, and she was saying that suddenly now it all made her feel unclean, and it wasn't supposed to be that way at all because it was supposed to be beautiful. Then he said that it wasn't unclean, it was very beautiful, and she said that it wasn't and then he became angered and shouted at her and she began to cry.

Well, they made up, right there, and it eventually became clear that she was married and he was not. He was a transatlantic airline pilot, but she had a young daughter at boarding school and a husband who was older and a New York department-store head, prominent and continually busy and heading charity fund-raising drives and hoping someday to become Governor.

It went on and on, in color, and I presume her husband thought her whole trouble was headaches, and finally there was

Flight 104. Her husband had to go to Paris on business and she knew her pilot was flying 104 and did not want to go to the airport. She could see, however, that her husband wanted her to see him off and so, while the chauffeur drove them, he suggested that she was just generally rundown, dear, and that she should visit her sister in Connecticut while he was gone.

At Idlewild airport the loud-speaker was calling Flight 104 and her husband was talking and her pilot walked by, in his uniform and cap and trench coat and carrying a brief case. He looked at her and she looked at him and her husband went on talking about what he hoped to accomplish in Paris and finally kissed her and went through the gate.

The next morning she was having coffee and toast when her maid came in and said a gentleman was there from the airline. It took a little acting then, when the airline man said that the plane had crashed and that her husband had been killed and when she asked if there were any survivors and the airline man said there were none.

When the airline man left he met a colleague, who was waiting in the lobby of the apartment house, and he remarked how well she took it and what a remarkable woman she was to have concern about the others on board at a time like this. In the final scene she walked out onto the terrace, high above the city, and the sky was pure blue and crossing it was a four-motor plane, silver in the sunlight, and she looked up at it and the plane was the last thing you saw as the music swelled into that song.

"You wanna see the beginning?" Penna said, when the theater lights came on. "I can tell you the beginning."

"Let's see it," Eddie said. "It can't be too long."

I had started watching the people sliding along the rows of seats and walking up the aisle and out of Neverland. I was thinking of those women, going back to their dishpans, and their men, in their plaid mackinaws, going back to their service stations or their chicken houses.

"You want to see it, Frank?"

"Sure, Eddie."

Certainly, I thought, I must see it. I must find out how Leander and Hero and Tristan and Isolde and the Prince and Rapunzel met. I am making book with myself that she dropped her glove and he said: "I believe this must belong to you."

They met in the canteen at the airport in Reykjavik, Iceland. There were Icelandic soldiers walking around in Russian-looking uniforms with shoulder boards and high collars, and she was flying back from Europe and he was buying a doll in native costume for his niece. She saw it and asked for one like it and it was the only one the woman running the counter had, so he insisted that she take it.

"That was all right," Eddie said, as the three of us walked up the small main street to his car. "I thought that was a pretty good picture."

"How about that broad?" Penna said. "How about a classy broad like that?"

"You like the picture, Frank?"

"Sure. It was fine."

"'Our love is forever,'" Penna sang, raising his voice again, "'no flighty, transient thing.'"

Yes, probably as forever as the ocean, I thought, and the mountains and the sky and have a small cry. There is no extra charge. That is the trouble with this business. I have a right to my ego, every man has, but no, you must establish what those psychiatrists and psychologists and those social-working people call rapport. Eddie must believe that you like what he likes and that you believe what he believes and then, without realizing it, he will believe in you and you will get out of him all that is in him and the editor won't know what it was like or that it was dishonest. He will think that you did it all with the questions and the typewriter, and why aren't they all so clever?

"How about that joint that broad lived in on Park Avenue?"

Penna said, on the drive back. "How would you like to shack up there?"

"Stop dreaming," Eddie said.

"You ever been in a joint like that, Frank?"

"Yes. Once."

"What was it like?" Penna said.

Trying to get to sleep that night I lay there a long while, picturing those people who made that movie.

The first two days that Eddie was in camp he slept late and just took it easy. After he had his breakfast we would take a walk and we would take another after dinner at night. The rest of the time he would play gin rummy with Polo or the pinball machine with Penna or watch television or just lie on his bed and read paper-covered westerns or the newspapers or a magazine.

"I found out it's good," he said the second afternoon, lying on the bed near the windows while I stood looking out at the lake. "The last couple of years I found out it's better if I come out two, three days early and just get away from the wife and the kid and, you know, relax."

It is a sort of transition period, I was thinking, a sort of interval in which to prepare to prepare, and basically sound.

"You know," he said. "So I can just do what I want to do."

"I understand. It's bound to be good for you."

"I never used to do it. First day in camp I'd start to work, but now I'm getting older, I like it this way."

He was twenty-nine.

"After a couple of weeks, though," he said, "I'm thinking about getting home again."

"Does your wife ever come out to camp?"

"A couple of times she did. Some friends of ours drove her out and they ate and looked around and went back. She might come out, but I call her up, two, three times a week. If she isn't home, I talk to her mother and find out how the kid is doing."

"How do she and Doc get along?"

"They never see each other."

"Does she like Doc?"

"Well, my wife is kind of different. I mean, she doesn't like everybody, and she doesn't understand this business."

"Few women do."

"I guess you're right," Eddie said.

About four o'clock the next afternoon I saw a beaten black Plymouth in the parking space, and when I went down to the bar a few minutes later, Johnny Jay was there. He was a bald little man, with a flat nose and the upper helix of his left ear slightly cauliflowered, and, with his friendly officiousness, he always seemed to be a challenge to anyone's capacity for collecting characters. He had been a featherweight, about forty years before, and Doc Carroll's first fighter, and he had been with Doc ever since.

"Hey, Hughes!" he called to me when I came in, and then, to the fat one standing at the bar with him: "This is that fella I was tellin' you about, that writer."

"Hello, Jay."

"Hello, Hughes. This is my friend Stanley."

"Hello, Stanley."

"Hello."

"He drove me up here," Jay said. "He's got his own car, so he drove me up."

Stanley was perspiring. It wasn't particularly warm in the bar, but they were drinking beer and Stanley was just standing there, fat and red-faced and perspiring under his eyes and where his nose met the rest of his face and in the crevice of his chin.

"What'll you have to drink?" Jay said.

"Give me some of that MacNaughton's in plain water, Girot."

"This fella is a great writer," Jay said, talking to Stanley and to Girot, who was standing behind the bar and pouring my drink.

"I know," Girot said, nodding, and then putting my drink down in front of me.

"Thank you, Girot," I said.

"He don't knock people," Jay said to Stanley. "He ain't like them other writers, knock people. He never knocks nobody."

"You mean almost never," I said.

"He writes for all the big magazines," he said, still making a show for Stanley. "All the big ones."

"Yeah?" Stanley said.

"I remember him when he was on the paper," Jay said, and then to me: "Don't I remember?"

"Sure."

"How many years do I know you?"

"I don't know. Too many."

"What, too many? You ain't so old."

"Well, since I can't get any younger, I hope I get older."

"You think you're gettin' older? How old you think I am?"

I know exactly, I said to myself. I happen to know that you're sixty-three.

"Oh, I don't know," I said. "About fifty-eight."

"You see?" he said, turning back to Stanley. "I don't look it, but I'm sixty-three. He thinks I'm fifty-eight. You see?"

"Yeah?" Stanley said.

"I'm sixty-three," Jay said, turning back to me. "Feel my belly. Go ahead."

"I believe you."

"Go ahead. Feel it."

I felt under his ribs in the front, and it was hard.

"Like a rock," he said. "Hit me a punch there."

"No. Have another beer."

"I'll have one, but hit me there. Go ahead. Hard."

I pushed a short right hand into his belly, not hard but harder than I would want anyone to hit me.

"Harder. Go ahead. Harder. That was nothin'."

"No, Jay. Please."

"You see, though? I'm in shape, hey? How many guys my age in that kind of shape? How many fighters, even, in that kind of shape today?"

"Not many."

"You see?" he said to Stanley. "Here's a guy knows boxin'. What'd I tell you on the way up? I mean about the old-time fighters and the fighters today?"

"That's right," Stanley said, putting down his beer glass and wiping his mouth with the back of his hand and nodding.

"Stanley could tell you," Jay said to me. "I was tellin' him how we thought nothin' of runnin' ten miles and boxin' twenty rounds in the gym."

"Fighters don't think much of that today, either," I said.

"You think I'm kiddin', hey?" Jay said.

"No."

"I'm not kiddin'. Today you ask a fighter to do half that and he looks at you like you're crazy. Today—"

"I know."

"You want the same, Mr. Hughes?" Girot said.

"Yes, and serve these gentlemen again, too."

"You know who's the best-conditioned fighter in the ring today?" Jay said.

"I can guess."

"Eddie Brown. Eddie Brown is far and gone the best-conditioned fighter in the ring today. You write a story on that, you'll have a good story that nobody ever wrote."

"Well, I'm not exactly going to write a story on conditioning."

"I know. Don't I know? You'll get a good story, because you write a story on Eddie Brown you'll have a story on the new middleweight champion of the world. Ain't that right, Stanley?"

"That's right," Stanley said, still perspiring.

"I mean you'll have the first. They'll sell a lot of them magazines."

"I'll bet."

"Sure. Why not? I'll tell everybody I know to buy the magazine. Stanley'll tell everybody he knows. Right, Stanley?"

"Sure. I'd like to read it," Stanley said.

"You see what I mean?" Jay said. "You gonna put me in that story?"

"Undoubtedly. I'm going to write about what a fighter goes through going into a fight and the people around him. You'll have to be in there, Jay."

"Yeah? I could tell you a lot of stories you could put in. You know what I used to do before a fight?"

"No."

"Listen to this, Stanley. You, too, Girot."

"I hear it," Girot said.

He was standing behind the bar with his arms crossed, and when I caught his eye he shook his head.

"Before a fight I used to eat garlic. You know why?"

"No."

"I didn't like to fight in close. You know? I mean, I could fight inside good enough. I could punch to the belly in close, but I liked to move around and box at a distance, you know? Everybody knew that, used to like to fight me in close, see? So I got the idea, eat garlic."

"What gave you the idea?"

"I used to eat it some, anyway. I'm Italian."

"I didn't know that."

"Sure. So—"

"What's your right name?"

"Don't put that in the story."

"I won't. What is it?"

"Giorno. Don't put it in."

"I won't. What's your first name?"

"Joe."

"Giuseppe Giorno. That's a nice name. It's musical."

"Johnny Jay. Put that in. Everybody knows me, Johnny Jay."

"I've promised."

"So, I fought a guy at the Pioneer. You remember Jimmy Muldane?"

"I remember the name. There were two brothers."

"For a featherweight a strong guy, liked to lay inside on you. So before I left for the club I ate garlic. Boy, I ate garlic, and in the dressing room Doc liked to die. He wouldn't even stay with me. He went out and walked up and down the hall. Ask him. He'll tell you.

"So, the fight starts and Muldane moved inside and I blew a little at him and he pulled out. In a couple of moves he comes in again and I breathed in his puss again and you shoulda seen his face and he says: 'You dirty, guinea punk.' He didn't come in again, and I licked him good."

"I like that, Jay," I said, winking at Girot, who shook his head.

"You think I'm kiddin'? I did that for every fight, maybe six or seven, and then one night, in the same club—the Pioneer—I'm fightin' another guy, but the only trouble is he's a Dago, too, and somebody must have told him, because I'm loaded and he likes to fight inside and comes in and I let him have a whole lungful, and nothin' happens. What I don't know, because I can't tell it, eatin' it myself, is that he's loaded, too. The referee steps in to break us, and he like to pass out. He don't break us again. He don't even come near us again, and this guy lays all over me and it's a lousy fight and everybody is booin' and hollerin' to throw us out."

"If I'm permitted the pun," I said, "you guys really smelled the joint out."

"You're right. But you know what happened? The referee complained to the commission, and I couldn't do it no more. You wanna put that in your article?"

"Well, I never know exactly what's going in until I write it, but I appreciate your story."

"I got plenty more."

"Stanley," I said. "How long did it take you to drive out from New York?"

"How long it took us?" Jay said. "It took us three hours. You know why? Traffic. Every day in the week now it's like a Sunday. Right, Stanley?"

Stanley nodded.

"Pretty soon the roads will all be filled with cars so nobody can move anywhere, so you know what they're doin'? You know what they're workin' on now?"

"No, Jay. What?"

"They're workin' on some way where man can move in the air."

"The airplane was invented some time ago."

"I don't mean like the airplane. I mean without wings, or motors. Just walk through the air. You don't think it's possible?"

"Anything is possible."

"I heard about it someplace. They're workin' on some way so that a man ain't held to the earth, so he can just walk off the earth through the air. I think I read it."

"You mean that they're trying to overcome gravity."

"Whatever it is, it's some kind of a secret, but some of the old-timers could do it. You know that, don't you?"

"No."

"I mean the real old-timers, like Jesus. Jesus could walk on the air, couldn't he?"

"It was written that he walked on the water."

"Water, air. One is as hard as the other, ain't it?"

"All right."

"The thing is, he knew the secret, but he didn't tell nobody. Now they're tryin' to find the secret, and when they do, everybody'll be able to go anyplace. There'll be plenty of room around for everybody, the whole sky and everything."

Girot was shaking his head again.

"Make me another, will you, Girot?" I said.

"Where you goin', Stanley?" Jay said.

"I'll be back," Stanley said.

"He's a hell of a guy, ain't he?" Jay said.

"I guess so, but he talks too much."

"What? He don't talk too much, but he's a hell of a guy, hey? He's got a real good job, too. You know?"

"What does he do?"

"I don't know what he does, but he works for the union, the electrical union. It's one of them real good jobs. I know him maybe fifteen years, and he's never out of work yet. He knows some of the higher-ups, too. Every year he gets three weeks' vacation, with pay, and him and his wife they go down to Rockaway. It's real nice there in the summer, but once, he was tellin' me, he and his wife took their vacation and drove down to Virginia. You know Virginia?"

"Virginia who?"

"You kiddin'?"

"All right, men. Attention!" Penna said.

He was walking in with Eddie. They shook hands with Jay and Penna asked Girot for a glass of water and Girot gave it to him.

"How you feel?" Jay said to Eddie.

"Good."

"You'll get in great shape. You'll be in the best shape of your life, and I was tellin' Hughes, here, that he'll have the first story about the new middleweight champion of the world."

"Swell," Eddie said, smiling and winking at me.

"You bring any dames up for us?" Penna said.

"Sure," Jay said. "I got three of them waitin' out in the car."

"'Our love is forever,'" Penna sang, throwing his arms, "'no flighty, transient thing.'"

"Hey, Stanley," Jay said, seeing Stanley back at his beer. "This is Eddie. Shake hands with Eddie."

"Hello, Stanley," Eddie said.

"I'm pleased to meet you," Stanley said, shaking Eddie's hand.

"This is Al Penna," Jay said.

"The uncrowned lightweight champion of the world," Penna said, shaking hands with Stanley.

"I'll crown you," Eddie said.

"Hey!" Penna said, letting go of Stanley's hand and looking at him. "Get a load of this guy. Here's a guy built like Schaeffer. How'd you like to spar a couple of rounds with a heavyweight we got up here, Paul Schaeffer?"

"No, thanks," Stanley said, shaking his head. "Not me."

"Is Schaeffer up here?" Jay said.

"Sure," Eddie said.

"Good. The first few days you can use him for a sparrin' partner."

"I bet this guy can out-eat Schaeffer, though," Penna said, still looking at Stanley. "How about we match him eatin' against Schaeffer? You like to eat?"

"I like to eat," Stanley said.

"Stanley wants your autograph," Jay said to Eddie. "Girot, give us one of them cards you got."

Girot reached behind some glasses behind the bar and handed over a postcard. On its face was a photograph, taken from the lake, of the inn.

"Write, 'To my friend, Stanley,'" Jay said to Eddie. "Then sign it, 'Eddie Brown.'"

"Sure," Eddie said, putting an arm around Jay's shoulder. "Who's got a pen?"

Without saying anything, Girot handed a pen over to Eddie. Eddie put the card down on the bar and wrote on it, and then he waved it to dry the ink.

"You write on it, too," Stanley said to Penna.

"Me? Sure," Penna said, and he took the card and started to write on it. "'The uncrowned lightweight champion of the world. Al Penna.' Don't ever lose this."

"You put your name on, too," Stanley said to me.

"Why me? I'm not a fighter."

"Put it on," Jay said. "When your story comes out in the magazine Stanley'll have your autograph, too. He can show it to people."

"You asked for it," I said.

"Thanks," Stanley said, when I gave him the card back. "I'll be right back."

"Where's he goin'?" Penna said.

"Out with our signatures to forge our names to three checks," I said.

"Him? Nah," Jay said. "He's gonna call his wife. Tell her he'll be late."

"What a build the guy's got," Penna said. "Wait'll Schaeffer sees him. He'll be jealous."

"Stanley's a hell of a guy," Jay said. "He works for the union."

"Wait'll Schaeffer sees him," Penna said. "I'll tell him: 'In ten years you'll look like that.' He'll be proud of it. I'll tell Polo he should manage this guy, too. He'd have the greatest stable of feeders in the world."

"You're forgetting Calumet," I said.

"What?"

"I'll tell you somethin' else about that garlic," Jay said to me. "The night after them fights I couldn't get a dame. You know? No dame would stay with me, and that's good. A fighter shouldn't get a dame right away after a fight. A fighter trains, he gets all wound up. He should unwind slow-like. A couple of nights later it's all right, but not right after a fight."

"You're crazy," Penna said.

6

The morning after Jay arrived, Eddie did his first roadwork. When I was younger and working for the paper and covering fight camps I would sometimes go out on the road with the fighters. I don't mean that I would keep up with them and run all the way with them, but at least, now and then, I would get up when they did and go maybe a mile or two. Then I would turn around and start walking back until they would pick me up, and I would try to stay with them coming back into camp.

It used to make me feel as if somebody had taken my insides apart and put them together again all wrong, but I was always glad when I did it, because it was a way of getting with the fighters. They would get to kidding me about it, and it would become the joke of the camp and sometimes it would last right up to the fight.

"Wake me when you wake Eddie, will you, Jay?" I said the night before.

"What for?"

"I want to get up when he does."

"Heck, I'm getting up at six-thirty," Eddie said.

We had been watching TV and now it was ten o'clock. Eddie was standing and stretching, and Jay was still sitting in one of the old overstuffed chairs and watching the commercial for an electric mixer and I could not conceive of him ever baking a cake.

"What do you want to get up for?" Jay said, standing up when the commercial had finished. "Relax. Get a good rest while you're up here. Just sleep and eat and breathe this air. Make the most of it."

"I haven't anything else to do. I just want to get up when Eddie does and watch him go out and be around when he comes back. That's all."

"Okay, I'll wake you. I wouldn't get up, though, if it was me."

"I understand, Frank," Eddie said. "I'll see you in the morning."

When Jay banged on my door I got up and got dressed and went into their room where Jay was walking around, busy looking for something on the tops of the two bureaus and on the card table where he had his boxes of gauze bandage and tape and a couple of small bottles. Eddie was sitting on his bed, seemingly removed from it all. He had on long underwear and Army khaki trousers, and he was pulling on a pair of heavy work shoes, and he looked sleepy.

"Now I bet you wish you didn't get up," Jay said, seeing me.

"I'll feel fine later. How are you, Eddie?"

"I'll let you know later, too."

"C'mon, let's get a move on," Jay said. He seemed to have found whatever he was looking for, and he was watching Eddie lacing the shoes. He was wearing old, chocolate brown trousers, worn shiny, and a brown-and-orange-striped Basque shirt and, over that, an old, dark blue Navy zippered jacket with the knitted collar and cuffs showing the wear. On his head he had a blue baseball cap with a white B on the front.

"Where'd you get the Brooklyn cap?" I said.

"This?" he said, taking it off and looking at it. "One of them sports writers knows the Dodgers got it for me. I was born in Brooklyn. Since the Dodgers win the pennant last year I wear it for luck."

"Go on," Eddie said. "You wear it to keep your bald head from showing."

"Sure, sure. Let's get goin'."

It was a fine, clean morning. The sun was just starting up over the hills across the lake, and it was the kind of morning that, they always say, makes you wish you would get up early more often. The lake was still in the shadows, but our shore was becoming sunlighted now and, when we got outside and I breathed in the clear, still, night-chilled air it made me think of a drink of mountain spring water.

As we walked up the driveway Eddie was pulling on an old gray sweater over his heavy khaki shirt, and we could see Barnum and Booker Boyd and Cardone and Penna waiting by the road. Barnum was saying something to Boyd and Penna was scaling rocks into the hillside across the road and Cardone was just standing, muffled up and with his hands in his trouser pockets.

"I'm ready," Eddie said. "Who's gonna lead?"

"I'll lead," Penna said. "I'll lead us to a nice soft spot where we can all lay down."

"You lead," Barnum said to Eddie.

"Not today. This is my first day."

"You lead," Barnum said to Boyd.

Booker Boyd said nothing, but he walked across the road, with Eddie and Penna and Cardone following him, and that was the way they started out. They ran in a line at an easy trot—Booker Boyd and Eddie and Penna and then Cardone—on the gravel at the edge of the blacktop, running north and to face any cars that might come down the road, running in step and their arms all moving and their bodies all swaying together. We watched them moving like that up the first rise, growing smaller until they reached the top and then disappeared over it.

"They'll be back in forty-five minutes, maybe an hour," Jay said.

"More like an hour," Barnum said, "the way they run and walk and run."

"It's like I said," Jay said. "In the old days we used to think nothin' of runnin' ten miles. I was tellin' Hughes, here, that."

"They run far enough," Barnum said, "if they run. That Penna, he don't like to run. He like to walk and talk."

"Eddie'll make 'em run," Jay said. "In a few days Eddie'll get his legs under him and they'll have to run to keep up with him."

"Eddie's a good boy," Barnum said.

"People think a fight is won in the ring," Jay said to me. "You know where a fight is won? Right here. Right here on the road and in the gym."

"I know."

"No use talkin' about it," Barnum said.

"Hey!" Jay said, stopping and pointing. "What's that?"

We had started down the driveway and we stopped. Where Jay was pointing a small olive-green bird with white-marked brownish wings had fluttered to a halt on the red twig end of a small, scrubby swamp maple. It was about thirty feet from us, the bird riding up and down on the swaying twig.

"It might be a goldfinch," I said, "but it isn't."

"It looks like a canary," Jay said. "Ain't it a canary?"

"You see that reddish cap? It's probably a ruby-crowned kinglet."

"Yeah?" Jay said.

As soon as I said it, the bird was gone. It had taken off among some pines, the yellow-green of its belly showing when it spread its wings in flight.

"It was a ruby-crowned kinglet. The reason its head was red is that it's either making a show for a dame or it's got an argument going with another male."

"You know about birds?" Jay said. "How do you know that?"

"I don't really know about birds. I just get it out of a book by John Kieran."

"John Kieran? You mean the guy used to be a sports writer?"

"That's right. He used to write the sports column in the *Times*."

"I remember the guy. I know him very good. Used to come around the fight camps years ago."

"That's right."

"He used to be on that radio program. You know that program?"

"Information Please."

"That's right. They asked them guys questions, and he used to answer."

"Sure."

"Was he as smart as they made him out?"

"Certainly. Nobody made him out. He's smart."

"He's that smart? I mean, he used to answer all them questions."

"Sure. Nobody goes around, Jay, fixing radio or television quiz programs."

"And he knows about birds, too, hey? I remember the guy."

"Here come Schaeffer now," Barnum said.

Schaeffer and Polo were coming out of the hotel. Schaeffer had on a gray flannel sweatsuit, the pants legs drawn tight around the tops of his shoes. He had a towel around his neck, tucked into the top of the sweatsuit, and Polo seemed small beside him.

"Where's everybody?" Schaeffer said, when he got up to us.

"Gone," Jay said. "They must be gone five minutes. Where you been?"

"Where's he been?" Polo said, looking disgusted. "In the sack. I woke him quarter after six. I woke him six-thirty. Five minutes later I come back out of the bathroom and he's asleep again."

"I slept good."

"You always sleep good," Polo said.

"If you hurry you might even catch them guys," Jay said. "Eddie ain't gonna take it too hard his first day."

"Can't you see him catchin' them?" Polo said.

"I won't run today, hey, Polo? I'll work twice as hard in the gym and run harder tomorrow."

"Nothin' doin'. You run today."

"I wanted to run with the other guys. I don't wanna run alone."

"C'mon. You run. Maybe tomorrow you get up when I tell you."

They walked up the driveway. We stood there and watched them for a moment, the big heavyweight, depressed now, and the little manager, disgusted.

"You see what fighters are like today?" Jay said.

"That ain't no fighter," Barnum said.

"He says he's a fighter, don't he?" Jay said. "I mean he fights. He gets paid. He makes out he's a fighter. Don't he?"

"No use talkin' about him," Barnum said.

I went in and took a shower and shaved. About forty minutes after the fighters had started out I looked for Jay and found him in the kitchen, talking to Girot's wife, who was busy working and only half listening. We walked back up the driveway, where Barnum was waiting by the road. After a while we saw Booker Boyd come trotting down the hill on our side of the road. Eddie was about a hundred yards behind him with Cardone right behind Eddie. By the time Eddie and Cardone reached us, Penna was just coming into sight over the top of the hill.

"You took it too hard your first day," Jay said. "You'll be stiff."

"Not bad," Eddie said, breathing and sweating. "God, Jay, I fought less than a month ago. I'm in pretty good shape already."

"I bet you took it too hard. You wanna bet?"

In their room Jay helped Eddie out of his sweater and threw him a towel. While Eddie sat on his bed, wiping his face and neck, Jay knelt down and took Eddie's heavy shoes off and then Eddie swung his legs up and lay back on the pillow.

"Now you just take it easy and cool out," Jay said.

"I know, Jay," Eddie said.

"Well, it don't hurt to tell you."

"Who put this here?" Eddie said.

There was a small white plastic radio on the gray-painted lamp table between the two beds.

"Girot lent it to you," Jay said. "His wife give it to me this morning. She says Girot wants you to have it while you're here."

"Hey, that's nice," Eddie said, motioning for me to see the radio. "I was thinking of getting one before I came up, and then I got all fouled up with things the last couple of days."

"So Girot likes you," Jay said.

"He's a nice guy, isn't he?" Eddie said, turning on the radio. "I'll have to thank him. He's all right."

"You're all right with him, too," Jay said. "You don't give him no trouble. He wants you to win this fight."

"Don't we all," Eddie said.

As the radio warmed up, Eddie tuned it in. An announcer was finishing the news, and then a disk jockey came on with some records. While Eddie lay there listening and perspiring, Jay went downstairs and in about five minutes he came back, carrying a cup of steaming hot tea with lemon in it. Eddie sipped that, slowly, and then he waited about ten minutes before he got out of his road clothes and took a shower.

"How often do you shave in camp?" I said when he came back.

"Every other day," he said. "Then I always shave at night before I go to bed. I mean, when I shave."

"So his face won't be sore if he boxes that next day," Jay said. "You see, in camp you got to do everything with a reason. You just don't do things. You got to have a reason."

"Sure, Jay," I said.

We went down to the dining room, where the fighters and Polo and Barnum were having breakfast at the long table. The room was bright now with the sun coming in the windows facing the lake and with the white tablecloths.

"I see Paul made it," Eddie said, looking at Schaeffer and winking at Polo.

"You surprised?" Polo said. "He makes all the meals."

"What?" Schaeffer said, spooning in his soft-boiled eggs.

"Nothing," Penna said. "Don't let nothin' bother you. Just eat."

"Pass me that sugar bowl, will you, Al?" Eddie said.

After his double orange juice, Eddie had a bowl of dry cereal with half a banana and cream on it. Then he had two soft-boiled eggs with toast and a cup of tea. When he had finished we walked out through the bar into the lobby where Girot was standing behind the high hotel desk, leaning on it and reading a morning tabloid.

"Girot," Eddie said.

"Yes, Eddie?"

"I want to thank you, bon ami, for the loan of that radio."

"That's all right."

"I appreciate it."

"For you I'd do it. Those other fighters I wouldn't give anything for."

"Thanks, anyway."

"I mean it, Eddie," Girot said, and then he shrugged his shoulders and you could see that he was embarrassed. "I have here the morning papers, if you want to read them."

"Thanks," Eddie said. "I was going to drive down into town for them."

That afternoon Eddie went into the gym. With Jay hovering around him with a towel over his shoulder and talking at him, Eddie exercised on the mat and skipped rope and shadowboxed a couple of rounds.

7

"Who wants to go to the movies?" Penna said.

We were finishing dinner. Eddie and Schaeffer and Cardone were still working on their stewed fruit, and we had been listening to Jay. He had been telling about a friend who had bought a chicken farm in the Berkshires, and the way Jay told it, it was a paradise in which only the chickens worked.

"What's playing?" Eddie said.

"*Eight Belles*," Penna said. "It's a good picture. It's about the Navy. It's one of them musicals."

I had seen a picture spread on it in one of the Sunday papers, and it had appeared to be about as much like the Navy as the Marx Brothers in *A Night at the Opera* was like the season at La Scala.

"I'll go," Schaeffer said.

"How about you, Polo?"

"If he goes, I gotta go."

"You don't trust him?"

"I trust him. I trust him to stop off at that bean wagon later and have four hamburgers and two Cokes."

"You want to go?" Jay said to Eddie.

"No thanks."

"What's the matter?"

"Nothing. I just want to take a walk, and go to bed early."

"Then I won't go," Jay said.

"Go ahead, Jay," I said. "I'll walk with Eddie."

"I don't know."

"Go ahead," Eddie said. "Frank will walk with me."

"I'd like to see it," Jay said. "I was in the Navy."

"Not that kind of a Navy," I said.

"You were in the Navy?" Penna said. "What Navy?"

"Whatta you mean, what Navy?"

"What war?"

"The World War. The First World War."

"It must have been some war."

"We won it, didn't we? Wait'll they get you in the Army or Navy. I could tell you some things about the Navy."

"You kill any Germans, Jay? Or were you just floppin' around on one of them South Sea islands with the broads?"

"He was in the Brooklyn Navy Yard," Eddie said. "Right, Jay?"

"Some admiral," Penna said.

"You want to go?" Jay said to Cardone.

"I don't know."

"Come on, Cardone," Penna said. "Live it up."

"All right," Cardone said.

"You had it pretty good, hey, Jay?" Penna said. "You worked in the Brooklyn Navy Yard and lived around the corner. You get any medals?"

"I didn't live in Brooklyn then. I lived in Harlem."

"You lived in Harlem?" Penna said.

I looked at Barnum and Booker Boyd at the end of the table. Barnum had stood up and Boyd was getting up, but it was always impossible to tell how much of the table talk they followed anyway.

"Sure," Jay said. "It was still mostly white in them days. There wasn't a lot of colored people in Harlem."

"Go on," Penna said.

"Ain't that right?" Jay said, turning to Barnum.

"What?" Barnum said. They had started to walk from the table.

"I was sayin' when I used to live in Harlem years ago there was mostly whites lived up there. Ain't that right?"

"That's right," Barnum said, nodding once.

"Is that right?" Penna said. "I never knew that."

"There's a lot of things you don't know," Jay said. "I could tell you a lot of things you don't know."

"Don't bother," Penna said.

Eddie and Penna played a couple of games of pinball and, when the others were ready to go, Eddie walked them out to the lobby. He handed the car keys to Penna, but Jay grabbed them out of Penna's hand and gave them to Polo, and they left, arguing.

Eddie and I went upstairs and I got a jacket and walked into Eddie's room, where he was putting on a new light-tan sailcloth windbreaker. I think that if he had worn a burlap sack he would have looked good in it, but perhaps that is merely the way Eddie seemed to me. I mean that the perfect proportions of that body and the skills trained into it would still, in my mind's eye, have been there behind anything, the way the art of one or two great writers I have worshiped has made even what were called their bad books seem, to me, for that same reason, good.

"We'll walk up about a mile," Eddie said, "and then turn around. All right?"

"It's fine with me."

It had been a day of sun, but now the sky was clouding and a mist was rising from the lake. We walked across the road and started north, walking side by side on the gravel beside the blacktop until a car would come bearing down on us. Then we would step off into the gravel and walk single file as the car sprayed the trees and road and then us with its light and its sound as it rushed by.

"When I used to walk with Graziano," I said, "he used to challenge the cars."

"He'd what?"

"He'd stop in the road and spread his feet and shake his fists at the cars and curse and make them go around him. It used to scare hell out of me."

"He wouldn't let them hit him."

"Of course not, but it used to scare me anyway. It would be before some big fight with $100,000 or maybe $200,000, in the till already. I used to think how the Garden people would die if they could see it, with some nameless guy in the night bearing down on the great Graziano at fifty miles an hour, unknowingly heading toward sudden fame."

"Rock was a character. Why do you think he did it?"

"I don't know. Maybe in revolt against training, against some guy making fifty dollars a week but riding in a rattletrap while he, who was going to make another eighty thousand or a hundred grand or whatever it was, had to walk."

"I suppose."

"Do you mind the roadwork, and the walking like this?"

"No, not any more. I used to, some, but I really don't mind it any more."

"What changed your mind?"

"When I started out I was a real eager kid. Good fighters were heroes to me, and I did everything Doc told me. Then, after a while, it got to be, you know, routine."

"You won a few fights."

"That's right. I don't mean I got cocky, but you know."

"Doc would never let you get cocky."

"You can say that again."

"So what made you accept training?"

"That's a good word for it, accept. That's what you do. You have a few tough fights where you don't think you can get out of your corner after eight rounds. I think that does something to the way you look at it."

"It doesn't for a lot of fighters."

"It did for me. At one time there, maybe you remember, Doc gave me a couple of those tough ones right in a row. That does it. At least, I think that's what does it. You've got it in your mind."

"What made you want to be a fighter?"

"Everything, I guess. I always liked to fight. That was a pretty tough neighborhood, and we used to get in street fights. We had this gang, and there was this kid, Tony, and he was a little older and kind of the leader and he and I used to handle everybody. I don't know why, but we just did. I just liked it."

"Did you have a temper then?"

"Sure. Like my old man. What they call a Dutch temper, but I lost that, even away back in the amateurs. You fight a kid, even in the amateurs, and you've got no argument with him, really."

"Fighting has cured a lot of tempers."

"That and my old man. Like I told you, he used to blow off at me and at my mother, and make her cry. I don't mean he was a bad guy. Afterward I could see it made him feel lousy himself. He just had that hot temper, and even before he died I made up my mind I wasn't going to get that way. Then I started fighting."

"How did you start?"

"Here comes a car."

We stepped off the blacktop and waited this time. The car was probably doing fifty, but standing as close to the road as we were, with me feeling naked in its lights and resenting it, it seemed to be doing a hundred as it went by.

"Zoom," Eddie said.

"How'd you start fighting?"

"In the PAL, and then the Golden Gloves. There was this little guy in our gang, Louie. You'll meet him. He always comes up one day when I'm training. He owns half a poolroom now in the neighborhood, and you'll meet him. He's a good guy and he used to train me in the gym and handle me in the Gloves. Then, when we decided I should turn pro, he still handled me. Doc bought him out."

"What'd he pay him? Do you remember?"

"Sure. He gave him fifteen hundred."

"That probably seemed like a lot of money then."

"It was, and it was a break for me. I'd had four fights. I got twenty-five bucks for the first three and fifty for the fourth. In the fourth fight I fought a guy in the Ridgewood and Doc was there and he liked something about me. I don't know what it was."

"It was what you are now, and he saw it way back then."

"I guess that's right."

"I don't suppose Louie knew much about training or managing."

"Louie? No. He's just a great little guy. Besides, after Doc took me, he took me in the gym for nine months. I mean, before he put me in another fight, and in those nine months, believe me, I found out I didn't know anything about fighting."

"I believe that."

"Any fighter who thinks he knows how to fight should spend a half hour in the gym with Doc. He'd take him down."

"There are no others like him."

"The man's a genius. I was scared of him, too. I was just a kid, and the night he came to our flat to pay Louie and meet my mother and sign me we were all sitting at the kitchen table, and he said to me: 'Look, if I take you, I'm the boss.' I said: 'Yes, sir.' He said: 'I mean that. If you don't like it say so, and I'll get out right now. Otherwise you do what I tell you the way I tell you. You can ask questions, but when I give you the answer, that's it. I don't like arguments. I'll tell you when you're fightin' and who you're fightin' and where. You just do the trainin' and the fightin'. I do the rest.' Then he said: 'That is, after you learn how to fight.'

"I thought I knew something about fighting. I figured I'd show this guy. I was pretty cocky, but for nine months he had me in the gym, and no fights. 'Step here. Step there. No. Stop. What are you tryin' to do, make me out a liar?' That's always his great saying. When you don't do something his way he says: 'What are you tryin' to do, make me out a liar?' He looks you right in the eye and kind of snarls it at you, and makes you feel about as big as nothing."

"What were you doing for dough, without any fights?"

"He was giving me twenty-five a week, for my mother, and I always ate my big meal with him. So he could watch what I ate, and talk more boxing to me, too. He really filled me with boxing."

"A lot of people don't know that about a good manager. All they know is that he's cutting into the big purses after the fighter makes it."

"Sure. Suppose I quit? Where would he be for the fifteen hundred and the twenty-five a week and the expenses? Many a time I thought to quit, too."

"Seriously?"

"I don't know. I'd come out of the gym some afternoons, and I'd think to myself about quitting. I mean Doc would be at me and at me, and I couldn't seem to get it and I was hating him and the whole thing."

"I can believe it."

"But what else could I do?"

"That's what makes fighters. The ones who can do something else better, do it—or should."

"What could I do? I quit school when I was sixteen. I didn't want that plastering, like I saw my old man. You look at the guys from my neighborhood. Good guys, but what could they do? Run a poolroom? Work loading beer trucks? Tend bar? Work on the tracks for the I.R.T.? Pump gas? That's what they do. What could I do? I didn't want those things."

"Oh, I don't know. You could do a lot of things now."

"Sure. If I win this title I've always got that. When I quit fighting I can get a job representing one of those liquor companies, going around. You know? What they call good will. Ruby Goldstein and Ray Miller and Joe Benjamin and Billy Graham do it and they're pretty good jobs. If I make some money with the title I might even invest in something, like a bowling alley. What could I do then, though, when I was a kid starting?"

"Not much."

"You can't do anything, so you don't quit."

"When do you stop thinking about quitting?"

"All of a sudden things start to come to you," he said, stopping and gesturing with his hands. "Doc keeps telling you: 'Do this. Do that. Throw it like this. Then step here.' It really doesn't mean anything to you. I mean you don't really understand it. He gets you a few fights and you're trying and you win, but you still don't feel good. You'd rather fight your own way. All of a sudden—I remember the fight—you try something and it works and you try something else and, just like that, it's like pieces of a jigsaw puzzle and everything fits into place. All of a sudden, for no reason, you've got it. You see the meaning of everything."

"I know what you mean. It's that way in anything. Ralph Branca, who used to pitch for the Dodgers, once told me that about learning to pitch, and what a great feeling it was when it all came to him. He won twenty-one games that year."

"The feeling is the greatest. All of a sudden you understand. Everything you do feels good. Your mind works good. When that happens in a fight it's the greatest feeling you ever have in your life. I can't explain it, but it really is."

"I know. I think, Eddie, that everyone, no matter what he does, has felt it at least once, at some time. It's why we all go on."

"Then Doc takes you down," he said, laughing. "He gives you that sourpuss, and shakes his head and goes at you again."

"But he knew it, too, the moment you found it. He liked it as much as you did."

"Sure, but he won't let you know. Two days later in the gym he's giving you something else, just as tough, but now you go along with it."

"As you said, a great man."

"You wouldn't believe this, but I think I want to win that title as much for him as for myself."

"I believe it. At his age he won't be up there again. He won't have another fighter like you. If he doesn't make it now he never will."

"He'll make it," Eddie said. "I'm sure I can lick this guy. I'm just as sure as we're walking here."

8

Two days later, just before noon, Doc Carroll arrived, cantankerous, vehement and vindictive, with every reason to be all of these things, and the best man with a fighter that I have ever known. I have known many who led their fighters to titles, and some who took them right to the end of the rainbow. I have found, however, that Destiny controls the passes to these places, and I keep telling myself, trying to believe it, that it is not important, really, how far you go but how you make the trip. Doc always paid his own way.

"So you really think so, do you?" Doc was saying to Girot when I walked into the lobby.

He was white-haired and bespectacled now, tall and thin, neatly dressed in a dark blue suit and somehow emitting an intimation of another time. He was standing at the desk, while Girot stood behind it and, off to one side, standing next to an old black Gladstone, Vince DeCorso was waiting. He was a six-round fighter who, in a dozen years in which he must have lost half of his eighty or ninety fights, had made most of the small clubs and the small towns of the East.

"I don't know," Girot was saying, and he shrugged his shoulders. "Eddie is a good fighter, and such a nice boy. He never makes no trouble. He has manners."

"Isn't that nice?" Doc said, nodding. "What do you think this is, a popularity contest, and the judges should give him four points for neatness and four more for being kind to his mother? Ah, Girot, you stick to your hotel."

"I don't know," Girot said.

"Hello, Doctor," I said.

"Hello, Frank," he said, turning and then shaking my hand. "How long have you been here?"

"All my life. Almost a week."

"I told you."

"I knew."

"You know Vince DeCorso?"

"Hello, Vince," I said, and we shook hands. He was a stocky, short-armed middleweight, starting to get bald, with the story of his career written over his eyes and under them and across his nose.

"I'm glad to know you," he said.

"Girot, tell him where he sleeps," Doc said, and then to DeCorso: "You can take your bag up. Johnny Jay's around somewhere."

"Sure."

"You have room four," Girot said. "You go to the top of the stairs and you turn right."

DeCorso went into the sitting room, carrying his bag.

"He's going to work with Eddie?" I said.

"Aah," Doc said. "What can you do? You go to the gym, there's nothing there. He'll do for a while."

"It's a living."

"Isn't that dreadful? There's a fella should have been talked out of it after a year. Going around and getting his brains scrambled. Dreadful. At least he won't get hurt up here."

"What do you give him, if I may ask?"

"Fifteen a day and his keep. For him it's a break. Next week I've got the Memphis Kid coming up. You know Memphis."

"I certainly do."

"Well, he's still got the brain. Girot?"

"Yes, Mister Doc?"

"Come in and give us a drink, will you?"

It was too early in the day for me, and I don't think Doc wanted to drink, either. I think he just wanted to talk.

"How'd you get here?" I said.

"My nephew. Thirty years old, with a college degree and a wife and two kids and a good job in a chemical plant in Jersey, and he wants to manage a fighter."

"That's your fault."

"My fault? It's my fault I put him through college."

Doc had six months in the City College of New York himself. That is why the fight game gave him the honorary degree of Doctor.

"When did he get the fight bug?"

"Ah, he's a kid, running around the streets in Brooklyn. I had Rusty Ryan then. You remember him."

"You know that."

"I'm getting old."

"What about Rusty Ryan?"

"I had him in camp on that lake in Pennsylvania."

"I remember."

"I had the kid out in camp with us for three weeks. Get him off the streets in the summer. Great idea. He shadowed that Ryan like a dog. Rusty made a mascot of him, let him walk with him, fish with him, bought him ice cream. He got him a pair of kid's gloves, and showed him a few punches. He never got over it."

"I can understand that."

"So, he wanted to be a fighter. That's why I sent him to college. He's out of high school then. I said: 'I'm promising you, Tommy. If I hear of you pulling on a pair of gloves I'll hit you right on the head with a baseball bat. I'm not kidding.' I'd have done it."

"I don't doubt it, but there was always that one chance he could have made it."

"Ah. If he could have been a good fighter, I'd have let him. Don't you know that? He couldn't make it. This is the worst business in the world for amateurs. They're liable to get killed. How many fighters do you think I've turned down in forty years?"

"Dozens."

"Dozens? I'll bet I've turned down a hundred. I say: 'Look, kid, you can't make it. Be a half-baked plumber, you won't get hurt. You'll make a living. You're a half-baked fighter, you may get killed.' The kid goes away hating me. Goes to somebody else. He's a better fighter because he hates me. He's gonna show that Doc Carroll, but that doesn't make him a fighter. Nothing can make him a fighter. The kid goes to one of those slobs who turns him over to one of those amateurs with a towel over his shoulder. He gets scrambled. There's about twelve thousand fighters in the world today. You know how many of them belong in it?"

"You tell me."

"About a hundred. Maybe less than a hundred."

"It's that way in anything."

"Hello, Doc!"

It was Polo. He walked up to Doc and pumped his hand, and smiled for the first time since I had been there.

"Hello, Polo," Doc said. "How are you?"

"All right. I'm glad to see you. You're gonna win the title, hey?"

"How's your fighter?"

"My fighter?" he said, sobering. "You tell me. He don't want to train. He don't want to do nothin' he should do. The way the heavyweight division is today I tell him: 'Look. You got a chance. Do what I ask you to do. Please, do me a favor, will you?' It's no good. All he wants to do is eat and sleep."

"Sure," Doc said.

"Eddie can work with him, if you want it. I mean my guy's big enough he'll just move around and Eddie can throw them in there, if you want it."

"All right, Polo. I'll let you know."

"Anything, Doc. You just tell me what I can do with my fighter. What can I do with him?"

"Sure, Polo."

"I'll see you later."

"What can he do with him?" Doc said, when Polo had left, and then he mimicked him: "'Please, do me a favor. Do what I ask you.' Can you imagine asking a fighter to do you a favor? Do what he asks him? Ask a fighter nothing. Tell him. You know what he should do with that Schaeffer?"

"I have several suggestions."

"That's no fighter."

"That's no manager, either."

"Dreadful."

He had a way of sliding the word out, as if it were a product of pain. His face would narrow and his eyes would grow smaller and sharper and he would slowly bare the word.

"How did he get in the business?" I said.

"I don't know. He can't manage a corner newsstand, but they all think they can manage a fighter. Who cares how he got in?"

"I do."

"How do they all get in? A kid is a street fighter, and he's got a pal. The kid goes into the amateurs and his pal goes into the corner with him. The kid wins a dozen fights and wants to turn pro, so he brings his pal along. His pal's gonna train him, maybe even manage him. They're friends, and it's a beautiful thing. The kid has a half-dozen fights and gets flattened. He quits, but does his pal quit? Oh, no. Of course not. He's a trainer now. He's up in the gym. He's got a towel over his shoulder. He's in for life. Some innocent kid comes walking in, wants to be a fighter. Now he's got another fighter."

"You make it sound real."

"Do you think, for a moment, that I'm making this up? Amateur fights don't make fighters. They make trainers and managers. Trainers? They know nothing about training. They're rubbers. Valets. They've got a towel and a lot of gall. Dreadful."

"What can you do?"

"Do? Nothing. All you need to be a trainer or a manager is fifteen dollars and a license. This entitles you to ruin a kid's life, maybe end it. You know this Al Penna who's up here?"

"I can't help but know him."

"You know who manages him?"

"No."

"A guy named Klein, from Long Island."

"I don't know him."

"Of course not. Guess what he does for a living?"

"Oh, he's a glass blower."

"Aah!"

"All right. He picks the dead petals off petunias in the Brooklyn Botanical Garden."

"He's a manufacturer. He's worth maybe a quarter million, but he manufactures falsies."

"It has never even occurred to me to wonder who did."

"Figure what he's doing in boxing."

"I pass."

"Say he's worth a quarter of a million. Wherever he goes, though, somebody says: 'Who's that?' Somebody else says: 'Klein. He's got money.' The first guy says: 'What's he do?' The other guy says: 'He makes falsies.' He could make ten million dollars, and they'd still laugh. So poor Klein—get this, poor Klein—he's gonna manage a few fighters now. Then they'll say: 'There goes Klein. He manages fighters.' Isn't that nice?"

"It's pathetic. There are a couple of people up here—Girot and Polo—who would prefer Klein's product to his pugilist."

"They're right, but Klein is staking him. Puts him up here.

Pays his bills. Lets him work with Barnum's fighter. Gets him a fight when he can. Buys a hundred tickets and gives them to his friends."

"And teaches him nothing."

"They ought to teach him to throw his cup and his ring shoes and his gloves and his mouthpiece in the lake, and flag a bus home."

"Speaking of buses, where's that nephew who brought you up? Talking with Eddie?"

"He's halfway home by now."

"You kidding?"

"I didn't even let him get out of the car. I gave him two ring-side tickets to the fight and I said: 'Turn this thing around and get going.'"

"You're a hard man, Doc."

"I told him once: 'Look at yourself, and look at me.' He put in four years in that lab, and now they've got him in the front of-fice. I said: 'In ten years, with your ability, you can own a piece of that place. What have I got? Forty-three years in the business and what have I got? Let's say I started out selling cars. By now I've got a Ford agency in Westchester. I've got a manager. I've got salesmen. I've got mechanics. I sit back. In the winter I go to Bermuda for a month. In the summer I go to Europe.' He wants to manage a fighter."

"I wouldn't mind managing a fighter named Eddie Brown myself."

"Not today. With that television today, you've got no chance. You're not a manager, you're an agent. They tell you who you have to fight and where you're gonna fight him and when."

Doc had a name for Eddie. To his face he called him Edward, but to others he always referred to him as the Pro.

"Suppose the Pro gets licked," he said. "In the old days you could take him to Chicago or Des Moines or St. Louis, and bring him back. They never saw him before. Today, if you get licked, you get licked in front of the whole country. Where are you gonna take him? They all say: 'Ah, we saw him get licked in his last fight on television.' You want another drink?"

"I'll have one more, if we can find Girot."

Doc walked out to the lobby and came back with Girot. Girot made the drinks and stood listening now.

"Television," Doc said. "Four weeks ago the Pro is in the Garden. Fifteen million people see it, and we get four grand for the TV and half that off the gate. In the old days we'd have put a hundred thousand dollars in there, and come away with twenty-five, at least. You put nine years of your life into a fighter, and the pay-off is in Indian beads."

"That's supposed to be progress."

"Progress? You read that story in the papers after the fight, about the guy on Central Park West?"

"What guy?"

"A big shot. The Pro is fighting in the Garden, so this guy is gonna be a big shot. He and his wife invite a half-dozen friends in to watch the fight. In the old days a guy like that would buy eight ringsides. Today what do we get out of him? Nothing. He pours out some whiskey, and that's all it costs him."

"I read the story. Somebody turned him over for $25,000."

"Well, that's what the papers said, but it'll probably come to fifteen. They're in there watching the fight and somebody works the fire escape and gets into a bedroom and lifts three fur coats and the dame's jewels."

"I refuse to celebrate the conquests of the forces of evil."

"I celebrated it. It serves him right. I read it in the paper the next day, and I called the guy up. I said: 'My name is Doc Carroll, and I manage Eddie Brown, who fought in the Garden last night. It serves you right.' He said: 'What?' I said: 'If you'd brought your friends to the fight this wouldn't have happened. Let that be a lesson for you.' He said: 'What? Who is this?' I said: 'Doc Carroll, and I manage Eddie Brown. It serves you right.' And I hung up."

"The poor guy probably thought it was all part of the plot."

"Poor? Like I'm rich, but you're right. He thinks I brought the Pro along and finally got him into the Garden just to set up the heist."

"I'm surprised you didn't have visitors from the law."

"Cops? Cops can't find anything. They can't even find their shoes and socks in the morning."

"I thought they sleep with them on."

"I had a brother was a cop. My old lady thought that was great. One of New York's Finest. I was a young fella, living home then. My brother and I slept in the same room, and he was a great cop. Handsome. Upright. A great parader, and with a twelve-inch eye. You know the twelve-inch eye?"

"No."

"He could walk along a sidewalk and tell whether a guy was parked twelve and a quarter inches from the curb, and give him a ticket. That takes talent. One night I came home, feeling a little high, and he's in the hay, getting his good nine hours, and he's got the uniform and everything laid out for the morning. I took his shoes and his socks and I tied them together and I hung them on the light in the middle of the ceiling.

"When I wake up it's just about getting light and he's making this racket, moving things around the room. He's on his hands and knees, looking under the bed, and he's in and out of the closet. I said: 'What are you doing, Sherlock?' He says: 'I can't find my shoes and socks. I put them right under that chair.' By now the old lady's there, too, looking.

"I'm lying in bed, and I said: 'Don't panic. Remember what they taught you. Make a systematic checkout.' He says: 'I did. I always leave them under that chair. I looked everywhere they could be.' I said: 'That's the trouble with you cops. You can't cope with the unexpected. Look someplace where they shouldn't be. Look up there on the ceiling. Maybe they're hanging from the light. Look.' He looked up there, and there they were. My old lady blew her top."

"But with that lesson he made a great detective."

"He died a detective. On West Forty-ninth Street, at one o'clock one morning, with a slug in his guts."

"Your brother was killed?" Girot said.

"Sure," Doc said, sipping his drink. "That was his kid drove me up here today."

Girot just shook his head.

"Speaking of law and order," I said after a while. "A couple of months ago I saw that an old friend of yours died."

"Who?"

"Pete Martin."

"Yeah," Doc said.

"I suppose you sent flowers."

"You want to know the truth?"

"Yes."

"I did."

"I'm not surprised."

"I sent him a wreath marked 'Bon Voyage.' I'm not kidding. It cost me twenty-five fish."

"I like that for a finish."

"Do you remember that night?"

"I'll never forget it," I said.

9

I shall remember it as long as I live. I was young then, and I had been on the paper about three years. They had me teething on boxing, and I had hit it off with Doc. Doc had a good-looking heavyweight at the time, a big blond, out of Des Moines and named Al Fraley.

Fraley's old man had been a Methodist minister, and that made a natural for Doc. The big kid was devout enough, but Doc made him wear dark suits and black ties and carry a Bible into the dressing room, and he called him Deacon Fraley. It was an era when you sold a fighter to the public in every way that you could.

This was right after Tunney retired with the title, and there was that confusion in the heavyweight ranks. There were three or four of the battleships with a chance, but the best of them all was the Deacon—or, rather, the Deacon and Doc.

When a kid starts out to become a fighter and, somewhere, walks into a gym, bag in hand, he is like a rough-cut block of marble emerged from the quarry that is the mass of man. In any block a stone mason can see many things, but a master sculptor can see but one. In his eye no two blocks of marble are alike, and the thing he sees is the thing for which the block was created and that is the way Winged Victory comes about.

That is the way it has always been, too, with Doc. In the boxing business, as in any business, there are hundreds of masons and three or four master sculptors, and the best was Doc. I watched him for years, with a dozen fighters, working carefully with reason and inspiration, shaping slowly and stepping back and looking at what he had done, hiding his excitement and his fear, too, behind that cynical front.

Until Eddie Brown came along, Deacon Fraley, even more than Rusty Ryan, was the one. The greatest sculptor in the world, working in marble, cannot add a thing. If it is not there, it is not there. No man makes it, and so no man is truly creative, but by subtraction from the whole he reveals it. That is the nearest that man can come to creation, and that is why the great are afraid. Only they can see all of it, and they are afraid that, in their process of subtraction, they will not reveal the all of it, and what is hidden will remain hidden forever. They are even more afraid that, in the process, they will cut too far and destroy that much of it forever. It is that way in the making of all things, including the making of a fighter.

At that time, Doc had the Deacon living in a boardinghouse on West Ninety-second Street, and Doc and I happened to be living in the same hotel. It was on West Forty-eighth Street, but it is not there any more, which is just as well. It was not much of a hotel.

It was in the fall of the year. At about 10:30 that night the phone in my room rang and it was Doc. He asked me to come down to his room, and when I got there the door was open and I walked in. He came out of the bathroom, pressing a strip of adhesive over a strip of gauze on his right hand.

"What happened to you?" I said.

"I've just had a visit from the Almighty," he said.

"Who?"

"Razor Pete Martin," he said.

It was a misnomer. I supposed he shaved with a razor, but he never used one in his work. Some romanticist named him and it stuck, but he definitely did not use a razor. He used a penknife, and he honed the tip of the blade until it was as sharp as a razor. He would grasp it about a quarter of an inch below that tip, so that it would not go any deeper than that, and he would slit you from the cheekbone to the jaw. It was always the right cheek, because he was left-handed. He was an enforcer.

This was, of course, during Prohibition, and two or three of the people in the mobs were playing with fighters. It was never quite as serious as they have made it in the bad books and motion pictures. It was rather the way a man of means will keep a show dog. It was a point toward prestige.

"What happened?" I said to Doc.

"Al Mele is trying to buy into my fighter."

"What did he offer?"

"What difference does it make what he offered? He offered me twenty-five grand. I told him: 'Look, Al, I put too much into a fighter to be satisfied with half. I've got to have all of any fighter I manage, and that goes for the Deacon.'"

"What did he say?"

"What did he say? He's not a debater. He's a thug. It was friendly."

"What happened with Pete?"

"I heard this knock on the door and I opened it and he was standing there. I stuck out my hand and he went for my cheek. I got my hand up, and I took it right there. It's not too bad. I hit him a hook in the belly as hard as I could, and when he dropped his hands I hit him a right on the chin."

Doc had wanted to be a fighter when he was a kid, but he had been too frail for it. His body could not take it, but knowing it and teaching it as he could, he could punch very well for his weight.

"You knock him out?"

"No, but the hook in the belly made him feel real bad. I'm lucky it's warm out and he didn't have a topcoat on. He'd have cut me sure, if the belly punch didn't fold him."

"Then what?"

"I picked his hat up and I helped him up and I took him to the elevator."

"Noblesse oblige. What did he say?"

"We didn't say a damn word. From the time he knocked on the door we didn't say a word. I just realized that."

"I believe that."

"What were we going to talk about?" Doc said, and he tossed something on the bed in front of me. "Here."

It was a small gold penknife, with the gold loop at one end to be attached to a watch chain. It was still open, the tip of the blade, as I have said, like a razor.

"Am I to have this?" I said.

"No," he said. "Let me have it again."

I handed it back to him. He was standing by the bathroom door and he pressed the tip of the blade against the door trim.

"Look out," I said. "When that blade breaks it may fly."

It snapped as I said it. I caught a glimpse of it in the light, and then it disappeared to the carpet.

"You'll enjoy stepping on that with your bare feet," I said.

"That would be the pay-off," Doc said, looking for it now.

"There it is, right by the leg of the bed."

Doc picked it up. He went into the bathroom and I heard the toilet go and he came out.

"I flushed it down the toilet," he said.

"Good."

"Before I called you," he said. "I called Fred Gardner."

Fred was writing the sports column even then. He has never made an enemy in his life, and he knew Doc and respected him and Al Mele knew Fred and respected him.

"I told him the whole story," Doc said. "I told him what I told you. Now I'm going over to see Mele, and I want you along."

"I'll go," I said. "I haven't heard that he's trying to buy into typewriters."

"I'll be honest with you," Doc said. "I want Fred and you for protection. These people aren't afraid of cops. They respect newspapers."

Mele had a cellar trap on East Fifty-third Street. The eye knew Doc, and after he let us in he disappeared and came back and led us to a small table in the back of the room where Mele was sitting with one of his sidearms.

It was a small room with a small band, a comedian, a canary and twelve legs in the line. Mele was not one of the suave ones. He was the almost complete thug. He did not become the complete thug until two years later when they found him in the gutter on the Lower East Side with enough lead in him to write his name down the middle of the Lincoln Highway from Paoli, Pennsylvania, to Point of Rocks, Wyoming. There are such places, you know.

"Hello, Doc," he said, not getting up. "Sit down."

"This is Frank Hughes, the sports writer," Doc said.

"I read your stories," Mele said.

"Thank you."

There were two empty chairs at the table and we sat down.

"You write good," Mele said to me. "You write like Fred Gardner."

"I try not to," I said, "but he's so damn good I can't help myself."

"He writes good because he's a good guy," Mele said.

"I just had Fred on the phone," Doc said.

"Yeah?" Mele said. "I never see him, except at fights. He never comes in here. He's one of them family men. He's all right?"

"He's fine," Doc said. "I told him you were interested in buying into Fraley. Then I told him I just had a visit from Pete Martin. I told him I still don't want to sell."

"Yeah?" Mele said. "You could be right. I don't want to buy no more, either."

"Good," Doc said, "and give this to Pete."

He tossed the knife on the table. Mele shoved it over to the sidearm, who picked it up and looked at it and closed the broken blade and put the knife in his pocket.

"You want a drink?" Mele said.

"You want a drink?" Doc said to me.

"I'll have one."

We stayed for two drinks. We didn't talk boxing. Mele wanted to talk baseball with me; he was a Cubs fan. Two weeks later they got to Deacon Fraley and he found a soft spot in the ring at the Garden and lay down on it until he was counted out. I was at the fight and I was in Doc's room in the hotel an hour later when he paid the Deacon off.

"I still have two years on your contract," he said, with the big blond kid sitting on the bed, still frightened and staring at the floor. "I don't want to hear about it. I don't even want to see you any more. You're through."

That was the last time I ever saw him and I last saw Pete Martin on a hot summer afternoon about two years before Doc and I stood at Girot's bar. There was a red-haired kid from a magazine who had the assignment to shoot some pictures to go with a piece of mine. He could not have been more than twenty-four or twenty-five, and he knew nothing about boxing and I took him up to the gym and introduced him to Lou Stillman. Lou winked at me and abused him to see how he would shape up, and when he made it Lou gave him the run of the place.

He must have shot fifty pictures, and when he was done I was going over to complain about life to my agent and we walked east together in the heat on West Fifty-fourth Street. When we came to Broadway and turned north I spotted Pete by the Automat, leaning against the glass. He looked like he was going to die right there.

He was never robust, but now his hair was absolutely white and his face looked gray. In all that heat he had on a good, but heavy, brown herringbone worsted suit, and he was even wearing a vest with a thin gold watch chain looped across it. It was obvious he was in trouble and I walked up to him with the red-haired kid following me.

"Hello, Pete," I said. "I'm Frank Hughes."

"Hello," he said, putting out his hand, but breathing in gasps. He had asthma and a bad heart and he was sixty-five at the time.

"Are you all right?"

"Yes," he said, gasping. "I'll be all right."

I introduced him to the red-haired kid and he gave him his hand. He was still leaning against the building.

"Let's go into the Automat where it's cool," I said.

"I'm all right," he said.

"Come on," I said, because I was afraid he was going to die right there.

I took him by the arm, and the photographer held the door open and we went to the first table. I sat Pete down, and the photographer and I sat down.

"Let me get you some iced tea?" I said.

"No, thank you," he said. "I don't care for tea."

"I'll get you a glass of water."

"Please don't bother. I'll be all right."

"I'll get it," the photographer said.

He went away and came back with a glass of water. He put it down on the table in front of Pete.

"Thank you, young man," Pete said, still breathing hard.

"You're welcome," the kid said.

"Go ahead and drink it," I said.

Pete picked up the glass, and his hand was shaking. He took it in both hands and took a couple of sips and set it down again. As hot as it was that day, though, and with that heavy suit and vest on, he wasn't sweating.

"Can I take you somewhere?" I said.

"No, thank you. I'm just going home."

"Let me take you."

"No, thank you. I'll be all right now."

"I'll call you a cab."

"No. I'll just rest here awhile. I'll be all right."

"Take some more of that water."

We sat with him for five or six more minutes. Then I stood up and the kid stood up.

"If I can't take you home, Pete, or get you a cab, we'll be going. Rest here now, will you?"

"Yes," he said, "and thank you very much."

He raised his hand slowly and I took it. Sitting there, he turned a little then and gave the photographer the hand.

"And thank you very much, young man," he said, "for the water."

"You're welcome," the kid said.

We walked out onto the sidewalk into the heat, and the last I saw of Pete he was sitting at that table, white-haired and gray-skinned, wearing that heavy suit but not sweating a bit and looking at that glass of water in front of him.

"Who is he?" the photographer said.

"Oh," I said, "he's been around for years."

"Will he be all right? I feel sorry for him."

"I guess so."

"What does he do?"

"He's got a job with the Teamsters Union."

"With the union?" the kid said. "He looks like he's some kind of a minister. He's so polite I thought he was some Methodist minister or something."

No, kid, I thought, you have the wrong man. Deacon Fraley's father was the Methodist minister.

"He used to be around the fight game," I said, "many years ago."

"Him?" the kid said. "I can't believe he was in a rough game like boxing."

"It's strange," I said.

I was thinking of Doc, and then I thought of Phil Arena. He runs a joint now in Las Vegas known as The Arena, but I remember him when he had a stable of fighters out of Boston. I see his name now in the New York and Hollywood gossip columns, and I guess he looks very distinguished in a dinner jacket and hosting all those names in all that plush and with his smooth black hair steel gray now and especially with that scar on his right cheek. You've read about him, kid, I was thinking, but he didn't get that scar in old Heidelberg. If I told you where he got it, kid, it would stand that red hair of yours right on its ends, but I won't tell you because you haven't lived long enough in this or, probably, in anything, to understand.

"This is where I'm going," I said. "If you need any more help, call me."

"Gee, thanks," the photographer said. "I'd like to do some more things with you."

He was such a kid, and he gave me his card.

"I remember it very well," I said now to Doc, standing there at the bar at Girot's. "Whatever became of Deacon Fraley?"

"He's an athletic instructor in one of the best clubs in Detroit."

"Do you mean it?"

"He's been there for years. He gets those big automobile guys and gives them exercises and teaches them how to hold up their hands. They send their kids to him, too. They think he's great."

"And I can hear them telling him he was smart to get out of boxing, that he was too good for it."

"You can bet on that," Doc said.

10

Eddie Brown was the fighter that Doc Carroll had wanted to be. To this union the one gave his youth and its riches and the other his years and his genius and now, as they approached together their moment, I felt, as I had known I would, the growing weight of my own involvement.

It is something that happens to most of us in my business. I have seen it happen over a ballplayer and even a racehorse, and I have felt its beginnings within myself in as small a thing as a gesture.

One day I sat in the press box in Yankee Stadium and watched, below us, Eddie Lopat going on the full count and with the tying run on third. I do not remember the hitter or the game, for in time they have become unimportant, but I watched Lopat chance that small, slow curve, and I remember the ball coming up there so big and then twisting high and foul to the circling first baseman. I remember, then, Lopat. I remember him not even glancing up at the flight of the ball, but taking one last look at the hitter before walking to the dugout and becoming, forever after, one of my pitchers.

We attempt to fight this in our business, but it is a losing struggle. We would maintain our poise and what we would wish to be our objectivity, but what we fight is the admission of our own defeat in the willingness with which we ascribe so quickly to another the remnants of what we once believed to be our own claim to success, even greatness.

I can no longer recall when I first met Doc Carroll, but I remember the night I first saw Eddie Brown. I was in Pittsburgh and researching a story, and it was late in July and there was an outdoor fight show at Forbes Field. It had been hot and humid for days, but about mid-afternoon the storm had come, darkening the daylight and the city, but cutting the air open with the flashing strokes of a huge cleaver. Now it was twilight and I walked over to the ball park from the Schenley through the greenery, feeling the air on my face and hands and in my lungs and watching it, after many almost breathless days, bring life back again into the people on the street with me. I watched it revive their eyes and saw them regaining the will to walk freely once more, and I heard it, uncontained now, breaking out in the beginning laughter of their voices.

At ringside I sat watching the preliminary bouts, not expecting much and so not asking much, and in the intervals between rounds and between bouts I listened to the crowd sound and felt the night come and tried to find the stars I knew were there above the ring lights and above the thin, blue-gray pall of cigarette smoke that lay, translucent, above us. Then the semi-final came into the ring, and there was Doc, climbing through the ropes and holding them open for a light-haired kid in a green and white satin robe.

He was not more than twenty feet from me and he and the other second were busy seating the kid on his stool and fussing around him and then Doc was leaning back against the ropes, his arms spread out along the top rope, squinting at the other corner where the other kid was just coming in. Then he straightened up and I saw him looking around the working press, nodding here and there, older than when I had last seen him and thin and narrow-shouldered in his white coat sweater. Then he saw me looking at him and he opened his mouth and threw his head back in evidence of surprise. He pointed at me and formed some words with his mouth, and I nodded to let him know that I would wait there for him later.

"And from New York City," the announcer said, "weighing 152 pounds, Eddie Brown!"

There was the small spattering of applause that comes from the polite irregulars, and I saw the kid, preoccupied, stand up and nod and turn and Doc take his robe. The kid had a good body, perhaps a little short in the arms, and I looked where he was looking, at the other kid, and saw that the other was about two inches taller and had the reach.

When the bell rang I watched Doc's kid walk out slowly and then start to circle, his hands low, looking out of the tops of his eyes, and there was no question about it. He was Doc's fighter. It is what a painter does in his paintings so that you would know them, even without his signature, and what the writer does in his writings, if he is enough of a writer, so you know that no one in the whole world but he could have been the writer.

For five rounds it was not too much of a fight, two earnest kids trying, the one patternless but inventive, desperately improvising as he went along, and Doc's kid always knowing what he wanted to do, but a little confused yet, making the other kid miss and then not quite being able to bring off the counter. In the sixth round it happened. Doc's kid, working underneath, missed a right hand, but slid his right foot forward with it and, rising with the punch, brought the left hand up and over to the other kid's jaw.

It was one of those sudden, picture punches, and it snapped the other kid's head back and he landed first on his rump and then on his back. He rolled over slowly and at nine he was up, shaking his head, trying to clear it, while the referee wiped his gloves. Then Doc's kid was on him again, throwing to the head until the referee stopped it.

In the main event two big maulers disqualified each other as serious heavyweight contenders, and when it was over I waited while the crowd thinned toward the exits and then I watched the newspapermen working at ringside under the yellow of the ring lights, and I envied them. I knew many of them, and I realized that what I envied was the assurance in the clicking of their typewriters, and their habits of concentration. Above them, in the center of the ring, a loud-mouthed Irish foreman was abusing an aging, muttering Italian who was one of the crew starting to roll the ring canvas, and yet the clicking of the typewriters and the higher, faster, tittering cicada-sound of the telegraphers' bugs went on.

In a while I saw Doc coming, with the kid following him and carrying his bag and Doc trying to pick a path toward me through the tree-stump disarray of the forest of wooden folding chairs. I signaled to him to wait there, and when I found my way out to them, I shook hands with Doc and he introduced me to the kid.

"Congratulations," I said, shaking the fighter's hand.

"Thanks," he said. His light-brown hair was crew cut, and he had young blue eyes.

"You have a live one," I said to Doc, motioning with my head toward the kid.

"Who can tell?"

"You can."

"Ah," Doc said, putting on that sour expression. "At my age you hate to start at the beginning again with another one."

"Where are you going?"

"I want to take him out and get him something to eat."

Outside the park we finally found a cab and went to a small restaurant where the fighter had some stewed prunes and a cup of hot tea and lemon. He was a quiet kid, and Doc and I had a drink and talked about people we hadn't seen in years, and then the three of us took a cab back to the Schenley and went up to the room Doc and the kid were sharing.

"You go in and take a hot tub," he said to the fighter.

"I already had a shower at the park," the kid said.

"I know that," Doc said. "Now take a tub. Put some of that Epsom salts in it, and soak about fifteen minutes."

"Okay," the kid said.

Doc pulled the spread off one of the twin beds and folded it at the foot. Then he pulled the covers back.

"You want to go out somewhere?" I said.

"Nah. I saw enough people for one night. I got a bottle of Scotch here, hardly touched. We'll go to your room and let this kid try to sleep."

"Fine."

Doc opened the bathroom door and said something to the kid above the sound of the running water and went to the closet and got the bottle. We went up to my room and Doc called room service and in a while a boy came up with a bucket of ice and a large bottle of club soda and two glasses.

"What kind of stuff is this?" Doc said, looking at the bottle of soda.

"It's very good," the bellhop said. "Everybody uses it."

"I never heard of it," Doc said.

"It's all right with me," I said, signing the tab. "I don't use any."

"You got nothing else?" Doc said.

"Everybody drinks this," the bellhop said.

"All right," Doc said, and then he tipped the boy a buck and the boy, surprised, thanked him and went out and closed the door.

"All a guy needs is a bathtub with running water and a tank of bottled gas and he's in the soda-water business," Doc said, showing me the bottle with the strange label. "I should have thought of something like this."

"That's not a bad-looking fighter you've got," I said.

"Ah," Doc said, pouring the Scotch. "He's a beginner."

He handed me mine, with the ice in it, and I went into the bathroom and added a little water. When I came out, Doc was sitting on one of the beds, his drink in his hand.

"Sure he's a beginner," I said. "They all are at one time."

"He's green," Doc said. "Got too much to learn."

"Sure," I said, "but I watched him carefully tonight. I could see the Doc Carroll in him."

"You could, hey?"

"Certainly."

"He executes pretty good at that, don't he, for a kid with less than two dozen fights."

"That's what I mean."

"That wasn't a bad sequence he dumped the other guy with, hey?"

"I thought it was great."

"You liked it, hey?"

"I did."

"You know he missed that right hand on purpose?"

"I was hoping he did."

"Sure. That's that shift to southpaw. The other guy is still thinking about that right hand that missed him when the hook unloads on him."

"It's a pretty thing to see."

"Name me the other fighters could do that."

"Dempsey."

"Right. Another."

"Petrolle."

"Another."

"I pass."

"McLarnin, and that's all. We named the only three in thirty years."

"Why don't you stop kidding me?"

"What?"

"You're really high on this kid."

"He should have had that other guy out of there in three."

"Possibly."

"Possibly? Absolutely. Definitely. From the second round on I told him: 'Now go out there and throw that shift into this guy. He won't know what hit him.' Do you think he'd do it? No. He's out there wading around like a guy lost in a swamp and coming back to the corner and I finally said to him: 'Look. What are you tryin' to do, make me out a liar? You're disgracing me here in front of a lot of people, and some of them are my friends. You throw that shift into him this round or when you come back I won't be here.'"

"I like that."

"So he finally threw it," Doc said, nodding. "Have another drink."

"I'll help myself."

"You know why he finally threw it?"

"Why?"

"Because he was more afraid of coming back to the corner and finding me gone than he was of throwing it. Dreadful."

He got up and mixed himself another drink and sat down again on the bed.

"I understand it, though," I said.

"Understand what?"

"The kid. Until he tried it he couldn't believe in it."

"Aah! Three months we worked on it in the gym between fights. He's got it down perfect."

"I know, but a fight is another thing. This is for real. You believe in it because of Dempsey and Petrolle and McLarnin and thirty-five years in the business. What has the kid got? Two years, and your word?"

"Did I ever lie to him?"

"Of course not, but a man has to find out for himself."

"They're not believers, none of them. I could name a half dozen—you can remember them—that could have been something if they just believed in it."

"I know."

"You don't just tell them. You show them. The only thing any man's afraid of is the unknown, so you try to show them and then there'll be no unknown. When a kid starts to fight he's like a newborn kitten. He can't see. All he sees in there is gloves. The air is full of them, until he learns he can ignore most of them. Then the mystery starts to disappear, and you really start to work on his own punches. You build up a sequence, and he won't throw the big one. It's the unknown again. He's afraid of what might happen if he commits himself. What can happen, if he'll just believe? Does he think I want to get his head knocked off? So you scare him into it. Understand?"

"Certainly. You're using fear to fight fear, and that's basic."

"That's right, but isn't that dreadful?"

"But the price is right. Now he knows. Now that's his move. As long as he's a fighter he'll have it, and believe in it."

"So you should have seen him when we got to the dressing room. He's alive. He's saying: 'It worked. It worked! Did you see that?' I said: 'Of course it worked, but you should have thrown it in the third round.' He said: 'I know. I know. I'll do it the next time.' I said: 'You should have done it this time. Look at the punches you took from the third round on.' He said: 'I didn't take too many.' I said: 'Of course not, because I taught you not to, but when you go to bed tonight just lie there and try to remember the punches you took from the third round till the sixth. Try to count them, and remember that you wouldn't have had to take a one, if you'd gotten that guy out of there when you should have.'

"And I told him something else, too. I said: 'When that guy got up, why didn't you hit him one shot in the belly?' He said: 'I know. I just got excited.' I looked at him and I said: 'Excitement is for amateurs. You're supposed to be a pro.'"

"You haven't changed, Doc," I said. I was enjoying it.

"So the kid is taking his shower and I walked out and I bumped into one of those pants pressers that have the other guy. He says: 'My kid wasn't right tonight.' I said: 'He looked all right to me.' He says: 'Well, you were lucky.' I said: 'How do you figure that?' He says: 'That kid of yours misses that right hand and gets lucky with the left.' I said: 'Sure.' I walked away. Isn't that dreadful?"

He had stood up and he walked to the bureau and was mixing himself another drink.

"Lucky," he said. "For months we worked on that—left foot, right foot, right hand, shift, spacing, leverage—and this guy calls it luck."

"Ignore him. You've already called him a pants presser. What do you expect from him?"

"Nothing. I used to ignore them."

He was beginning to feel the drinks a little now.

"I used to ignore them," he said. "Ignore them. All my life I ignored them, but can you imagine that?"

"What?"

"That SOB. Can you imagine? 'You were lucky,' he says."

"Forget him. He's not worth it."

"That's what I used to think, but how the hell are you going to ignore them?"

"Why not?"

"There's too many of them. You can't ignore them. They outnumber us ten thousand to one. You know that, don't you?"

"Certainly, but that's nothing new. They were always ten thousand to one. Why do you think Ted Williams, at 31, with eight years in the majors and the best of them all with that stick, makes what they call those insulting gestures at the fans?"

"Why?"

"Because once, when he was young, he was going to show the world with that big bat. He was going to walk up there and keep hitting that ball and the world would know he was a great hitter. He's done it for all these years, and finally, when the world still boos him, he can think of nothing except to display to them his contempt."

"You think that's why he did it?"

"I know it's why. So they boo him all the more. You mustn't insult the amateurs."

"Amateurs. How many people in that park tonight could read what my kid was doing out there?"

"I don't know. Very few."

"Two? Three?"

"Possibly."

"Isn't that dreadful?"

"But it doesn't really make any difference."

"That's what I used to say. I used to say: 'I'm Doc Carroll, and this is the way you do it.' The hell with the rest of them, I used to think. I'll put it right up there, and they can see it. I'll walk right through them, and where the hell am I?"

"You're in Pittsburgh right now."

"I'm fifty-eight years old in Pittsburgh with another green fighter. That's where I am."

"Oh, come off it. The amateurs have always crowded the highways to everywhere, so it's never been easy for the pros to get through. Now you've got a real good-looking kid who looked fine tonight. If I was a fight manager I'd wish I had him."

"You liked him, hey?"

"I think he's got a hell of a chance."

It seemed to pick him up.

"He's got a chance, all right," he said.

"A hell of a one. You're just afraid to let yourself enthuse."

"I've had so goddamn many disappointments."

"Who hasn't? This is a new deal."

"He likes to fight, too. You know?"

"I could see that."

"He got that guy hurt, he wanted to kill him."

"I saw it. So you bawl him out, telling him excitement is for amateurs."

"You know what I mean."

"Sure I know."

"A fighter's got to feel excitement, or he's nothing."

"Sure. He'd just be a guy going through the motions."

"But he's got to learn to control it, and let it go in the right place."

"Certainly."

"I wanted him to put that excitement into one good shot in the belly."

"I know."

"That's the hardest thing in the world to do. People don't know that. It's the hardest thing in the world to teach a fighter to control that excitement without killing it."

"It's the secret of everything, from painting to, hell, selling."

"It's the hardest thing in the world to teach."

"Or to do."

"Do? Hell, if I can teach it, he can do it."

"Yes."

"This kid might, too. This kid's a learner. I abuse hell out of him, but he's a good kid."

"I can see that."

"You have to abuse them. You can't let them think it's easy. This kid has never had an easy fight, and he never will. I won't let him. I get him guys he can lick, but guys who look to knock his block off. I get him guys like that one tonight, that he can learn on, but no cousins. This is the toughest business in the world, and one easy fight could ruin him."

"You worry too much. You wouldn't let it ruin him. You'd find a way to bring him back to size."

"You can't always do that. Guys in this business, they worry about bringing a kid back if he gets licked. Hell, that's no problem. You match him right and he gets licked in a tough fight, so he either comes back or he doesn't. If he don't, he's not enough fighter and you can forget it."

"I suppose so."

"It's the other ones. I've lost fighters the other way. You've seen it."

"I have."

"You put a kid in with a guy figures to be tough and something happens. Maybe your guy gets lucky or the other guy is off his feed and takes a couple of good punches and resigns. You look at your kid, and you can see it in his face. 'Oh, boy!' he's saying. 'This is for me.'"

He was room-walking now, his glass in his hand, and he stopped at the foot of my bed and looked down at me sitting there and watching him.

"He's gone," he said. "You're looking at a fighter that just left. Gone."

I know, I was thinking. I've seen it happen to fighters and to ballplayers, too. I could tell you about some writers.

"I lie awake nights over this kid. Every fight I take for him I worry. Half the time I'm in the corner there rooting for the other guy to belt him a couple. Isn't that dreadful?"

"It's the way it should be."

"It's hard as hell to make matches for a kid like this."

"It's like Granny Rice said about horse racing. There's a slight element of chance involved."

"Can you imagine?"

"What?"

"He wants to get married."

"They usually do."

"Kids. They can't understand. They got one chance. They got ten years. They make it in ten years, or they don't. So they want to get married."

He had finished his drink and he stood up and walked over to the bureau and put the glass down on it.

"Doc, you're going against the laws of nature and civilization. It's quite normal for a normal human being to want to get married."

"Fighters aren't normal human beings," he said, staring down at me through those rimless glasses, and raising his voice at me. "Get that out of your head. You should know that. A fighter is a freak. He's got ten years in the toughest business in the world, a business that calls for every ounce of his strength and every second of his life. There isn't a goddamn thing he does that doesn't affect his business. He's not a paper hanger, a lawyer, a writer. He can't spread it over thirty, forty years. He's got to give it all now, or never."

You have always asked too much, I was thinking. There have been many of us who have asked that of ourselves or others at one time or another, but we have deserted you in compromise and now you are the only one I know who, after all this time, still carries on that lonesome crusade against reality.

"Goddamn dames," he said. "What do they want?"

"They only want what everyone else wants. They're bound by the same laws, too."

"What does she want with a fighter?"

"Maybe she doesn't want anything with a fighter. Maybe she just wants a nice young guy named Eddie Brown, who happens to be a fighter."

"Not this one. I met her."

"And didn't like her."

"Of course not. She's a good-looking kid, with big brown eyes and a nice figure. I can read her."

"I suppose so."

"She wants Eddie Brown, the fighter. He's the best grab she knows. He's a fighter. It's glamorous. He's starting to get his name in the paper. He might even become a champion. 'There's Eddie Brown's wife,' people will say. She'll have a mink coat. They'll go to nightclubs. The head waiter'll know them. It'll be a ball. The hell it will."

"You're imagining all this."

"The hell I am. I met her. She's got a head of her own. That's the trouble. If she was some cow-eyed little thing I'd say maybe this'll work, as long as she keeps looking up at him that way. Not this one. This one has a mind, but she don't know she's marrying a freak.

"What can it be? Hell, he'll be home two weeks and gone for three. What kind of a marriage can that be? He's a long shot to make it at best, right? Now let's say he doesn't make it. Twenty years from now he's still trying to figure out why. There he sits some night, a working stiff just trying to meet expenses, his dreams gone and hers, too. He looks over at her. She's put on twenty pounds, and she's sitting there in some old house dress and he says to himself: 'Maybe if I didn't marry her I'd have made it.' They do that, you know. The ones that don't make it are always grabbing at something. Won't that be a beautiful marriage?"

He picked up the bottle. There was still some Scotch in it.

"I'll leave it here," he said. "You can finish it."

"I'm not a lonesome drinker, either."

"The hell with it."

"When you leaving?" he said as I walked him to the door and we shook hands.

"Oh, I may be here two or three more days."

"We're flying back at eleven."

"I'll see you back in town."

He walked out into the hall and turned back to me.

"Can you imagine that?" he said.

"What?"

"That guy says: 'Well, you were lucky tonight.' Can you imagine? Amateurs."

I watched him start down the hall, and then I closed the door.

11

Somewhere seven years had gone, somewhere between a night in Pittsburgh and an afternoon in the small dressing room at Girot's. What the years take from the old they give to the young, and so in seventy fights in seven years Eddie Brown had become many fighters I had known.

There is a ritual about any form of art, and I had seen this one so many times. It is the way a man, preoccupied, prepares his paints with his palette knife or inserts two sheets of blank paper into a typewriter or strips out of his street clothes and puts his body into the things of the ring. For another this would be an awkward act, embarrassing in its fraudulence, but for this man it has become one of the most natural of rites.

Eddie had hung his jacket over the back of the chair, and then he sat down and took off his loafers and his socks. Jay handed him a clean pair of white woolen socks and he put those on and then put on his ring shoes. Resting first one foot and then the other against the edge of the rubbing table he laced the shoes in silence, and now he stood up and pulled his white T-shirt over his head and tossed it on the chair and he started to get out of his gray flannel slacks.

"Where you supposed to hang things around here?" Jay said, looking at the array of hooks with clothes draped on them.

He had been mothering his bandages and jars at one end of the bench. At the other end Vince DeCorso had got into his ring clothes and wrapped his hands in gray-soiled gym bandages and taped them. Now he was just sitting on the bench and waiting.

"Where you put your stuff?" Jay said to him.

"Me?" DeCorso said. "Here."

He reached over and put his hand on his slacks and shorts and T-shirt and sweater hanging from one of the hooks.

"You want me to take them off?" he said.

"No," Eddie said, looking over. "Leave them there."

"The sparring partner got a place to hang his clothes," Jay said. "The fighter got nothing."

DeCorso looked at me and shrugged his shoulders.

"Forget it," Eddie said. He was folding his slacks and placing them over the top of the jacket on the back of the chair.

"Somebody's got to take charge around here," Jay said. "I bet that Girot never comes out here. What kind of a place is he runnin'? Who's fightin' for the title here, anyway? You're the most important guy he's got here."

"Hand me the gauze, will you, Jay?" Eddie said.

Jay handed Eddie the first roll and I watched him bandage the right hand, around the wrist and then down and around over the body of the hand, between the fingers and back over the body, flexing the hand now and then, the white bandage building like a cast. Jay handed him a strip of the wide tape and he wrapped it over the bandage at the wrist. Then Jay handed him, one at a time, the narrow strips, and he took each one and pinched it in the middle, then stuck it to the back of the hand, brought it over between the two fingers and stuck the other end to the gauze covering the palm.

"You always bandage your own hands?" I said, when he had started on the left hand.

"Always," he said, wrapping the tape.

"Since he first come around," Jay said, standing there and

watching, waiting with a small strip. "Not for fights, though. Doc always bandages him for fights, but Doc and me, we taught him to do his own hands soon as he come around. While he's doin' it, a fighter can tell himself how it feels. You know?"

"No matter how often I watch fighters do it," I said to Eddie, "I still marvel at the sureness and neatness of it."

"Hands are a fighter's tools," Jay said. "He's got to take care of his tools. A fighter busts his hands and he's nothin'. I see many a good fighter have to tap out with bad hands. You remember Danny Bartfield?"

"Yes," I said.

Jay was talking about Danny Bartfield and I was watching Eddie. He was not even hearing the conversation, and I know that kind and I never press them at such a time. Often the newspapermen will descend upon them in a pack at a moment like this and flush them out, but it really isn't any good.

"First he couldn't do the right hand so good," Jay was saying, talking about Eddie again now. "You know what I mean, tryin' to work with the left hand? So we told him always do that hand first. Now he does one about as good as the other. Right, Eddie?"

"Right," Eddie said, taking the tape from Jay.

When he had finished the hand he pulled on a pair of brief, tight, white woolen trunks and a white T-shirt and picked up the use-darkened brown leather harness of his cup. Jay collected the jar with Eddie's mouthpiece in it and a jar of Vaseline and a towel, and with Vince DeCorso following us and carrying his own mouthpiece jar and towel and protective cup we walked out.

It is the fighter's place. The dressing room and the gym and the ring are the fighter's kingdom and in them the good fighter is supreme. He breathes and walks and talks in many places, but this is where he belongs, formed so right for this that he himself is not aware of it, and will never be until years after it is over and then it will come to disturb him that something has gone out of his life forever, not just the fights but something. The something is all of it.

Eddie walked through the gym, a part of all the other fighters and yet apart from them, as they were one with, yet apart from, him. In the ring Schaeffer was mauling with a young heavy-weight who came up from Jersey each afternoon with two other fighters and Charley Keener, who managed them and managed Cardone, and Charley's kid, who helped train them. At the big bag Booker Boyd was shouldering it and then throwing hooks and short right hands into it, and at the speed bag Cardone stood, blank-faced and sweating, rhythm-clubbing the bag over his head, louder and then louder, first one knee and then the other coming up, the two like pistons and in perfect cadence. Near the corner formed by the dressing room and the outside wall, Keener's two other fighters, a middleweight and a welter-weight, did sit-ups on the mat, their hands locked behind their heads, and in the open space near the bar only Penna was alone, rope-skipping in place, sweating, too, and the only one un-watched.

On the ring apron Polo leaned on the top rope, watching Schaeffer and shouting to him. Ten feet from him, Keener's kid leaned, watching the other heavyweight. Near the big bag Bar-num, his face unchanging, watched Boyd. Keener stood be-tween the speed bag and the mat, talking with Doc, but watch-ing Cardone, the current hope of the stable, but at the same time lending his presence to the two others on the mat.

When Eddie walked through this, with Jay and DeCorso fol-lowing him, he moved to the open floor by the bar. Penna stopped the rope to say something to him, and then he went back to skipping and Eddie moved around, rotating his arms and shoulders, stopping to bend over, feet spread, to touch his toes, stopping again to do a deep knee bend, coming up and walking again, rotating his arms and shoulders, with Jay leaning on the bar and watching him and DeCorso moving around and doing the same but always with an eye on Eddie and always keeping out of his way.

"Hey, Frank!"

It was Keener, and I walked over to where he and Doc were standing, and we shook hands. Keener stabled in New Jersey, because he lived there, but he worked out of New York and was regarded as one of the most successful of all of them and looked it. He was a semi-short, pink-faced, immaculate man who bought his clothes at Martin's, next to Lindy's, and ate his steaks in Gallagher's and worked both sides of the street. I have seen him bellied up to a West Side bar with a known hood and the next night I have not been surprised to see him pick up the tab at Leone's for an assistant DA. Without even trying I can recall a couple of occasions when he explained to me, for no particular reason, how important it is that a man have friends.

"Doc tells me you're writing a story about Eddie," he said. He had to raise his voice to be heard above the noise of the speed bag.

I nodded in the noise, and he turned and walked a couple of steps and put his hand on Cardone's shoulder. Cardone stopped the bag with one hand and turned.

"That's enough," Keener said. "Cool out and take your shower."

Cardone nodded and, without saying anything, walked over to the ring, pulling off his bag-punching gloves. He picked his towel up from the ring apron and wiped his face and neck.

"You can both go in now, too," Keener said to the two on the mat.

He was in his fifties and had been at it for thirty years and was one of the great merchandisers. He was often referred to by the boxing writers as an astute student of styles and abilities, but his business really was buying and selling. One of his best fighters had been built by old Barnum, another had been self-made, and the truth was that Keener knew no more about fighters than the best of race-track clockers knows about the horses that flash before his eyes and live only in the sweep second hand of his watch. What our world mistook for genius was merely a handicapper's knack.

"Eddie's a good boy," he said.

"I like him, but I can't stand his manager," I said.

I was trying to bring Doc into it. In the presence of success I was trying to let both of them know that my man was still Doc.

"You want me?" Doc said, turning from us.

Schaeffer and Keener's heavyweight were finished in the ring, and Polo had walked over. He had been standing there listening and looking to Doc.

"You want my guy to work with Eddie?"

"With Eddie? No thanks."

"I thought you wanted him. I mean Jay said you might use him. You remember I mentioned it?"

"He's too big, Polo."

"But just to move around."

"I got DeCorso," Doc said. "Charley'll let me use that middle-weight of his if I need him. I got Memphis Kid coming up. Thanks, Polo."

"Whatever you say," Polo said, shrugging but waiting for Doc or someone to say something else.

"Thanks," Doc said.

"I got to look after my guy," Polo said and, the towel over his shoulder, he walked over to where Schaeffer was whanging the big bag.

"Can you imagine?" Doc said. "Can you imagine the Pro pushing that tub of lard around?"

"Well, he wants to be helpful," I said.

"Amateurs," Doc said.

He saw Jay coming out of the dressing room now with the headgear for Eddie and DeCorso, and he walked over to him and took Eddie's. While Keener and I watched, the two fighters climbed into the ring. Eddie stepped into his cup and tugged it up over the white woolen tights, and DeCorso climbed into the sweat-blackened leather carcass of his.

"How do you like my kid?" Keener said to me.

DeCorso was fitting on his own headguard, but Doc was leaning across the ropes and fastening the strap on Eddie's. Jay was standing on the apron with Doc, holding Eddie's gloves, ready to give them to Doc.

"Cardone?"

"He's gonna be a good fighter."

"He's got talent."

"You keep an eye on him," Keener said. "Remember I told you."

It is the least of my concerns, I thought. I am involved here in a crisis, and you want to show me card tricks.

"You like Eddie in this fight, hey?" Keener said, looking at me out of the sides of his eyes.

"Yes."

"The other guy's a good fighter. You know that."

"So is Eddie."

"That's right. Old Doc could stand a break."

"Yes," I said. "Just don't tell him that."

"He's an odd guy."

"He just doesn't play for the breaks. He never has, and I don't think he ever will."

"In this business you have to."

"You can say that of any business," I said.

There can be no use in talking about it, I thought. The play for the break, the dependence on it has come to be regarded as almost a mathematical factor, but to the few, even in the winning, it is the admission of defeat.

"Time!"

It was Jay, standing on the ring apron with Doc, looking up from his wrist watch and shouting to Eddie and DeCorso. When he called it, the two fighters turned toward each other, top-heavy in their headguards, Eddie with his hands low, head down and looking out of the tops of his eyes, and DeCorso sticking out the big pillow of his left.

"I have to go and pick up my crew and get back," Keener said. "I'll see you tomorrow."

"Good."

"Remember what I told you about Vic. If you ever want to write something about him just let me know. He's yours."

"Sure, Charley."

"Always glad to help," he said.

I watched Eddie and DeCorso work three rounds, the gym quiet now except for the shuffle of their shoes on the canvas, the thap-thud of their punches and the low, short rushing of their breathing. Eddie was saving all the time, never wasting a thing. When it was over he worked a couple of rounds on the big bag and two more on the light bag, and then I followed them into the dressing room.

"Close the door, will you, Frank?" Doc said.

"Sure."

Only Penna was still there, in an old pair of green-gray slacks and a white T-shirt and over it a soiled brown suède unbuttoned jacket. He was sitting on the bench, his long black hair still wet from his shower and still sweating a little just below the hairline in front, and he pulled his legs in to let the others by.

"Now I'm gonna tell you this once and for all," Doc said.

Eddie had his white terrycloth robe on, pulled close under his chin. The perspiration was beaded on his forehead and he sat down on the chair and extended his legs.

"I know," he said.

"Don't tell me you know," Doc said, standing in front of him and squinting down at him. "The only way to tell me anything is to show me."

"All right," Eddie said, looking up at him.

"Now I don't want to see you take one single step back in this camp. Not a one. Understand?"

"I understand."

"I don't care what this guy does."

He motioned back with one arm toward DeCorso, who was sitting on the bench next to Penna and sweating in a soiled dark-blue satin robe and starting to peel the gym wrappings off one hand.

"I don't care how this guy or anybody else up here moves to you. I want them to move to you, but don't let me catch you taking one step back."

"I know," Eddie said, nodding and looking down along his legs.

"Give him that towel."

"Sure," Jay said, serious-faced and handing Eddie the towel.

Doc waited while Eddie wiped himself, his face and his neck.

"Move to this side, move to that. Circle him, but don't ever give him his angle and don't ever step back."

"I know," Eddie said, still wiping. "I mean, sure."

"Look at me."

"Sure," Eddie said, looking up at him, his hands with the towel suspended in front of him.

"They think this other guy can fight. Sure he can fight, if you let him. Anybody can fight if you let him, but you never let him. What they don't know, but you and I know, is that the other guy can't do anything with you if you don't give him the room he wants, and he'll be absolutely nothing if you back him up."

"I understand, Doc."

"Get him his hot tea, John."

"I thought he'd have it when he comes out of his shower," Jay said.

"I want him to have it now. I want him to keep that sweat longer."

"Whatever you say, Doc."

He was cutting open the bandages on Eddie's hands, and when he finished he put the scissors down on the bench next to his jars and went out.

"That was all right today, Vince," Doc said to DeCorso.

"Thanks."

When Doc walked out I sat down on the other chair and watched Eddie sweat. On the rest of us sweat is the visible, often repulsive evidence of our unsuitability, but on the trained athlete it is the finely balanced weighing of the water content and the exact equating of the chemical formula and so it belongs.

"That's not a bad head of steam," I said to him.

"Yeah," he said, wiping his hands now with the towel. "I wanted it today. I haven't felt quite right, you know? I mean, not loose. I think a good sweat like this will get me going right."

"You can have it," Penna said.

"You were sweatin' good today," Eddie said.

"Who wants it?" Penna said. "There's only one thing I ever wanna get up a sweat doing."

"Forget it," Eddie said.

"Who can forget it?"

"Hey, Penna," DeCorso said, "why don't you get a good close haircut?"

"A what?"

"He's right," Jay said. He had come in carrying the tea, a cup balanced on a saucer in each hand, with a slice of lemon floating in each. He kicked the door shut behind him, and handed one steaming cup to Eddie and the other to DeCorso.

"He's right, what?"

"Get one of them crew haircuts like Eddie got."

"Why?"

"Then it don't look so bad when you get hit a punch. You get hit a punch now, your hair flies up. It makes the punch look good."

"Are you kiddin'?"

"No. The way you got your hair long now, it could lose you a close fight."

"You're crazy."

"No, he's not," DeCorso, sipping the hot tea, said.

"Sure," Jay said. "You see a guy's long hair fly when he gets hit and everybody in the crowd lets out a holler. Them judges got ears."

"Yeah, but you two guys got no hair. You two guys are just jealous. Don't con me. Nobody's cuttin' my hair short."

"What are you tryin' to be?" Jay said. "A fighter or a sheik?"

"A fighter or a what?"

"A sheik."

"A sheik!" Penna said, laughing and turning to Eddie. "You hear that? You get that? Here's a guy still thinks that Rudolph Valentino, or whatever his name was, is still alive. Hey, Jay?"

"What?"

"Nobody ever tell you Rudolph Valentino is dead? You know he's dead?"

"Sure I know he's dead."

"Where'd you get that word? You got any more words like that?"

"Like what?"

"Like sheik. What a word! You got any more old words like that. Sheik. Oh, Jay."

"What?"

"I'll bet you were some sheik, hey? I'll bet you wanted to be some Rudolph Valentino, hey?"

"I did all right."

"You did all right, hey? Tell us about it, Jay."

"I'll see you gentlemen later," I said.

"Okay, Frank," Eddie said.

I walked out through the gym and when I got to the lobby I saw Doc sitting on the porch in one of the red-painted metal tubular chairs. It was the warmest afternoon we had had, and the sun was just nearing the tree line and Doc was sitting there, looking up the avenue of the driveway toward the road.

"You're right about not backing up with that other guy," I said, sitting down.

"Of course I'm right."

"The moment you said it I could see his fights, and I knew you were right."

"You want to know something?"

"Yes."

"He's made for Eddie."

"It'll be great if it works out that way."

"If? It has to. People have the idea the other guy's a great fighter. That's a joke."

"He's a pretty good one, Doc. Let's give him that."

"Sure he is. He's champion of the world, isn't he?"

"That's what I mean."

"But not a great fighter. Let's not get confused about that. Quicker than the rest, so he covers better. He looks good at it, but he's not what he looks. You've got to see through all that."

"I can see it, now that you say it."

I meant it. I could see that lithe brown body and the fast hands and all the natural grace, but I could see now that always, without it being a conscious thought, there had been the impression lying dormant within me that something was not there. It is the way a passage of music will raise you and then leave you up there all alone, feeling but not quite knowing that something is missing and wondering what is wrong.

"Window dressing," Doc said.

"Yes, it's pretty."

"Made for the Pro. For nine years I've fed him every guy I could find who'd come to him. That's why I've made every one of my fighters a counter puncher. It's the only way you can con the other guy into thinking you're fighting his fight. When he finds out you're not, it's too late. Surprise. Christmas is over. Ante up. It'll be the same with this great champion."

"But a bit tougher."

"Naturally. That's the way it's supposed to be, isn't it?"

"Sure."

"Listen. After forty-three years I've got a guy who's learned everything I could teach him. He's even learned how to walk out there and make it look tough. He makes it look like it's close, but it isn't. He's just inside those punches or outside them. The ones he's taking he's taking where it doesn't matter. He's even kept the secret. That's the great talent, because nobody knows this except the guys who've fought him. Ask any one of those guys. Ask them. I can give you three, four, a half dozen that came to Eddie after he fought them and told him they never had it done to them before. They still aren't sure what happened, but whatever it was they never thought anybody could do it to them. I'll give them to you, if you want them."

"You know me for a believer."

"Who are those dames? You know them?"

I had seen them as soon as I had stepped onto the porch, but I had had it in my mind then to go at Doc and, half turned from them, I had forgotten them. They were sitting in a tomato-red Buick convertible, the top down, sitting in the last spread of sun in the parking space and about sixty feet from us.

"What are they doing here?" Doc said.

The one at the wheel was a blonde, about thirty, and she seemed to be reading a book. The other was a brunette, older but only they knew how much, and she was smoking and occasionally, without turning her head, saying something to the blonde, who would then raise her eyes, looking straight ahead, and then go back to the book.

"Who are they?" Doc said.

"Ma-me!" Penna said.

He had come through the doorway behind us, and he was standing now between Doc and me.

"Ma-me!" he said. "How do you like that?"

"Who are they?" Doc said.

"Top secret. This information is classified. Ain't that what they say in the F.B.I.?"

"Who are they?"

"I ain't allowed to give out this information. You screws can put me in solitary and torture me all you want, but I ain't gonna sing. I'll just give you one clue."

"What?"

"Ask Cardone."

"Cardone knows them?" Doc said.

"Knows them? And how!"

"How do you know?"

"Oh, no you don't. You know who that dark-haired one is?"

"Who?"

"She's the blonde's mother."

"Isn't that dreadful?" Doc said, looking at me.

"I told that Cardone. I told him: 'Just knock me down to that mother. That's all. I never had a mother like that.' Two good-looking broads, ain't they?"

"Why, she's got to be old enough to be your own mother," Doc said.

"My mother was never like that. How about that? Every day could be Mother's Day. Right?"

"Cardone," Doc said, disgusted.

"They must have some pretty interesting conversations," I said. "I mean, discussing things like the lasting evidence of the transcendentalist influence in modern American literature."

"What?" Penna said. "What?"

"Do you believe in transcendentalism, Penna?"

"I believe in that," Penna said, still looking at the two.

Booker Boyd had come out of the door behind us, and he walked down the front steps. He was carrying a sweatsuit and a pair of white woolen socks, apparently taking them from his room to hang them out and, without even glancing at the two, he walked by the car and around the corner of the building. As he walked by, the brunette glanced at him and then leaned forward and, apparently, snuffed her cigarette out in the ash tray on the dashboard.

"Some car, too, hey?" Penna said.

"If it's a fighter they want," I said to Doc, "they just saw one. Booker Boyd."

"That's right."

"I should tell them," I said. "I should say: 'Look. If you're specializing in fighters, that was Booker Boyd. One of these days, in a year or so, he's going into a ring for real with your boy, and he's going to knock your boy out. In fact, he's going to destroy your boy. Meet Booker Boyd."

"The dirty bitches that can't keep their hands off fighters," Doc said. "Why, that Cardone's just a kid."

"Come on," Penna said. "Just 'cause you guys can't do it, don't knock it."

We were playing them so hard, sitting there on the porch with our eyes and all our thoughts on them, that I knew they knew it. You could not tell it, though, the way they sat there, each holed up behind her own indifference.

"Who are they?" Girot said, walking out onto the porch.

"There," Doc said.

Cardone had come out of the gym door, and walked up to the car on the brunette's side. He couldn't have said more than three words, but the blonde turned toward him and, leaning over a little, said something to him across the other, and then the other said something and smiled and Cardone turned and, without looking at us, went back into the gym. When he did the blonde started the car and the back wheels ground into the gravel and they went by us and up the driveway, looking straight ahead.

"Ma-me!" Penna said.

"So that's who they are?" Girot said. "They should be arrested."

"Go on," Penna said. "'What do you wanna do, play jailer?'"

"That new fellow who has those cabins down the road," Girot said to Doc and me, "he called me last week. He said: 'You know, one of your fighters comes here.' He told me what he looked like. I knew who it was. I said to him: 'You shouldn't allow that. That's against the law.' He said: 'I have to make a living.' I think I'll tell Mr. Charley Keener."

"You tell him nothing," Doc said.

"Mr. Charley Keener has money invested in that boy. He sends him up here to get in condition. He has a fight coming up. That's not right to Mr. Charley Keener. I should tell him."

"Tell him nothing," Doc said. "Let him find out for himself."

"I don't know," Girot said, shaking his head. "That's terrible."

"You're just jealous," Penna said. "I know you foreign guys."

"I know you, too," Girot said.

He walked back into the lobby and Penna followed him, talking at him.

"What's that going to be like between that mother and daughter in a few years," Doc said. "I mean when that mother can't go any more? Isn't that dreadful?"

"I'm thinking of Charley Keener," I said. "I like what you told Girot."

"Keener'll find out for himself."

"Sure, but he's so surfeited with his own success. The great Charley Keener knows everybody and knows everything. I just want to look at him tomorrow, knowing everybody else knows that Keener's fighter is playing house, and Keener doesn't know it himself. I'm enjoying this, and you should be, too."

"I don't give a damn about Charley Keener," Doc said.

12

Eddie had come back off the road with the others and had had his breakfast, and I had left him lying on his bed and reading the morning papers and listening to the radio while Jay sat at the table writing postcards. After three days of good weather, it had just started to rain, hard, and I was standing on the porch, looking out through it, when I heard the bus stop on the road. Then I heard it backfire and start up again, and then Memphis Kid came walking down the driveway through the rain.

He had on an old dark gray sharkskin suit and he was bareheaded. He was carrying an Army khaki barracks bag slung over his left shoulder and, under his right arm, a cardboard suitbox tied with twine. I watched him, walking through the rain and looking the hotel over, and then, as he got closer, looking at me.

"Hello, Memphis," I said, when he came up the steps. "My name's Frank Hughes."

"Why, sure," he said, putting the cardboard box down and shaking my hand and smiling and showing his white teeth. "I remember you, Mr. Hughes."

"Thank you."

The rain had soaked the tight curls of his hair and wet his face and darkened the shoulders of his jacket, but he seemed not to notice it.

"I remember. Once you wrote a story about me in the paper. That was quite a time ago, but you remember that?"

"I remember."

"That was a good story. I got it home still. My wife, she like it, too, and she put it in the scrapbook she keep of me."

"I'm pleased, but I don't like the weather you brought."

"You know somethin' about this weather?"

"What?"

"I used to say that, too. When it rain I liked to say it's bad weather, but then I come to figure that when it's bad weather for some people it got to be good weather for others. It all depend."

"That's right, Memphis."

"Since then I read a story in the paper about Texas, and it don't rain there for a long time. I forget for how long a time, but I boxed out there some. You know?"

"I know you did."

"Even then it don't look too good to me. I mean you see all that country out there and it ain't like here, green the way we got it, and I noticed the people they don't look happy to me even then. I just figure they don't get enough rain, so I figure you got to have rain to be happy. That's why I never call it bad weather no more."

"You're right, Memphis."

"I sure didn't look to meet you up here, Mr. Hughes."

"I'm writing a magazine story about Eddie."

"That's good. I'm glad to hear that. Eddie's a good fighter."

"He's lucky to get you to work with him, Memphis."

"I don't know. I just hope to stay in there with him. I hope I don't disappoint Mister Doc Carroll."

"You won't. You want to go in?"

"I guess I should sometime."

He was about the right size for a middleweight, about five feet nine inches and solid and never any fat on him, even at his age. He was what they call a tan, not a black, with a face, widespread by nature, that neither gave him away as a fighter nor denied it and that was truly amazing. It is as rare to find such life still playing in the face of a fighter going nowhere after almost two hundred fights as it is to find it in the look of a very old man.

"Let me carry that."

"No. I make it fine."

I held the door open for him and walked up to the desk with him. Girot was behind it, heavily engaged again with a pencil and another sheaf of papers.

"You know Memphis Kid, Girot."

"I know Mr. Girot. I been here before."

"Memphis Kid?" Girot said, looking at him. "Today you come?"

"That's right," I said. "See for yourself."

"They tell me he's coming tomorrow," Girot said, talking to me.

"Mister Doc Carroll tell me come today," Memphis said, "I come today."

"I don't know," Girot said, spreading his hands and shrugging his shoulders to me.

"Where does he stay, Girot?"

"How do they expect me to run a place like this if they do not tell me when this one or that one is coming?"

"I don't mean to cause no trouble, Mr. Girot."

"You're not causing any trouble, Memphis," I said. "Girot's got room for you."

"He will have to stay with Barnum and that Booker Boyd."

"That be fine with me."

"Now I must go to the attic and bring down a cot."

"I'll bring it down, Mr. Girot. You show me, and I'll bring it down."

"I will have to show you later."

"Come on, Memphis," I said. "I'll show you where the room is."

"Thank you, Mr. Hughes."

He picked up his things and Girot went back to his papers and I led Memphis up the stairs. At the top I pointed down the hall to the room where Barnum and Booker Boyd were staying, and he went down the hall and I turned the other way and looked into Eddie's room and went in.

Eddie was lying on the bed, his eyes closed, but the radio still playing. Jay was still sitting at the table, still writing postcards, and Penna was sitting near the window reading one of the morning papers.

"I'm writing a few cards," Jay said, looking up at me.

"A few dozen," Penna said.

"You get my Christmas card?" Jay said to me.

"Pardon?"

"You get my Christmas card?"

"Oh, sure. Thanks, Jay. I thought I thanked you."

"Did he get your what?" Penna said.

"My Christmas card."

"Four months later you're askin' him did he get your Christmas card?"

"Sure. Why not?"

"Man, you're nutty. You know? Real fruitcake."

"What time is it?" Eddie said, still lying there but stretching.

"You sleep?" Jay said.

"I don't know. What time is it?"

"Quarter after one."

"I guess I dropped off. Maybe a half hour."

"It's rainin'," Penna said. "Lousy rain."

"Memphis Kid is here," I said.

"He is?" Eddie said, sitting up and swinging his feet to the floor. "That's good. When did he get in?"

"Just now."

"Where is he?" Jay said. "I gotta see him."

"Rooming with Barnum and Booker Boyd."

"Three spades," Penna said.

"He was a great fighter," Eddie said.

"That's right," Jay said.

"What?" Penna said. "Who?"

"Memphis Kid," Jay said. "He was some fighter."

"Are you kiddin'?"

"That's the truth," Eddie said, looking at Penna. "When I first started fighting he was a great fighter."

"How come in those days I never even heard of him then?"

"I'm telling you," Eddie said, "when he used to box at Stillman's everything stopped. I mean the other fighters used to stop boxing or whatever they were doing and just watch. Is that right, Frank?"

"That's exactly right. The managers even stopped arguing."

"I used to watch him," Eddie said. "I mean, when I was just beginning, Doc never liked to have me watch other fighters. When he'd catch me watching in the gym he'd give me something to do, but one day he saw me watching Memphis and he said: 'That's all right. You can watch this guy.' I can remember the day."

"How come he never won a title then?" Penna said.

"What?"

"If he was such a great fighter, how come he never won a title?"

"What's that got to do with it?" Jay said.

"Man, are you rocky? What's it got to do with it? If you're a great fighter you win a title, don't you?"

I looked at Eddie and Eddie looked at me and shrugged.

"Not always," Eddie said.

"Why not?"

"Memphis never got the breaks."

"So he's a great fighter, he makes his own breaks."

"It's not so easy. It's very complicated, Al."

"What's so complicated?"

"Let Frank explain it to you."

"Why me?"

"Somebody explain it to me."

"I'll explain it to you," Jay said.

"No, thanks," Penna said. "I want to believe this."

"Go ahead, Frank," Eddie said.

"Well, in the first place, Memphis was never a sensational fighter. He was never a crowd pleaser, because he knew too much. He never went out to make a show. He went out to get a job done. For the few people who hang around Stillman's he was a pro. The people who go to fights don't know a pro from an amateur."

"I still don't get it."

"You're in the entertainment business, Al."

"Who, me?"

"All of you. Why do you think it's taken Eddie so long to get a title shot? He's too solid to be a showman. The crowd wants a fighter who goes out there and risks his life every time the bell rings. Memphis might spend eight rounds just lousing the other guy up, if that was the way to fight that particular guy on that night."

"I don't know. You guys still ain't sellin' me. I still think if he was such a great fighter he'd have won a title."

"All right. He's also colored."

"What's that got to do with it? We got more colored champions than white guys."

"For one thing, we're going back a dozen years, Al. We're talking about a colored fighter nobody wants to fight because he doesn't make a show. Besides, he's too good, and you can't do anything with him."

"You ought to see how he could louse you up with those gloves and arms," Eddie said.

"Also, he was mishandled. He had two or three different managers who should have been selling insurance, or something, and who had no idea what they had. No white guys would fight him unless he carried them—and he did that, too. None of the first half-dozen middleweights would fight him, for anything, so he had to go in with a lot of guys who outweighed him twenty pounds. Look at his record. He boxed all over the world. He fought all the tough ones."

"He ever get knocked out?"

"Five or six times."

"For real, or he go in the tank?"

"I've never asked him. Why don't you?"

"No thanks."

"You convinced now?" Jay said.

"Maybe. I ain't sayin'."

"Listen," Jay said. "I can tell you a lot of good fighters never won a title. How about Charley Burley? From way back, I can name you—"

"Yeah, I know you can. Some of them sheiks, hey?"

"What?"

"Sheiks," Penna said, turning to Eddie. "Yesterday he drops that on me. The great Jay. He says: 'What you wanna be, a fighter or a sheik?' Can you imagine? A sheik. Why don't you lie down, Jay. You're dead, you and your sheiks. Here's a guy don't know he's dead."

"Listen—"

"I'm not listenin'," Penna said, and he got up and walked out.

"He really is crazy," Jay said.

"He's a kid," Eddie said. "Not really a bad guy."

"What good is he?" Jay said. "He's just one of them wise guys. One of these days I'm gonna tell him off."

"You know something?" Eddie said to me.

"What?"

"It's really a crime he never won a title."

"Who?" Jay said.

"Memphis Kid. You know, everything you told Al was the truth, but I still don't understand it myself."

"You don't understand what?" Jay said.

"I just don't understand it. A fighter like Memphis Kid. He never made a bad move. I used to get a kick just watching him pick off punches. You never saw anybody could do that like him."

"I knew some others," Jay said. "Years ago we had fighters like that."

"I don't get it. What do the people want? Why couldn't they see how good Memphis Kid was?"

"It's too intricate an art, Eddie."

"How do you mean?"

"It's just too intricate for the average person, fight fan or not, to comprehend. All they see is the result. If it's a war in there, great. If a guy gets knocked out, greater. That's all they're equipped to understand."

"But there's some guys you can't knock out. There's guys nobody can look good in there with. You know that."

"Certainly."

"It's not right. Maybe you fight the toughest guy in the world for you, because of his style, and you lick him and people don't like it. Is that right?"

"No, but that's because the fighter, of all the practitioners of the arts, is in the most peculiar and unfortunate position."

"How do you mean?"

"Because every fight is in front of an audience. You don't think a painter has to perform that way."

"I don't know."

"A painter picks out a tough one for himself, and if it doesn't go and he looks bad in it, he hides it. It never gets shown. Nobody looks at it and says: 'He's a bum. He can't paint.' Painters—great painters—have attics full of stuff they never show. Maybe some of that stuff they liked better than anything they're famous for, because they licked a tough one in a way nobody else ever licked it. It doesn't come off as a great fight, though, because it never could, but they don't have to show it in front of an audience of amateurs who wouldn't understand. You guys have to show every time out."

"I never thought of it that way."

"I'm gonna see Memphis," Jay said, and he went out and closed the door.

"I really feel sorry for Memphis," Eddie said.

"What about yourself?"

"Well, I've made some money."

"Stop conning me."

"What?"

I've got to get you to talk to me now, I was thinking.

"Stop conning me," I said.

"I'm not conning you."

"Look, I'm your friend. I like you. I'm Doc's friend. I've known him for twenty-five years. He's the greatest in the business. You're the best fighter, pound for pound and punch for punch, in the ring today. People don't know that. They can't even find it in the newspapers. Don't tell me you've made some money. You should have made ten times as much. You should be champion of the world."

"I know it."

"You've got to be sore about that."

"I read in the papers what a great fighter this other guy is."

"Everybody reads that."

"It's like a crap game. You got to be lucky."

"You're wrong."

"How do you mean?"

"It's not a crap game. It's a card game. You've got to be lucky, but only in the deal. After forty years in the business, Doc finally got dealt a fighter who could learn and do all the things Doc has been trying to teach for all those years. Where were you dealt in? You were dealt the body and the mind and the reflexes to be that fighter. Now you two guys are holding the winning cards. That's why it's not a crap game. You've just got to play them right."

"We'll play them."

"I know you will."

"Everybody always talks about this other guy, and they write in the papers, like he's a great fighter. Sometimes that makes me a little sore."

"It should."

"He's not a great fighter. He's a great showboat. You want to know the truth?"

"Certainly."

"The guy is made for me."

"I know he is."

"Doc and I know exactly how to lick him. They say he's a puncher. He can't punch with me. I'll back him off in any exchange. You watch who backs off in the very first exchange."

"I'll be watching."

"That'll show you how great a fighter he is. I'm sick of hearing that. I just want to show people."

"Well, you will."

"I will."

"You see? Finally, after all, you're very lucky. You've got the chance now and the cards to do it. Many guys in life never get that chance."

"I suppose that's right."

The door opened and Penna came in.

"Hey!" he said, to Eddie. "Big news."

"What?"

"Your wife and your kid and your brother-in-law are here."

"No kidding?" Eddie said. "Let's go down, Frank."

"I want to wash up," I said.

13

I guess they had been talking for about fifteen minutes when I came into the dining room. They were sitting at a table for four by one of the windows that look onto the lake and the kid was running back and forth among the other tables, from one end of the room to the other.

"Come on over, Frank," Eddie said.

Apparently they had exhausted whatever it was they had been talking about, because Helen and her brother were just sitting there with their drinks in front of them, and Eddie was scribing lines on the table cloth with the tip of one of the table knives.

"You know Helen, and this is her brother, Herb."

"Hello, Helen."

"Hello," she said, nodding.

"I'm glad to meet you," I said to her brother, and he half rose and we shook hands.

He looked to be about thirty-five, about a head taller than Helen and, although he wasn't thin, there was a drawn look to his face and he was getting bald. He had on a glen-plaid cotton-flannel sports shirt, and clipped to the breast pocket were a ball-point pen and a mechanical pencil. Crowded into the pocket behind them, with the pocket hanging forward from the weight of it all, was a small black leather notebook.

"Was the driving bad in the rain?" I said to the two of them.

"It wasn't any fun," Herb said.

He's got to be a supply clerk, I was thinking, or I can't make people any more.

"You want a drink, Frank?" Eddie said.

"I'll get it," I said. "Helen?"

"Well, I suppose so."

"What are you drinking?"

"Scotch, and soda."

"You, sir?"

"No, thanks," Herb said.

Girot poured some McNaughton's over some ice for me and mixed Helen's drink and I brought them back. Through the window behind Herb I could see that it was still raining hard.

"My God," Eddie said, "can't you make him stop?"

The kid was still running up and down as hard as he could go, and now he was stamping his feet, with each step, on the bare wooden floor.

"What can I do?" Helen said.

"Hey, Slugger!" Eddie said, calling the kid.

The kid, running, heard him but paid no attention. On the next trip past us, though, he ran close to our table and, as he was about to duck out again, Eddie reached out and caught him about the waist.

"C'mon," he said, pulling the kid to him with the kid squirming to get loose. "I want you to meet Mr. Hughes."

"Hello," I said.

"I wanna run," the kid said.

"How about us having a party?" Eddie said. "We'll have a party right here, and you can have ice cream. How would you like some ice cream?"

The kid was short and wiry, with short brown hair, and he had brown eyes like his mother. He had on new red shoes and a gray flannel suit, short pants and a short lapel-less jacket and I realized that he and his mother were dressed as a pair. She had on a gray flannel suit and a red blouse and there was a red ribbon holding the pony tail at the back of her head.

"I don't want ice cream," he said, wrestling to get away from Eddie.

"C'mon, I'll get you some ice cream."

"All right," the kid said and, taking him by the hand, Eddie led him out to the kitchen.

"Can you remember, Helen, when you first met Eddie?" I said after a while.

"When I first met him?"

"Yes."

"Who knows?" she said.

"We all lived on the same block," Herb said.

"I know that."

"She always knew him. They were kids."

"What's the first thing you can recall about Eddie? I mean, going back in your mind, what do you remember about him? Maybe it's something he said to you, or you said to him, or that you saw him do."

"All the kids were together," Herb said. "She wouldn't remember things like that."

Big brother has got to be a supply clerk, I was thinking, when Eddie came back, still holding the kid's hand and, with his left hand, carrying the dish of ice cream and a spoon.

"Now," he said, putting the dish on the table and pulling another chair up for the kid. "This'll taste good."

"I was asking Helen," I said to Eddie, when he sat down, "what she first remembers about you."

"What do you mean?"

"Oh, when she and you first became aware of each other."

"I can tell you when I first paid any attention to her," he said, smiling and looking at her.

The kid was kicking one of the legs of the table, and Eddie became aware of it just as I did.

"C'mon," he said. "Eat some more of your ice cream."

"I don't want it."

"What's wrong with it? You like ice cream."

"I don't like it."

"Since when doesn't he like ice cream?" Eddie said to Helen.

"I don't know."

"All right, but just don't kick the table."

"You were saying," I said, "that you remember when you first noticed Helen."

"That's right," Eddie said. "We were playing stickball. You know? Somebody—I don't remember who, but probably Tony—hit one real good, and up the street there was this car parked."

The kid was kicking the table again.

"Look, Slugger," Eddie said to him. "You want me to flatten you?"

"Don't talk to him like that," Helen said.

"All right. Then you tell him to stop. He shouldn't be kicking the table."

"Then guess," the kid said.

"Guess? Guess what?"

"Billy's cousin's name."

"Who?"

"Billy's cousin's name."

"What's he talking about?"

"Billy Murphy's cousin," Helen said. "He was playing with Billy Murphy the other day, and his cousin was there."

"Guess," the kid said, kicking the table leg again.

"All right, but just stop the kicking. Is it a girl or a boy?"

"I don't know."

"You don't know? You were playing with him, or her, or whatever Billy Murphy's cousin is, weren't you?"

"It's a girl," Helen said. "He knows it's a girl."

"It's a girl?" Eddie said to the kid.

"Guess her name," the kid said.

"Betty," Eddie said.

"Nope," the kid said, drawing it out and smiling and shaking his head slowly.

"Alice?"

"Nope."

"Helen?"

"Nope."

"I can't even think of any girls' names," Eddie said to the rest of us.

"Ruth," Herb said.

"Nope. Guess."

"Florence," Eddie said.

"Nope."

"Grace," Herb said.

"Nope."

"What's the kid's name?" Eddie said to Helen.

"I don't know. I never even saw her. He just came home and said he was playing with Billy Murphy's cousin."

"Guess."

"And he didn't say the name?"

"I told you not."

"Guess," the kid said, starting to kick the table leg again. "Guess."

"Oh," Eddie said. "Frances."

"Nope. Guess."

"This is silly," Eddie said. "We could guess all day. What were you asking me, Frank?"

"You were telling me about the stickball game."

"Guess."

"That's right. Somebody—probably Tony—hit one a mile up the street and it hit the back of this car that was parked there and—"

"Guess."

"—and, where the back sloped up by the back window, it hit there and bounced up in the air, over the top of the car—"

"Guess. Guess," the kid was saying, keeping time with his shoe on the table leg now. "Guess. Guess."

"Oh, Alice."

"Nope."

"You guessed that before," I said.

"I don't know any more."

"Guess."

"Why don't you guess?" Eddie said to Helen.

"I don't know the name. I told you I don't know."

"But I don't know it, either. He's the only one that knows."

"Guess. Guess," the kid said, still kicking in time.

"Oh, I don't know. Jane?"

"Nope," the kid said, at least stopping the kicking.

"Judy?"

"Nope."

"Janet?"

"Nope."

"Jean?"

"Nope."

"How are we going to guess it?" Eddie said to the rest of us.

"Take it alphabetically," Herb said. "That's the only way to do it."

"Guess."

"Even I'm getting interested now," I said.

"Guess."

"Abby," Herb said.

"Nope."

"Aachen," I said.

"What?" Herb said.

"It's a town in Germany."

"Guess."

"Barbara," Eddie said.

"Nope."

"It's impossible," Eddie said.

"Nope."

"I like that one," I said. "Impossible Murphy."

"Nope," the kid said, looking at me.

"Adele," Herb said.

"Nope."

"We've got to think of something else to get his mind off it," Eddie said.

"Guess."

"Well, if anybody knows the phone number," I said, "I'll gladly call Mrs. Murphy."

"Guess. Guess."

"Look," Eddie said to him. "We're not going to guess any more. Now the game's over."

"Guess. Guess. Guess."

"We did. We can't guess any more. You have to tell us."

"Nope."

"I'd like to know," I said to the kid. "Won't you tell me?"

"Nope."

"Tell Mr. Hughes," Eddie said. "Come on."

"Nope."

"Look!" Eddie said, raising his voice a little. "Tell him."

"Nope," the kid said, and then he dropped his head and started to cry.

"Now look what you did," Helen said.

"Look what I did?" Eddie said. "What did I do? He's got us all going nuts here, trying to think of the name of a kid we don't even know and now he starts to cry. I didn't make him cry."

"I certainly didn't," Helen said.

"Come on," Eddie said, and he picked the kid up. The kid was still crying, sitting on Eddie's lap, Eddie trying to rock him. "Just stop crying. What are you crying about?"

"I don't know," the kid said, breathing it now, between the sobs that were shaking him. "I don't know."

"You don't know? You don't know what?"

"I don't know the name," the kid was sobbing. "I don't know the girl's name. I don't know the girl's name."

"How do you like that?" Eddie said, looking at Helen. "He drives us all crazy trying to guess a name he doesn't even know himself."

"That's the way he is," Helen said.

"We don't care what the name is," Eddie said to the kid, rocking him, the kid still sobbing. "We don't care. Who cares about that old name?"

"You know you should never have started that guessing business with him," Herb said.

"You know you're right?" I said to him, hoping my face was expressing awe. "You're absolutely right."

"Of course I'm right."

"Do you have any children of your own?"

"You don't have to have children. All you have to have is common sense."

"I know what we'll do," Eddie said, bending over and trying to look into the kid's face. "I know what we'll do. We'll play the pinball machine. Do you want to play the pinball machine?"

"I don't know," the kid said, crying.

"Come on," Eddie said.

He stood up and bounced the kid up toward his shoulder and he carried him off toward the bar, the kid still sobbing.

"It's never easy," I said to Helen. "I guess it's not supposed to be."

"You're telling me?"

"If you just use common sense," Herb said, "you won't have any trouble."

"No trouble at all?" I said.

"Well, you know what I mean."

"What was Eddie trying to tell me about the stickball game?" I said to Helen.

"I don't know."

"You don't remember that particular game with which, apparently, you had something to do?"

"There were a million stickball games on the block," Herb said.

"I remember them playing stickball," Helen said. "They used to play it half the summer."

"What's so important about a stickball game?" Herb said.

"I don't know. I haven't heard Eddie's story yet."

"But what difference would it make? Eddie's a fighter now. That's what you're writing about, isn't it?"

"That's right."

"I don't understand how you writers work."

"So I judge," I said, and then to Helen: "May I get you another drink?"

"You might as well."

"And you?" I said to Herb.

"No," he said, and then, thinking: "Well, all right. Rye and ginger."

I brought the drinks back and sat down. Helen was lighting another cigarette, adept and behind that pane of clear glass I had seen at the house.

"Do you enjoy watching fights?" I said to her.

She inhaled from the cigarette, and then streamed the smoke out slowly. It is a device all those glaziers use.

"To be honest, I can take them or leave them."

"Do you go to Eddie's fights in New York?"

"I have."

"How many have you seen?"

"Oh, three or four."

"Are you planning to write about Helen?" Herb said.

"Yes. To some extent."

"Why do you have to bring her into it?"

"Because she's Eddie's wife."

"There's a lot of fighters that aren't even married."

"What was the first fight you ever saw Eddie in?" I said to Helen. "Was it before you were married?"

"Yes. It was at that place at Fort Hamilton."

"What do you remember about it?"

"Well, he fought a colored fighter."

"Toby Arnold," Herb said. "Eddie knocked him out in the fourth round."

"Tell me about it," I said to Helen. "How did you happen to go to the fight, and who did you go with? What kind of a night was it? You weren't married to Eddie yet, and you may remember the dress you decided to wear. You'd never been to a fight before, so it was either the way you expected it to be, or it wasn't. How was it?"

"Well, I went with a girl friend. Eddie gave me two tickets."

"What's the name of the girl friend?"

"It was Alice Jenkins. Now she's married."

"What kind of a night was it?"

"It was in the summer. I don't remember what kind of a night it was particularly."

"Is that important?" Herb said. "The kind of a night it was?"

"It might be."

"Why?"

"Because this was the start of Helen becoming a part of Eddie's way of making a living, his career."

"But Eddie's a fighter."

"What difference does that make? Eddie leaves home, has a pair of gloves laced onto his hands, and fights. Somebody else picks up a brief case and kisses his wife good-bye. They're all in the same tournament. Each man rides out wearing the colors of his house. I'm merely trying to reconstruct the beginnings of the relationship that grew to involve Helen and now their child— just to give you two people—in Eddie's fights."

"What magazine did you say this is for?"

"I didn't say."

"Well, what magazine is it for?"

"The *Tel Aviv Chuzpah*."

"What?"

"You're afraid of this story, aren't you?" I said to Helen.

"Why do you say that?" she said.

"Because I feel it. I'd have to be pretty dull not to."

"She's got a right to be," Herb said.

"Why?"

"The things they write about boxing," Helen said.

"All those movies they make," Herb said. "Eddie was never in a fixed fight."

"Of course not," I said. "Not one fighter in a thousand ever is."

"Then why do they write those things?" Helen said.

"To make a living."

"People don't know what it's like, married to a fighter."

"I'm sure of that."

"He's away half the time. When he's home he's not like other men."

"Naturally, he's a fighter."

"There's a lot of things we don't do. There's a lot of places we don't go."

"Believe me, Helen doesn't have any easy time of it," Herb said.

"I never suspected that she did."

"Then the things they're always writing about boxing," Helen said. "At least if Eddie was in another business it would be respected."

"When he wins the title he'll be respected. Millions of people will watch it on TV and, in spite of what they've heard about fighting, they'll respect him."

"I don't know," she said.

"Sure, if he could win the title," Herb said. "Then he could make something of his name, but the other guy's some fighter. Don't forget that."

I didn't have to answer. Eddie was walking back to us, holding the kid by the hand.

"Some pinball player," he said when they got to us. "He's a champ."

"I wanna play some more," the kid said, pulling at Eddie's hand.

"I have to go in and work," Eddie said. "I'll take him in with me and he can watch everybody. He'll like that."

"Nothing doing," Helen said.

"I wanna play some more."

"Why? What's the matter? He'll like it."

"Sure he'll like it. Do you think I want him watching his father punching other people?"

"Why not?"

"What does he know about boxing? All he'll see is his father punching other people. Then he'll start doing it on the block."

"No he won't."

"Listen I know him better than you do. I'm the one who'll have to put up with him, and it's bad enough as it is."

"I wanna play some more."

"Okay," Eddie said, shrugging. "I'll see you later."

"I wanna play some more."

"Your mother'll play with you," Eddie said, over his shoulder and walking out.

"All right. All right," Helen said. "I'll play with you."

"Well, I'm glad to have seen you again," I said to her.

"Thank you."

"And you, too," I said, nodding to Herb.

"Wait. I'm going in to watch Eddie box."

I walked into the gym with Herb following me. Cardone was in the ring, boxing with Keener's other welterweight, and Doc was standing alone near the chairs, watching.

"Did you rest?" I said.

"Yeah. I lay down for a while."

"You know Eddie's brother-in-law?"

"I've met him," Doc said, nodding to Herb.

"Say," Herb said. "What kind of shape is Eddie in?"

"What kind of shape?" Doc said, looking at him.

"That's right."

"Lousy shape," Doc said.

"What?"

"He's getting in great shape," I said.

"He'd better be," Herb said.

"Had he?" Doc said, giving Herb that look.

"Sure he'd better be. He's fighting a tough fighter. The other guy is some fighter."

"You think so?" Doc said.

"I certainly do."

"What business did you once tell me you're in?" Doc said, giving him that look again.

"Wholesale hardware. Why?"

"Good," Doc said, and he turned and walked away and I followed him.

"Thanks," I said.

"For what?"

"Big brother."

"Isn't that dreadful?" Doc said.

When Eddie came out, DeCorso and Memphis Kid were with him, and they loosened up for about fifteen minutes with Jay mothering around Eddie. In the ring Eddie went the first round with Keener's middleweight, just hounding him, and then he worked two with DeCorso, starting to sweat. When DeCorso finished and Memphis Kid climbed in, I got up on the ring apron and stood next to Doc.

"Mind if I join you on the bridge?"

"Any time," Doc said. "Memphis!"

Jay had finished fingering the Vaseline on Memphis' face and then he put the mouthpiece in. Eddie was circling the ring, walking around loose-armed, breathing in through his nose and out through his mouth, and Memphis walked over to where Doc and I were standing.

"Eddie'll let you set your own pace," Doc said to him. "Don't kill yourself the first day."

Memphis nodded and then hooked his white rubber mouthpiece out with the thumb of his left glove.

"Don't worry 'bout me, Mister Doc," he said. "I keep in shape. I'll keep his sweat for him."

"All right," Doc said to Jay.

"Time!" Jay said, shouting it.

Memphis put the mouthpiece back in and turned and Eddie turned and they boxed the round. Memphis set the pace, not fast but even, moving in and out with that left playing at Eddie and with Eddie making his own moves off it and Memphis catching almost all of them on the elbow or forearm or on one of the big gloves.

"What are you looking for?" Doc said to me.

"Penna."

I could see Keener watching with Cardone, and Barnum and Booker Boyd standing together and watching and Eddie's brother-in-law sitting in the front row of chairs, looking up at the two in the ring. I judged that Penna had gone in for his shower.

"What do you want him for?"

"We were trying to convince him that Memphis knows something about fighting. With the big gloves on Memphis, even Penna should be able to see it."

"Time!" Jay said, shouting it.

Eddie came over, his mouthpiece in his left glove, and Doc took a towel off the top rope and wiped the sweat off Eddie's face. Jay did the same for Memphis and, with Eddie pacing the ring again, Memphis walked over to us.

"Mister Doc?"

"Yes?"

"I believe I can hit him with the straight right hand."

"Why don't you?"

"You want me to try it?"

"What do you think I've got you up here for?"

"Yes, sir," Memphis said, nodding and putting the mouthpiece back in.

"Time!"

"Watch this," Doc said to me.

"He's giving a great imitation of the respected champion," I said, watching.

Memphis was, at that. He was jabbing, then doubling the jab, head-feinting and picking off Eddie's jabs with the right hand.

"Memphis can imitate any well-known fighter of the last fifteen years," Doc said. "You name him, and he can ape him."

As he said it, Memphis let the right hand go. He leaned his upper body a little to his left and let it go straight from the shoulder. When he did, Eddie turned his head so that it just grazed the left side of his headguard and, pivoting back, he drove his own right, hard, under the heart.

"Hold it!" Doc hollered.

The punch had driven Memphis against the ropes and the follow-up hook caught him flush on the cheekbone as his head dropped as Doc hollered. Now Eddie grabbed Memphis under the arms, and Memphis held Eddie and straightened up.

"Now let's take it easy," Doc said, calling it to them.

"How'd you like that?" Jay said, walking over to us.

"Fine," I said.

"Eddie'll do that to the champion, too. They'll see who's a great champion. Eddie is liable to kill him."

"Watch the time," Doc said. "How's the time?"

"Time!" Jay said, shouting it.

"You all right?" Doc said to Memphis.

"I'm all right," Memphis said, breathing hard and about to crawl through the ropes, but stopping now and straightening up. "He sure did time me, Mister Doc. He's real sharp."

"He'll be sharper."

"Nobody figures to counter my straight right. They figure to slip it or block it now, but not to counter it. Nobody ever did."

"All right, Memphis. Thanks."

Eddie worked only one round on the big bag and one round on the speed bag and then went in to cool out. Doc and I had started out toward the kitchen to avoid Eddie's brother-in-law, when Penna came after me.

"Hey!" he said. "Eddie wants you. He's in the dressing room."

"Where were you when Memphis was boxing?"

"Right under a good old shower."

"I'll see you later," I said to Doc. "Why don't you buy Herb a drink?"

"I'll buy him a mickey," Doc said.

When I got into the dressing room, Eddie and Memphis and DeCorso were having their hot tea. Jay was making a project of picking up around the room.

"Whose towel is this?" he was saying, holding up a towel.

"That's mine," DeCorso said.

"How about that punch?" Jay said to me.

"Good."

"How about it, Memphis?" Jay said.

"Skip it," Eddie said.

"You want me?" I said to Eddie.

"Sure. I want to finish telling you about the stickball game."

"Good. I'm listening."

"We played stickball a lot, and this Tony could hit them a mile. I think it was Tony hit it this day, and it hit the back of this car—a parked car—near where the back slopes up by the back window. It was a rubber ball—you know?—and it took off up into the air. Well, Helen and this other girl—I think her name was Alice—were walking down the sidewalk and we hollered and they looked up and they could see the ball starting to come down. This other girl, she put her arms up over her head, like girls do, but I remember that Helen just stood there, looking up and waiting for that ball, and when it came down she just stuck her hands out and she caught it, just like nothing."

"How come you're telling him that?" Jay said.

"Because he asked me if I could remember the first time I ever noticed Helen. That was the first time, when she caught that ball. I remember that all the guys cheered."

"Thanks, Eddie," I said.

"Does that help you? I mean, can you use that?"

"I might. Do you, by any chance, remember what Helen was wearing?"

"It was the summertime. I think she had on a light blue dress."

"Thanks."

"I'm just trying to be helpful," he said.

14

I awakened as soon as the hand turned the knob. It was deep dusk in the room, with the dark green shades drawn, and I was conscious of the rain dripping somewhere outside and then of the light from the bulb in the hall reaching into the room and the silhouette of Jay standing in it and straining to see me.

"You awake?"

"Yes, Jay."

"It's still rainin'."

"So I hear."

"It's seven-thirty."

"Oh?"

"We didn't go on the road, but we're goin' down to the gym. Eddie's gonna loosen up."

"Good. I'll be down."

"He's not gonna do anything, just loosen up and skip rope, but you said you wanted to be around, whatever we do."

"That's right, Jay."

"If I was you, I'd sleep."

"I'll be down, Jay. Thanks."

"Okay, but I'll close this door. Maybe you'll go back to sleep."

When he shut the door and the room was darkened again, I lay just listening to the rain. I had left the window open about six inches below the shade, and the rain dripping on the sill sounded like it was falling right in the room.

I wanted to lie there and just listen to it and then, perhaps, fall into sleep again, but after a couple of minutes I got up and found the door and opened it halfway, so that the light from the hall would come in, but not too bright, because I did not want to raise the shades and see the rain. Then I dressed up to the waist and took my towel and soap and went down the hall to the bathroom and then washed and came back and finished dressing.

In the gym Eddie was skipping rope, wearing a gray sweatsuit and his ring shoes. The four ceiling lights were on, up among the red white and blue paper streamers, and Jay was leaning against the bar, the towel over his shoulder, and Doc was sitting on one of the wooden folding chairs near the ring, the two of them watching Eddie.

"What are you doing here?" Doc said, when I walked up to him.

He had on a pair of dark blue trousers and a light blue V-necked sweater and he needed a shave. Sitting there, in the pale mixture of the yellow light from above and the gray light coming through the windows, he looked very old.

"Don't you remember me? I'm a member of the club, too."

"You work at this, don't you?"

"Not any harder than you do."

"I don't want him to break the schedule," Doc said. "I let him sleep an hour longer, but if he doesn't do something in place of the roadwork and sleeps all morning it'll throw him all off."

"Let's hope we don't get three or four days of this rain."

"It's raining for the other guy, too."

There is always the other guy. You do not just turn in your corner and walk out and meet a stranger. Even if you never saw him before the weigh-in, you have known him and he has known you for all of this long while, and I watched Eddie and listened to the tick of the rope and the pat of his feet in the big quiet room. Then, in the rhythm of it, my mind moved away from me and I saw the room as from a high, far rafter and in the room the three of us focused upon the one, the one, spring-footed and loose-wristed, sweating in his circular cage of rope and staring, darkly, out through it.

"All right!" Doc hollered to him. "Break it up."

Eddie gave the rope a half-dozen double-timed whirls, and on the last one turned toward the bar, passed the rope into his right hand and, whirling it a half turn, flung it in an arc toward Jay. Jay put his hands up, and got one hand into it as it hit him and the wooden handles clacked on the floor.

"What are you tryin' to do, kill me?"

"All right," Doc said. "Walk around a while."

I watched Eddie walk, sweating, rotating his head, walking past the bar, rotating his shoulders, making a tour around the chairs in front of the ring and starting the circuit again. When a man runs or walks on the road it is conceivable that he is finding a world bigger than his room, but when he walks in a place like this it is for only one reason, and I tried to picture the other man in his own place but in this same moment.

On such a morning of rain and grayness there in Summit, I wondered, did he lie in bed in one of the bare rooms above and behind the gym on the side of the hill? I wondered if he, too, walked his gym, for it is important. When a match is made what each man does with the same moment is a part of it, just as every act a man has ever performed, every thought he has ever possessed and that made him as he now stands become moves in it, for time has now revealed that these two have been in combat forever.

"All right," Doc said. "That's enough of it."

"Good," Eddie said, walking over to us. "Hello, Frank."

"Good morning."

"You want your tea in your room or down here?" Jay said.

"In the room," Eddie said. "My clothes are up there."

He was sitting on the bed now, with just the white terrycloth robe on and a towel around his neck, the hot teacup cradled in both hands, blowing across the top of it and sipping from it.

"What do you think of my brother-in-law?" he said.

"He's quite a brain," I said.

"What?"

"He has what they call a good head on his shoulders."

"Are you kidding?"

"Yes."

"Who?" Jay said. He was sorting his rolls of gauze and tape again on the table.

"My brother-in-law."

"What's the matter with him?"

"You tell me."

"When he was here yesterday," Jay said, "he was asking me how many rounds you worked every day since you're here. He wrote it down in a notebook. He wanted to know how far you run on the road, to write that down, too. What's he want all that for?"

"Don't ask me," Eddie said. "You should have asked him."

"I make it all now," I said. "He's not in wholesale hardware. That's just a front. He makes book, and he's getting ready to establish his line on the fight."

"I can just see that," Eddie said. "A guy like him."

"He says to me," Jay said, "he says: 'How does he sleep?' I said: 'Whatta you mean, how does he sleep? On his back, on his side. I don't know.' He says: 'I mean, does he sleep good all night long.' So I said: 'Sure, he sleeps good.' What does he think I do, sit up all night and watch you sleep?'"

"It reminds me of the second Louis-Walcott fight," I said.

"What about it?" Eddie said.

"The AP sent a psychiatrist to both camps to analyze the two fighters. Walcott's people didn't want to let him talk to Walcott, so he started on Dan Florio. When Fred Gardner and I got out there Dan was blowing his top. He said: 'You know what the guy asks me?' We said: 'What?' He said: 'How many times a day does Walcott go to the bathroom? What does the guy think I do here?'"

"What happened then?" Eddie said.

"The last we saw of the psychiatrist, he was sitting at one of those tables under the trees in that kind of a picnic area, interviewing Curtis Hatchet Man Sheppard, who was one of Walcott's sparring partners."

"What could he get from him?" Jay said.

"So yesterday," Eddie said, "we're sitting there talking, Helen and Herb and me, and he says: 'Now, if you win, you should have one or two more fights and then retire.' I said: 'If I win? Whatta you mean, if I win?' He says: 'Well, you know what I mean. The other guy is a good fighter, and accidents can happen.' I said: 'Stop it, will you?'"

"So Helen says: 'Don't get sore.' I said: 'Who's sore?' So she says: 'Well, the other fighter feels the same as you do, too. He's just as sure he's going to win as you are.' I said: 'What? What's that got to do with it?'"

"Finish your tea," Jay said.

"How do you like that?" Eddie said, looking at me.

"I don't."

"Why do they act that way?"

"Well, I can't speak for your brother-in-law."

"Believe me, nobody has to."

"I prefer to believe, though, that your wife is just instinctively preparing herself, and you, too, for the possibility that exists in her mind that the other guy, who has a chance to win, might. That's all it is."

"When you're a fighter you never think of that. Believe me, I never once think anybody I fight can lick me, especially this guy in this fight."

"But your wife isn't a fighter and, if something goes wrong, she doesn't want her whole world, and yours, to collapse."

"Nothing's going wrong."

"Of course not, but you asked a question."

He drank the last of the tea and put the cup down next to the radio on the bed table. He turned on the radio and waited for it to warm up and tuned in music.

"Many's the time," he said, "I wished I was in some other business for just that reason. I mean when other guys come home from work they can talk about it with their wives and their wives understand what they go through."

"Don't be so sure."

"You don't think so?"

"How can they understand? I don't care what the business is. Unless they're in it themselves they can't really understand what it's like."

"So Herb says: 'If you win, have a fight or two and retire.' Right now I'm fighting the best I ever fought. I win the title, I'm on top. Why retire? I like it. I spent nine years learning the business and he wants me to retire. What else can I do as good as I can fight?"

"I agree," I said, "but what intrigues me is the thought that probably not one person in the thousands—millions on TV—who watch a fight even thinks that a fighter has a brother-in-law."

"I suppose they think you just go and fight."

"That's right."

We could hear a pounding on a door or a wall somewhere, and some muffled shouts.

"What's that?" Jay said, looking around.

"I don't know," Eddie said. "Let's see."

When we got out into the hall, Doc, in a flannel robe, was opening his door, and Memphis, Booker Boyd and Barnum were coming out of their room. We were all looking at the door to the room where Polo and Schaeffer slept, and wedged across it was a piece of two-by-four, with one end sharpened, that appeared to have been used once as a stake. Wrapped around the stake and around the dooknob, with a glob of knots, was a heavy twist of old clothesline.

"What's goin' on?" Jay said.

"Somebody's in there," Memphis said, above the pounding.

"Hey! Let us out!" Polo's voice came through the door.

"Go get your scissors," Doc said to Jay.

"How about that?" Eddie said to me, laughing.

When Jay came out with the scissors, Penna showed in the hall, with DeCorso. As Jay started for the door, Penna, shirtless but wearing a pair of slacks, grabbed the scissors from him.

"Here, let me do it," he said.

"Come on," Jay said, trying to get the scissors back again.

"Let us out!" Polo's voice came through the door, and now the pounding started again.

"Oh, no," Penna said, holding the scissors away from Jay. "Those are my pals in there. I'm the guy to let 'em out."

"You're the guy did it," Jay said.

"Come on! Come on!" Polo was hollering. "Let us out!"

"Relax, relax," Penna said, shouting it at the door. "I'll rescue you."

"I'll get you for this, Penna," Polo's voice came back. "Open it!"

"What is it? What is it?" Girot said, coming around the corner from the stairs.

"Let us out! Let us out!"

"I'll handle it, Girot," Penna said. "I got friends in there."

"We're no friends of yours," Polo's voice came back. "Open it!"

"Look at this," Penna said, pointing with the scissors to the rope. "Some genius must have done this. He soaked the rope, so it would shrink and be tight. The guy had to be a genius."

On the sill and in front of the door on the floor there was a small puddle of water.

"Open the door!" Polo was shouting, pounding again.

"Open it, Penna," Doc said.

"Sure, Doc," Penna said, slowly, looking at Doc. "I'll open it."

"Open this door!"

"This'll take a little time," Penna said, sawing at the rope and calling to the door. "Just relax, friends. Al Penna's got everything in hand."

"Open it!" Polo said, pounding on the door.

"Please. You'll make me nervous," Penna said, sawing. "There."

When he cut the rope the two-by-four fell and Penna turned the knob and pushed the door open. As he did, Polo, in a pair of striped, rumpled pajamas came through and Penna, backing off, held the scissors in front of himself and pointing at Polo.

"What a minute, friend. I rescued you."

"If you didn't have those scissors," Polo said, still moving toward Penna, "I'd kill you."

"Why me?" Penna said, circling a little now, the scissors in front of him as Polo still moved at him.

"Polo, back off," Doc said. "Jay, take those scissors."

"Here, I'll take them," Eddie said. He walked between the two and took the scissors from Penna and held Polo off with the other hand.

"I oughta kill you," Polo said to Penna.

"No thanks. No thanks a guy gets," Penna said, addressing the rest of us, but watching Polo.

"I'll give you thanks," Polo said, pressing against Eddie's arm.

"Whatta you so sore about?" Penna said. "I didn't do it. Besides, you weren't gonna get up to run, anyway."

"You did it all right," Schaeffer's voice came out of the room. He was still lying in one of the beds. "We know you did it."

"Me?"

"Yes, you," Polo said, cooling a little now. "Suppose the place caught fire and we were caught in there? Did you ever think of that?"

"You and your fires. I rescued you from one, didn't I? I'd rescue you again, but in case I died trying, you could jump out the window. What's to worry about?"

"Yeah?" Polo said. "You can get killed jumping from this high."

"What's get killed? Let Schaeffer jump first, and you jump on top of him. He's soft."

"I ain't so soft," Schaeffer said, from the bed.

"Oh, you hear that?" Penna said, addressing the rest of us again.

Doc had gone back into his room and shut the door and Barnum had disappeared from the other doorway although Memphis and Booker Boyd still stood there watching. Polo turned to me.

"I'm glad we're leavin' tomorrow," he said. "I got enough of this guy."

"You're going tomorrow?" I said.

"Sure. Who's there to work with here? That one heavyweight Keener brings up? The fight's next Thursday, so we go into Stillman's for a couple of days. What my guy needs is a lot of work."

"Is that what he needs?" Penna said.

"Why don't you shut up?" Polo said.

"Yeah, Penna," Jay said.

"Take your shower," Doc said to Eddie. He was standing in his doorway again. "Don't stand around out there."

"Yeah, take your shower," Jay said to Eddie.

15

The next morning Eddie and Memphis and I walked up the driveway with Polo and Schaeffer to see them off on the 9:25 bus. After a day and a half of rain the world was washed clean. The sky was a spotless blue, but there was a cool, steady breeze blowing out of the northwest to mean that, at least by noon, we would be getting those high-piled banks of swift white clouds.

To anyone seeing us and not knowing us we would have appeared a curious group. Polo, worrying about missing the bus, led us, carrying his suitcase. Eddie walked with his hands in his pants pockets, his jacket zipped to the neck. Memphis, walking behind Eddie and me, carried the smaller of Schaeffer's two suitcases, and Schaeffer trailed us carrying the big one loaded with his gear.

"Maybe we missed it," Polo said.

"No," Eddie said, looking at his wrist watch. "They run like trains. They're late, but they're never early."

We had crossed the road, and stood in the lee of the hillside and in the sun.

"Here it come now," Memphis said.

We saw it coming, blue in the sunlight, down the rise of the road to the north.

"So good luck," Eddie said, shaking Schaeffer's hand. "You can lick that guy."

"Thanks, Eddie," Schaeffer said.

"He better lick him," Polo said. "The money it cost me up here."

"Good luck, Paul," I said, shaking his hand, and then Memphis shook his hand and I could see that Schaeffer was pleased that we had walked up to see him off but that he was trying to cover his embarrassment like a big child. Then we all shook hands with Polo and he remembered to wish Eddie luck, and that was the way we bundled them off, with the little guy in the almost threadbare topcoat and old brown fedora and the big one in a new gray tweed topcoat and bareheaded following him down the aisle of the half-filled bus, the two of them lugging their bags and lurching together as the bus started off.

"Well, that's that," Eddie said as we watched the rear of the bus going away, the blue-gray exhaust swirling back from the flatulent bursts.

"That's that," Memphis said. "You're right."

We walked back down the driveway and I noticed then for the first time that the seed pods of the swamp maples had put out their dark red dollhouse chandeliers and that the forsythia along the driveway was chartreuse, ready to break out into yellow. Beyond and above the roof line of the hotel the long, thin, crowded branches of the top of the big willow by the lake hung in yellow fronds so that the whole, moving in the breeze and the bright sun, seemed a golden fountain.

"You just lost two customers," Eddie said to Girot when we got to the porch.

I had seen Girot come out onto the porch and then just stand there, his arms folded across the front of his butcher's apron, and watch us ambling down the driveway toward him.

"Yes," he said. "Some customers."

"What's the matter with them," Eddie said.

"What's the matter with them?" Girot said. "When it comes time to pay the bill this morning, that Polo he says: 'I am sorry, but I don't have the money now. I will pay you after my fighter fights on Thursday.'"

"So he'll pay you," Eddie said.

"So he'll pay me. Now when my meat man comes today I suppose I am to tell him: 'Don't worry. I will pay you after Schaeffer fights someplace on Thursday.'"

"In Holyoke," Eddie said.

"Yes. My meat man would be happy to hear that. Holyoke."

"Ah, Girot," I said. "You are indeed one of the world's privileged minority."

"I am privileged?"

"Certainly. You are one of that small but all-powerful group of holders who control the destinies of the rest of us. By exacting the privilege of extending credit to Polo you will on Thursday, without lacing on a glove or throwing a punch or selling a ticket, become a party to the profits of a prize fight. Schaeffer will now be fighting for you, too, and it's in exactly that fashion that all of the world's great fortunes have been amassed."

"Sure," Girot said, disgusted.

"From Schaeffer you may branch out into railroads or munitions or whatever. You've got to decide what you're going to do with all your money."

"That's right, bon ami," Eddie said. "What will you do with all your money?"

"Money? You think I make any money on that Schaeffer?"

"Sure," Eddie said. "Why not?"

"The way he eats? Who can make money?"

"Now you're trying deception," I said. "You know you're flattered."

"I am flattered?"

"Absolutely. Every time you see Schaeffer eat you know he is paying his most sincere compliments to the wonders of your wife's cooking."

"Compliments. With him that's no compliment. Schaeffer would eat anything."

"Let's go around and sit in the sun," Eddie said.

"Fine," I said. "Memphis?"

"Thank you," Memphis said. "I'd like that."

"I would like it, too," Girot said, "but I have to work."

"But remember you're holding," I said. "We're not."

The gray, weathered dock reached about fifteen feet out into the water, and moored to the end of it was an old, heavy-planked, flat-bottomed rowboat that had been freshly painted in Girot's hotel colors, white with dark red trim. At the land end of the dock there was an unpainted single-plank bench, and we sat there, sheltered from the wind by the hotel and warm in the sun.

"Holyoke," Eddie said. "I fought there four times."

"How many times did you fight there, Memphis?" I said.

"Oh, seven-eight times, I guess. I don't rightly remember."

Along our shore the water was calm, but the rest of the lake was alive with small, sun-dappled waves.

"How many fights have you had, anyway?" Eddie said.

"Oh, maybe a hundred fifty-sixty. I had a lot that's not in the book. I fought a lot in the bootleg amateurs and a lot of fights in Australia, more than it shows in the book. I never did figure it out exactly how many I got."

"How come you went to Australia?"

"I couldn't get no fights around here so my manager at that time booked me a couple of fights in California—in San Francisco, California—and, after I knocked those two boys out, there wasn't anybody would fight me around there either. Then I figured I had just enough money left from my purses to get back to New York, so I sent that money to my wife and I found me a job as a mess boy on a freighter ship and I went to Australia."

"Who managed you there?"

"I manage myself. There was this gentleman work on the ship, 'way down in that engine room, and he was a fight fan and he been to Australia before so when we got to Melbourne he took me to the gym, where he'd been to visit before, and I found me the promoter there and I told him I was a fighter. He said to me: 'Just comin' off that ship can you fight six rounds the day after tomorrow?' I said: 'Mister, I can fight six rounds right now.'

"So I told my friend from the ship, I said: 'How about you get-tin' one of them other gentlemen from that engine room and you two be my seconds?' So he said: 'Me? I just like to watch fights. I don't know what you supposed to do in the corner.' I said: 'You just get another gentleman and I'll tell you what to do. It's easy.'

"Then the night of the fight there must have come, I guess, more than a dozen gentlemen from the ship that come to the club. When it come about time to go down to the ring my friend he was scared. He had this other gentleman from the ship with him and they're in the dressin' room with me and I said: 'What make you worried? There's nothing to be scared.' So he said: 'But we don't know what we're supposed to do.' I said: 'I'll tell you what to do. You gentlemen just follow me down to the ring, carryin' that pail there with that bottle in it and with the sponge and my mouthpiece and my towel. Then I'll tell you what to do.' Then he said: 'But supposin' you get cut? I don't know what to do.' I said: 'Get cut? Gentlemen, I never been cut in my whole life. I ain't gonna get cut tonight. You got nothin' to worry about that.' That was the truth, too."

"How was the fight?" Eddie said. "What happened?"

"They had me fightin' some red-headed boy that I guess he didn't have more than ten or twelve, maybe, fights. By now I only been in Australia a couple of days, but I kinda like it—the people they seem nice to me—so I have it in my mind that I might like to stay here a while. Then I figure that, if I'm gonna stay here and get work, I better be careful in this fight. I mean that this better look like it's a good fight—you know what I mean—and that I better not hurt this red-headed boy too much because he was just like a child, almost, when you come to think about it."

"So what did you do?" Eddie said.

"So I make it a real good fight. This red-headed boy he was a professional fighter there, but he was like what we call an amateur here."

"Can you imagine?" Eddie said to me. "Memphis in with an amateur?"

"I wish I'd seen it," I said. "What about the fight, Memphis?"

"Well, that boy was game. When the bell ring he come out punchin' and lookin' to knock me out. The people, they like that right from the start. They was hollerin', and I figure that if they like this, I go along with it, too. I let him come to me, but you know how you do it. You make it look like a war, but those punches he was throwin' they only look good to the people because yourself you're catchin' most of them on the arms or with a part of the glove, and once in a while I would let one through to me to see how much this boy could punch. You know how you do it."

"I know," Eddie said, grinning. "Nobody could do it like you, Memphis."

"The people, they love it, but when I come back to my corner each round I like to laugh. I would take my mouthpiece out myself and just sit there and hold it in my glove until it time to put it back in and my friend from the engine room would say: 'But what do we do now? What are we supposed to do now?' So I would say: 'Now one of you gentlemen give me the bottle to wrench out my mouth, and then the other sponge my face a little, if you don't mind.' Then I remember my friend lookin' at me scared and he said: 'But are you all right? Don't get hurt now, will you? That other fella's tough.'

"They were so scared, I like to laugh. I said: 'Now don't you worry. I be all right.' So at the end of the fourth round I figure I better do somethin'. By now I make that red-headed boy look so good that, to win, I got to knock him out, but I got to be careful how I do that if I'm gonna stay here in Australia. I mean you can't offend the people, can you?"

"No, Memphis," I said. "You can't."

"That's right, and also I don't want to hurt that red-headed boy none. I mean he seem like a nice boy, so I start pressin' him a little more in the fifth round, and the people are goin' crazy and stampin' their feet and then I stepped inside him and I hit him a right hand in the body as hard, real solid, as I could. Well, his hands they come down and he just start to fold forward and then, for the people, I hit him a hook on the chin, but not hard because the body punch already done for him, and he went down on his face and the referee he just count him out."

"How did it go over?"

"It go over fine. I mean the fight it was so close in the eyes of the people that they like it even if their boy don't win. In Australia they're nice people, and now they're all standin' and cheerin' me."

"How about your friends from the ship?"

"They was shakin' hands with one another in the corner and jumpin' up and down, they was so happy. After the fight I guess there was a dozen of them gentlemen from the ship that come to the fight and I guess they bet on me because they all took me out and we went to a restaurant and they bought me a dinner and they had a time. They wanted me I should stay with the ship and they had it figured that every time we'd go to some port I'd get me a fight and they'd all go to it and second me and bet on me like they did that night. They really wanted me to do that."

"I'll bet they did," I said. "They had it figured that, in time, they could sack every seaport in the free world."

"They were even gonna speak to the captain. They were gonna find me a place to train on the ship. They figured that even the captain he'd like that, too, and I sure was sorry, when they treated me like that, to have to disappoint those gentlemen on that ship."

"You told them you wouldn't do it?" Eddie said.

"I explained to those gentlemen that I couldn't train on no ship, and that I was really a fighter. I just had to stay someplace and fight, and I was gonna stay, I made up my mind, in Australia."

"How long were you there?"

"I guess I was there almost two years. The people they were real nice to me."

"And how many fights did you have there?"

"I don't know for sure, but I guess about two dozen maybe."

"Did you play ping-pong with all of them, like with the red-haired kid?"

"No, sir. I did for most of them. I made them real good fights, right up until I knocked out the middleweight champion of Australia. Then I fought the light heavyweight champion and I outpointed him. Then I had to fight the heavyweight champion. He wasn't a boy knew too much about fightin' but he was big. He had more than twenty-five pounds on me, and he kept hittin' me on the arms until I couldn't lift 'em, just blockin' his punches, and he got the decision in fifteen rounds. Then I come home, because I wanted to see my wife and my daughter, and there wasn't nobody else for me to fight down there neither."

"How long have you been married, Memphis?" I said.

"Oh, fifteen years. My wife she works in a laundry."

"How old is your daughter?"

"She's twelve years old now already. In the school they say she's smart, too."

"What's she going to do when she gets out of school?"

"She says she's gonna be a nurse. I like that."

"I like it, too. That's fine."

"Would you excuse me now?"

"Sure, Memphis."

"Speakin' of the laundry, I gotta get my own."

Memphis left us then, and I asked Eddie what he meant about the laundry.

"He does his own laundry every day up here. You know?"

"No. I don't know."

"Well, the only clothes he brought, besides what he wears on the road mornings, is the gray suit he's got and that sweater he has on today. Then he's got a change of shorts and socks and two T-shirts, and I guess, some handkerchiefs. Every day after the workout he washes out his shorts and socks and T-shirt and a handkerchief. He hangs them out in the furnace room off the kitchen and then, every day after he takes his shower, he has clean clothes to put on."

"He's a wonderful guy."

"He should have been champion and made some money."

"I know, and one of the most amazing things to me about him and his type is that they never seem to resent us whites. We're the ones who did it to him, you know."

"I suppose."

"Sure we are."

"I noticed today he looks something like that Louie Armstrong."

"And if he could have played a trumpet like he used to fight he'd have been another Louie Armstrong."

"That's right."

I wanted to ask Eddie how, believing as he did about Memphis, he felt in using him as a sparring partner and banging him around. I could not find the right way to express it, however, and then he stood up and I put it away.

"Doc got him a six-rounder on the card," he said. "Memphis will make himself four hundred plus what he's getting up here. At least it's something."

"Yes, it is."

We walked around between the cascade of the willow, moving in the wind, and the south end of the hotel and started across the parking space to the front porch. A new light-blue, two-door Ford had apparently just pulled in, and a small, thin young woman got out and shut the door and walked toward us.

"Excuse me," she said, "but can you tell me where I can find Eddie Brown?"

"I'm Eddie Brown."

"Oh, fine. I'm Ethel Morse from the Bunny Williams show."

"The what?" Eddie said, shaking hands with her.

"The Bunny Williams show on television. Don't you know about it?"

"Oh, yes. Doc spoke to me. This is Frank Hughes, Miss—"

"Ethel Morse. I'm glad to know you, Frank."

"Thank you."

"I trust you'll be with us on Monday," she said to Eddie, "so I thought I'd just run up and ask you a few questions about your background and—"

"Well," Eddie said, "I don't know."

"But as I understand it, you're going to be in town on Monday, aren't you?"

"Yes, sure. We have to go in for the preliminary examination, but I don't know about the show. You've got to talk to Doc about that."

"Doc? I'm afraid I'm not familiar with Doc."

"He's my manager," Eddie said, smiling, "and he's against television."

"He's against television?"

She was a very plain thing, about thirty, with not enough chin and a little too much nose and black-rimmed eyeglasses, and the way she looked right then you would have thought that Eddie had said that Doc was against God.

"You're not serious?"

"Well, you better talk to Doc. I don't know anything about television. Frank, here, is a magazine writer, so probably he knows more about it than Doc or I do."

"I pass."

"Frank Hughes?" she said. "You write for magazines?"

"I confess."

"I know your name. I'm sure I've seen your articles."

"Thank you."

She could be playing a hand, I thought, but for some reason I'm always inclined to believe them when they're plain or homely. Why, I was wondering, do I always believe this kind and suspect the lookers?

"Why don't we go in," Eddie said, "and find Doc?"

"Fine," she said, "although I must confess I'm a little nervous about meeting this ogre."

"Oh, no," Eddie said. "Doc's all right. He's a wonderful guy."

"Lead on," she said.

She had on a dark green tweed suit that came off Fifth Avenue and not Fourteenth Street and a pair of flat-heeled, brown suède sports shoes with fringed, flap-over tongues for her day in the country. Over one shoulder she was lugging a large saddle-leather bag and she walked with a real stride for such a small woman.

When we had ushered her into the lobby Eddie went upstairs to find Doc and I took her into the dining room and sat her down at one of the tables by a window. She refused a drink and asked me a couple of questions about the camp and who ran it, and then Doc came in, peering at her, and Eddie introduced them and we all sat down.

"Now what do you want me to buy?" Doc said.

"Really!" she said, looking at Eddie and me. "Now I am frightened."

"Easy, Doc," I said.

"I hate television," Doc said.

"So I've been told," she said, "although I can't say I really believe it."

"You can believe anything I tell you, lady."

"But, really, you can't hate television. What's there to hate? What did it ever do to you?"

"Everything, to both questions. Your business eats mine. Four years after your business started televising my business, forty-three small fight clubs in this country had folded because even a sucker won't pay for something that somebody else is giving away for free. Why do I hate it?"

"But I can't see what earthly difference that makes to you. After all, Eddie Brown doesn't box in these small clubs you're speaking of."

"But where do you think he learned how to fight? Do you know that you may be sitting at this table right now with the last of the real professional fighters, because my business isn't like your business where they tear a piece of bark off a tree and the first thing that crawls out they make into a—what do you call it?"

"I'm sure I don't know what you mean."

"A television personality," I said.

"That's right," Doc said. "A television personality. The first thing that crawls out they make into a television personality. Look at me."

"I am," she said.

"You're looking at a guy who's got a fighter and the sports pages and that's all I've ever had for over forty years. I'm not married because I never wanted to be, and for the last fifteen years I've been living in the same hotel. I know every cabbie that works that stand there, day or night. I know how many kids they've got and what troubles they got with their wives. So one night when your business was just starting to catch on I came out and got in a cab. You listening?"

"I most certainly am."

She was, too, because she couldn't figure Doc at all.

"So I sit back and the cabbie says: 'Say, Doc, how about that Wally Johns?' I say to myself that he's not a fighter. 'Willie Jones?' I said. 'Ballplayer?' He starts to laugh. For the first time in my life a cabbie laughs at me. He says: 'Doc, are you kidding?' I said: 'No. Who is he?' He says: 'Who is Wally Johns? He's famous. He's the guy announces the wrestling on television. He's great.' I said: 'Stop the cab.' He says: 'Why? We're not there yet.' I said: 'Yes, we are. We just passed it.' I got out and slammed the door and walked six blocks in the rain. Television? What do you want from me?"

"Well, we want Eddie Brown on the Bunny Williams show on

Monday. Eddie has confirmed what they informed us at Madison Square Garden—that he has to be in New York on Monday anyway."

"We shouldn't even be going in for the examination," Doc said turning to me. "I told them: 'Send that doctor out here.' So they said: 'We want Eddie and the other guy together for the photographers. If you both come to town we can start the fire under the fight.' Now we should go on television, too."

"It was Madison Square Garden that suggested it," she said. "They called us and said they'd spoken with you."

"Why don't you get the other guy? The other guy is the great champion. Since when is television interested in the second man?"

"Well, the people at Madison Square Garden suggested Eddie. The gentleman there who handles the publicity explained that Eddie is intelligent and makes a good appearance, and now that I've met him I'm convinced that he's just what we want."

"Thanks," Eddie said.

"Ah, come on now. Level with me," Doc said.

"What?"

"You know you don't want the other guy because he's colored. Admit it."

"That's not so. We've had Negroes on the show."

"Who?"

"We've had Negro musicians."

"What kind of a show is this, anyway?"

"Well, it's a half-hour show from two to two-thirty, Monday through Friday. Bunny is a grand person and she does a wonderful job. It's basically an interview show and we have two guests each week. We may have someone who's just written a book or is appearing in a new show or we may have someone who's in the news. We've had baseball players. That Mr. Farrell of the Yankees has been very nice about sending us a player when the team isn't playing that day."

"But it's for women, isn't it?"

"Yes, basically, but you'd be surprised at the number of women who have become interested in what used to be just men's things. Since boxing has been on television you'd be surprised at the number of women who enjoy it now."

"I wouldn't be surprised at anything," Doc said. "What time does Eddie have to be there?"

"Well, we'd like him there at one-thirty, to meet Bunny and to see the setup and get a picture of what we'll want him to do. All he'll have to do will be to walk in and sit down and Bunny will chat with him about his career. We're honestly excited about having a prominent boxer."

"All right," Doc said. "We'll be there."

"Well, thank you. You had me scared, but you're not so bad after all."

"I'm worse."

"Are you married?" she said to Eddie.

"Yes. That's right."

"Say, there's a thought. Could we get your wife on with you?"

"I don't know," Eddie said.

"I know," Doc said. "No."

"Really? It would help the show. Why not?"

"Because he's a fighter in training."

"I don't understand."

No, I thought, looking at her, I can believe that. I'm sure you don't.

"You don't?" Doc said. "Well, let's just put it this way. He doesn't look at his wife from now until after the fight. All right?"

"Yes, if that's your rule."

"My rule? It isn't only my rule."

"I'd like to ask you a few questions," she said to Eddie, "if I might."

"Sure," Eddie said. "Go right ahead."

She reached into the shoulder bag and brought out a pack of

cigarettes and took one and I lighted it for her. Then she came out with a stenographer's notebook and flipped it open professionally and sat forward with a small gold pencil poised.

"First of all, how old are you?"

"Twenty-nine."

"How many prize fights have you had?"

"Ninety."

"How many have you won?"

"Eighty-seven."

"How did you start to be a fighter?"

Eddie told her about the boy's club and the amateurs and how Doc discovered him. She was asking Doc about this when we heard the shout and turned.

"Hey! Where's the next champion of the world!"

"Hey, Louie!" Eddie said, his face breaking into a big grin, and then he stood up. "Come over here!"

It was a little guy, dark-haired, in a dark blue suit, with the open collar of his white sports shirt folded down outside the collar of his jacket. Behind him were four others, all in their late twenties or early thirties and all of them grinning, and they stood there while Louie came over.

"This was my first manager," Eddie said, after he and Louie shook hands. "Louie is the one I was telling you about, had me in the amateurs. All these guys are from the old neighborhood."

Louie shook hands with Doc, and then Eddie introduced him formally to Miss Morse and to me.

"Look," Eddie said to him. "I'm busy for a few minutes, so take the guys into the bar. Take Frank with you, too. Tell him about the old neighborhood. I'll be in."

"Sure," Louie said, grinning at Eddie. "Sure."

"Fine," I said. "I'm glad to have met you, Miss Morse."

16

So you're all from Eddie's old neighborhood," I said.

"That's right," Louie said.

"And the best neighborhood in the world," the one named Frankie said. "We're not kiddin'. It was the greatest. The best neighborhood in the world."

"It used to be, when we were kids," the big husky one named Pretzauer, but called Pretzel, said. "It ain't the same no more."

"What is?" Frankie said. "But it still ain't bad."

We were spread along the bar while Girot served us. Pretzel and one named Pete had asked for beer, but Louie and Frankie and a quiet, good-looking one dressed in brown sports clothes and wearing a tie and named Harry had ordered whiskey.

"Well, here's to Eddie Brown, the next middleweight champion of the world," Louie said.

"Right," Frankie said.

We all drank to Eddie.

"These guys you're lookin' at here now," Louie said, "we're all Eddie's gang. Since we're kids, we're all the same gang."

"All except Dom ain't here," Frankie said. "Dom had to work today."

"Oh?" I said. "What does Dom do?"

"He's got an important post with the City Transit Authority," Frankie said, and a couple of the others laughed.

"He's with the I.R.T.," Louie said. "He's a track worker."

"But a real good guy," Frankie said.

"The best," the one named Pete said. "He wanted to come up, too. He really wanted to see Eddie."

"It's too bad," Frankie said.

"So what do the rest of you guys do for a living?"

"Me, I got a piece of a poolroom," Louie said. "Frankie, here, owns a gas station."

"Half a gas station," Frankie said.

"Pretzel drives for a beer distributor, Harry's a fireman and Pete tends bar at the Stanton."

"That's a nice hotel," I said to Pete.

"You ever drop in?"

"I have, but probably not in a couple of years."

"Drop in and look for me. I'm there nights."

"I'll do that."

"But Eddie's the one," Frankie said. "Eddie's our boy."

"We go to all of Eddie's fights," Louie said, "except the ones away out of town. You know. I mean we couldn't go to Pittsburgh and Chicago and Omaha, but we all started with his first fight, when I put Eddie in his first four-rounders at the Ridgewood, and all these guys went. We never missed any fight of Eddie's we could get to. We even drove up to Holyoke the times he fought there, and we'd be drivin' home all night."

"Hey! How about that first fight Eddie had in Holyoke, hey, Pretzel?" Frankie said.

"Yeah," Pretzel said.

"What about it?" Louie said.

"There was this guy there wanted to bet us," Pretzel said.

"Wanted to bet us?" Frankie said. "He didn't want to bet us."

"That's right," Pete said. "He didn't want to, but he did."

"A guy sittin' right behind us," Frankie said to me. "A loud mouth. He's rootin' for the guy's fightin' Eddie. You seen Eddie fight, right?"

"Right."

"He don't look to kill the other guy the first round or two. I mean, usually he don't. He usually goes out to figure the other guy out, first."

"Doc taught him that right from the start, how to case a guy," Louie said. "Doc's some manager."

"He's the best," Frankie said, "but this loud mouth is rootin' for the other guy. He's hollerin': 'Kill him! Knock him out! He's from New York, so he can't fight! Knock that bum out!' This keeps up all the first round, and when he starts it again in the second I turned around to him and I said: 'Look, Mac, why don't you tune that volume down?' He says: 'Whatta ya mean?' I said: 'You're disturbin' people. The fighter can't hear you anyway.' He says: 'He can hear me all right and he'll knock that bum right back to New York and you know what you can do.'

"Now I'm not a very big guy, see, and this guy don't know we're all together. So when he says that, Louie is sittin' next to me and he ain't big either, but Pretzel leans behind Louie and he puts that big paw of his on the guy's shoulder and he pushes him right back in his seat. Ain't that right, Pretzel?"

"Yeah, that's right."

"So Pretzel says: 'He don't know what he can do, Mister, but you know what you can do?' The guy says: 'Whatta ya mean?' Pretzel says: 'Put up or shut up.' The guy says: 'All right, if you wanna bet.'

"So I say: 'How much?' He says: 'I'll bet ten bucks.' I said: 'Are you kiddin'? All that noise you're makin' and you're gonna bet a lousy ten. I'll bet you fifty, even.' The guy says: 'I ain't got that much with me.' I said: 'Whatta ya got?' He says: 'I'll bet twenty.' I said: 'You're on.'"

"So what happened?"

"So what happened? Eddie knocked that other guy out in the fifth round."

"Good punches," Louie said, and the rest nodded. "Eddie kept hittin' him in the belly and in the fourth round he raised up and hit him a hook on the chin and I said: 'Oh boy, here it comes.' He let him go then, but in the fifth round he raised up again and that guy's head went right under the bottom rope. What a punch Eddie hit him."

"Yeah," Frankie said. "I took the guy's twenty. He wasn't a bad guy."

"No," I said, "not after Pretzel leaned on him."

"We bet all of Eddie's fights. We always place some before the fight and then we always find some sucker at the fight, makin' noise or somethin', so we oblige him. You know?"

"Except in Philadelphia," Pete said.

"Yeah," Pretzel said. "That wasn't right."

"I understand that was a bad decision," I said.

"A bad decision?" Frankie said. "That's what you call it?"

"It was the worst decision there ever was," Louie said. "Two of the officials give it to the other guy and, believe me, Eddie won eight of the ten rounds. Absolutely won them."

"How about Harry that night?" Frankie said, looking at Harry.

"Don't embarrass him," Louie said.

I looked at Harry and Harry looked at me and shrugged and looked away.

"After the fight we're comin' out to catch the train back to New York and we look and we don't see no Harry."

"I had to go to the men's room," Harry said, looking at me and shrugging again.

"So Louie and I go lookin' for him, and we find him in the men's room. Tell him, Louie."

"Ah, forget it."

"No. We find him in the men's room, and he's the only guy there by now and you know what he's doin'?"

"No."

"He's cryin', I mean Harry had tears in his eyes."

"And he's the only guy don't bet," Louie said. "He didn't even bet the fight."

I looked at Harry. He was facing the bar and he had his head down a little and he was sipping his drink.

"Well," I said, "that just shows what Eddie means to Harry and to all of you."

"Right," Frankie said. "Eddie is the greatest, and after he becomes champion and people get to know it they'll see. How come them sports writers don't write better about Eddie?"

"They don't knock him."

"I know, but they write what a fighter the other guy is. Eddie'll knock him out. Why don't they write that about Eddie?"

"Well, the other guy is champion and he's had most of his fights in New York. Doc has moved Eddie around the country and brought him along slowly. They haven't seen Eddie in many of his fights, and they haven't seen him in his best ones."

"They'll see him," Frankie said. "He'll show 'em. He'll show all the wise guys."

"Tell me about Eddie when all you guys were growing up."

"How do you mean?" Louie said.

"Was he a tough kid?"

"We didn't live on no Park Avenue," Frankie said.

"Eddie could always fight," Louie said. "He liked to fight. I mean he didn't go lookin' for fights, but he had what you call a temper."

"Yeah, you remember what a temper he had?" Frankie said. "Wow! And now he don't have it no more. You ever notice that?"

"Now he's a pro," I said.

"He had a temper all right," Louie said, "but he was right. He wasn't a mean guy. If some guy did somethin' wrong then Eddie would blow his top. He licked a lot of guys that way, especially in some of them fights we had with guys from the other neighborhoods."

"Was Eddie the toughest guy on your block, then?"

"Eddie?" Frankie said. "No. Tony was. He was a couple years older than Eddie, and Eddie was never crazy like Tony."

"Tony?"

"Tony Marino," Louie said. "Dom, that couldn't come here to-day—the guy that works on the tracks—was Tony's younger brother. Tony was the toughest."

"I remember now," I said. "Eddie has mentioned Tony."

"The toughest that ever was," Frankie said. "There was no-body as tough."

"Except his brother," Pete said. "Angelo."

"Go on," Frankie said. "Angelo wasn't tough. Them guys pack guns ain't really tough. Tony was ten times tougher with just his fists."

"Angelo was two years older than Tony," Louie said to me. "He's in Sing Sing now."

"Twenty to life," Frankie said. "He killed some poor slob run a candy store. They shoulda juiced him, but they give him twenty to life. Just a hood."

"Tell me more about Tony."

"He was the leader," Louie said, laughing.

"What a guy," Frankie said. "You remember that day we're all up on the roof and that cop come down the street lookin' for us?"

"Yeah," Pretzel said.

"He's walkin' along lookin' around and we're all lookin' down. Tony—like Louie says, he was the leader—he says: 'Watch me drop this on his potata.' You know what he done?"

"No."

"There was this brick there. He dropped it right on him."

"Hit him?"

"On the shoulder. Lucky for us he don't hit him on the head. He might of killed him, he hit him on the head."

"How we run," Louie said.

"Right over the roofs. We come down where Harry lived."

"Were you in on this?" I said to Harry.

"Not that day."

"He was probably readin'," Louie said. "Harry used to read a lot."

"I'm all for readers," I said.

"I still like to read," Harry said.

"The cop knew who done it," Frankie said. "About a week later he catches us on the street and he grabbed Tony. Remember?"

"Sure."

"He made a pass at him with the stick and Tony ducked under it and give the cop the knee. He give him the knee as hard as he could and that cop went white. He grabbed himself and doubled right over and went into a store. He went into that Dutchman's. You remember? We all run."

"I remember," Harry said. "I said: 'Tony, he'll get you for this. He'll take you in.' Tony said: 'Take me in? If he takes me in it'll be a joke in the station house. They'll laugh at him, that a kid like me give it to him. He don't dare take me in.'"

"He was right," Louie said.

"Tony was always right," Frankie said. "He had a good head. What a fighter he could have made. He could punch like Graziano. He'd have been champion of the world."

"What happened to him?"

"He's dead," Louie said. "He got killed in the war."

"On Iwo Jimi," Frankie said.

"Iwo Jima," Louie said.

"Jimi Jima," Frankie said. "Tony was there. He was a hero. Can you imagine? Tony was a hero."

"I can believe it."

"He was a sergeant," Frankie said. "Some guy come back told us. At night he used to go around where they had the guys posted to see if they were all right. Everything was dark and quiet, you know? The guy said them Japs used to come out of some caves, or somethin', at night, so this one night Tony sees this Jap sneakin' up on one of Tony's guys and Tony didn't want to make no noise because he didn't know how many Japs there were so he just sprung on this Jap and the guy says he choked him to death with his bare hands. What a fighter Tony was."

"That's not how he got killed, though," Harry said.

"He got killed helpin' a guy. Some guy was wounded and layin' out in the open and Tony run out and picked him up and started to bring him back and the Japs opened up with a machine gun and killed Tony."

"It's a screwy thing," Louie said. "A lot of people didn't think Tony was any good, because of Angelo and the way Tony acted wild. I mean the old people on the block."

"I saw his mother a couple of weeks ago," Harry said. "One Sunday afternoon my mother said to me: 'Why don't you go see old Mrs. Marino. Since Dom got married she lives alone now and she's not so well.' So I went up to her flat and she was just sitting there in a rocking chair and she's got Tony's picture there on the table, in his uniform, and right by the picture she's got the Purple Heart and the Silver Star that they sent her."

"Yeah," Frankie said. "Tony got the Silver Star."

"What's the matter with the drinks?" Louie said.

"Pretzel and me have been puttin' in this beer," Pete said.

"Girot's making another round now," I said. "Tell me about Helen."

"Who?"

"Eddie's wife. Helen. She lived on the block."

"You ever meet Helen?" Louie said.

"Yes."

"Well?"

"To tell you the truth," Frankie said, "I was surprised when Eddie started goin' with Helen. Eddie never paid too much attention to girls."

"Yeah, not like you," Pete said.

"Helen never paid too much attention to Eddie, either," Louie said, "until he became a fighter. Then he became somebody in our neighborhood."

"Her old lady didn't think so," Pete said.

"Louie was the best man when Eddie got married," Frankie said. "Right, Louie?"

"Where did they get married?" I said.

"In City Hall," Frankie said.

"No," Louie said. "In the Municipal Building."

"How did they happen to get married there?"

"They were gonna get married by a justice of the peace," Louie said. "Helen's old lady wasn't too hot for Helen gettin' married to Eddie, so Helen had the idea they should go up some place in Westchester and get married by the justice of the peace. You know? Real romantic?"

"Yeah," Frankie said.

"So Eddie had this secondhand Ford, and one night in the summer he got the car out and picked me up and then he picked up Helen. They had their blood test certificates and everything, and we drove up to Yonkers. You know Yonkers?"

"Yes. An old vaudeville joke."

"We're in the north part of Yonkers, a nice neighborhood, and we don't know where we're goin'. Up ahead there's this Good Humor ice-cream guy got his truck parked under a street light and Helen says: 'Stop and ask him. He'll know where there's a justice of the peace.'

"Now Eddie stops the car and the guy comes over and stands there. I'm sittin' on the side by the guy, and Helen is sittin' in the middle and I'm waitin' for Eddie to say something. The guy says: 'What'll it be, folks?' So Helen says to Eddie: 'Go ahead. Ask him.'"

"Wait'll you hear this," Frankie said to me. "This is Eddie for you."

"So Eddie says: 'What flavors you got?' I'd like to die."

"How do you like that?" Frankie said to me.

"So the guy reels off a whole list of flavors and Eddie says to Helen: 'What'll you have?' Helen says: 'Nothing.' She was steamin'. So Eddie says to me: 'How about you, Louie?' I said: 'No, thanks.' Then Eddie says to the guy: 'I'll have a toasted almond.' I'll never forget he said a toasted almond.

"While the guy went to get the Good Humor I figured I better do something. Eddie and Helen are just sittin' there and sayin' nothing, and I feel sorry for Eddie. When the guy comes back and gives Eddie the ice cream I said to the guy; 'Say, where's there a justice of the peace around here?' The guy says: 'I don't know. I don't live here. I just work here, and I never saw any justice of the peace.'

"So we drove back home, nobody saying anything, and they dropped me off at my place and the next morning Eddie came around and picked me up and we picked up Helen and we took the subway down to the Municipal Building and some judge married them. I don't remember his name. Then they went to Atlantic City for a couple of days."

"When they come back, Helen's old man had a blowout at his bar," Frankie said. "We all went. It was a pretty good party."

"Eddie's got his own home in the Bronx now," Pete said. "You ever been there?"

"Yes," I said. "I met him there the day we came up here."

"It's a real nice place, ain't it?" Frankie said.

"Yes, it is. Do you guys visit him up there?"

"We been there once," Louie said.

"Eddie called us up one night," Frankie said. "Helen was going out and he called us and we all went up. It's a nice place."

"Give us another round, will you, Girot?" Louie said.

"What are you guys talking about, anyway?" Eddie said, walking up to us.

"Who's that dame you been sittin' with?" Frankie said. "You can do better than that."

"Television," Eddie said. "She's from television."

"You're gonna be on television?"

"On Monday afternoon."

"What time?"

"Two o'clock. The Bunny Williams show."

"I heard that name," Frankie said.

"We'll all get away and watch it," Louie said.

"Hey!" Frankie said to me. "You'll have to come down to the neighborhood right after the fight. When Eddie wins that title we're gonna have a real blowout that night. Be sure to come."

"It'll be a real blowout, too," Eddie said to me.

"Where do you have it? At Helen's father's bar?"

"Hell, no," Frankie said. "We got another place."

"You can come down with me, Frank," Eddie said. "You'll see these guys as they really are."

"I'll be there."

"How come you guys came up today?" Eddie said.

"It's Saturday, ain't it?" Louie said.

"Is it?" Eddie said. "That shows you. Up here I don't have any idea what day it is. Every day is the same."

17

By Monday it was raining again. It was just a fine mist when Jay got me up and Eddie went out on the road with the others, but by the time they had all come back and Eddie had cooled out and we had had breakfast it had turned into a steady spring fall.

We left just before nine o'clock, in Eddie's car, and Doc sat in front with Eddie and I sat in the back with Jay. The change of routine and of scenery seemed to spark Jay and he talked almost incessantly, about a car he once owned until the finance company claimed it, about his trip up to camp with his friend Stanley, about the kind of camp he would run if he were Girot, about the kind of place to buy if you want to live in the country and, when we crossed the bridge at Bear Mountain, about the George Washington Bridge and the hazards of being a steelworker. Now and then, while Jay was talking, Doc would say something to Eddie and Eddie would nod and say something to Doc. I doubt that they heard much of what Jay was saying.

When we got to New York, Eddie finally put the car in the new lot on the corner west of Shor's. It was 11:45, and in the rain, we were lucky to get a cab to go the six blocks to the commission.

"This is better than the old place," Jay was saying, as the four of us rode up in the elevator. "You remember the old place, where you had to go all the way down to Foley Square?"

"Yes. I remember."

"I remember once—"

The elevator stopped and we followed Doc out. Mel Nathan, from the Garden, was sitting on the bench and when he saw us stepping out he stood up and shook hands all the way around.

"Gee, I'm glad you're here," he said to Doc.

"Ah. What were you worried about? That we wouldn't show?"

"No, but Eddie's gonna be on that television show this afternoon, right?"

"No," Doc said. "He's not."

"What? He's not gonna be on? I was just talking this morning to some gal over there who said it was all set. She was up to see you."

"Relax, Mel," Eddie said.

"Then you'll be on?"

"Sure."

"What are you trying to do, kid me?" Mel said to Doc.

"Kid you? The smartest publicity man in boxing? Where would I get off trying to kid you?"

"We might as well go in. The doctor's in there."

There were three photographers sitting on the bench inside, their cameras in their laps, and they got up and shook hands with Eddie and with Doc. Doctor Martin was sitting on the corner of a desk, talking to a mousy middle-aged Civil Service secretary, who kept nodding as he talked, and when he finished he walked over to us and shook hands.

"You look good," he said to Eddie.

"Thanks. So do you."

"He should," Doc said. "He dies his hair. He's as old as I am."

"But I'm in shape," Martin said.

"His name's not Martin, either. He's a dago, but he won't admit it."

"Who won't admit it? Listen, I saved a few of your fighters."

"I know you did," Doc said, smiling. "You're all right."

"Let's go in."

"Where's the other guy?" Doc said.

"He's not here yet. I'll look at Eddie, and get it over with."

He led us through the other office and into the small room. There was a scale there and a desk and a couple of chairs, and Eddie sat down and the doctor, using the pocket flashlight, looked into his eyes and then down Eddie's throat and into his ears. Then Eddie stripped to the waist and the doctor put the stethoscope on the chest and then on the back. When he finished that he wrapped the blood pressure cuff around Eddie's left upper arm and squeezed on the bulb and read the dial.

"Okay," he said. "Strip down to your shorts and I'll weigh you."

"As you were, Edward," Doc said. "Nix on that."

"What?" Martin said. "What's the matter?"

"He's not going to weigh. He makes the weight a week from Friday."

"He's got to weigh. It's a title fight."

"Not today it isn't. The fight's a week from Friday. What difference does it make what he weighs today? Are you afraid he won't make the weight?"

"Of course not."

"He'll make sixty, a week from Friday. In fact, I'll tell you exactly. He'll come in at 159."

"The law says that for a title fight both contestants must weigh at the preliminary examination. He doesn't have to weigh 160 today. I just have to have a record of his weight."

"Now the lawyers are writing laws to make work for doctors, too," Doc said to me, and then to Martin: "They used to just write laws to make work for themselves, so how come they're cutting the doctors in, too?"

"The commission has to protect the public. The public is buying tickets for a title fight. The commission has to have some proof that both contestants, on this date of examination, are within reach of 160 pounds."

"Ah, don't give me that about the commission and the public. As soon as you try for a title the commission wants to manage your fighter. Why do you think I never let one of my guys go for a title before? I've been bringing fighters in at their best weight for over forty years. When I bring a fighter in on the day of a fight all he has to do is spit once and step on that scale and he makes exactly what I wanted him to make the day we signed for the fight. You don't think I'm going to blow this one, do you?"

"I know you're not. I just have to have the weight in my report. What have you got against that?"

"Plenty. I manage my own fighter. The commission doesn't manage him, and the newspapermen don't manage him. I don't want it in the papers what Eddie Brown weighs."

"It's not going to be in the papers. This is for our own records."

"You might just as well publish it in Parker's column or on the front page of the *Daily News*. There are more leaks in this office than there were in the *Andrea Doria* after she came off second best with that other boat. The Pro doesn't weigh."

"Then what do you expect me to put down?"

"Put down 161½."

"I can't do that."

"How long do you know me?"

"I don't know. Thirty years."

"Did I ever lie to you?"

"No."

"Eddie Brown weighed 161½ pounds yesterday afternoon. Put it down."

"You're a tough man, Doc," Martin said, looking Eddie over and then feeling him around the stomach and then the hips. "I'll do it for you, but don't say anything."

"You're all right, doctor," Doc said, and then to Eddie: "Put your shirt and things on."

"Gentlemen! Gentlemen! Gentlemen!"

It was the champion. He came through the door with three others from his camp and Mel Nathan. There was a big smile on his face and a day's growth of beard, and he was wearing road clothes—heavy shoes and khaki trousers, a gray woolen shirt and an Army khaki zipper jacket. He was perhaps an inch taller than Eddie, with a good slim build that showed in spite of the clothes, and on his head was a red woolen toque.

"There's my man," he said, walking over to Eddie with that big smile still on and his hand out. "How are you, Eddie?"

"I'm fine. You?"

"Man, you look good."

"You're late," Martin said to him.

"Hello, doctor," he said, shaking Martin's hand. "Man, I got things to do. You can't expect a man to always be on time."

"You're never on time."

"C'mon," Doc said, motioning with his head to Eddie.

"Hello, Mr. Carroll."

"Hello."

We walked through to the outer office where the photographers were still waiting. Eddie put his tie back on and got into his jacket again. Jay was talking with the photographers.

"What did he really weigh yesterday?" I said to Doc.

"Sixty-one and a half. Martin's all right. I level with him."

"I just wondered."

"I'll bet that champion has to weigh in there," Doc said, nodding back toward the other room. "You know that, don't you?"

"How about that big greeting I got?" Eddie said.

"The phony SOB," Doc said. "Dreadful."

"Who does he think he's impressing, showing up in those clothes, like he just came off the road."

"Dreadful."

In about ten minutes Mel Nathan came out, leading the others.

"Now, what have you got in mind?" one of the photographers said, as the three of them stood up. "What do you want us to do?"

"Just relax," Nathan said. "You know I get paid for thinking, too."

"We're here to do a job," the same photographer said. "Get it up."

Nathan went back into the other office and came out carrying a gilt-painted cardboard crown, on the front of which was painted, in black letters: CHAMP. He took the red toque off the champion's head and put the crown on.

"Man, dig that crazy hat," one of them with the champion said.

"Man, how about this?" the champion said, grinning.

"So you two guys get over here," the same photographer said.

"No. Get them over here," another said. "We don't want the windows in the back."

"So have it your way," the first said.

They posed the two of them, Eddie with the left hand cocked and reaching for the crown on the champion's head with his right hand, the champion blocking the right with his left and about to throw his own right.

"Isn't that dreadful?" Doc said to me, as we stood there, the flash bulbs going and the photographers working.

"Go on, you've done worse than that."

"Thirty years ago. Don't they ever come up with anything new?"

"What's the matter?" Nathan said.

"Nothing," Doc said. "It's great."

"It'll get in the papers."

"Now what do you want?" the first photographer said to him.

"Doc Martin!"

"Hello?"

"Lend us that stethoscope a minute, will you?"

The photographers had the champion discard the crown and take off his jacket and open his shirt and they posed the two of them with Eddie, neat in his light gray sports jacket, dark slacks, blue shirt and gray tie, using the stethoscope on the champion's chest. Then they posed the doctor using the stethoscope on the champion, with Eddie looking over the doctor's shoulder.

"Now what?" the first photographer said.

"Now go back to your offices," Nathan said.

"That's all?"

"What did you expect, Marilyn Monroe?"

"It's up to you."

"So I'll be seein' you," the champion said to Eddie, smiling and shaking his hand.

"That's right," Eddie said.

When we got outside the rain had stopped, so we walked the half block to Broadway and up the two and a half blocks to Dempsey's, the traffic slurring on the wet pavement and the dampness hanging over it and over the people on the sidewalks. We took the first booth on the right and Doc and I ordered a drink and a sandwich apiece and Eddie had a cup of tea and dry toast and Jay had corned beef hash with a poached egg on it.

"What time is it?" Doc said, as we were finishing.

"One-twenty," I said.

"That's right," Eddie said. "We better get to that studio."

"You know why I'm doing this, don't you?" Doc said to me.

"No."

"I'm a kindly old man. I felt sorry for that dame."

"Ethel Morse?"

"Whatever her name is."

We took a cab the seven blocks to the studio. It was on the West Side, and when we got out and I looked at the place I made it out to be a remodeled loft building, a flat-roofed three stories, like the rest of the block, but the front redone in new red brick with plate-glass doors and aluminum trim. There was a small, semicircular lobby with the walls painted light green and with a cork-tiled floor, and we walked up to a kid in his teens who was sitting at the reception desk, talking into the phone.

"Can I help you?" he said, taking the phone away from his face, but ready to go back to it.

"What's that dame's name?" Doc said to me.

"Ethel Morse."

"Will you have a seat?" the kid said.

We spread ourselves along a long, curved, tan, plastic-covered sectional sofa that fitted the curve of the wall. The kid put the phone back on the cradle, waited, picked it up again, listened and dialed.

"So this is what these places are like," Jay said.

"No," I said. "It's just what this place is like."

"How do you mean?"

"This business is still so new nothing is like anything else."

Ethel Morse came out of the hallway behind the desk. She had on a dark blue suit and a light blue mannish shirt with a round silver clip at the neck.

"So you're here!" she said, all smiles and shaking hands with Eddie and then Doc. "Good!"

"Is it?" Doc said.

"Let's go back. Bunny will want to meet you."

"Bunny," Doc said to me. "What's our business coming to?"

"You don't want to go back to fighting on barges, do you?"

"Yes."

It was a big room, undoubtedly an old warehouse, with a frightening air, now, of calculated disarray. Deep into the room, slightly to our left, a group of parochial-school girls, not yet in their teens and dressed in Navy blue skirts and white blouses, sat on a three-tiered bleacher flooded with lights. At either end of the top row of girls a nun sat, and in front of the group a guitar player in a black cowboy costume stood, his back to them and facing a TV camera. He was playing and singing and smiling at the camera, and to the right, off camera, a piano player and a bass-fiddle man, also in cowboy costumes, were accompanying him.

"Just wait right here," Ethel Morse said to Eddie. "I'll find Bunny."

"Who's that cowboy singing?" Jay said to me. "I bet I seen him somewhere."

"William S. Hart," I said.

"Go on," Jay said. "I'll bet I've heard of this guy."

Off into the vast room there was a kitchen set and, at another angle, an office, or study, set. To the right of that there was a corner of a living room, two brick-red upholstered love seats with a blond corner table with a modern, chartreuse lamp on it. Across the floor coursed the heavy black cables to the cameras and the stand-up flood lamps, and moving around, stepping over the cables, were a half-dozen people, male and female, all of them young, a couple of the men with headsets on, one or two of the women carrying clip boards and all of them studiously harassed.

"This is a madhouse," Doc said.

"What's Eddie's mother doing here?" Jay said.

"Where?"

"Right there."

Eddie had moved about fifteen feet from us and was talking with a small, gray-haired woman wearing a black cloth coat and a small, black felt hat. She was fingering a black leather handbag and seemed worried, and Eddie was doing the talking, shrugging and explaining something.

"Tell them to come over here," Doc said to Jay. "What's going on here, anyway?"

Jay went over and shook hands with Eddie's mother and then

brought them over. Doc shook hands with her and then Eddie introduced her to me.

"We didn't know you were going to be here, Mrs. Braun," Doc said.

"She didn't know, either," Eddie said. "That gal—Morse—called her Saturday night. Then she called her this morning and told her to come up."

"I don't know," Mrs. Braun said, shrugging. "She told me she saw Eddie, and I should come here."

"She didn't tell me she was going to call my mother," Eddie said to Doc. "You were there."

"Well, you're here," Doc said.

"But I don't know what to do," she said.

"There's nothing to worry about, Mrs. Braun," I said. "They'll tell you what to do."

We stood in an awkward silence, watching the guitar player in the cowboy clothes finish his number.

"And now," he said, grinning into the camera, "we're all going to join in a song that's my favorite and probably one of your favorites, too. 'Harvest Moon'!"

He turned slightly and looked toward the parochial-school group on the bleacher.

"Am I right about that?" he said. "Isn't that one of your favorites?"

"Yes," several of them said, most of the others nodding.

"Then you'll all join in with me. Dick!"

He signaled to the piano player and the piano player led into it with the bass man, and the guitar player picked it up and then started to sing.

"'Shine on, shine on harvest moon, up in the sky . . .'"

Behind him all the lips moved and the voices sounded small and far away. I looked at the two sisters, flanking the top row, and their lips were moving, too, and my mind moved ahead to the next line and my eyes stayed on them.

"'I ain't had no lovin' since January, February, June or July.'"

"My God!" Doc said, nudging me. "Did you just see what I saw?"

"The sisters singing it?"

"Sure. Let's get out of here. What is this?"

"This is the brave new world."

"Dreadful."

"Bunny will be right here," Ethel Morse said. "You people enjoying watching this show?"

"This is Mrs. Braun," Doc said.

"Yes, I know. She got here before you did."

"Why didn't you tell us she was coming?"

"To tell you the truth, I didn't know it myself, not until this morning. Oh, Charley!"

A young man, wearing a white shirt and a black knitted tie and charcoal gray trousers, turned and walked toward us. He had a sheaf of papers in one hand and was making marks on them with a pencil.

"This is Charley Adams, our A.D. This is Eddie Brown, and his mother, Mrs. Braun, and his manager, Mr. Carroll."

"Hello," Charley Adams said, nodding a couple of times, and then he turned and walked away, studying his sheaf of papers again.

"Who's he?" Doc said to me.

"Our A.D.," Ethel Morse said. "Assistant Director."

"Isn't that dreadful?" Doc said to me. "A.D."

"Here comes Bunny now."

She came, stepping over the cables, toward us, about five feet three inches at the most, a good-looking little blonde wearing a blue dress with a flared skirt.

"Bunny," Ethel Morse said. "Mrs. Braun, Eddie Brown, Mr. Carroll and—"

"Johnny Jay," Jay said. "Hello."

"Johnny Jay and Frank Hughes."

"How do you do?" Bunny said. "All of you."

She had on pancake make-up, which gave her that orange look, but she had a small, turned-up nose and big blue eyes and seemed to be in her early thirties.

"Now who's going on, anyway?" she said, looking at Ethel Morse and then at some papers she was carrying. "Not all of them?"

"Oh, no," Ethel Morse said. "It's right there. First Mrs. Braun, and then Eddie. The rest of them are just watching."

"Good," Bunny said, and then to Eddie and his mother, "I'll see you on, then."

"Wait a minute," Doc said. "What are they going to do?"

"Why I'm sure Ethel's explained that. Haven't you explained that?"

"No, but I'm going to now."

"Good. Then it's nice to have met the rest of you."

She turned and walked back across the floor to where the young man named Charley Adams and identified as the A.D. was waiting for her. In front of the camera the guitar player in the cowboy clothes was sitting on the bottom step of the bleachers, smiling and nodding and talking with two of the parochial-school girls.

"What about this?" Doc said.

"It's very simple," Ethel Morse said. "There's nothing to worry about. Bunny's very good at this, and she'll lead them."

"Lead them where?"

"Well, they're on the second segment. Bunny has a piano player from the Embers on the first half. He's over there, getting ready now. In the second half, Mrs. Braun, the announcer will take you in. Perhaps you'd better leave your coat and your handbag here. Here, let me take them."

"I don't know," Eddie's mother said. "My dress?"

"Oh, it'll be fine. It's just fine. Here."

It was a black dress, plain except for a small white-lace collar.

With her coat off, Eddie's mother was smoothing the dress, the front and the sleeves.

"I don't know," she said.

"Then what?" Doc said. "This woman doesn't know what she's supposed to do."

"She'll sit down with Bunny on that love seat over there. We're using that for this bit. Bunny will just ask her some questions."

"About what?" Doc said.

"About Eddie, naturally. About his boyhood. That's why we wanted her on the show. After all, no one knows Eddie's boyhood better than she does, and this is a home show. I mean it's largely a woman audience, and they'll appreciate this."

"I'll bet," Doc said.

"What do I do?" Eddie said.

"Yeah," Jay said. "What does Eddie do?"

"Then you'll be told when to walk in. You just walk in and sit down, and Bunny will talk with you. Haven't you ever been on television before?"

"Some of my fights, sure, and a couple of sports shows. Not like this."

"This will be the same as those shows, I'm quite sure. You'll be splendid."

"I should have my head examined," Doc said.

"We'd better go over there now," Ethel Morse said, taking Mrs. Braun by the arm and Eddie following. The guitar player in the cowboy clothes was smiling his sign-off melody into the camera, and when he finished and the parochial-school girls started to file off the bleachers, Doc and Jay and I moved to where we could see and hear an announcer introducing the Bunny Williams show.

"—and here's Bunny herself!" he said. "Bunny?"

She was standing at the end of the blond spinet piano, leaning on it with her right arm. At the piano sat a young man, poised.

"Thank you, Don, and hi!" Bunny said, smiling into the camera. "It's a kind of a damp spring day here in New York, but we're all quite cozy here with a special bag of treats to help you spend the next half hour wherever you are in this wonderful big land of ours. First of all, I want to introduce my friend at the piano here. . . ."

She introduced the young man and he nodded into the camera. Then she went into a commercial and walked over to a table in the kitchen set. On it were a box of flour, an empty cake tin and a cake, covered with light blue icing. She said something about being able to go from this—the empty tin and the box of flour—to this—the cake—in almost no time and with almost no effort. Then, still smiling, she walked back to the piano and the young man played.

He played four numbers. After each, Bunny chatted with him, leaning on the piano. She asked him about his beginnings as a musician and plugged the place that had sent him and they talked about modern jazz, about which she appeared to know quite a bit.

After she had thanked him again she seemed to be off the air, because she turned from the camera and said something to someone off to one side. Then she nodded and walked over to the kitchen set and picked up two bottles of milk, one in each hand, and stood smiling at the refrigerator and into the camera.

"Are you ever caught like this?" she said, smiling and holding out the two bottles. "Not enough hands? Certainly you are, every time you bring in the milk. Well, it's no problem at all today, with a refrigerator like this. You just—"

She nudged the door handle of the refrigerator with her left elbow, and the door opened. She put the milk into the refrigerator, talking all the while, and then, in passing, pushed the door closed behind her, still talking.

"And now," she said, "we're going to meet a very special kind of guest—Mrs. Augusta Braun, the mother of Eddie Brown. Eddie Brown is a prize fighter who, a week from Friday night, will fight for the middleweight championship of the world, and we thought that, because so many of you, thanks to television, have become interested in prize fighting and probably have wondered about it and about prize fighters, we would bring you a fighter's mother."

Again she seemed to be off the air, because she turned from that camera and walked to the corner setting where Mrs. Braun was sitting on one of the love seats, turning a white handkerchief in her hands. Then, at a signal, Bunny Williams, smiling and her hand out, walked into the set.

"Mrs. Braun," she said, shaking hands and sitting down beside Eddie's mother. "We're so happy to have you with us."

"Yes," Eddie's mother said nodding. She looked frightened.

"We want you to tell us all about Eddie. We've never met the mother of a fighter before, and so we're most anxious to hear how long he's been a fighter and how he became a fighter and whether you attend his fights and a lot of other things. How long *has* he been a fighter?"

"How long? Exactly I don't know. For years. Eddie could tell you."

"Then you could tell us how he became a fighter. How did that happen?"

"He liked to fight, I guess. He always seemed to like to fight."

"You mean as a boy? That he fought with the other boys in, perhaps, the neighborhood where you lived?"

"That's right. They were wild boys, but that's where we had to live."

"That was here in New York?"

"Yes. On the West Side."

"But did you try to stop him from fighting with the other boys?"

"I tried to stop him. I told him that was no good, that fighting, but he had a temper. Like his father, he had a temper."

She kept twisting the handkerchief in her hands in her lap.

"Tell me, Mrs. Braun, what did your husband do? What was his business?"

"He was a plasterer. Then he died."

"Well, plastering is a good and noble trade. I'm sure, too, that he was a good man."

"Yes. He was a good man."

"When Eddie became a professional fighter, did you try to stop him?"

"I couldn't stop him. He had it in his mind. He was grown then."

"Have you ever gone to any of your son, Eddie's, fights?"

"I go? No."

"Do you watch on television when he fights?"

"I don't have a television."

"Do you listen on the radio?"

"Sometimes. Once or twice I tried."

"You say you tried. You didn't enjoy it?"

"I turned it off."

"Are you afraid that your son will be hurt?"

"Yes, always. He could be hurt."

"Tell me this. You gave birth to a son, and watched him grow, and you must have had certain dreams for him. All mothers do. What did you dream that your son might become?"

"I don't know about dreams. Dreams I never had. I just thought he would get a job."

"What sort of a job?"

"I don't know. He was learning to be a plasterer. My husband was teaching him. My husband was not well, and Eddie he helped him. Eddie is a good boy."

"I'm sure he is, Mrs. Braun. Then you hoped that he might become a plasterer like his father?"

"Yes. It's a good job. Today they get big pay, plasterers."

"Indeed they do, Mrs. Braun, and I want to thank you. Now you just wait right here, because we have a surprise for you."

She turned, then, into the camera and said something about the refrigerator. Then she got up and hurried over to it and stood waiting, smiling.

"Why, she's a dirty little bitch," Doc said to me. "What is she trying to do, make him out a criminal?"

"That seems to be the idea."

"Eddie's not going in there. I'm pulling him out."

"Wait a minute, Doc," I said, putting my hand on him. "You can't do that now."

"Why can't I?"

"It's too late. He's in there."

"Where?"

I pointed to one of the floor monitors that showed Eddie standing there, waiting to walk on. Actually Bunny Williams was still talking about the refrigerator, demonstrating something about the freezer compartment, and then she shut the door and walked back to the set, paused a moment, got a signal and walked in.

"And now Mrs. Braun," she said, smiling, "this is our surprise. Here with us today, to tell us himself what it's like to be a prize fighter, is your own son, Eddie Brown."

Eddie walked in. He shook hands with Bunny Williams and then walked over to his mother and gave her his hand and sat down beside her. Bunny had seated herself on the other love seat, and she was leaning forward, smiling at the other two.

"This *is* a surprise, isn't it, Mrs. Braun?"

"Yes," Eddie's mother said, nodding.

"How long had it been since you'd last seen your son?"

"I don't know. Three weeks."

"You've been in your training camp, haven't you?" she said to Eddie. "Training to fight for the middleweight championship a week from Friday?"

"That's right," Eddie said, nodding.

"And you're going to win?"

"Well, I certainly think so."

"But in your profession one can never be certain. Am I right?"

"I suppose so."

"It *is* a precarious business, isn't it?" she said, smiling.

"I guess you're right."

"How long have you been preparing for this fight?"

"You mean training?"

"Yes," she said, smiling, "if that's what you call it. I'm not familiar with all the terminology."

"I've been in camp, I guess, two weeks."

"We've been talking here with your mother, Eddie, about your boyhood and what made you become a fighter. Your mother isn't quite sure. Can you yourself tell us now why you became a fighter?"

"Well, I just liked to fight. I guess that's why."

"Didn't you ever want to be anything else but a fighter?"

"How do you mean?"

"Well, did you ever want to be a lawyer or a policeman or whatever it is that small boys want to be?"

"I couldn't be a lawyer. I didn't like school much, and I had to quit when my father died. I didn't want to be a cop. Is that what you mean?"

"Well, yes, but did you ever want to be, say, a baseball player?"

"Oh, yes. When I was a kid."

"Why didn't you? I mean, become a baseball player?"

"Well, where we lived there wasn't any place to play ball. We played stickball on the street, but that's not the same. I never even owned a glove. I couldn't be a ballplayer."

"Tell us, how many fights have you had?"

"Professional? Ninety."

"How many have you won?"

"All but three. I lost three decisions."

"Have you ever been knocked out?"

"No, ma'm."

"Do you ever think about being knocked out?"

"No, ma'm."

"You know your mother, here, worries about you when you fight. She thinks about you being knocked out."

"I suppose that's right."

"Now, I want to get to the heart of this, Eddie, if you don't mind."

"That's all right."

"Do you really mean that you never think about being knocked out?"

"That's right. I take a good punch. That's what we call it. I just don't think I can be knocked out, so I don't even think of it."

"But you've knocked out others. Your opponents?"

"That's right."

"How many opponents have you knocked out?"

"Oh, let's see. I think it's forty-eight, or nine."

"Tell us, how do you feel when you knock an opponent out?"

"How do you mean?"

"Well, isn't there some sort of a sadistic impulse in a fighter that makes him want to hurt another man, to knock him out? I'm just asking."

"I don't know. I don't want to hurt him."

"But that's what you set out to do, isn't it? You try to render him senseless. Isn't that right?"

She was doing this with a smile. It was a small, tender smile, to imply sympathy.

"I suppose so. You put it that way."

"So what do you feel when you see him lying there on the floor, after you've knocked him out? Do you feel glad, or sad, or what?"

"Well, you feel glad, I guess. He's been trying to knock you out and you've been trying to knock him out. You won. You got your moves and your punches across. So it makes you feel good."

"Exactly."

"It isn't that you're trying to hurt him. You're trying to lick him. It's fighting, boxing."

"But you know you do hurt him. You know, for example, that ten fighters were killed in boxing last year."

"I don't know how many. I know it isn't as many as it used to be, since they got better matting on the ring and they changed the size of the gloves, except for championship fights."

"Now, Eddie Brown, you're married, aren't you?"

"That's right."

"Do you have any children?"

"We have a boy."

"How old is he?"

"Five."

"Do you want him to become a fighter?"

"He can't be."

"Oh, he can't? Why not?"

"He's not well. He's all right, but he couldn't be a fighter."

"I didn't know that. What's wrong with him?"

"Well, we found out he has epilepsy. He's all right, but he has that."

"Oh, I'm sorry to learn that. I truly am, and I'm sure we all are."

"Thank you. He'll be all right."

"But if he were perfectly healthy, would you want him to be a fighter?"

"I don't know. That's hard to say."

"Is it hard to say? Don't you really mean that you have your doubts and, having them, you wouldn't want him to be a fighter. Is that right?"

"I suppose so. Probably I couldn't take it."

"Exactly. You're a fighter and you know the truth of it, and this is it. You wouldn't want your own son to follow in your own footsteps."

"I don't know."

"Well, unfortunately, I see our time is up. I want to thank you, though, Eddie Brown, for visiting with us, and to wish you luck. You've chosen your profession, fighting, and I know we all hope you may make the best of it, when you fight for the middle-weight title and after that."

"Thank you."

She stood up, and Eddie and his mother stood up.

"And to you, Mrs. Braun, you're a wonderful little lady, and to you our hearts go out. And now—"

She walked off, talking, in front of another camera, and Eddie and his mother came off toward us.

"Well, what do you suggest?" Doc said to me.

"Getting drunk. It was inevitable."

"But why did I have to play sucker and be a part of it?"

"I did the best I could," Eddie said.

"It's not your fault, Edward," Doc said. "I was the sucker, going for it."

"But what did she mean, anyway?" Jay said.

Ethel Morse came up, all smiles and in a hurry.

"You were fine, Mrs. Braun," she said, putting her arm around Eddie's mother.

"I don't know," Mrs. Braun said. "I didn't know what to do."

"Listen," Doc said. "Get that dame over here."

"Who?"

"Bunny whatever-her-name-is. Get her over here."

"Oh, I'm sorry," Ethel Morse said. "She's got a meeting with the agency in fifteen minutes and has to get over there. I'm sure she'd have liked to say good-bye to all of you, but she's a terribly busy person."

"You see?" Doc said to me.

"Forget it."

"Listen," Doc said to Ethel Morse. "I'm not going to jump on you. I just feel sorry for you."

"For me? Really. I don't understand. I thought it was a grand show."

"Let's get out of here," Doc said.

"Please. You'll be surprised at the impact this could have throughout the country. This is a very popular show, and after this I'm sure there will be many more people who'll be interested in Eddie Brown and the fight."

"And stay home and watch it on TV for free," Doc said. "Please. Just don't con me any more. I'll repeat myself. I just feel sorry for you."

We left Ethel Morse standing there and walked out and down the hall and out onto the sidewalk. It was misting again, and Doc called a cab and Eddie and Doc put Mrs. Braun in it.

"So you'll be careful?" she said to Eddie, when he bent down to kiss her on the cheek.

"Sure, Mom. Don't worry. I'll be down to see you the day after the fight."

"He'll be the champion then, Mrs. Braun," Jay said.

"I don't know," she said.

We waited for another cab and got in and started for the parking lot.

"I should have known that," Doc said on the way. "All my life I've had one rule. When they send a homely dame or a cripple to shill for something, walk away from it."

"That's right."

"Walk away from it. All my life I've had that one, so I play sucker."

"There's one thing that Ethel Morse said that was the truth," I said.

"What?"

"If those viewers could really be made to believe it's as bad as that, they'd walk through machine-gun fire to get to the fight."

"Isn't that dreadful?" Doc said.

"Speaking of sadistic impulses, Miss Bunny doesn't even need to climb into a ring."

"Dreadful. Thumbs you, spins you, knees you, butts you. It's my fault."

On the ride back to camp even Jay was suppressed. When we got in it was 5:30 and Eddie and Jay ate dinner with the others, but Doc and I stood at the bar a long time so that Doc could get rid of his steam.

"You know that ten fighters were killed in boxing last year?" he'd say, mimicking the voice. "You know that ten fighters were killed in boxing last year? What does he know, except to fight?"

"Have another drink."

"I will, but I wish I'd got on that television."

"You'd have had no chance."

"I wouldn't? With that little Stork Club snob?"

"Of course not. Not even you. They're pros at that racket, and you're not. They inflate their egos by picking on amateurs. They write their own rules. She could do the same thing in there with you or me or any one of us."

"You know that ten fighters were killed in boxing last year? That's for the whole world, and seven of them were amateurs. How many got killed in football? How about that auto racing?"

"How about that drink?"

"Hey, what's the matter with you guys?" Jay said, walking up to us. "We're finished eatin' already, and you guys don't even start. Ain't you gonna eat?"

"Is it still raining out?" Doc said.

"I don't know," Jay said.

"Do me a favor," Doc said. "Go see."

At nine o'clock we went into the kitchen. Girot's wife, Katie, had just finished cleaning up, but she made us a hamburger apiece and coffee. Then we went back to the bar, and at ten o'clock Eddie and Jay and Penna stopped by. They had been watching television, and were on the way to bed.

"Are you two guys still at it?" Jay said.

"Is it still raining?" Doc said.

"I already told you before. It stopped. I think it's gonna be nice tomorrow."

"Good. Then we can celebrate that, too. The good old weather, and the good old Bunny Williams show, too."

"Some broad, hey?" Penna said to me. "I watched it, and I'd like to get on that show."

"Frankie called me," Eddie said. "He watched it, too. He didn't think it was so bad."

"See if it's raining out, will you?" Doc said to Jay.

"Sure," Jay said, and then to me: "You don't want me to wake you tomorrow, do you?"

"If you don't I'll excommunicate you."

"What?"

"I'll leave you out of the story. So help me, I will."

"You want to get waked, I'll wake you. It's up to you."

18

The next morning I felt the hand on my shoulder. I felt it and then I felt it again, this time shaking me, and then, finally, I made out a figure bending over me and I knew where I was.

"Frank?"

"Yes? Jay?"

"No. It's Eddie."

"Oh. I thought you were Jay."

"Doc wants you."

"Who?"

"Doc?"

"Yes, sure. Doc? What's the matter with him? Is he all right?"

Eddie was gone, the door open and the light from the hall coming in. I got up and got into my slippers and put on my robe. Doc was standing in the doorway of Eddie's and Jay's room, with his blue flannel robe on over his pajamas, and he looked terrible. His hair was uncombed and he needed a shave and his eyes were baggy and his face was almost as white as his hair and he looked a hundred years old.

"You all right?" I said to him. "What's the matter?"

"It's Jay," he said. "Come in here."

"What's the matter with him?"

"He's dead."

"He's what?"

The overhead light was on in the room, bright, and I looked at Jay's bed against the wall and he was lying there with the khaki Army blanket up to his chin, the white sheet folded down over the edge of the blanket. Just his face was showing, the eyes closed, the head on the pillow, all of it, Jay and the bed, in that corner against the wall.

"He's dead?" I said. "How do you know he's dead?"

"He's dead," Doc said.

"But why is he dead? How could he be dead?"

"A heart attack," Doc said. "A heart attack, I guess."

"A heart attack? Did he have a bad heart?"

"Sure. Two years ago he had an attack."

"I didn't know that. Nobody ever told me."

Doc was sitting on the straight-backed chair near the table with Jay's tape and bandages and bottles on it. Eddie was sitting on the edge of his bed, his robe over his pajamas, staring at the floor, and they said nothing.

"I never knew that," I said. "What do you want me to do?"

"He told me the doctor said he should take it easy," Doc said. "I told him to listen to the doctor. I always brought another man into the corner to do all the carrying. Maybe he shouldn't even have been here?"

"Where else would he be? This would have happened wherever he was."

"Eddie woke me. He said: 'You better get up. There's something the matter with Jay.'"

"I didn't know what it was," Eddie said. "The alarm clock went off and Jay always gets up. He didn't get up and I got up and shut it off, and I tried to wake him up. How did I know he was dead?"

"C'mon, men!" Penna said. "Hit the road!"

He was standing in the doorway in his road clothes. He could see that something was wrong, and he came into the room.

"What's the matter?"

"Jay's dead," Eddie said.

"What?"

The others were in the hallway now, crowded in the doorway and looking in—Barnum and Memphis and Booker Boyd and DeCorso and Cardone—all of them heavy in their road clothes.

"Jay's dead," Penna said to them. "Eddie said Jay's dead."

"He's what?" Barnum, in the beret, said.

They followed him into the room, then, cautiously. They seemed almost to fill the room and they looked at Jay. I looked at him again, too, at the form under the khaki blanket and at the head on the pillow, bald, with that bashed, broken nose and that gnarled left ear. Now that I knew he was dead, he seemed a yellowing, curious figure out of a wax museum. He was so still. Move, Jay, I was thinking. All you have to do is move.

"What happened to him?" DeCorso said.

"He had a heart attack," I said.

"Why don't we all get out of here?" Memphis said.

"Yes," Doc said.

"You goin' on the road?" Penna said to Eddie.

"No."

"Yes, you are," Doc said.

"I don't want to go. I don't feel like it."

"You're going," Doc said. "You had yesterday off."

"That's right," I said. "Doc's right. You're in training here, and the sooner you get back into it, the better."

"But I'm not even dressed."

"We'll wait," Barnum, in the doorway, said. "We'll wait downstairs."

"Sure," Penna said. "We'll wait for you."

They left and Eddie got out of his robe and pajamas and dressed slowly. When he went out, Doc closed the door and sat down again.

"Well," I said, "what do you want me to do?"

"I don't know. What do we do?"

"Is there any family? Did Jay have any relatives?"

"No. He had a sister, married, but she died a couple of years ago. There's her husband—if he's still alive—but he's old and wouldn't give a damn."

"Where did Jay live?"

"He's got a room on West Ninety-third Street. I'll have to take care of that, too."

"Forget it for now. I suppose we should get Girot. I suppose he knows an undertaker in this town."

"What time is it?"

"That clock says five of seven."

"We kept Girot up until one o'clock. He'll like this."

"He doesn't like anything. Katie will be in the kitchen by now. I'll tell her."

"I'll get dressed," Doc said.

When I told Girot's wife she threw up her hands and sat down and kept slapping her hands onto her lap and shaking her head. I got her to go and wake Girot, in the cottage where they slept, beyond the south end of the parking space, and I went upstairs and dressed quickly and went into Doc's room. He was just finishing dressing when Girot came up the stairs.

"Do you mean he's dead?" he said. "This is terrible. Where is he?"

"In his bed," Doc said. "Go see for yourself."

Girot went across the hall and, in a moment, came out, closing the door behind him and shaking his head.

"This is terrible," he said. "Why did this have to happen here?"

"Do you know an undertaker in town?" I said.

"There's only one."

"One's enough," Doc said. "Call him, will you?"

"I'll call him," Girot said. "This is terrible."

Doc and I went down to the kitchen and Girot's wife commiserated with Doc and poured us coffee. We carried it out into the dining room and sat at a table by a window on the lake side with the new sunlight flooding the white tablecloth. When we finished the coffee, Girot's wife came out and refilled the cups, and finally we heard the fighters come back and we went out into the lobby.

"Go up and use my room," Doc said to Eddie. "Cool out in my room."

"All right," Eddie said, and he followed the others into the sitting room and we could hear them going up the stairs.

"I'll go up with him," I said.

Doc went to the kitchen to get the cup of hot tea for Eddie, and I followed Eddie into the room and closed the door. There was a wicker armchair with a cretonne-covered cushion in it by the window, and Eddie, sweating, sat down in it.

"How was the road?" I said.

"All right."

"Here. Use Doc's towel."

"Thanks."

"Look. I know how you feel about Jay, but you have to forget it. It may sound unfeeling, but the only important thing is the fight. You don't want to blow the fight."

"I'm not gonna blow the fight, but Jay was a nice little guy. Why did it have to be Jay?"

"Who knows?"

"He was with me for all my fights. From the time Doc took me, Jay was with me for every fight except one or two out of town the first couple of years."

"I know."

"How did I know he was dead? I was shaking him and saying: 'Jay, come on and get up.' I didn't know he was dead."

"Of course not."

Doc came in with the tea and gave it to Eddie. Then he went across the hall and came back with Eddie's robe and shower clogs and another towel.

"After you've had your shower I'll get your clothes," he said to Eddie.

We heard feet on the stairs and Girot came up with a man in a blue serge suit. He was short and fairly stout and looked about sixty. He had a round, pink face that was expressionless, and his hair, gray now, was plastered back in a pompadour with a straight part right down the middle.

"This is Mr. Edwards," Girot said. "The undertaker. This is Mr. Doc Carroll and Eddie Brown and Mr. Hughes."

"May I extend my sympathy?" Mr. Edwards said.

"Thanks," Doc said.

"Tell me," Mr. Edwards said to Girot, "where is the deceased now?"

"Across the hall," Doc said. "It's that room right there."

"I understand. Would you, uh, prefer to talk here or shall we go somewhere else?"

"If you're going across the hall we'll talk there," Doc said. "Eddie doesn't have to be a part of this."

"I understand. Fine."

"Will you come with us, Frank?"

"If you want."

We left Eddie, and Girot went back downstairs and Doc led the way into the room. Mr. Edwards walked over to the bed and looked down at Jay and then turned back to us.

"As I understand it, there was no physician in attendance at the time of death?"

"That's right," Doc said. "He must have died in his sleep. Eddie—my fighter—found him just like that. He had heart trouble."

"Well, I shall need a certificate of death. Is there a doctor here who was treating him?"

"Up here? No."

"Then I'll call the coroner."

"Why the coroner?"

"Well, that's the law. It's just a matter of procedure. In the absence of a physician the coroner must certify to the death."

"So call him."

"I'll do that. Have you informed the surviving relatives?"

"There are none. I'll handle everything."

"Oh. Well, have you had a chance to think about the funeral and interment? Where it will be?"

"I don't know," Doc said. "This thing just happened."

"I suppose he should be buried in New York," I said.

"I suppose so," Doc said. "In Woodlawn, I guess. How do I go about getting him in there?"

"I judge Mr. Jay owned no plot?" Mr. Edwards said.

"No."

"Well, I can arrange that for you. Will there be a church service?"

"No. He didn't go to church. Can't we use Cooke's or one of those funeral parlors somewhere around midtown?"

"Certainly. I'll make my call now and then go back to my office—I have a burial later today—but I'll be back. I'll see to everything."

"Thanks," Doc said.

"I suggest that this room be locked. I imagine the coroner will want to see everything as it is."

"Whatever you say," Doc said.

"But he wants to get Eddie Brown's clothes out of here," I said.

"Clothes?"

"Yes. He ran on the road this morning. He's probably getting out of those clothes now. After he's had his shower he wants to put on other clothes—slacks and a shirt and sweater. They're probably right there in the closet."

"He couldn't wait? It probably won't be long."

"Wait?" Doc said. "Wait for what? What difference does it make?"

"Well, it would be better to leave everything."

"Look," I said. "I'll pick out the clothes right now, while you're here. Then we'll all go out together and close the door."

"There aren't any keys for these doors anyway," Doc said.

That seemed to convince him, so I went over to the closet and opened it. I saw some of the things Eddie had been wearing, and I took a pair of slacks and a plaid shirt and a light-blue sweater and shoes with socks stuffed into them. There were a pair of shorts and a T-shirt on a hook, and I took them, too.

"That's all," I said, showing Mr. Edwards.

"All right," he said. "You understand that I just want to avoid any complications later."

We all walked out and Doc shut the door. Mr. Edwards went downstairs, after telling us again that he would handle everything, and Doc and I went into his room and I put the clothes down on the bed.

"Is it all right?" Eddie said.

"What's this about the coroner and everything being left where it was?" Doc said to me.

"I don't know. It's standard operational procedure, I suppose."

"The law. Always the law. The politicians and the lawyers haunt a guy right to his grave. Can't they ever leave him alone?"

After Eddie had had his shower and dressed we went down to the dining room. The others were finishing breakfast, and we sat by one of the windows again. Eddie passed up his cereal but had a couple of soft-boiled eggs, and Doc and I had coffee and toast.

"Anyway," I said, "the weather is nice. It's beautiful out."

"Yeah," Doc said.

"What are we going to do?" Eddie said.

"I'll have to go into the city," Doc said. "Is there a bus this afternoon or tonight?"

"If you could drive," Eddie said, "you could take my car."

"Go in tomorrow morning," I said. "You won't have the funeral until Thursday. Tomorrow's Wednesday. I'd drive you, but for the purposes of this thing I'm supposed to be doing here I should stay with Eddie."

"I want you with him anyway. Funeral. Can you get out of having a funeral?"

"Sure. You can call it private."

"Private. It'll be private enough, even when it's public."

"Mr. Edwards is here again," Girot said, walking over to us.

Mr. Edwards was waiting in the lobby with the coroner. He introduced the coroner as Doctor Bernardi. The doctor seemed to be in his early thirties, stern-faced and black-haired, wearing a dark gray suit and carrying a black medical bag and a black brief case.

"You want to go upstairs?" Doc said.

"I've already seen the body," the doctor said. "There are some questions to be answered, so I'd like to find a place to sit down."

"You go upstairs," Doc said to Eddie. "Go to my room."

"I'll go with him," I said.

"I'd rather have you here," Doc said. "Eddie'll be all right."

We went back into the dining room with the doctor and Mr. Edwards following us. We sat down at one end of the long table that had been cleared of the breakfast dishes, and the doctor took a printed form out of his brief case and placed it on the table and took out a fountain pen.

"To begin with, the name of the deceased?"

"Johnny Jay," Doc said.

"He'll want his legal name," I said.

"Yes, his legal name."

"That's right," Doc said. "Joseph Giorno. G-i-o-r-n-o."

"He had an alias?"

"Not an alias," Doc said.

"Well, what was it, if it wasn't an alias?"

"It was his fighting name."

"He was a fighter?"

"Years ago."

"Was he a good fighter? Well known?"

"Does that have to go down there, too? Do you mean to tell me you've got a line on that form for that?"

"I'm merely asking."

"What else do you want to know?"

"Was there a middle initial?"

"Not that I know of."

The doctor filled in a couple of lines on his own.

"Was he married?"

"No."

"Ever?"

"No."

"Date of birth?"

"July 14th, sixty-three years ago. Figure it out."

The doctor took a piece of blank paper out of his brief case and did the subtraction on that. Then he marked the date on the form.

"Place of birth? Do you know that?"

"Brooklyn."

"Father's name?"

"Tony. Anthony, or Antonio. Whatever you want to make it."

"Mother's maiden name?"

"God, I don't know."

"As I understand, there are no relatives who would know?"

"Correct."

"Usual occupation?"

"Prize-fight trainer."

"Kind of business or industry?"

"What? Prize fighting. Boxing. Make it boxing."

"Is there a difference?"

"Yes. As long as we're being so legal, prize fighting is out-lawed. It's boxing. Boxing is legalized."

"Was the deceased ever in the U.S. armed forces?"

"Yes. In the Navy."

"When?"

"World War One."

"Now, as to cause of death."

"A heart attack."

"That's merely your supposition."

"Well, what else would it be?"

"It might be any number of things. We don't know."

"What do you mean?"

"It could have been a cerebral hemorrhage, a ruptured aneurysm, an intestinal hemorrhage. It could have been many things."

"He had heart trouble."

"As a matter of fact, Mr. Carroll, we don't know but that it might have been foul play."

"Foul play? Are you kidding?"

"No. Until I've got evidence to the contrary this man might have been poisoned for all I know. He might have died by strangulation. He might have been struck a blow on the head. There is no evidence of that at the moment, but it may be a fact."

"Did you ever hear anything like this?" Doc said to me.

"That's why I'm going to perform an autopsy."

"An autopsy? You mean you're going to cut the poor guy open?"

"You can be sure, Mr. Carroll, that it doesn't make any difference to him."

"It does to me."

"I'm sorry, but that's my ruling. It's the law."

"How long will this take?" I said.

"I'll do it this afternoon. Mr. Edwards will remove the body to his funeral home."

"How long will it take?"

"Oh, an hour and a half. I'll call with my finding, if all goes well."

"If all goes well?" Doc said. "What does that mean?"

"All right," I said. "It's all right, Doc."

"It is like hell," Doc said.

The doctor put his papers back in his brief case and we walked out into the lobby. Doc was talking with Mr. Edwards about the cemetery plot and the doctor motioned to me and I followed him out onto the porch.

"You understand the necessity for this, don't you?" he said.

"I understand."

"After all, you recognize the circumstances. The cause of death has to be established. Besides, this Mr. Giorno, or Jay, was in the boxing business. Right?"

"What's that got to do with it?"

"Are you in the business?"

"No."

"I didn't think so, but you're familiar with the business. You've read about it."

"About what?"

"What sort of business it is, the types that are in it. How do I know who this man was, or what went on here?"

"All right, doctor. You'll call us later?"

"I'm not particularly keen about this myself. Performing an autopsy is no novelty to me. I was going to play golf this after-noon, the first time this season."

"I know. We were going to have some gangsters up for tea."

"What?"

"Call us when you're ready."

"Listen, we have a fellow in this town who used to be a fighter. You should see him."

"Why?"

"A drunk. A no-good."

"Is he the only drunk in this town?"

"No, but he's one of them. That's what it did for him."

When I went back into the lobby Doc was still standing there, and Mr. Edwards was coming out of one of the phone booths.

"I've just called my son," he said. "He'll be right over and we'll take the body. I'd like to go up now with you gentlemen and check anything that's on the body. I mean any jewelry or what-ever."

We went up to the room, and Mr. Edwards pulled the covers off Jay. I merely glanced at what he was doing, and looked at Doc, who was looking around the room.

"Nothing on the body," Mr. Edwards said. "Except, of course, the pajamas."

"All right," Doc said.

"My son will be here shortly."

"Wait a minute," Doc said. "There's a ring. Jay had a ring."

"There's no ring here," Mr. Edwards said. "There's no ring on either hand."

Doc and I walked over and we looked at both hands. There was no ring.

"There should be a ring," Doc said. "A ring with a ruby in it. He wore it on his left hand."

"It isn't here."

"I gave it to him myself, about twenty years ago, on his birthday. He was born in July, and that's the birthstone."

"Maybe he took it off," Mr. Edwards said.

"He never took it off. Since I gave it to him he never took it off."

"You'll probably find it here somewhere," Mr. Edwards said.

"Maybe Eddie took it off," I said.

"No," Doc said. "Why would he take it off? He wouldn't think of that."

I heard the front door slam. Then we could hear someone coming up the stairs.

"That's my son, probably," Mr. Edwards said.

"Let's get out of here," I said to Doc. "We'll look for the ring later."

We passed the young man carrying a stretcher in the hallway, and went into Doc's room. Eddie was lying on the bed, looking at the ceiling.

"Everything all right?" he said.

"Yes," Doc said. "Did you see anything of Jay's ring?"

"His ring?"

"Yes. It's not on him."

"It's got to be. He never took it off."

"Some SOB took it," Doc said. "Can you imagine that?"

"You're not sure," I said. "When they leave we'll look around the room and through Jay's stuff. It may be there."

"But I never saw him take it off, ever," Eddie said.

When we heard them go out and slowly down the stairs, Doc and I went back into the room. We looked all over the room and in the bureau drawers and the table drawer and in the pockets of Jay's clothes.

"Some SOB took it," Doc said. "Can you imagine a thing like that?"

"Who would take it?"

"Anybody. Who knows? This is some business."

"Well, not anybody. Who would steal a ring off a dead body? Not Girot or his wife. That's two out of the way."

"I don't know."

"Suppose we say nothing about it?"

"I don't care. I need a drink."

We went back to Doc's room, and Doc told Eddie to keep quiet about the ring. We sat with Eddie for a few minutes, and then Penna came in with the morning papers and Doc and I went down and got Girot from behind the desk in the lobby. I think that desk gave Girot the same sense of security that the Maginot line once gave the French, but it was just as false, and we went into the bar.

"Make us doubles," Doc said to Girot, "and that'll be all. Then you can get back to your work."

"All right."

"I feel lousy," Doc said.

"I do, too. After what we had last night we'd feel lousy under the best of circumstances."

"To Jay," Doc said, when Girot had left.

"To Jay."

"Jay and I went through a lot together. Over forty years."

"I know, and now I'm feeling a little ashamed."

"Ashamed? Of what?"

"Of myself."

"Why? What's the matter?"

"Oh, about Jay. Jay was a nice little guy. I liked him, but I used to think how he weighed on everybody. Now I'm ashamed."

"God how he liked to talk."

"I probably shouldn't say this now, but I used to wonder sometimes how you put up with it."

"You want to know how?"

"Yes."

"You ever look at that busted nose? That beat-up ear?"

"Yes."

"I put them there."

"You?"

"Certainly. Jay was my first fighter."

"I know that."

"I learned on Jay. I was a punk kid, managing him. I put that busted nose there. I put that beat-up ear there. I was learning—on Jay. Many a time Jay used to get on my nerves, too, but I'd look at that nose and that ear, and I'd say to myself: 'You're with me. As long as you live, you're with me.'"

"I should have figured that out for myself."

"It's something, talking about it now. 'As long as you live.' That's the way it worked out."

"Yes. Suddenly today was the day."

"I should have been arrested, the fights I put him in. Some of those great old-timers they use to write about—those grand old managers—what they did to me when I had Jay. He might have been a good fighter."

"Really?"

"Not a great one, but a good one. A lot better than he was. I was real brave with Jay. I put him into wars. I'll tell you one thing. When he was finished, I was finished being a brave manager. I outgrew that with one fighter. Jay."

"Some of them never do."

"I'll tell you another thing. Every fighter I've had since Jay was a better fighter because of Jay, because of what I learned on Jay. Every one of them, and that goes for the Pro, too, and I told every one of them. Jay never knew it, but I told them. I told the Pro. He was very fond of Jay."

"I know. He used to go along with him the same as you did."

"A lot of guys at Stillman's probably wondered why I kept Jay. He talked too much. He got excited in the corner. I could have got ten better trainers. I didn't need a trainer. I do that. I needed a pickup guy for the towels and the pail and to give a rubdown."

"I know."

"I thought a lot about Jay in the last few years. You ever ride along in a train, or drive along, and see one of those junk yards packed with old cars, rusting, one on top of the other?"

"Yes."

"I used to see those old car bodies and think of Jay. Every one of those old wrecks has a piece of every new car on the road. They learned on those old ones the way I learned on Jay. As long as I lived there could never be any junk heap for Jay. You know something else?"

"What?"

"Don't get me wrong. This was no charity. Jay did what he was supposed to do, and he was loyal. He was the most loyal guy in the world."

"I know."

"Right after he had that first heart attack, a couple of years ago, I asked him about it and he says: 'The doctor says I should take it easy. I shouldn't get excited.' Do you think I could keep him out of the corner?"

"No."

"About ten days later we're in Boston. Eddie got a bad decision—dreadful. He had the other guy almost out at the end, and where's Jay? Jumping up and down and screaming at the referee, ten days after the doctor warned him to take it easy."

"I believe that."

"A loyal little guy. He had nothing. You know what was a big thing with him?"

"No."

"Christmas cards. He sent Christmas cards to everybody."

"I know. He always sent me one."

"Half of the people never sent any back to him."

"I never did. You make me ashamed again."

"It makes no difference. He got some. He used to hang them on a string in his room. There was an old, bricked-up fireplace there, and he'd hang the cards on a string over the fireplace. He'd keep them there all year, until the next Christmas when the new ones came. Then he'd save the old ones in boxes under his bed. Over thirty years or more he had boxes full of them. That was his Christmas. I'll have to clean them out now."

"Let it go until after the fight."

"I will. I'll have to. He had nothing. That's why, one birthday, I gave him that ring. I thought he was going to cry. Nobody ever gave him anything. Who the hell would take that ring?"

"I don't know."

"Who would do it? Figure it out."

"Well, if you want to go into it, you've got the fighters and old Barnum. One of them must have gone back into the room while we were in your room."

"Not Barnum."

"No."

"Penna?"

"I don't think so."

"Why not?"

"That wise-guy type wouldn't do it."

"He's just the type."

"No, Doc. He's out in the open. Practical jokes and kidding, yes. Not taking a ring off a body. How about DeCorso? I don't know much about him."

"Vince? Listen, he's so glad that I gave him a few weeks' work he wouldn't take the chance. I know him."

"Not Memphis."

"No. Of course not."

"Booker Boyd?"

"I don't know."

"A possibility, but my candidate is Cardone."

"Cardone? Why Cardone?"

"Well, I know Charley Keener, and the way he keeps his fighters, Doc. Cardone's probably got nothing in his pockets right now—except, possibly, the ring—and when he's in Jersey I bet Keener gives him a ten a week. He has all his fighters eat with him, you know, so he can watch them."

"It's possible."

"Certainly. Cardone's got those two dames, or they've got him."

"Ah, he doesn't need dough for them. You can be sure they pick up everything. Maybe they're even paying him, for all I know."

"Nevertheless, picture the kid. He's got some pride. He'd like to be able to make one show, have some dough."

"That ring is worth a couple of hundred."

"I recall seeing it on Jay, now that it's come up. Does Keener know about those dames?"

"I don't know. My suspect is still Penna, in spite of what you say."

"You may be right, but I doubt it. Too open. Not knowing anything about Booker Boyd, mine is Cardone."

"We'll never see that ring again."

"I believe you're right."

We saw Barnum come through the door, looking for someone, and then he saw us at the bar and walked over.

"'Scuse me, Doc," he said.

"Sure, Barnum."

"You goin' to New York?"

"Yes. Tonight or tomorrow morning."

"I'm sorry about Jay, and I'll take care of Eddie while you're gone. I mean I'll handle him in the gym, and don't worry about it while you're gone."

"Thanks, Barnum. Thanks. I'll bring somebody out with me. Freddie Thomas, if I can get him. I'll get somebody. I appreciate it, Barnum."

"Don't worry about it. I'm glad to do it, because Eddie's gonna win this fight."

"Sure he is."

"I know. I know the other boy. I know him since he start. He ain't the fighter people think he is. He got dog in him, but he don't show it to them yet. Eddie, he'll make him show it."

"He will, for sure."

"Nobody fought that other boy right yet. I been watchin' Eddie in the gym, and the way he's boxin' in the gym is the way he's gonna lick him. You got that other boy just right."

"I know."

"You back him up, he can't fight you. The way Eddie counters and punches to the body he's gonna make it easy. I know the other boy and I been watchin' Eddie. What Eddie knows and the way he punches he's too much for him, sure."

"Thanks, Barnum."

"The people in our business, they don't know. They may think Eddie gets lucky, but I know you for years, Doc. You got the good one now, and he ain't gonna miss."

"Fine, Barnum."

"I'll take care of him. It's a pleasure."

Eddie went into the gym that afternoon stony-faced, and Doc worked him harder than he had worked since we had come into camp. No one kidded around, and it seemed to me that they all were working harder and that there was an air of resentment over it all. Charley Keener said a few words to Doc about Jay and let it go at that, and Eddie and Memphis were boxing the last round, with Doc and me standing together on the apron, when Girot tapped me on the leg and I climbed down.

"Doctor Bernardi is on the telephone."

"I'll take it."

I went out into the lobby and into the booth and shut the door and identified myself.

"Oh yes, Mr. Hughes," he said. "I'm ascribing cause of death to coronary thrombosis with infarction—"

"Wait a minute. I'm trying to write this down. Did you say infraction?"

"No. Infarction. I-n-f-a-r-c-t-i-o-n. That's an obstruction. With infarction due to arteriosclerotic heart disease. Have you got that?"

"In other words, he died of a heart attack."

"To all appearances."

"Wait a minute. What do you mean, to all appearances? You performed an autopsy, didn't you?"

"Yes. Of course."

"Then appearances have nothing to do with it. You were going on appearances before. This is your professional finding, isn't it?"

"Yes."

"Good."

I hung up and, when I got back to the gym, Doc had Eddie banging at the big bag. Doc was standing with his arms folded across his chest, watching.

"That coroner just called."

"He did? What did he say?"

"Jay died of a heart attack."

"Surprised?"

"Hardly. I don't really think that that doctor was, either."

"Political SOB. He'd like to have made a big thing out of it, wouldn't he? He might even have gotten his picture in the paper."

Doc took the 9:25 bus to New York that night. Eddie and I walked up the driveway to see him off, and then Eddie went into the kitchen and had a glass of warm milk and went to bed in Doc's room. In my own room I lay awake in the darkness for a long while, seeing Jay. He wanted to be sure I'd put him in the story. Then I remembered Jay's fat friend Stanley, and I felt sorry for Stanley, too.

19

The next morning I slept until I heard the fighters come back off the road, their feet heavy on the stairs. By the time I had showered and shaved and dressed, Barnum was coming up the stairs carrying a tray with five cups of steaming tea on it. He took one in for Eddie, and then went down the hall with the others.

"How did you sleep?" I said to Eddie.

Eddie was sitting in the wicker chair, holding the cup and saucer in both hands and blowing on the tea. Through the window I could see that it was another clear day.

"I don't know. It must have been midnight before I got to sleep. I didn't feel like getting up this morning. How about you?"

"The same, except that I didn't get up."

"Eddie Brown!" Girot's voice came up the stairs. "The telephone!"

"All right, Girot."

"You can't go down with that sweat on you. You'd better take that tea."

"Find out who it is, will you?"

I walked to the top of the stairs.

"Girot? Find out who it is."

"It's the telephone operator. She said somebody wants Eddie."

"Tell her to call back in a half hour."

I walked back to the room.

"Maybe it's Doc," Eddie said.

"No. He wouldn't call at this time. He knows you just came off the road."

"This tea is almost too hot to drink."

"You remind me of Tony Zale."

"Why?"

"He was in Stillman's one day, training for Graziano—just before they postponed that first fight. He'd finished his work and we were back in one of those little dressing rooms and Tony was sitting on a stool and Lester Bromberg was bending over him and interviewing him—you know the way Lester does. Art Winch came through the door, carrying a cup of hot tea for Tony in one hand. It was a warm day, and Art was stripped to his undershirt, and just as he went to hand the tea to Tony, Lester straightened up, and the cup and the tea went up into the air. It made a complete loop, and the tea spilled out and came down right inside the front of Winch's undershirt, the slice of lemon and all.

"Well, Winch jumped about three feet off the floor. He ripped off the undershirt and the lemon fell to the floor and he's jumping around there, screaming and grabbing a towel and Tony is sitting there, clapping his hands and laughing and shouting: 'Stay in there, Art! Stay in there! You gotta be able to take it!'"

"Tony did?"

"That's right. You know how quiet he was."

"I know."

"That's why I remember it. It was the only time—in or out of the ring—that I ever saw him show any emotion."

"So what happened?"

"Well, Winch is drying himself off—his chest was all red from the scalding—and Tony is still laughing, with his head back, and

Winch says to him: 'What's the matter with you? You crazy? What's so funny?' And Tony said: 'You. You're always telling me how tough I gotta be. You're always telling me that you gotta stay in there. So stay in there, Art. Stay in there yourself. You see?'"

"He made a lot of money, didn't he, with Graziano and Cerdan?"

"Tony? He was a good fighter, and he had the right people around him—Pian and Winch and Ray Arcel."

"He was plenty tough."

"Winch was right. You've got to stay in there, otherwise find another business."

"That's right. You'd be surprised, though, at the number of fighters that aren't that way at all. I mean, pretty good fighters. Anyway, people think they're good. They don't like it. I mean, how they got in the business I don't know."

"They have a manual dexterity—great reflexes, fast hands. They cover up."

"That's right, but that's not enough. Not if you're in there with a real good fighter. He'll show you up."

"Certainly. That's the truth of it all. If it wasn't so, boxing wouldn't mean anything."

"This other guy isn't so tough. From the fights I've seen him in I know he's not tough enough, and I'll prove it."

"Of course you will. You've got the equipment to do it."

"I wish the fight was this Friday. I'm getting sick of it around here."

"I know."

It wasn't a half hour. It was about twenty minutes after the first call that Girot shouted up the stairs again. Eddie had just come back from his shower and was finishing dressing, and I walked downstairs with him and stood talking with Girot while Eddie went into the booth.

"I need some change," Eddie said, coming out of the booth. "It's collect."

Girot gave him some quarters, dimes and nickels, and Eddie was in the booth for five or six minutes.

"That was Ernie Gordon," he said. "He wants to write something about Jay for today's paper. Doc called him. I guess he called all the newspapermen."

"That's good."

"He wanted me to say something about Jay. I didn't know what to say."

"I know."

"I said he was with me for all those fights, and he was a great little guy, and I wish it didn't happen. That sounds stupid."

"What else could you say?"

"So you know what he asked me then?"

"What?"

"He said: 'What does this mean to the fight?' I said: 'What do you mean?' He said: 'How do you feel about the fight now?' I said: 'I feel the same. I'm gonna lick the guy, only more so.' What else could I say?"

"Nothing else. You did well."

"Why does he call collect? He always calls collect."

"He does it with all the fighters," Girot said, shaking his head. "That's no good."

"He must make money, doesn't he?"

"You know that, Eddie. You should know that."

"I know what you mean. Plenty. So can't he afford to pay for the call? I don't care about the dollar-sixty, or whatever it is. Can't he even pay that?"

"That isn't all."

"What isn't?"

"When he writes his story he'll dateline himself here in camp, and then he can collect expenses from his office."

"Even when he is here he has no expenses," Girot said.

"Is that right to do that?" Eddie said.

"He's still a good reporter in that paper," I said. "Why don't we have our breakfast?"

After breakfast I walked with Eddie. When we got to the top of the driveway I suggested that we might walk south to the town.

"No," he said. "It's too flat. If I'm going to walk, the hills are better."

"I just thought you might be bored with it. How many times do you see it, running it every morning and walking twice a day?"

"I don't know. I'm not here to have fun."

We walked to the top of the rise of the road north of the camp. I was trying to think of something to say to get Eddie out of it, and as we started down the gentle, curving-to-the-right slope of the other side, I looked at the vista, limited by the pines on the lake shore, half hiding the roofs of the summer homes and cottages and the lake itself, but open on the left, where two sloping fields lay bare in the sun. Once, long ago, they had been stripped of wood and growth and stone, and now they lay bare brown, waiting for a planting, probably in corn. To me they seemed to be breathing the warm spring sun the way a man breathes the air after a long try under water at the end of a long dive.

"Who do you think took Jay's ring?" Eddie said.

It is inevitable. When a man has just died he is suddenly, for a time, more alive than he had ever been in his life.

"I don't know," I said.

"Doc thinks it might have been Penna."

"I don't think so."

"I know. He told me. I don't think so, either. Penna's not a bad guy. Doc says you think it might have been Cardone or Boyd."

"There's no one else. I don't necessarily think one of them took it. I've just eliminated the others."

"How could anybody take a ring off somebody that just died?"

"I don't know. During the war I passed up I don't know how many rings and wrist watches and good German binoculars. I just couldn't take them off the bodies, but some guys could. I might just as well have taken them. Somebody was going to."

"I couldn't have done it, either."

"In the war, at least, I didn't resent the guys who did it. I rather admired that ability."

"How do you mean?"

It was a chance to take his mind off Jay.

"They were realists," I said, "and it was one of the things that made them good in combat. I never heard of a one of them having to go back to see the division psychiatrist because of what they called combat fatigue. That type won the war for us, and there's really no basic difference between men in war and men in peace. When a thing is done it's done. When a man dies he's dead. If you can see things that way, and accept them, you've got life licked."

"I still don't see it."

"You do in your own business."

"How?"

"Take that dame who interviewed you the other day on television. To her it seems just as horrible for one man to punch another man into insensibility as it seems now, to you and me, for someone to strip a ring off Jay's finger."

"But that's stealing."

"I know, but that's not what bothers us. If this ring or some money or a watch were stolen from Jay last week we wouldn't be so aroused. We recognize that some people are crooks. What really gets us is that the ring was taken off the hand of a man who had just died. Am I right?"

"That's right."

"So, feeling as most people do about death, we can't understand how anyone could do such a thing."

"I sure can't understand it."

"And that television dame—that Bunny Williams—feeling as most people do about hurting other people physically, can't understand how you can punch another man until you knock him out."

"It's not the same."

"Of course not, because you have one attitude about the one, and another about the other. Suppose that television dame had given you a chance to explain what you feel about fighting another man, and hitting him. Suppose she had really been trying to find out the truth of you, and of fighting, instead of just trying to make her own point. If she had led you into expressing what you feel about hitting an opponent and knocking him out, what would you have said?"

"I don't know."

"All right, I'll frame the question. You're Eddie Brown—as Jimmy Cannon would say—and a week from Friday you're going to fight for the middleweight championship of the world. To win this fight you're going to have to hurt the other man more than he hurts you. Do you enjoy hurting other people?"

"No. I don't think of it that way."

"How do you think of it? What's in your mind when you punch another man, as hard as you can?"

"I want to beat him. He's trying to beat me, and I'm trying to beat him. That's what it's all about."

"Is that all? Don't you want to hurt him?"

"I don't know. I don't think of that. I think of beating him, like you do in anything else."

"And when you knock him out, how do you feel? There he is, lying there. How do you feel?"

"I feel good, great. You try to get a knockout."

"Ezzard Charles once told me that, after he had knocked a man out, he often started to think, that night or the next day, that maybe he could have won without knocking him out. He began to regret the knockout."

"I don't."

"That was one of the flaws in Charles as a fighter. He wasn't the complete fighter, and that showed in his fights and was one of the reasons why the people never rose to him. He could never understand that, and late in his career when he tried to turn slugger and go for the knockout he floundered because he was going against his true nature."

"I know that. I could see it."

"I don't want to keep going back to Graziano and Zale, but if anyone saw their three fights he saw most of the truth of fighting. After the second one—the one that Rocky won—he was in the shower room in the basement of the Chicago Stadium. One eye was closed and there was a metal clip holding the cut over the other one, and the newspapermen were crowded around him asking him how he felt. He kept saying: 'I wanted to kill him. I like him, but I wanted to kill him. I wanted to kill him.' That was all he could say."

"I know. I remember reading that. I was just a kid, starting to fight."

"Did you believe that? Did you believe that he could like the other guy, and still want to kill him in there?"

"I don't know if I believed it then. I believe it now. I've felt that way."

"You have?"

"It's just that you get so worked up in a fight. I mean, if it's a tough fight, and the other guy is a good fighter and you're both trying to take one another out. You like him for that, but the funny thing is it makes you want to kill him at the same time."

"Rocky liked Tony and Tony liked Rocky. Each still thinks more of the other than he does of any other fighter. Three times they were ready to fight to the death, but do you know why they like one another?"

"Why?"

"Because of those fights. Each guy brought out the best in the other guy, and gave him his greatest fight and his greatest moment."

"I go with that. I like the guys that gave me my good fights. I think of them a lot. I'd even like to see them again. I mean, someday just sit around and talk."

"Marciano once told me the same thing."

"He did?"

"He feels that way about Walcott, off their Philadelphia fight. He said: 'It was my greatest fight, and I couldn't have done it alone. I'll always like Walcott for that.'"

"I feel the same way. I fought Al Morrow in St. Louis."

"A real good fighter."

"I'll say. In the first round he hit me a punch under the heart I could feel in my legs. We fought that way for ten rounds. We never let up, and when I got the decision you know what I wanted to do?"

"No."

"I wanted to kiss him. What would that look like?"

"I've seen fighters do it."

"I mean, for ten rounds I wanted to kill him and he fought like he wanted to kill me, and then I wanted to kiss him. First I wanted to kill him. Explain that."

"Suppose you had?"

"What?"

"Killed him."

"I don't know."

"Don't get me wrong. I understand this. I'm just trying to be an honest Bunny Williams, if there is such a thing, and bring out the truth in you. This is what she should have done on that show."

"So why didn't she? Why did she have to do it the way she did?"

"Because there isn't enough truth in her to bring it out in someone else."

"How come you like boxing so much?"

"Because I find so much in it."

"How do you mean?"

"The basic law of man. The truth of life. It's a fight, man against man, and if you're going to defeat another man, defeat him completely. Don't starve him to death, like they try to do in the fine, clean competitive world of commerce. Leave him lying there, senseless, on the floor."

"I guess that's it. I don't know."

"Look. I'm not supporting this. I'm not saying it's good. I'm just saying it's there. It's in man, all men. I'm against violence. I hate arguments. I believe in a world where everything will be done through reason and with honesty and where force will be nothing. Centuries from now we may have this, but as of now there is still that remnant of the animal in man and the law of life is still in the law of the jungle—the survival of the fittest. As long as that's true, I find man revealing himself more completely in fighting than in any other form of expressive endeavor. It's the war all over again, and they license it and sell tickets to it and people go to see it because, without even realizing it, they see this truth in it."

"I never thought of it like that."

"I'll go back to Zale and Graziano for one last time. I'll go back to their first fight in the Yankee Stadium. It was the best of the three."

"It was?"

"I say it was, and it set the pace for the others. That same year the Dodgers and the Cardinals tied for the National League pennant, when the Dodgers blew their last game of the season. After the game we all went down to the clubhouse at Ebbets Field and the ballplayers were scowling and staring at their lockers.

"We went into Leo Durocher's office. Now I'm for Durocher as a baseball manager. I think he represented, better than any other manager since John McGraw, the competitive essence of the game. Durocher was a symbol of what baseball—any game—is all about, the overwhelming desire to win, and as we walked in he was standing in the middle of his office, pulling on a pair of peach silk undershorts, and somebody said: 'Well, Leo, what about it?'

"'What about it?' Leo said, straightening up and looking at us.

'I'll tell you what about it. We'll play 'em till the snow flies.' So there stood the baseball writers, writing this down, and, as I said, I'm not knocking baseball or Leo. This was a fine, fighting quote—for baseball—but as I walked away I was thinking of something else. You know what?"

"You said Zale and Graziano."

"That's right. Leo was going to play them till the snow flew, and one week before I'd seen Zale and Graziano, two men standing toe to toe under the lights in Yankee Stadium, literally trying to take one another apart with that mass of mankind sitting in the darkness around them and screaming for more. It was like two prehistoric monsters, knee deep in the primeval ooze, ready to fight to the death and with the jungle all around them echoing to the noise and the horror of it."

"It was that good a fight?"

"Yes, and it was the truth. When you want to beat another man, you try to beat him, literally. You don't try to hit behind the runner, or work the pitcher for a walk or break a curve over the corner of the plate. These are the refinements of civilization."

"They're two different things. A fighter is a fighter, and a ballplayer is a ballplayer."

"No. A ballplayer is a fighter, too. What does the ballplayer do, when it comes down to essentials? When hitting behind the runner, or breaking off the curve isn't enough? You've seen them do it. When it all becomes too much, they strip off their gloves and drop their bats and go at one another with their bare fists."

"You're right about that."

"Certainly. It's the truth, but their game doesn't allow it and yours does. I like baseball. I like most of the refinements of civilization, but I have to believe that of all games—if that's what we're talking about—yours goes the deepest and, going deepest, goes the furthest toward the truth."

"I still envy those ballplayers."

"I know. Do you want to turn around and start back?"

"All right, but nobody knocks their game. I wish you'd explain it to Helen sometime, the way you just explained it to me."

"I wasn't explaining it to you. I was just talking. I can't explain it to anyone."

"Helen's got a good head."

"I know she has."

"She seemed to like it at first. I mean she went to three or four of my early fights."

"Certainly, but how can a woman—a wife—sitting outside a ring come away from a fight with the same feeling about it as you who were in there doing it?"

"I suppose that's right. Many times I think that if I was in some other business she'd understand it."

"Not really, and I don't mean to apply that just to Helen."

"How do you mean?"

"Every man's in a fight, Eddie, no matter what business he's in. The woman can try to understand, but she's really just a spectator."

"Then Helen reads all that stuff they write about the fight game. If you read it, and you don't know anything about it, you have to believe a lot of it. She'd like me to be in something everybody looks up to."

"Everybody looks up to the champion of the world, in spite of what they read or think about it."

"That's right, too."

At least his mind was off Jay.

20

That was Cardone's last day of boxing, and after he had finished his three rounds, Eddie went in. Charley Keener handled Memphis, and Vince DeCorso and Barnum handled Eddie, and that night Keener stayed in camp. Eddie and the sparring partners and Penna and I went to the movies—a war thing about a G.I. who got mixed up with a German girl in a cellar and then had to fight with himself about what the war was all about. He accomplished his mission, though, lieutenant, and when we got back to Girot's, Eddie went right to bed, and I went into the bar.

Keener was there. He was talking with a middle-aged man and woman who, apparently, had just stopped in for a couple of beers, but when he saw me he finished his conversation with them and sat down on the stool next to mine.

"How did my guy look today?" he said.

"Fine. He looked fine."

"He'll lick that other guy easy."

"He should."

"Why?"

"You know why. The other guy is a short-armed club fighter who'll keep trying, but he'll never be able to reach Cardone."

"I know. That's why I made the match."

"Of course."

"See what Mr. Hughes will have, Girot."

"He knows."

Girot set the drink down in front of me.

"That's why I picked him. It'll look good on that TV, and my guy will look great."

"Agreed."

"That's the way you've got to do it."

"Is it?"

"Sure. What do the people know? They'll see a good fight."

I started on my drink.

"You still like Eddie in his fight?" he said.

"I do."

"The other guy is seven-eight to five."

"It'll come down. He opened higher than that. The newspapermen will be up in a day or two and get a look at Eddie. He'll come out of his depression about Jay, and they'll see him as he is."

"The other guy will still close as the favorite. He'll be at least six to five."

"That's because he's the champion."

"Well, that's a good reason, isn't it?"

"Not necessarily."

"Look, I like Eddie and I like Doc, but look at the records."

"What does that prove? There's nothing wrong with Eddie's record, but you can't read a fighter in black and white, won and lost in a record book."

"You remember that fight Eddie had in Chicago about a year ago, that was on TV?"

"Yes. It was a good fight. Eddie licked him good."

"But he had a tough time doing it. The champ fought the same guy later and licked him easy, eight rounds out of ten."

"Come off it, Charley, will you? He outboxed him, proving what?"

"You tell me."

"Gladly. I can name you two or three other fighters—including Eddie Brown himself—who can lick that guy outboxing him, but you can't name me another one who ever licked him the way Eddie did."

"I don't get that."

"The guy in Chicago is a southpaw."

"Of course."

"The left hand is his big punch."

"Sure. When he fought the champ he never landed it."

"All right. All you people are always saying that the way to fight a southpaw is with right hands. Right?"

"Sure. Then you take his left hand away at the same time."

"You know how Eddie fought him?"

"How?"

"Right to his strength. With left hands. He licked that guy standing in there, drawing the left hand, slipping it or taking it high and belting the guy's brains out and blasting his body apart with hooks."

"So he made it a tougher fight."

"Sure, but he and Doc wrote a book for all you others to read. Eddie could have outboxed him, too, but if you're basically a counter puncher the way to lick a southpaw is with hooks. It's a risk, sure, because you're inviting him to fire his big gun, but that's the only way to open him up. Eddie gave him a worse licking than that champion did, winning his eight rounds, and he wrote something new."

"But he made it tougher for himself."

"So does any explorer. Doc made it tougher. You people don't understand Doc."

"I understand him. I know him for years."

"So do I, and I've watched him all those years. Doc isn't looking for the easy way to do things, because he tries to build fighters, and there's no easy way to do that. For nine years he's been building Eddie Brown. He finally found a kid who could learn it all and do it all, and he taught it to him in the gym and, most of all, fighting tough fights the tough way—going to the other guy's strength and licking him there, and then, once you've proved it and taken all there was out of it for yourself as a fighter, handling him any way you want."

"You think he'll try to outbox the other guy in this one?"

"No. Not in this one. He's arrived now. Eddie'll make the other guy fight this one the way Eddie wants it fought."

"He'd better."

Girot motioned toward my glass, but I shook him off.

"Look. What you say about Doc may be true. I like Doc."

"He's the last of the old guard."

"That's the trouble. Times change. The fight game isn't what it used to be."

"That's the trouble, not Doc."

"With everything you say about Doc, how many times has Eddie fought on TV?"

"Three."

"Cardone has been on five times already, and he's fighting half as long as Eddie."

"Congratulations."

"The big thing today is to get those TV shots. I'm telling you. Within two years, at the most, Vic Cardone will be the welterweight champion of the world."

"I won't be surprised."

"Like I told you. You'll get a good magazine story out of him."

"How, Charley? It's a real sacrifice for him to say good morning, and that's the last thing he says all day."

"He's not that bad. He's just shy. He's a kid."

"Obviously."

"Listen. It's a good story. You should see the mail he gets. They love him on TV. He's a good-looking kid. They've even got bobby-soxers' fan clubs for him. Vic Cardone clubs. I'm not kidding."

"I know you're not. You probably started the first one."

"What one?"

"The first bobby-soxers' fan club. Did you stake it?"

"Well, I send them all pictures. That's all. The women are crazy about him. They really are."

"How's he about women?"

"Cardone? He's a kid. What does he know?"

"He knows there are men and women, and that there's a difference."

"He pays no attention to them. He's a fighter. You don't think I'd let him get loused up, do you, all the years I've had fighters?"

"No. I'm sure not."

I was sure then, too, that he knew nothing about it. If he had, he would have known that we all knew and he would have found a way to explain it, and this pleased me.

The next morning Cardone went on the road with Eddie and the others. In the gym he exercised lightly and then, when he went to the dressing room, Keener handled the sparring partners again for Eddie. Eddie was hitting the light bag when Cardone came out, ready to go to Keener's home in Jersey for the night. When he saw Cardone, he stopped the bag.

"Good luck, Vic," Eddie said.

"Yeah. Thanks," Cardone said.

"Hey, Silent," Penna said, walking over with the jump rope in one hand and sweating. "If the guy gets too tough in there, just talk him out of it. Give him a little speech. Say: 'Look, Mac.' You're a good talker."

"Good luck," I said, shaking Cardone's hand.

"Thanks."

"Can you imagine him talkin' in a fight?" Penna said to Eddie. "Ain't that a laugh?"

"You watch tomorrow night," Keener said to me. "You'll see a good fighter."

"Yes. One good fighter. Yours."

"So?" Keener said, winking. "What do you want from me?"

They walked across the gym and out, Cardone carrying his luggage and Keener striding ahead of him. I got Eddie's robe off a chair and helped him into it, and Penna followed us into the dressing room while Barnum went for the hot tea.

"He looked nervous to me," Penna said. "Cardone."

"He'll win easy," Eddie said. "I'm not even going to watch it."

"You'll be better off in bed," I said.

After dinner we all took a walk for a half hour and then went in and watched television. We were watching Groucho Marx when Doc came in. He had Freddie Thomas with him and a middleweight named Artie Winant, and they had driven out in Winant's car.

"How do you feel?" I said to Doc.

"All right."

He looked tired. Even the dark blue suit he was wearing looked too heavy on him.

"Have you eaten?"

"No."

"We'd better have Katie make you something. Some scrambled eggs and toast and tea?"

"All right. I'm going up and wash."

"I'll tell Katie," Eddie said.

"Where do you want us?" Freddie Thomas said to Girot, who was standing in the doorway, with his arms crossed, listening.

"There is the room Eddie and Johnny Jay had," Girot said, shrugging. "The big room in the back corner by the lake."

"I know the room," Winant said. "I know all the rooms here."

"I'm glad to see you," I said, shaking Winant's hand.

"Thanks," he said. "It's been a while, no?"

I wasn't glad to see him. Four or five years before he had been a pretty good middleweight. He had been good enough to fight for the title and almost take it, and then Eddie had taken a decision from him and Winant had managed to win his next one and had retired. Now he was heavy, and even his face looked a little soft.

"I'll take the stuff up, hey?" he said to Freddie Thomas.

"Fine, Artie."

"Why don't you move in with me?" I said to Doc. "Let Eddie stay in your room. There's two beds in my room."

"That's what I was going to suggest. I'll be down in a minute."

He went upstairs, carrying his bag and following Winant.

"I'm glad Doc was able to get you," I said to Freddie Thomas.

In thirty years he had worked with nine or ten champions. He was the best conditioner in the business and had great hands in a corner. He was a quiet, immaculate man of medium build who came as a surprise to any stranger who, having heard his name and knowing his business, met him for the first time.

"Listen, I'm glad to be able to do it. These are nice people— Doc and Eddie—and I felt terrible when I heard about Jay."

"We all did."

"I was coming up with Artie in a couple of days anyway. The extra time will do him good."

"I didn't even know he was coming back."

"What can you do?" he said, shrugging. "Somebody conned him into putting everything he made fighting for ten years into some roller-skating rink out on Long Island. Now they need some more money, or they'll lose everything he's got in it."

"It's a shame."

"So they came to me. What else can I do? How else can he make any money? He was good to me when he had it, so I said I'd try to get him into some kind of shape."

"But how much can he make?"

"You tell me. He'll win a few tune-up fights out of town some-where, and then to get some money he'll have to fight somebody who'll lick him good. It's terrible, but what can you do? I've seen it happen to a lot of them. They get out of this business, and they're suckers for everybody. I feel sorry for him."

"So do I."

When Doc came down, Eddie and I sat with him while he ate his eggs slowly and had one piece of toast and drank his tea.

"So how did it go?" I said.

"All right."

"Was there a funeral?" Eddie said.

"Yes, sort of."

"What happened?" Eddie said.

"We had a service last night at the funeral parlor. I remembered there was some minister Jay knew when they were kids. He used to get him tickets to the fights, some Protestant minister in New York, and I got him. He was glad to do it."

"Was anybody there?"

"Yes, a few. About a dozen guys from Stillman's. Freddie Thomas was there. Jay's brother-in-law was there—an old Italian. My nephew was there, and that friend of Jay's came."

"Stanley?"

"That's right. He had his wife with him. This morning the minister and I rode out to the cemetery with the fella from the funeral parlor. We were the only ones there."

"Where's he buried?"

"In Woodlawn. I got him a small plot—the funeral man from up here arranged it. I'm having a stone made for the grave."

"I'd like to go in on that," Eddie said.

"Forget it. It's taken care of."

"But I want to, Doc."

"All right. We'll take it off the top after the fight."

21

At about eleven o'clock the next morning Doc and Freddie Thomas had gone into town for tape and gauze and Eddie was lying in his room, reading the morning papers, when I came up the stairs and saw him there and stopped by the door.

"There's nothing in the out-of-town fight results about Schaeffer's fight," he said.

"Those are the early editions we get up here. They come out too early to carry all the results."

"I wish I knew how he made out. He's a nice guy."

"I'll call the AP in New York."

"It'll be in the afternoon papers, won't it?"

"Probably, but why wait?"

I called the AP and got the sports desk. It took the kid who answered a couple of minutes to find what I wanted, and then I went back upstairs and told Eddie.

"Schaeffer lost," I said. "A decision."

"He did? Gee, I'm sorry about that. I didn't think that guy he was fighting was much of a fighter."

"Let's be honest. Neither is Schaeffer."

"He's a nice guy, though. Did they say what kind of a fight it was?"

"No. All they sent out of New York was the result, and it took the kid a couple of minutes to find that."

"Poor Polo, too."

"He shouldn't be in the business, either."

"I know, but when guys are in camp with you, you get to like them. You know?"

"I know."

I went into my room and lay down. I had brought *I Cover the Waterfront* to camp and I was reading it when Penna came in. It is something I do every two or three years—get it out and read it once more. I was reading that chapter about the Navy diver, the one whose wife was plaguing him for back alimony and whose buddies would hurry him into the decompression chamber every time his wife showed up at ship side. I prize that book the way you prize a great recording that you take out and play again when you feel just right for it and need it.

"Hey!" Penna said. "Your two buddies are here."

"Who?"

"Them two aces. Them sports columnists. Fred Gardner and that little guy, Scott. He's some writer, huh?"

"Dave? Yes, they both are. Thanks, Al."

When I went down they were already in the dining room, at one of the small tables by the windows, and Girot was bringing them dry martinis.

"Make me one of mine, will you, Girot?"

"Yes, Mr. Hughes."

"Doctor Livingstone, I presume?" Fred said, the two of them standing up while we shook hands.

"Precisely," I said.

"How long you in for?" Dave said, as we sat down.

"The duration. Until the fight."

"God, you're as loyal as—I don't know—but I'll say Lassie," Dave said.

"Not a bit. She's smarter than I am. I hang around because I can't discover a quicker way of doing this kind of a piece."

"Getting stir crazy?"

"Just about. Thanks for coming."

"Don't thank us," Fred said. "We have to work for a living, too. You don't suppose we could find a couple of columns around here?"

"Any number of them."

Girot brought my drink and left.

"What's the matter with him?" Fred said.

"Nothing. He's just perpetually sad. On the wagon for years."

"You see? That proves it. Let's not get that way."

"No chance."

"It's a pleasure to have you aboard, sirs," I said. It is one of our gags out of the war.

"It's a pleasure to be aboard, sir."

"What have you been doing up here?"

"You heard about Jay."

"Yes," Dave said. "I was sorry to hear it. We were talking about it driving up."

Fred just sat there, shaking his head slowly.

"And, talking about it, got lost?"

"Not then. We got lost later, talking about something else. About Jay, I was saying what a nice little guy he was, I'm sure, but he used to bend my ear something awful."

"Don't say it," Fred said.

"Well, I don't think I'm being irreverent. I liked him. He was a nice little guy, but half the time I didn't know what he was talking about, and I don't think he did, either."

"You've already told me that," Fred said, shaking his head.

"Don't pay any attention to him," Dave said to me. "He's been complaining all morning. He also cries at movies. I remember at one boxing writers' dinner I had to go to the boys' room and Jay collared me there and started telling me some long story about one of his fights thirty years before. I thought I'd never get back to hear the rest of the speeches."

"If you were wise you wouldn't have," Fred said. "I don't

know which boxing writers' dinner you're talking about, but whatever Jay was telling you, it was better than the speeches."

"I agree."

"Will you stop, then, and finish that drink?"

I motioned to Girot to make three more.

"How are you doing on the story?" Fred said.

"Who knows? I'm walking around and looking and listening and living it as much as I can. How do you know until you've written it?"

"You'll do all right."

"So then Jay dies. If you'll excuse me, Fred, I felt lousy, too, for thinking just what Dave's been saying. Then, today, I wake up realizing I'm even worse. I'm supposed to be writing a piece about a typical, good fighter and how he lives and thinks and feels getting ready to fight for a title. In the middle of it the trainer dies. What's typical about this? Now I regret Jay dying, first of all because he died, but also—I'll be honest with you— because I'm going to have to find a way to handle this in the piece. How do you like that?"

"I don't like it," Fred said, "but I understand it."

"It's our business," Dave said. "The piece has to be first."

"It reminds me of one day during the war. After the break-through at St. Lo, the Germans were trying to get back to the Rhine, and we were trying to cut them off. A half dozen of us were with the Third Armored, through the rest of France and into Belgium. We're just about to Mons and the press camp is still back in Paris, so they're flying our copy out each afternoon in a Piper Cub.

"Late one afternoon the P.R.O. calls us all over to his half-track. He was a nice young major out of the South, named Haynes Dugan, and the half-track was in this apple orchard be-hind this château, and he says: 'Gentlemen, I have some bad news. The Piper Cub that takes the copy back was shot down.'

"Well, four or five of us said, in one voice: 'Was he going or

coming?' So Dugan says: 'He was coming. The copy got through.'
We said: 'Oh.' I felt I'd just resigned from the human race, and I
still feel I did."

"It's the business."

"I'll tell you something else about the business."

"What?"

"I'm getting tired of becoming emotionally involved with the
people I have to write about. I've had too much of it for too
long. I've liked Doc for years and Eddie before I came up here.
Now I spend a month with them, and after all the fighters I've
known and the fights I've seen—you count them—I've got to go
to one more and die again for two nice guys to whom it means
everything. I like fights where I don't know either guy, or give a
damn about them. Why do I have to get involved in this?"

"That's what you're getting paid for."

"Suppose Eddie loses?"

"I don't think he will," Fred said.

"I don't think he will, either, but if he does it's the end for both
of them. You know that. It took Doc two years to get this shot.
They'll never get another one. How would you like to have everything hanging for you on one hour on one Friday night?"

"I still say he'll win," Fred said.

"I do, too, but forgetting what happens to Doc and Eddie—
which is most important—what happens to my piece if he
loses?"

"Well, somebody wins and somebody loses. There's as much
of a story in a fighter losing as in a fighter winning, maybe more."

"Sure. You get the best stories in the loser's dressing room,
but that's not the magazine business."

"How not?"

"I had lunch with a nice little guy works on a magazine one
day—I won't tell you who—and he was telling me about a piece
some writer did for them. He had the idea to do one about a
kid's first fight, to be called 'The Kid's First Fight.'"

"A good one."

"Fine. He hung around the kid and his family for a few days. On the day of the fight he stayed with him, and the mother cooked the kid's last meal and, when he left, she kissed him good-bye. The kid's father went with him to the club—the Sunnyside—and there was the dressing-room scene. The kid was in the second bout—a four-rounder—and when the call came he got up and started for the door. Then he stopped. The trainer said: 'Let's go. Come on.' The kid said: 'No. I'm not going. I'm too scared. I don't want to be a fighter.' He never did go. He put on his clothes and went home with his old man."

"Great. 'The Kid's First Fight.'"

"Absolutely. So the presiding genius on the magazine says: 'We can't use it.' The guy telling me said: 'Why not?' The big guy said: 'He didn't fight. It was supposed to be his first fight, but he didn't go through with it. We can't use it.'"

"I don't believe it," Fred said.

"I do," Dave said. "It's unspeakable, but maybe the piece was badly done."

"I don't care how badly it was done. Put a good writer on it to rewrite it. He'll get the quotes he needs, and set the scenes. I'm talking about the business."

"But Eddie's not going to lose," Fred said.

"I agree."

"I haven't seen enough of him," Dave said. "In the two fights I saw him he looked good."

"Eddie's married, isn't he?" Fred said.

"Yes."

"You know his wife?"

"Yes."

"What's she like?"

"Yes and no."

"You don't like her?" Dave said.

"Not especially, but I hope I understand her."

"What's the matter with her? What's she like?"

"She's a good-looking doll with a temperature about two degrees below everyone else's normal who gives the impression that she's very competent and self-sufficient."

"Is she?"

"No."

"Why not?"

"Well, if you insist, I'll give you the rundown."

"Please do," Fred said.

"Well, they're both from the same neighborhood. I judge she was attracted to Eddie because he was the best grab on the block. I think he was attracted to her because of her looks and then because, like most fighters who are so competent in that ring, he's a little shy and lost outside of it. He was looking for outside strength. Now—are you guys still interested, or shall we just skip it?"

"No, Doctor Hughes," Dave said. "I want to hear this. I'm fascinated."

"Let's drop it," I said.

"No, I want to hear it, too," Fred said.

"All right. You asked for it. Now, this poor doll—and I think I feel a little sorry for her—is also a victim of the literary crime of our time. I mean cinema, slick-paper, twenty-one-inch tube portrayal of the husband-wife relationship."

"What?" Fred said.

"Togetherness," Dave said.

"You know what I mean. The husband comes home and divorces his work and remarries his wife every night. 'And what did you do today, darling?' he says, drawing her down onto his lap."

"I see."

"In this case, it's particularly cruel because there's a triangle—Eddie and his wife and Doc Carroll."

"Ah, Pythagoras, I see the geometry now," Dave said.

"Fighting is Eddie's big thing and Doc's his man and she's just outside. This is a dame who needs to be needed."

"Who doesn't?" Fred said.

"Right. As far as I know, she went to three or four of Eddie's pro fights. I'm sure that what he felt in there and what she felt outside of it and watching it were two different things. I think that's the last try she made."

"This is too bad," Fred said.

"That's right," I said.

I decided not to tell them about the kid, because it was getting me down as it was. I had signaled Girot again, and he brought us another round and walked back to the bar.

"No matter how sad this character is," Dave said, "he makes a good dry murder."

"He should. He's an expert."

"He is?"

"Yes. When he was drinking he had enough of those to fill this lake out here."

"He never should have stopped."

"A doctor scared him. He used to drink them out of milk bottles."

"Who?" Dave said. "The doctor?"

"No, Girot."

"Please," Fred said. "Drinking martinis out of milk bottles. Don't spoil these."

"Are you kidding about that?"

"No. Years ago there was a dinner here one night. The Lions Club, or something in town, was having its annual Volksfest or bonspiel or whatever, and Girot made up a batch of martinis in milk bottles beforehand. He had them in the refrigerator behind the bar, and when he came down the next morning he remembered one bottle was left. So, in the course of the day, he got to sneaking that. He told me about it once, when he was still drinking, and I used to see him nip the bottle. He got to like them that way. He always had a bottle of them in there—and banged them like that, right out of it."

"Now I like him less than ever," Fred said. "What a way to treat a martini."

"I know what you mean," Dave said. "The dry martini—to be sipped from shell-thin, prefrosted glasses in the quiet dignity of the Ritz men's bar late of a sparkling autumn afternoon."

"Precisely," I said. "It has always seemed to me that the dry martini is the épée of alcoholic weapons, to be handled as such."

"No. The épée in the armory of alcohol."

"All right, let's stop writing, and don't you guys want to eat?"

"Yes."

"Girot!" I said, and he started over.

"He has guts, though," Dave said.

"What?" Fred said. "Out of milk bottles? It's sacrilegious."

"No. An ex-alcoholic tending bar. I admire it."

"Yes?" Girot said.

"They'd like to eat."

"And those were fine martinis, Girot," Dave said. "This other little bum won't admit it, but they were."

They ordered cold roast-beef sandwiches and coffee and then Dave remembered it was Friday and ordered a toasted cheese sandwich instead. They were just starting to eat when Doc and Freddie Thomas came in and shook hands and sat down. I was glad of all this then, too, for Doc.

"We're sorry about Jay," Dave said.

"Thanks," Doc said. "I know. I'm putting that away now. There's a fight."

"That's good," Fred said. "How's your tiger?"

"He's fine. Fine. I've been in New York for two days, but he'll be ready. There'll be a fight."

"Good. There's a lot of enthusiasm for this one."

"It's about time."

"Yes. It's a pleasure to be writing about a fight somebody cares about for a change."

"What do you think of the other guy, Doc?"

"He's a good fighter. He's the champion, isn't he?"

"You've worked against him, haven't you, Freddie?"

"Yes," Freddie Thomas said. "A couple of times. He's got a lot of ability."

"For some reason he doesn't excite me like he should," Dave said.

"I don't go with all the raves about him," Fred said. "I'd rather watch your fighter any day."

"Thank you."

"How many fighters have you had, Doc?"

"How many have I had? The Pro is the tenth."

"Ten fighters in over forty years?"

"That's right, and when I started in the business there were managers who had that many fighters at one time. They were chain-store operators. They had somebody fighting for them somewhere almost every night in the week. They managed by telephone. Dreadful."

"And often used someone's else's phone," Fred said.

"What could they give a fighter?" Doc said. "Two round-trip tickets, somebody along to carry the pail and a fast count on the finances."

"Did you ever go for a title before, Doc?"

"No."

"You could have had it with Rusty Ryan," Fred said.

"I never saw him fight," Dave said. "I was in St. Louis then, covering loft fires and businessmen's luncheons, but I used to read about him. Really how good was he?"

"The best lightweight in the world for four or five years," I said.

"That's right," Fred said, nodding.

"Why didn't you get him the title, Doc?"

"I offered it to him one day. I sat down with him and I said:

'Rusty, you've done everything I've asked you to do, and I owe you this. If you want the title I can get you the match and you know you can lick the guy. Do you want it?' So he said: 'Doc, it's up to you. What do you think?' I said: 'Forget it. You're better off as you are.' He was, too."

"Why?"

"I explained it to him. I said: 'If you win that title do you know who'll be managing you?' He said: 'Why, you will, Doc.' I said: 'No. I'll still be taking my cut, but those politicians down at the boxing commission will be managing you. They'll tell you who to fight and when and where. They'll force you in with every slob who's got an in up at Albany—all the grabbers and runners and guys who'll make you look bad—and you'll have one lousy fight after the other. You'll be the champion, though. On the other hand, if you want to go along the way we're going, we'll move around the country and make more money fighting guys looking to get strong trying to lick you and you'll be a better fighter because of it. It's up to you.'

"He said: 'Doc, I'm for doing it the way we're doing it right now.' He was wise. After ten years he walked out of it with a hundred and fifty grand, clear. That was money in those days. Those three guys who held the title while Rusty was around, what happened to them? One of them has been on the bum for the last five years. Another one works on the docks, and I don't know what happened to the third. Don't put that in the paper about them, though."

"What's Rusty doing?" Dave said.

"He got a partner and they own that summer resort for years. They do very well."

"Do you ever go up there?" Fred said.

"Me? No. What would I do up there? Go out on the lake and paddle a canoe? Take a walk in the woods? That's not my stuff. I see him whenever he comes to New York. We have dinner. He'll be at this fight."

"Good. I'd like to see him again."

"He'll be there, but if Eddie wins this title I'll wonder about Rusty. He knows he did the right thing, but take that place he owns. The people that come up there, they probably know he was some kind of a fighter once."

"I'll say he was," Fred said.

"What do the people know? He may think now that if he'd held the title it would mean something big today."

"Not Rusty. I doubt that he thinks of that."

"Is that why you're going for the title with Eddie?"

"Ah. It's conditions. That television has closed down the country. Where are you going to take a fighter? I've taken the Pro everywhere you can still go, and we've fought everybody he can fight and he's learned everything I or anybody else can teach him. I'll tell you something else, but don't put this in, either. Eddie Brown is a better Rusty Ryan. For two reasons. He had it in him—the gift, even more than Rusty—and I've got twenty more years at it. Things I was just getting to try with Rusty when he started to slow up I picked right up later with this kid. Any good fighter a teacher has grows right out of the others."

"That makes sense."

"So what have I got? I've got a guy can do everything now. No commission can louse him up. No fighter can louse him up."

"I've never seen him in a bad fight."

"Because he goes to the other guy's strength. He licks him at that, and it's a good fight. Even the clutchers can't grab him, because when they spread their arms to grab he drops down and unloads two hands into the body. That's the last time they try it that way. With that kind of a fighter going for me I'm not afraid of any commissions. Besides, what can you make without a title today?"

"Not much."

"When we get that title I can go to the Garden with this kind of a fighter and say: 'Listen. Tell those razor-blade people it'll cost them an extra ninety Gs.' You can get it with this kind of a champion. Robinson got it."

"That's right."

"You want to talk to him? He's in his room, and I'll get him down."

"I'd rather talk to him up there," Fred said.

"Finish your coffee. I'll go up and see what he's doing."

Doc and Freddie Thomas went out.

"What a man," Dave said.

"Now you see?" Fred said, nodding.

"I think I'll write about that, about why you don't go for a title or why you do."

"Good. Then you'll leave your column-pickin' paws off Eddie."

"But I want to go along and listen. Please?"

"I'll permit it."

"There's something he didn't tell you," I said.

"What?"

"He wants that title for himself, too."

"Why not?"

"That's the shame of it. He's getting old. Years ago he wouldn't have given a damn. You know that, Fred. All this time, over forty years, he had one philosophy—do it right and let the spoils fall where they may, mostly into the laps of the amateurs. In those days there were a few guys around who could appreciate it. Today, in Stillman's, what do they know? Did you ever have a champion? It's a crime, and a defeat, but Doc wants it for that, too. He's human, and I'm complaining."

"Let's hope he gets it."

"He'll get it," Fred said.

"He'll have to," I said. "I told you I'm involved. I am. It's a cause. The other guy's not a fighter, compared with Eddie. He's all show and no meaning, but who knows the difference? Eddie's our standard bearer. He's just a fighter, but this is a fight against all the shoddy they sell and celebrate today in boxing and on TV and in the bookstores and in our newspapers and magazines and everywhere else. You see that, don't you?"

"I agree," Dave said.

"Please," Fred said. "Two guys are going to have at each other in a contest with gloves."

"He's a stubborn little bum, isn't he?" Dave said, nodding at Fred.

"He is. He has no causes to talk about because he lives them all his life. If there is such a thing, he's a purer Doc."

"Please."

"He can't see himself. For twenty-five years he's been writing the purest prose ever to appear in a newspaper, and the purest dialogue to appear anywhere, Poppa and O'Hara notwithstanding. Do the lights turn red on all sides when he wants to cross Fifth Avenue, though?"

"Are you finished?" Fred said. "Do you mind if we go up and see Eddie?"

Eddie was lying on the bed reading a paperback, and when we came in he put it aside and got up and shook hands. Then he sat down at the head of the bed again, with the pillow at his back, and Doc came in, bringing a couple of straight-back chairs.

"How do you feel?" Fred said.

"Fine. All right."

"He asked you that," Dave said, "because we asked Marciano in camp once how he felt, and he said: 'Great, but I have to laugh. Everybody asks me how I feel. I'm up here, getting up early, running on the road, training, eating, and sleeping right. How else could I feel?'"

"He was right," Eddie said, smiling.

"What were you reading?"

"Just a western. I like to read them once in a while in camp."

"What else do you read?"

"Mostly magazines. I like to read magazines."

"The articles, or the short stories?"

"Both. I like some of those stories, not all of them."

"You mean, not the fight stories?"

"That's right. They usually have the fighter, during the fight, thinking about his girl or his mother or some mobster. Believe me, when you're in there you don't have much chance to think about anything else. Of course, I never had any mobster threaten me. Maybe if I did I'd think about that, hey?"

"What do you think about? I mean, specifically what kind of thing?"

"Well, I'm thinking of what the other guy is doing, that I can use. You know? I mean, Doc has always studied the guys I fight and we've pretty much worked it out, but you actually have to fight the guy to find out."

"They all have patterns," Doc said. "I don't care who they are."

"Then fighters are like writers," Dave said.

"The good ones have more patterns than the others," Doc said. "That's all."

"So that's what you're thinking about, Eddie?"

"A lot of things, but that's it. The way Doc has taught me—I don't know whether it's all right to say this or not."

He looked at Doc.

"It's all right. The good fighters you fought knew what you were doing to them, but they couldn't help themselves. What the other guy discovers in the newspapers isn't going to help him."

"Well, what I mean is that the way Doc has taught me, you give the other guy the impression that he's in charge. That's so he'll fight his fight, and follow his patterns. I mean, as Doc says: 'Let him perform.' For example, when I'm pressing a guy a certain way he may jab me a couple of times, and then hook off it. Well, he does this a few times in the first couple of rounds and then, when I see it's the pattern, I'm thinking whether I'll try to beat the hook with a straight right hand or if I'll drop down and slip the hook and counter with a hook in the belly. I mean that's what you're thinking about."

"I like that," Dave said. "Cite us another one. I don't mean to pry into your secrets, but I've never heard a fighter talk like this before."

"That's all right," Doc said.

"I don't know," Eddie said. "There's so many. Say, like I can't get the guy to open up. He'll throw a few punches, but nothing that you can go off. Maybe the only pattern will be a double jab. He'll jab twice and move. So I take those—one-two, on the forehead, one-two. He gets real confident now, because I lean into them a little to help him think he's going good. Then, when I'm ready, I take the first one, but on the second one I lean over to my right so I slip it over my left shoulder and I cross a right over it. It's a good punch because, leaning to the right, I've got my weight on that side and behind it."

"The punch is standard," Doc said. "The big thing is the trap. There's only so many punches. Everybody knows what they are. You've got to con the other guy into walking into them. It's thinking, first of all. Then, when he's committed, it's timing and placement. That's all."

"That's all?" Eddie said, shaking his head. "I've been at it for nine years and I'm still learning."

"You'll still be learning the day you quit," Doc said.

"What about the other guy?" Fred said. "Have you seen him fight much?"

"I've seen him a couple of times and once on TV. Doc and I went to his last fight in the Garden."

"What do you think of him?"

"He's a good fighter. Lots of natural ability. He's got fast hands, and he moves good."

"While you're up here," Dave said, "how much do you think about him? You're in camp, working every day toward just one thing. Do you ever dream about the fight?"

"Here we go," I said. "Dave Scott's Dream Book."

"We're laughing," Fred said to Doc and Eddie, "because, sooner or later, one of us asks this of all of them—Marciano, LaStarza, Charles, Saxton, Patterson. You can't escape."

"Amateur psychology," Dave said. "I mean, do you ever see the other guy in your mind, like when you're boxing up here?"

"No," Eddie said. "I mean, not when I'm boxing. I've got Memphis Kid up here—"

"He's here?"

"Sure, and he does a real good imitation of the other guy. When you're boxing, though, you're thinking of what's going on, like I said, so I don't see the other guy then."

"When do you see him, if you do?"

"You see?" Fred said. "You can't get away."

"I know what you mean. I'd say I think of him when I'm running on the road in the morning, and when I'm punching the big bag. That stuff gets kind of monotonous, and I think of him then."

"What do you think? Do you see the fight?"

"That's right. You guys must be psychologists. I keep making up the fight. Sometimes when I'm falling asleep, too. I mean, I see the guy make a move and I make a move. We fight like that."

"How long does it last? The fight."

"Oh, I don't see the whole fight. I just see a part of it. Maybe it's something that happened in boxing in the gym that day. I see that happening in the fight."

"Do you see the fight end?"

"Oh, sure. Especially at night. No matter what moves I'm thinking about, when I see the two of us I can't stop thinking about it until the fight ends in my mind."

"How does it end?"

"He's flat on his back," Eddie said smiling.

"I like that," Fred said, laughing. "You knock him out."

"Sure. Then I can get to sleep."

"You see?" Dave said. "Don't knock the Dream Book."

"Eddie," Fred said, "I don't think you've ever been knocked down, have you?"

"Once," Eddie said, looking at Doc. "About four years ago. Doc'll tell you about that."

"Dreadful," Doc said, that pained expression on his face. "He's fighting that Art Matso in Cleveland. I don't know what he was thinking about. All of a sudden he's got his feet too close together, and all his weight on his left foot. That Matso hits him a hook high on the head that wouldn't topple a tenpin. Down he goes on his left side. Dreadful."

"I got right up. I knocked the guy out two rounds later."

"Never mind that. Tell them what I made you do, Edward."

"Well," Eddie said, shaking his head. "For a week after that Doc made me wear a slipper—one of those bedroom slippers—on my right foot. Everywhere I went I had to wear it for a week, one shoe and one slipper. I was embarrassed."

"You should have been," Doc said, still disgusted. "You embarrassed me. It taught you that you have a right foot, though. It taught you to keep your weight on both feet, though, didn't it?"

"I'll say. Every place I went, up in the gym and every place, people asked me: 'What's the matter with your foot?' For a whole week."

"What did you say?"

"I lied. I told them I sprained my big toe."

"I love this," Dave said.

"Yes," Fred said, "but remember, it's mine."

"I know."

"So let's leave him alone now," Fred said, standing up. "He's got to work soon."

"All right."

"You writers amaze me," Eddie said.

"How?"

"You two. You never take any notes, and when I read it in the paper it's just what I said."

"That's what you think," Fred said.

"I don't understand how you do it."

"We don't understand how you do what you do either, Eddie," Dave said.

After they watched Eddie work, Fred and Dave wrote their copy. Dave phoned his in, and then we drove into town and filed Fred's at the Western Union. After dinner we had a couple of drinks, sitting in the dining room with Eddie and Doc and swapping baseball stories for Eddie's benefit until it was ten o'clock.

"So I'll see you all tomorrow," Eddie said, getting up.

"You're not going to watch the warriors on TV?" Dave said.

"No. I need my sleep."

The rest of us watched the fight, and it was just about what it had promised to be. For the first six rounds Cardone moved around, picking at the other guy and, when he saw a safe opening, taking potshots. Cardone's claque seemed to like it anyway, if you could tell anything from the screams on the TV.

"The little guy has no chance," Dave said. "He can't reach him."

"Dreadful," Doc said.

"He'll do a little better from now on," I said. "Cardone will start to run out of gas."

"I know what you mean," Doc said.

He did, and by the ninth round the other guy was getting inside and hitting Cardone in the body. When he did, Cardone would grab, his head back and out of the way, but, as it was, he won it big on all cards.

"After that, I'm the one needs a drink," Doc said.

22

That night Fred and Dave stayed in one of the cabins down the road. They came up the next morning for breakfast and then said good-bye to Eddie and Doc and Freddie Thomas and left for the other camp.

"We'll see you when you get sprung," Dave said, when I walked them to Dave's car.

"Don't worry about it," Fred said. "He'll win."

"Good."

"Whatever happens," Dave said, "you'll get a good piece. I never knew the guy was such a good talker."

"He's great on boxing. On the rest he's thin, but I don't press him. With a month to give to it I try to let him emerge as if I'm almost not here. It's not the easiest thing to do."

"Stop weeping. Do you think the boys in the Tombs have it better?"

"All right. Take your eighty papers and your eight million readers and get out of here."

That afternoon Doc sent Eddie eight rounds. Enough had been in the papers about the fight by now so that there were a couple of dozen men and women and a half-dozen kids sitting on the chairs and watching while Freddie Thomas kept after the sparring partners to press more and Doc leaned on the top rope watching Eddie turn it on. Now and then one of the men would say something in a low voice to the woman next to him and the woman, stony-faced and watching the fighters, would nod or shrug.

"Excuse me," one of them said, walking up to me, when Eddie climbed out of the ring and walked over to the big bag.

"Yes?"

He was about thirty years old, with a mop of blond hair, and he needed a shave. He had on a red-and-black-checkered woolen shirt, the tails worn outside of his brown corduroy trousers, and he had a boy about three by the hand.

"I'm a boxing fan."

"Good."

"Is the fight going to be on television? Eddie Brown's fight?"

"Not around here."

"Not around here? We get the fights here."

"Not this one. They're blacking it out north to Albany and south through Philadelphia."

"How come? We seen it the last time Eddie Brown fought."

"Not this one. This is for the title."

"So what are we supposed to do?"

"You're supposed to go to the fight."

"Them tickets cost a lot of money, don't they?"

"Thirty dollars ringside, but you can get up in the gallery for five dollars."

"Who's got that much money for a fight? You pay a lot of money for a television set, you should get all the fights."

"If it'll make you feel any better, you can watch that fella in the ring now box on television on Monday night."

Penna and Booker Boyd were moving around the ring, Boyd stalking Penna.

"Yeah? Which one?"

"The white boy."

"What's his name?"

"Al Penna."

"Is he good?"

"You can see for yourself. He fights the semifinal at the St. Nick, and the semifinal goes on around nine-thirty on Channel 5."

"Yeah? Good. Thanks a lot."

Eddie was lying face down on the rubbing table in the dressing room, naked except for a towel brought up like a loin cloth, Freddie Thomas working on him and the air in the small room sharp but, at the same time heavy, with the smell of the oil of wintergreen. Freddie had finished with the thighs and calves, and was starting on the shoulders.

"This is one of those times I envy fighters," I said.

"I'll give you a rub," Freddie said.

"No. I'd be ashamed, an impostor. A fighter earns it."

"Phew!" Penna said, coming in and closing the door behind him. "That stinks."

"You don't know what's good," Freddie said.

Penna's face, above the white terrycloth robe and the towel around his neck, was running with sweat.

"'Our love is forever—'" he started to sing, standing there and throwing his arms out. "'No—'"

"That isn't so good, either," Eddie said, turning his head to look back at Penna. "How about getting another station?"

"What's the matter? You gettin' touchy?"

"No."

"Listen. If I wasn't such a good fighter, you know what I'd be."

"No."

"One of them airline Charlies. One of them pilots. You go to all them foreign countries and you have a broad in every one."

"Listen, Penna," I said. "I just met a fan of yours."

"Yeah? Who?"

"A guy out there in a red-and-black shirt. He thinks you're a great fighter."

"Yeah? Tell him to be at the St. Nicholas Monday night. One-two. Bam-bam. Raise me hand, ref. I'm your boy."

"He'll be there."

"Yeah? I'll give him my autograph. Cheap. For a buck."

After breakfast the next morning Booker Boyd and Barnum and Penna left, in an old Ford. A friend of Barnum's—a Negro kid about eighteen and a Golden Glover—had driven it up the night before, and they were going to drop Penna off at the Jersey end of the George Washington Bridge so that he could get a bus into New York while they went on to Philadelphia.

"You just fight your fight," Barnum said to Eddie, when they shook hands at the car. "You'll take that boy."

"Thanks. Good luck to you guys."

"Fight that fight you been workin' on. You'll show the people."

"Thanks."

"Tune in tomorrow night and watch this boy go," Penna said. "I'll see you Friday at the weigh-in, anyway."

"Good," Eddie said. "Good luck, Al."

"You guys will miss me around here. You'll be sorry I'm gone."

At about 12:30 I was lying on my bed and reading and Doc was napping on his. The window was open and I heard car wheels on the gravel and got up and looked out. It was one of those big black for-hire Cadillacs, with driver, and the newspapermen—six of them—were getting out.

"What is it?" Doc said, sitting up. I hadn't said anything, so he must have sensed it.

"The riot squad. The gentlemen of the press."

"It's about time they showed."

"It'll be a riot, too. Tom White's with them."

"I was afraid of that, but I was hoping he didn't come to camps any more."

"He doesn't. Just for the big ones. I haven't seen him in a year. You're supposed to be honored."

"A year is too soon. Why does he have to be like that?"

"You know as well as I do. He's getting old."

Doc had put on a tie, and was getting into his jacket.

"We all are, but not like that. What's the matter with him?"

"He can't take the competition. His seams are showing."

"Then he should quit."

"Don't get drunk and tell him that."

"I'm not crazy."

Doc went down and I washed and thought about it. When I was just starting in New York, Tom White had already come down from Syracuse and it was all new then and he was new and he took the town. You should never take those years from him because he was the best, but then it became the second time around for him and the third, and somewhere along the way, he got tired of working and resorted to the impression that he owned it all—that the ball games were played for him and the fights fought for him. I could see him starting to resent the new ones among us and, when I read him, I could taste that tangy wine turning to vinegar and the whole thing spoiling before the bottom of the barrel and the grave.

I looked in on Eddie, but he was asleep, with the white candlewick spread pulled up over him, so I closed the door again and went down. They were spread along the bar, Doc in the middle with Tom White, Tom doing the talking and Ernie Gordon hovering at his side, calling him "boss" and making certain to be listening and to light Tom's cigarette and to signal Girot for another martini for Tom.

"What the hell are you doing here?" Tom said, and we shook hands.

"Hello, Tom."

"What are you doing here?"

"I want to ask the same about you."

He was a good-looking guy, even at sixty and dissipated, and he still dressed with the best.

"Well, I thought I'd write a few columns about this damn fight.

I don't think it's going to be so much but, for some reason, there's a lot of interest in it."

"It'll be a good fight."

"It better be, after those stinkers they've been putting on that television. What are you doing here?"

"I'm doing a magazine piece about Eddie."

"Still with that magazine stuff? Why don't you get back in an honest business, like ours? Those magazine editors don't know what they're doing."

In the time they've been here, I was thinking, he can't have had more than one. He sure comes out of the gate fast these days.

"Magazine editors. What the hell do they know about sports?"

I watched him. He had three at the bar, and kept insisting that Doc keep up with him. When we sat down he had another, and ordered another one for Doc. He seemed in a pretty good humor, talking about the old days and what he once told Kearns, in front of Dempsey, but he just picked at his food.

By the time we had finished eating, Eddie was going into the gym, so we all went in there. They were too many for the small dressing room, so they waited for Eddie to come out, and then he sat on the ring apron, with Doc sitting next to him, and they sat in the chairs. There were four of them in the first row and I sat in the second row with Tom and Ernie Gordon.

It was so warm in the gym, even with a couple of windows open, that Eddie did not need his robe, and he sat there in just his white T-shirt and brief white-knitted trunks and white woolen socks and his ring shoes. Freddie Thomas handed him some gauze, and he started wrapping the right hand, his legs dangling, while they asked him the questions. It was so warm, in fact, that when I looked over at Tom his eyelids were heavy, and I figured that, with the drinks in him, he might fall asleep.

"So what makes you think you can win this fight?" he said suddenly, stirring.

"I just believe I can," Eddie said, still bandaging.

"Great! That'll make big news. You ask him something, Ernie."

"Eddie," Ernie said, "what do you think of the other guy, technically? I mean, what do you think is his best hand?"

"Who the hell cares about that?" Tom said, turning on Ernie.

"His best hand?" Eddie said. "His left."

"What do you want me to ask him?" Ernie said to Tom.

"Get a story! Get a story! What the hell do you think I got you up here for?"

This is going to be great, I was thinking. The only trouble is that I've seen this play before.

"You say his left hand?" one of them in the front row said. "He's knocked a few of them out with his right."

"I know," Eddie said. "He's got two hands, but I think his left—that jab and hook—is his best."

"The left is the fighter's working hand," Doc said. "The right just comes in for the pay-off."

"Like you," Tom said. "You ought to know."

I looked at Doc and saw him look at Tom, and his face set. I was thinking that I ought to go out and get Tom another drink. If he didn't knock it out of my hand it would put him to sleep, and that would be a way out of it.

"What about those three fights you lost, Eddie?" one of them in the front said.

"I lost three. I won eighty-seven."

"I don't mean that."

"I'll answer that," Doc said. "He got two bad decisions, one in Philadelphia and one in Boston."

"That's right," Ernie Gordon said. "I saw the one in Boston."

"What are you siding with him for?" Tom said, turning on Ernie.

"The other fight he lost," Doc said, "I got him licked on purpose."

"I'll bet," Tom said, raising his voice.

"What do you mean, Doc?" one of them in front said.

"About seven years ago he licked a guy pretty good in a semifinal in Pittsburgh. It was outdoors, with a couple of heavy-weights on top. He started to think he was pretty good."

"I'll bet," Tom said, again loudly.

"The next fight he had he looked lousy. He beat the guy, but he was trying to make me out a liar and—"

"That's no great feat," Tom said.

"He thought he knew it all, now, so I got him a semifinal in Cleveland. I got him a guy licked him, not bad, but he licked him. He needed it."

"That's right," Eddie said, smoothing the tape on the hand and nodding. "I know it now."

"You want us to believe that?" Tom said.

"What?" Doc said, and I could see it all over his face now.

"You know what."

"Look, Tom. I don't give a damn whether you believe it or not."

"Oh, you don't?"

"No."

"You think I'm going to believe that stuff, like that line you handed Dave Scott in that column he had yesterday morning?"

So that's it, I thought. It's that competition and how he resents Dave.

"I don't give a damn what you believe."

"Let's forget it," I said. "Let's have a drink."

"I'm not going to forget it," Tom said. "That stuff about why he never had a champion before. Why, you couldn't have won that title with Rusty Ryan or anybody, and you won't win it with this guy, either. You're nothing but a loud mouth."

"If you weren't drunk," Doc said, "I'd belt you."

"Easy, Doc," Eddie said, sliding off the ring apron with Doc.

"Who's drunk?" Tom said, standing up, Ernie holding him by the right arm. We were all standing now.

"You are," Doc said. "You're a miserable, goddamn dirty drunk, who stands on corners and abuses people in that column. You don't know the first goddamn thing about boxing and you never did. You can't even write good any more because the rot has set in from the inside and you're dead and you don't know it. Don't think you can intimidate me with your lousy column. Not any more."

"Come on, Doc," I said. "Knock it off."

I knew it was not only the drinks talking, but the fight and Jay and many years and everything.

"Knock it off?" Tom said, sneering at me. "He's going to get knocked off. That fighter of his there is going to get flattened, and I'm going to say it in that paper tomorrow—that and a few more things."

"I don't give a damn what you say," Doc said.

"Come on," one of those in front with Doc said.

"You'll see all right. You'll see it in the paper."

"No I won't," Doc said, "because I haven't read that stinking column of yours for five years, and I won't read it tomorrow. And I'll tell you something else. Don't talk like that about this fighter here."

"Forget it, Doc," Eddie said.

"Why not? I'll say and write what I want about him."

"And show your stupidity. He's not only gonna knock that other guy out but, when he does it, the other guy will go down with his face right in front of yours. Print that."

With that Doc pulled his arm away from Eddie and turned and walked to the back of the gym. Freddie Thomas followed him, and I looked at Eddie and he shrugged at me.

"I'm getting out of here," Tom said. "I'm going down to that other camp. Where's that damn driver?"

"He's in the bar," Ernie Gordon said. "What are the rest of us supposed to do?"

"I don't give a damn what you do. I'll send him back."

After Tom left, Eddie boxed four rounds and Doc said nothing to him the whole time. Then the rest of them went into the dining room and found their typewriters and started to write their pieces. When I came into the dressing room Freddie Thomas had just brought the tea and Doc was trying to make work for himself, picking things up and putting them down again, while the fighters drank their tea.

"Well," I said, "now that it's over I'm glad I was here to hear it."

"I'm glad you were, too," Doc said.

"I'd have done anything I could to have stopped it, but I couldn't think of anything."

"What difference does it make?"

"He'll rap you in the column tomorrow," Eddie said.

"He'll rap you, too," Doc said, "but what difference does it make? It's about time somebody in this business told him off."

"That's right," I said, "but you really burned that bridge."

"Who needs it? What do I have to worry about him for any more? I've got a fighter that'll stand up for me in there. You knock that guy out and you're the champion, and what have I got to worry about? Tom White? He only picks on little people."

The next day, right after the workout, I took Eddie's car and drove into the town and got the paper. I read the column, standing in the cigar store, and when I got back Doc was in the room and I handed it to him.

"He never mentions you or Eddie," I said. "He just datelines himself from the other camp and writes about the other guy."

Doc read the column, quickly, and then threw the paper on the bed.

"I knew he had no guts," he said.

"Of course not. He's afraid Eddie's going to win."

"No guts," Doc said. "Absolutely no guts."

23

Then came the quiet days, the quiet days loud with implication.

"All right," Doc said. "That's enough."

It was that Monday afternoon, in the gym.

"How many rounds was that?" Eddie said, when Doc took the mouthpiece out.

"Seven."

"I feel like more."

"Good. Never mind the bags today. Go in and cool out. We'll weigh after your shower."

It is one of the most difficult of scientific endeavors, this struggle to bring an athlete up the mountain of his efforts to the peak of his performance at the precise moment when he must perform. That peak place is no bigger than the head of a pin, shrouded in the clouded mysteries of a living being, and so, although all try, most fail, for it requires not only the most diligent of climbers but the greatest of guides.

"You have to play the probability," Doc said, explaining it, standing by the window and looking out across the parking space at the fresh greenery beyond and waiting for Eddie. "You ask a fighter how he feels and he says: 'Good,' or 'All right.'

Does he know for sure? You got to be able to see your fighter better than he can see himself, and play the probability.

"Most of them, they go wrong trying to bring a fighter right up to some fine point the last day. Figure the chances of the miss, under or over. Either way you're just as bad off. You can't ask for odds in this life. You've got to make them. I found out. You hit a level where he's almost where you want him to be four or five days before the fight. It's not as hard to hold that. Then the next step he takes is the step into the ring, and he's there and that's where he fights."

The scale was in the room with the frosted rectangular light with the silhouette of the Colonial dame over the door. Eddie slipped out of his shower clogs and Freddie Thomas took the robe off him and Eddie stood naked and statuesque on the scale. We waited while Doc moved the weights along the bars.

"One sixty and a half," he said.

"That's good," Eddie said.

He stepped down and Freddie helped him into the robe and then Eddie slipped his feet back into the shower clogs. I held the door for him, and Freddie and Doc followed him out.

"You trust that scale?" I said to Doc.

"I should. It cost me fifteen bucks for Girot to get the guy up here to test it and set it right. He'll make fifty-nine and a half, exactly what I told that Doc Martin. So don't hold any more doors for him."

Freddie Thomas was following Eddie into the dressing room.

"What do you mean?" I said.

"He's no invalid. He can open his own doors."

"I was just being polite. What's eating you?"

"Nothing. The last few days before a fight everybody bows and scrapes for a fighter so you'd think he was Prince Rainier. There's enough pressure building up inside him as it is."

"Sorry."

"When I'm not thinking, I do it myself. Let's have a drink."

It was that evening and in the sitting room we sat, all of us—
Eddie and Doc and Freddie Thomas and Artie Winant and Memphis and DeCorso and Girot—and watched Al Penna fight his
semifinal. They were two green kids, all arms and elbows and
gloves, trying to knock each other out in a hurry, their heads
snapping back with the punches and the crowd hollering, and in
the fifth round Penna was cut over the left eye.

"Oh-oh," Eddie said. "Come on, Al."

"Dreadful," Doc said.

They were trying to stop the bleeding in the corner, but in the
sixth round it opened again. Now the other kid was going for
the eye, and the referee was looking at Penna every time he
broke them, and after that round, and after the seventh, the doctor was in the corner. In the eighth round Penna hurt the other
kid, the two of them flailing away and the crowd across the ring
on its feet, screaming.

"Al made some fight," Eddie said, while we waited for the decision. "I think he won it."

"The guts of a burglar," Doc said.

"I still think you've got him wrong," I said.

"The decision," the announcer said, "is a draw! A draw!"

The crowd was still standing and applauding.

"I thought he won it, cut and all," Eddie said.

"The other guy lost it," Doc said, "going for the eye."

"That's no fighter," Girot said, shaking his head. "Al Penna,
he's crazy. He keeps fighting and he'll be hurt. You watch."

"Come on, bon ami. You know you were rooting for him."

"For him? I don't root for him. I root for you."

"Thanks, and good night," Eddie said.

It was that Tuesday, and it rained all day. It was coming down
as early-morning mist when Freddie Thomas and I walked with
Eddie and the sparring partners and Artie Winant up the driveway to the road. It was building on the new leaves and on the
branches, and the only sound was the sound of the feet on the

gravel and of the dripping from the leaves and from the branches.

"Let's just walk to the top of the hill," I said to Freddie, when the fighters started off. "I want to see how it looks today where they're running."

From the top of the rise of the road we could see them making the curve, beyond and below, Eddie in the lead and the three of them in the rhythm of it but Artie Winant lagging. Then they ran into that gray-blue mist that hung so low.

When it was time for them to get back we walked back up the driveway and, when they came in, the mist was on Eddie's wind jacket in droplets and on his face like sweat and on his short hair like hoarfrost. His breath hung in front of him like cigarette smoke until it mingled, lost, with the mist, and as we walked down the driveway I noticed the small swamp maple, green now, where the ruby-crowned kinglet that Jay had thought was a canary had rested. I thought to the willow beyond the roof line of the hotel, the willow light green now, too, and I wished we were sitting in the sun again, listening to Memphis tell about Australia. I wanted us once more to have all that time.

It was that Wednesday, and I called the AP in New York again and found out that Booker Boyd had knocked his man out in three rounds and I told Eddie. That afternoon he boxed his last in the silence of the gym, just the squeak of the shoes on the canvas and the thud of the big gloves and the sound of the breathing for two rounds, one with DeCorso and the last with Memphis. In that round he turned it on and was the complete fighter and spoke as eloquently as I ever heard a man speak.

"Time!" Freddie Thomas called.

"That's all," Doc said, standing on the ring apron and motioning.

"One more," Eddie said. "How about just one more?"

"Come out of there," Doc said, shaking his head, and then to me: "Now I can breathe again."

It was that Thursday, a day of pale sun and cool. After they came off the road and had breakfast we walked Memphis up the driveway to meet the 9:25 bus. Memphis, in that same old gray sharkskin suit, carried his barracks bag over his shoulder. DeCorso walked on one side of him, carrying Memphis' cardboard suitbox tied with that twine, and Eddie walked on the other. We stood across the road again in the sun.

"Here it comes," DeCorso said.

"You're gonna beat that boy," Memphis said, shaking Eddie's hand. "You're gonna be the new champion of the whole world."

"That's right. Thanks, Memphis."

"I always know that boy got some geezer in him. He try to be Robinson. I know him since he start. Once I see him punch the big bag in the gym and, when I first come in, I thought it was Robinson, but he ain't. Robinson mean it. This boy don't."

"Thanks, Memphis. Thanks for everything."

"I'm glad to do it. I'm glad."

"And good luck yourself. You win your own fight."

"Sure," Memphis said, winking.

The bus had stopped and the door was open, waiting for Memphis.

"Is somebody gettin' on or not?" The driver said. "I haven't got all day."

"Sure, mister," Memphis said. "I'm sorry."

We watched Memphis get aboard and go down the aisle, looking out at us once and smiling as the bus started, and then we watched it disappear.

"How will you get back?" I said to DeCorso.

"I won't," he said. "Artie Winant wants me to work with him. I'm gonna stay with Artie."

That evening at dinner Katie came out of the kitchen and asked Eddie about the steak and stood there for a couple of minutes, smiling and nodding and watching him eat, while Doc looked at me and shook his head once. After dinner Freddie

Thomas and I walked with Eddie. We walked for an hour, just taking it easy and talking about the stars and new cars and every baseball story I could remember. When we got back we watched *Dragnet* and then Jackie Cooper and *Playhouse 90*, and Eddie stayed up until eleven o'clock for the first time in camp.

In bed that night I lay for a long while in the darkness, listening to Doc turning and then hearing his breathing even out. Then I thought of Eddie, lying alone in Doc's old room.

It was the last of the quiet days.

24

When the alarm clock went off I was floating on my back, suspended half in sleep and half in wakefulness. Now, with it ringing, it was as if I were trying to sit up in the water, until suddenly it stopped and I got my feet down and realized that I could stand up in it and that there was no need for panic.

"You awake?" Doc said.

"Yes."

"How did you sleep?"

"Not too well. You sleep much?"

"No."

"You will, after it's over."

"Not right away. It takes me two or three nights to unwind after a fight."

He was up now, in his rumpled, light-blue pajamas, his white hair shaggy, raising the dark shade at one of the windows.

"It's not a bad day," he said. "It looks nice out."

I waited, half dressed and cold and sitting on the bed, until he came out of the bathroom. Then I went in and, when we were finished dressing, it was 8:15 and I followed him into Eddie's room.

"Doc?" Eddie said, sitting up in the bed, the light from the hall playing across him and the bed.

"It's a nice day," Doc said, raising one shade and then the other.

"Is it?"

He was still sitting up in the bed, and then he pulled the covers off and swung his legs over the side. He had on white pajamas, with dark red piping edging the collar and down the front, and he sat there a moment, the pajama top failing to hide the bulk of his shoulders. With his right hand he rubbed the back of that good neck.

"Close the window, will you?" he said to Doc.

"I am. You sleep all right?"

"I guess so. If Artie and Vince went on the road I never heard them."

"They went, and they're back already and having breakfast," Freddie Thomas said.

He was standing, slim and neat, in the doorway. He had on a single-breasted gray suit and white shirt and dark blue tie, and he looked like a businessman about to leave for the office.

"Get him a large glass of orange juice, will you?" Doc said to Freddie.

"Sure thing."

Eddie put his robe on then and slid into a pair of slippers and went to the bathroom. When he came back he sat down in the wicker chair and waited, still looking like he had just awakened.

"We'll go down and weigh now," Doc said. "Get out of those slippers."

"Why?" Eddie said. "I don't want to walk downstairs barefooted."

"I don't want you slipping on those stairs. Put those other things on with heels on them."

Eddie kicked his slippers off and put on his loafers and we went down. We walked through the empty quiet of the gym into the small room and Eddie took off his robe and took his loafers off.

"Shall I take off the pajamas? They don't weigh much."

"Take them off."

Freddie Thomas took the pajama top and then the pants and Eddie stepped up onto the scale, naked and standing straight with just his head bowed, watching Doc slide the weights on the bars.

"One-fifty-nine and a quarter," Doc said.

"I hope this scale is right," Eddie said, watching the bar suspended in balance.

"You move your bowels this morning?"

"No. You know I just got up."

"Put your robe and those shoes on. You're all right. You're just what we tried for."

Freddie Thomas helped Eddie back into the robe and Eddie put the loafers back on. Freddie held the door open and Doc and I followed Eddie back upstairs. Then Freddie Thomas came up with the orange juice, and Eddie sat in the wicker chair and drank it slowly.

"This tastes good," he said.

Doc and I had packed our things the night before, and now he started taking Eddie's clothes out of the closet, folding them on the bed and packing them into Eddie's bag. By the time he was finished, Eddie was dressed. He had put on the light gray flannel slacks and the light wool maroon sports shirt and the almost cream-colored sports jacket he had worn to camp. He had shaved the afternoon before, but he still looked clean enough.

"How are you today, Frank?" he said, seeming really to notice me for the first time.

"I'm fine. I was just thinking you might pose for one of those fashion ads in *Esquire*."

"No chance."

"Never mind that fashion stuff," Doc said. "Anything in the drawers of that bureau?"

"Just some shirts and underwear in the top drawer. There's

that stuff on the top of the dresser, too. It goes in that kit. I'll do it."

When he had finished putting it in the kit he closed the kit and handed it to Doc and looked around the room.

"That's all. I'll be glad to get out of here."

"You take care of his foot locker?" Doc said to Freddie.

"All taken care of. When we go down I'll get Artie and Vince to help me move it out."

"Don't forget to leave the cup and the ring shoes and that stuff out," Eddie said.

"All taken care of. I brought along a zipper bag and it's all in there. Your robe's in there, too, and the guy from Everlast is bringing the trunks to the weigh-in. Don't worry about a thing."

Freddie took Eddie's bag from Doc, and Doc and I went into our room and got our own bags. When we came out of our room, Eddie was taking a last look around, and we went down to the lobby. Girot, in his butcher's apron, was standing there and Freddie Thomas came out of the dining room followed by Artie Winant and Vince.

"My wife wants to say good-bye, Eddie," Girot said.

"We'll be out by the car," Doc said.

Eddie held the front door open while we went through with the bags. In the parking space he got out his keys and opened the luggage compartment of the car. Freddie Thomas and Artie Winant and Vince DeCorso had gone back into the gym for the foot locker.

"Give Frank the keys," Doc said to Eddie.

"Why?"

"He'll drive."

"I can drive."

"I know you can. I want you to sit in front with Frank and be able to stretch your legs."

"Twenty-five years without an accident," I said.

"I'm not worried," Eddie said. "I just thought I'd drive."

"So, Eddie," Girot said. His wife was with him, her butcher's apron on over her dark green coat sweater, a short, stocky, gray-haired, red-faced woman, smiling too obviously now.

"Right, bon ami," Eddie said, giving it that same pronunciation and shaking Girot's hand.

"Some Eddie. You could learn to speak French if you wanted to."

"Thanks for everything, Katie," Eddie said, holding out his hand to Girot's wife.

"God bless you," she said, and, taking Eddie's hand, she pulled him down. With her left arm around his neck she kissed him on the right cheek. "God bless you, Eddie."

"Put that foot locker in first," Doc said.

Freddie Thomas was removing the bag he had placed in the luggage compartment. One end of the foot locker rested on the bumper, and Artie Winant held the strap handle at the other end.

"Some difference, hey, Eddie?" he said. "I mean, from the day you and I fought."

"That's right. You'll do all right, Artie."

"Four or five fights, that's all for me. This is too tough."

"Good luck, Eddie," DeCorso said, shaking Eddie's hand. "You'll flatten him."

"Thanks for everything, Vince."

"You'll win it," Artie Winant said, shaking Eddie's hand.

Eddie had to tell me again how to start the car, and I stalled it once, backing it up. Then we left the four of them standing there in the parking space, Girot's wife still holding that smile and waving with just her hand, like a small child, as we pulled out.

"It's a good camp," Eddie said, "but I'm glad to get out of here."

"I know," I said. "So am I."

"I'll bet. Tell me one thing."

"Sure."

"Did you really get what you wanted up here? I mean, for the article?"

"Yes, thanks to you. It's been fine and I appreciate it."

"How long will it take you to write it?"

"Oh, about two weeks. I'll walk around and around for about five days, thinking about it. Just about the time when I start getting scared that nothing will come, something will happen—I hope. Then it'll take me a week to write it and a couple of days to rewrite it."

"I'm glad I don't have to do it," Eddie said. "Can you imagine me trying to write something?"

In the town we passed the movie theater and took the next right and left the town and followed the winding blacktop through the rolling country, the hills light green and, here and there where they opened out and always within sight of a house and a barn or two, the sloping land tilled fresh brown. Once or twice at such vistas I had the impulse to stop the car and announce that this would be where we would all get out and live our years, for it is foolish for a man to have to fight.

"Now we'll make time," Eddie said, when we came in sight of the Thruway. "I should have thought of this before."

"It's so new that I still don't think of it."

"I don't either, but they say you can cut a half hour off the time, easy."

We did. As the monotony set in, Eddie settled down in the seat and stretched his legs and put his head back and, when I looked over at him, his eyes were closed. I could hear Doc and Freddie Thomas talking in the back seat, although I could not hear what they were saying, and finally Eddie sat up.

"Were you asleep?"

"No. That's some bridge, isn't it?"

It was the Tappan Zee Bridge just ahead, slightly to the left and below us, reaching across the widest point of the Hudson, risen from the waters like the skeleton of some Loch Ness monster, stripped clean and dry and shining now in the bright sun. When we crossed it, Eddie turned and looked up and down the river.

"Some view," he said.

"We'll go right to the hotel first," Doc said, on the West Side Highway. The traffic had slowed us now, and I was trying to measure the engine drag to the distance to the next car and Eddie was looking ahead and to the right at the build-up of the big, docked liners.

"Have we got time?" he said. "We're supposed to be there at twelve."

"It's eleven-twenty-five," Doc said. "There's plenty of time. The other guy will play it late for effect anyway. The big shot."

I pulled up in the small clearing space in front of the hotel. I left the engine running and slid out behind Eddie.

"You gentlemen registered here?" the doorman said, looking from one to the other of us.

"I got a reservation," Doc said. "You take care of the car?"

"We use a garage around the corner for our guests. Who takes the ticket?"

"I'll take it," Eddie said.

"Say," the doorman said, handing him the ticket. "You're Eddie Brown, aren't you?"

"That's right."

"Well, good luck to you," the doorman said, smiling and shaking Eddie's hand. "Good luck."

"No handshaking," Doc said to Eddie. "You know better than that with strangers."

"I know," Eddie said, nodding.

"Gee, I'm sorry," the doorman said.

We waited in the compact, busy lobby while Doc registered. Then we got into the elevator with three or four other people, and I noticed the bellhop carrying the zipper bags nudge the elevator operator and nod back toward Eddie and say something in a low voice.

"How do you feel, Edward?" Doc said, when we got to the room.

"Okay."

"You better go to the bathroom."

"I know. I have to."

The two beds, the night table with the lamp on it, the bureau, the writing table and one easy chair just about filled the room. Doc opened one of the two windows that looked out on the small, bleak brick quadrangle formed by the other three sides of the hotel.

"All right?" he said when Eddie came out.

"Sure. Good."

"We might as well get down to the commission. It's twelve now."

We walked the four blocks, through the noonday crowds, the noise of the car traffic beside us. Doc walked with Eddie, and Freddie Thomas and I followed them, and in New York, as everywhere, you can always pick out the tourists. As we passed Dempsey's, three of them had stopped in the middle of the sidewalk—a man with the collar of his open-necked sports shirt worn outside the collar of his jacket, a camera hung over one shoulder, a woman and a girl of about ten. He was pointing to Dempsey's name over the big windows and the woman was nodding, and just as Eddie and Doc tried to get by, the man turned and bumped into Eddie.

"I'm very sorry," he was saying as we walked up.

"That's all right," Eddie said, and we walked on. I should tell him, I was thinking, that he bumped into Eddie Brown. Then when he got back to Indianapolis it would be one of the highlights of the trip and someone would think out loud about the probability of such a thing happening and someone else would end it by remarking about it being, really, such a small world.

As we turned off Broadway and approached the commission we could see the crowd on the sidewalk. There were about a hundred there, just a few of them women and at least a couple of dozen of them teen-aged kids. One of the kids spotted Eddie while we were still fifty yards out and ran toward him with a half-dozen others following.

"No," Doc said, shaking his head. "No autographs."

"Aw, come on," the first kid said.

One of the photographers came up and two others spread the crowd. Doc and Eddie waited, and Freddie Thomas and I moved to the side. Here and there Eddie's name was being called to him, and Eddie was nodding and he waved a couple of times when he recognized someone.

"Will you wave like that again?" a photographer, on one knee, said.

"Please," another of the photographers said, pushing back against the crowd. "Will you give us a chance to work?"

"Knock him out, Eddie!" someone shouted. "Flatten him!"

Doc made the way then, and Freddie Thomas followed close behind Eddie. They were still calling to Eddie from the crowd, and one of them reached over and slapped him on the back.

"I don't think I even got it," one photographer was saying to another in the elevator, going up. "I better send over for yours."

"I don't know what I got myself," the other said.

The narrow hallway was crowded and we pushed through them and through the doorway. There was a crowd in the big room, but inside a square formed by benches only the newspapermen and the people from the Garden and from the commission were standing.

"Hello, Eddie . . . Say, Eddie? . . . Good luck to you, Eddie."

"Good," Doctor Martin said. "You're late."

"The other guy here yet?" Doc said.

"No, but he'll be here. I'll examine Eddie, meanwhile."

"You can weigh him, too. If the other guy isn't here, never mind the pictures. We're leaving as soon as you're through."

"You come in here, Eddie."

Eddie and Doc started to follow the doctor into the next room.

"I'm sorry, Doc," the doctor said, turning at the door as Eddie walked past him. "Only the fighter."

"Just a minute, Edward," Doc said. "Come back out here."

"It's that new rule," the doctor said. "Only the fighter goes in. I examine the fighter alone."

"Not my fighter. Any place my fighter goes, I go."

"I can't help it."

"Get the commissioner. Nobody touches my fighter if I'm not present."

"Will you please, Doc?"

"Get him."

The doctor walked over to the desk next to the scale. One of the commissioners was sitting there, talking with a couple of the newspapermen. In a moment the doctor came back.

"All right," he said, but shaking his head. "You can come in. I was only doing what they told me. I wish they'd make up their minds."

"You can come in, too, Frank," Doc said.

"No thanks. I'll wait here."

"I'm sorry," the doctor said to me, closing the door.

When the three of them finally came out, the champion was just coming in, his retinue of a half dozen behind him. He had on a chocolate brown sports jacket, cut long, and light tan slacks. Under the jacket he had on a bright yellow shirt, buttoned at the neck, and he walked around the square, loose and brown and smiling and shaking hands.

"There's my boy," he said when he saw Eddie, walking up to him and smiling and sticking out his hand.

"Hello," Eddie said, taking the hand.

"You want to come in now?" the doctor said.

Doc had Eddie sit down on one of the benches, and Ernie Gordon walked over and sat down next to him. One of the other newspapermen was talking to me about that scene between Doc and Tom White in the camp, so I could not hear what Ernie was telling Eddie, but Eddie was listening and now and then saying something and nodding.

"All right," the doctor said, coming out of the room. "Tell the commissioner they're ready to weigh."

The champion stood in the doorway, wearing the black trunks with white and his street shoes. One of those with him was putting the brown sports jacket over the champion's shoulders. As Eddie stripped he handed his clothes to Doc and Doc placed them on the bench and, when Eddie was naked, Freddie Thomas handed him the white trunks with black and he put those on.

"Gentlemen!" the commissioner said, walking in and nodding around. "Are we ready?"

He shook hands with the champion, who gave him the big smile, and then he came over and shook hands with Eddie. The photographers were motioning the others back to the sides and away from the front of the scale.

"Eddie Brown first!" one of the deputies said.

Eddie walked over, barefooted, and stepped on the scale. The commissioner moved the balances along the scale arms. Doc and the champion and one of his people stood watching.

"Quiet!" someone in the back said. "We won't be able to hear."

"One-fifty-nine and three-quarters," the commissioner said, announcing it. "Eddie Brown, one-five-nine and three-quarters!"

There was a murmur through the room and Eddie stepped down and then the champion kicked his shoes off and stepped up onto the scale. He said something with a smile to the commissioner, who moved the balance back and then, watching it, moved it forward again.

"One-fifty-eight and a half! One-five-eight and a half!"

"All right, you people," one of the photographers said. "How about stepping back now, so we can have a chance?"

They took pictures of first the champion and then Eddie on the scale, with the other watching and the commissioner behind the scale and beaming. Then they squared them off, the champion looking right at Eddie and Eddie a little lower and looking at the champion but turned southpaw so that his face would show.

"That's enough," Doc said.

"One more."

"Come on," Doc said to Eddie.

When they were both dressed again the commissioner called both parties over to the desk and he gave them the routine about the big crowd and the vast nationwide audience and the good, clean fight with the good luck to both of them. Then he shook hands all around and left, and one of the deputies brought in the gloves. Eddie tried his on and Doc asked him about them and then Doc nodded and the commission deputy took the gloves from Eddie and wrote Eddie's name on the white lining inside of each of them.

"So let's get out of here," Doc said.

"Good luck to you, boy," the champion said, nodding to Eddie.

"The same to you," Eddie said.

We were waiting for the elevator in the crowd in the narrow hallway when the doctor came out and found me. He wanted to apologize about not letting me in at the examination.

"I understand," I said. "Forget it."

"Listen," he said. "Some people have been telling me about what a story I've got. I mean, thirty years in this business. The fighters I knew, what they were like. We could do some of those magazine articles."

"I'm sure we could."

"The things fighters say, and the way they behave. Nobody else saw them like I did. I mean, before fights and in the dressing room afterward. I sewed up a lot of fighters, you know. You'd be surprised—"

The elevator was there, and Doc was holding a place for me.

"Sure, doctor, but right now I'm busy."

"So call me. Call me any time."

"Sure."

"We might make a lot of money out of it."

I left him standing there.

"Now what did he want?" Doc said, as we rode down.

"Nothing. He just wants me to make him famous and wealthy."

We had to push through the sidewalk crowd again, the voices calling to Eddie and wishing him luck. Then we walked up to Dempsey's and took the only vacant booth on the right. I noticed the heads turning, and the three of us had juice and eggs and coffee while Eddie had stewed prunes and two soft-boiled eggs and hot tea and one piece of toast.

We walked back to the hotel and killed a couple of hours. Eddie and Doc played gin for a while and we talked and finally left to eat again. We walked just three blocks from the hotel to a small Italian restaurant where Doc and Eddie knew the proprietor. It was one of those places where you go down a couple of steps from the sidewalk, and the proprietor was looking through the glass of the door as we arrived.

"So!" he said, smiling and shaking hands with Eddie and then Doc. "I was afraid you weren't coming."

He was about thirty-five, slim and with a fine head of black hair and dark eyes. He had on an Oxford-gray single-breasted suit and a white shirt with a rather high, small-tabbed collar and a black knitted tie. His nails had been done professionally but, with it all, his thin face was strong.

"This is Vito," Doc said, introducing Freddie Thomas and me. "Vito's an old friend."

"Always. Excuse me, gentlemen," Vito said, and he stepped around us and turned the lock on the door. Then he took a white card from a shelf in the check room and hung it against the door.

"So we won't be disturbed," he said to me. "We are closed at this time, but I keep the chef and the waiter on for Eddie and Doc."

"I'm sorry," Doc said.

"For what? They are delighted. They love Eddie."

There were about fifteen tables in the room, and he led us to one back near the small bar. He held the chair for Eddie.

"We always come here before a fight in New York," Doc said to me. "Vito's a good man. He takes good care of us. Picks out the best steaks, the best vegetables. He goes every morning to the market himself. You'd be surprised what time he gets up."

"Four o'clock," Vito said, nodding. "You have to, if you want to get the best."

"You see?" Doc said. "Every morning, six days a week."

"I know Doc for years," Vito said, smiling on Doc. "Since he managed my brother."

"You managed his brother?" I said.

"Sure. Joey Napp."

"I knew him. The featherweight. He was your brother?"

"Napoletano. Doc changed the name."

"He was a pretty good little fighter," I said.

"Only pretty good," Vito said, "but he liked to fight."

"He wasn't bad," Doc said. "He was a game, honest kid."

"He was older than me, so I was young and thought he was great. He would like, though, to have been the fighter that Eddie is."

"Thanks, Vito," Eddie said, smiling.

"I wish he could be here for tonight."

"Where is he?" I said.

"In Italy. He was in the Army there during the war and found a girl and went back. Her father owned a little restaurant in Naples, so it's the same thing there as here. Do all you gentlemen want what Eddie gets, or shall I bring the menu?"

"Frank?"

"Let's have the same as Eddie."

"That's all right with me," Freddie Thomas said.

"Then Dino and the waiter want to say hello to Eddie. Then we will leave you alone."

"That's all right."

Dino came out smiling, in his white apron and white chef's hat. He couldn't have been much over five feet tall, and I made him to be about sixty years old. The waiter was about the same age but, of course, taller, and he had on a white mess jacket and tuxedo trousers.

"So, tonight you champion?" Dino said, shaking Eddie's hand and nodding and smiling.

"I hope, Dino."

"What, you hope? You know. You eat what Dino prepare, you become champion. Be sure."

"Then we'll all become champions," Freddie Thomas said.

"That's right," Dino said, nodding and smiling at Freddie. "Eddie to be the champion tonight."

"Dino's hero was Carnera," Doc said to me.

"That's right," Dino said, nodding. "A good fighter. Never mind what they have say."

"Well, he wasn't quite the bum they've made him out since," Doc said.

"That's right," Dino said. "The champion of the world."

"How about Enzo Fiermonte?" Doc said to him.

"Too bad," Dino said. "Could be good."

"All you have to do to be a good fighter with Dino," Doc said, "is get off the boat from Italy."

"Good fighters," Dino said, nodding. "All Italian."

"So they eat now," Vito said, clapping his hands once. "Do you want something to drink, Doc, or Mr. Hughes or Mr. Thomas? Something before you eat, or wine with the meal?"

"Not me," Doc said. "Frank?"

"No. We'll play it clean, like Eddie."

We had small bowls of minestrone and then went right into the steak and broccoli and green beans. They were good-sized steaks and Doc and I quit on ours about halfway through but Freddie Thomas finished his and I watched Eddie eating well until there was just one good piece of meat left.

"Don't force yourself," Doc said. "If you feel it's enough, it's enough."

"It was good," Eddie said, "but that's all I can take."

They brought Eddie his tea, then, and the rest of us had coffee. While we were having that, Vito came back, with three menus and a ballpoint pen.

"So, how did it taste?"

"Fine," Eddie said. "Just as good as ever, Vito."

"So, then. Would you sign these menus, one for me and one for Dino and one for the waiter?"

"Sure."

Eddie inscribed a message and then his name on two of the menus. Vito stood over him, watching him write.

"I'm sorry, but I don't remember the waiter's name."

"Joe. Believe me, after the fight tonight I'll be showing this around the bar. Maybe, if you feel like it, you'll stop in."

"I can't, Vito. We're having a blowout in my old neighborhood. My old gang."

"I understand. Maybe next week you'll stop in for dinner, and you will bring your wife."

"Fine."

Dino, small and smiling, was standing by the door to the kitchen. The waiter was with him, smiling too, and Dino called something and Eddie waved back and then Vito wished Eddie luck and invited us all to come in again and we climbed the two steps to the sidewalk.

"How does the little guy ever look into what he's cooking?" I said to Doc.

"You'd be surprised. You should have gone back there. They've got a long step that runs along in front of the stoves and another one in front of the table. He steps up on that. He's a good chef."

We walked back to the front of the hotel and the doorman smiled and nodded to Eddie. Doc said he wanted to get the papers and rest, so Freddie Thomas and I walked with Eddie. We must have walked almost two miles, over to Park Avenue and along there, stopping to look at the foreign sports cars in the two showrooms. The streets were in shadow now, but the tops of the tallest of the far buildings were orange in the late sun and against the blue sky, and when we got back to the room Doc was lying on the bed, his coat off, the papers strewn around him.

"Your wife called," he said to Eddie, getting up.

"She did. What'd she say?"

"Nothing."

"She want me to call her back?"

"If it's not too much trouble."

Eddie went to the phone and gave the operator the number and sat down on the bed. I was trying to think of conversation to make.

"What are you people going to do now?" I said to Doc and Freddie.

"I have to meet a couple of guys at the Garden and give them their tickets," Doc said.

"I've got to meet somebody at the Garden, too," Freddie Thomas said. "Is that all right with you, Doc?"

"He'll take his nap now," Doc said, nodding at Eddie, who was speaking into the phone. "You don't have to be with him."

"All right," Eddie was saying into the phone. "Okay."

He put the phone back in its cradle and turned toward us, still sitting on the bed.

"She wants to go tonight. She wants two tickets."

"Great," Doc said. "Why didn't she wait to call at eight o'clock?"

"I can't help it," Eddie said.

"This is great," Doc said.

"All right, Doc," I said. "Let's just get the tickets for her."

Doc didn't say anything.

"She wants them left at one of the windows at the Garden?" I said to Eddie.

"I don't know. I'd be worried about that. With all the confusion something might go wrong and she might get shut out. I'd be wondering if she got in or not."

"This beats me," Doc said.

"Look," I said. "I'll grab a cab and take a couple of tickets up to her."

"Don't be silly," Doc said.

"I'm not doing a thing for the next couple of hours," I said to Doc. "Have you got a couple with you?"

"I've got these two promised."

"So you'll give me those and go over to the Garden and get two more. All right?"

Doc reached into the inside pocket of his coat, that was still lying on the bed, and took out his wallet. He handed me two tickets and then reached into a pants pocket and came out with a ten-dollar bill.

"For the cab."

"Don't be silly."

"You try to take your nap," he said to Eddie.

"All right, but I want to look at the papers awhile."

"You're sure you don't want me with him?" Freddie Thomas said to Doc.

"He'd rather be alone," Doc said.

Doc had his coat on now, and he and Freddie were at the door.

"I'll see you down in the bar in about an hour and a half?" I said to Doc.

"All right," he said, and they went out.

"Thanks, Frank," Eddie said.

"I'm glad to do it."

"I don't know why she decided to come tonight. She hasn't been to a fight in years. She's coming with a girl friend of hers."

"Good."

"I'll call her and tell her you're bringing the tickets up."

He gave the operator the number and I went into the bathroom. When I came out he had taken his jacket off and had slipped out of his loafers and he was trying to straighten out the three afternoon newspapers jumbled on the bed and on the floor.

"She has to go out for an hour," he said, "so you can wait a half hour."

"Fine."

He was still trying to sort the papers.

"That Doc," he said. "I like to read a neat paper. When I read it, I keep it neat."

"That's your Teutonic heritage."

"What?"

"Neatness."

"Doc is so exact about everything you do in fighting, but he throws the papers around."

"It might be in contempt."

He took one paper and turned to the sports section and lay down on the bed. I took one of the others and sat in the chair to read it.

"It says here the other guy is seven to five," Eddie said.

"That's what it says here, too."

When he finished the first paper and put it down I took it and put the one I was reading on the bed beside him. When he finished with the second one I looked at that.

"Well," he said, "your friend Fred Gardner picks me."

"Not because he's my friend."

"That Tom White picks the other guy."

"You had to expect that."

"Ernie Gordon picks the other guy, too."

"He works for Tom White."

"I know. He told me that at the weigh-in, but I think he'd have picked the other guy anyway."

There was a knock at the door. Eddie looked up from the paper.

"See who it is, will you?" he said.

I got up and opened the door part way. Al Penna was standing there, a patch of white bandage and tape bulked over his left eye.

"Hello," he said. "Can I come in?"

"It's Al Penna," I said.

"Sure. Come in, Al."

He walked into the room and looked around. He put his hands in his pockets.

"How are you, Al?" Eddie said, sitting up. "That was a good fight."

"Can I see you a minute, Eddie?"

"Sure."

"I'll get out," I said.

"No," Eddie said, and then to Penna: "You want to see me alone?"

"Yeah."

"Then we'll go in the bathroom," Eddie said.

He stood up and led Penna into the bathroom. Penna turned and closed the door behind them. In less than a minute they came out.

"I'll see you," Penna said, and left without looking toward me.

"What's eating him?" I said.

"This," Eddie said, and he handed me something. As it dropped into my hand I could see it was a ring. Then I turned it and saw that it was a man's gold ring, with a ruby set in it.

"What's this?" I said, and then it came to me. "Was this Jay's?"

"That's right."

"How about that? It was Penna after all."

"That's right. I didn't think he took it, either."

"You know I didn't think so. So what made him bring it back?"

"Who knows?"

I gave the ring back to Eddie, and he looked at it.

"What did he say?"

"I don't know. He said he doesn't know why he did it. He said he was going to hock it, and then bet it on me in the fight. Then he said today he decided to give it back."

"What did you say to all this?"

"I don't know. I said: 'Thanks, Al.' What could I say?"

"Nothing. I think I'll take those tickets up now."

"You know where it is?"

"Sure. I met you there the day we went up to camp."

"That's right. I forgot. Thanks, Frank."

"Forget it."

I told the cabbie what I wanted, and made him feel better by telling him he could wait for me and bring me right back. He stayed off the West Side Highway to avoid the first of the evening exodus and went up through Harlem and across the river into the Bronx and onto North Broadway and worked in off that, so that we made much better time than I had thought we would.

"Just leave it running," I said, when I got out, "because I won't even be going into the house."

There was a light on in the living room, but I had to ring the bell twice before she came to the door. She was wearing gray slacks and a light blue sweater.

"Your tickets, madame," I said, handing them to her.

"Oh, hello," she said. "Thanks. Thanks a lot."

"Don't thank me. I got them from Doc."

"And broke his heart, I'll bet."

"Oh, I wouldn't say that. Anyway, you know I'll be rooting hard for all of you tonight. Eddie'll be fine."

"Thanks," she said.

Well, I thought when I got back in the cab, I tried, anyway. At the hotel I went into the bar and was halfway through a drink when Doc and Freddie Thomas came in. Doc ordered a Scotch,

straight with a water chaser, and Freddie Thomas ordered a
Coke.

"You all straightened out?" I said to Doc.

"Yeah. Tickets make more trouble than the opponent. I'm
sorry you had to get involved with that."

"You were right about Al Penna."

"What about him?"

"He was up to see Eddie, and he gave him Jay's ring back."

"He did?"

"That's right."

"When?"

"Shortly after you two left. I should apologize to my candidate, Cardone."

"How about that no-good SOB."

"What happened?" Freddie Thomas said.

I explained it to him. He kept shaking his head.

"So what did he give it back for?" Doc said. "He'd already
scored."

"Who knows?" I said. "I like to feel that, this day of the fight,
he felt something for Eddie. Penna's a screwball and a brigand,
but when it came up to today he felt something. He found out
he's on your side. That's just my theory, of course."

"Who needs him?" Doc said.

"That's right," Freddie Thomas said. "Some business we're
in."

"Yes, but you're wrong about the business here. If anything, it
led him to give the ring back. That took a little guts."

"Let's have one more drink," Doc said. "I could use another
one."

"If we can sit down, and you'll take yours in the water. I don't
want you drinking it straight."

"I could finish a quart tonight and still be sober," Doc said.

I paid for the drinks at the bar and we went to a small black-
topped table in a corner of the dark room. Doc went out once to

be sure the phone was cut off in Eddie's room, and we nursed that second drink for about forty-five minutes. Then we ordered again, and Freddie Thomas had a second Coke and we nursed those.

"You feel all right?" I said to Doc, finally.

"What do you think? Forty-five years comes down to one night."

"I know. I don't know what I'm doing, getting involved with un-nice people like you and that fighter of yours. Right now I'd like to walk out of here and go to some remote bar and get drunk and not even see the fight. I'd read about it tomorrow."

"Believe me, I would, if I were you."

"I don't believe you."

"For four years I've watched that other guy every time I could. I knew they'd move him into that title. If he can find a way to lick the Pro tonight it just doesn't add. Forty-five years don't add. There has got to come a time in that fight tonight when that other guy will know that there's nothing he can do to win, and when he knows it he'll show it and everybody will know it. That will be the moment."

"It's what the bull fighters call the Moment of Truth," I said.

"They do?"

"There's Eddie now," Freddie Thomas said.

Eddie was standing near the bar. A nicely dressed young man, with a girl, had turned on his bar stool and was holding his hand out to Eddie. Eddie avoided the hand by placing his two hands on the other's shoulders and nodding and saying something. Then he turned and came over to our table and we made room for him and he sat down.

"What's the matter with you?" Doc said.

"Nothing. I rested. I was looking for you guys."

"You sleep any?"

"I don't know. Maybe. I feel all right."

Under the slim, indirect lighting in the dark room I could see heads turning at the bar to look at him. The two bartenders were watching him, too.

"It's about time to go to the Garden, isn't it?" he said.

"What time is it?" Doc said.

"Up there," Eddie said, pointing. "A quarter to eight."

Where he pointed there was a clock on the wall above and behind the bar. It was set flat into the dark wall, just gilded hands and small rectangular markers, like second lieutenant's bars, for the numbers, that part of the wall serving as the face of the clock.

"In a few minutes," Doc said. "We've got time."

"I got the tickets to Helen," I said to Eddie.

"Gee, thanks. I called her again and she said you were there. She put the kid on the phone."

"How is he?"

"Fine. Helen promised him I'd buy him something tomorrow."

"He didn't want you to guess the name of his playmate's cousin?"

"No," Eddie said, smiling. "Thank God he forgot that."

The young man from the bar came over with a postcard for Eddie to sign. Then a woman came over with another card.

"We might as well get out of here," Doc said.

"I'll go up and get the bags," Freddie Thomas said.

Eddie signed two more cards and we walked out into the lobby. Eddie stood at the newsstand, scanning the front-page headlines and looking at the magazine covers until Freddie Thomas came down carrying the two zipper bags.

"Get us a cab," Doc said to the doorman on the sidewalk.

"Right away," he said, walking to the curb and giving a big motion for the cab to pull up from the stand.

"Madison Square Garden," Doc said to the cabbie, and he followed Eddie into the back seat. "Go over to Ninth and come back on Fiftieth Street. We want that entrance."

"Thanks, and good luck, Eddie," the doorman said, closing the door.

Freddie Thomas and I were on the jump seats. At the corner the driver had to stop for the light.

"You fellas going to the fight?" he said.

"Yes," I said.

"I hope it's a good one," he said. "Some of them they had lately have been lousy."

25

When we stepped out of the cab onto the curb I could feel the surface tension that held the crowd. Invisible, untouchable, nowhere but everywhere, fragile but all-imprisoning, I have felt it hold an infantry company before an attack, the witnesses before an execution, a courtroom before a verdict, a family before the moment of death. Now it held this crowd, the moving bodies milling on the sidewalk and the still bodies and the turning faces, black and white, in the balcony line. It held the mounted cop and horse walking the gutter and confined the low murmur, rent only by the police whistles and the car horns, that is distinctive of fight mobs. Inside the Garden and within two hours, a little more or a little less, something would happen and then this thinnest unseen film of oneness would burst and it would all come out.

"There's Eddie Brown!" . . . "Hey, Eddie!" . . . "Eddie Brown!" . . . "Eddie Brown!" . . . "Get him, Eddie!" . . . "Good luck, Eddie!" . . . "Eddie Brown!"

We pushed through quickly, Doc and Freddie Thomas leading the way, Eddie with his head down, the crowd parting and calling. Ahead of us the ticket taker signaled and a man stepped quickly aside to let us by. Then another shook his finger at Eddie, and called after him.

"Hey, Eddie! I got all my dough goin' on you! Remember that, Eddie!"

In the molecular movement of the crowded lobby a path opened, some of them calling, and then we were out of it, walking the long gray catacomb and up the step into the dressing room at the Ninth Avenue end. Behind us the uniformed guard closed the door.

This is the place, I was thinking, the gray walls and the steel lockers, the rubbing table in the middle of the rectangular room, the benches against the walls. There it is, the door to the toilet and the shower, and that is all.

"They keep it plenty warm in here," Eddie said, looking around.

"Good," Doc said. "Take off your coat."

"Here, I'll take it," Freddie Thomas said.

"Doc!" the uniformed guard said, his head through the partially opened door. "Somebody out here."

Doc went to the door and looked out. The door opened and Louie came in, in a dark blue suit and forcing a smile.

"How are you, kid?" he said, walking up to Eddie.

"Fine," Eddie said. He was sitting on one of the benches. "Good. I thought you'd come up to the hotel."

"I couldn't. My old lady's sick, so when I got away from the place I went over to see her. I'd rather see you here, anyway."

"Good."

"Some difference from the first fight I put you in, hey?" Louie said, looking around and saying it to the room and then sitting down next to Eddie.

"That's right," Eddie said. "Remember that night?"

"The whole mob's here. They all send their best."

"Thanks, Louie. Tell them thanks."

"So we'll be in after the fight, and we'll all go over together, hey?"

"Good."

"You're all invited," Louie said to the rest of us. "A real blowout."

"Thanks, Louie," I said.

"So I better go," he said, standing up and then looking down at Eddie and slapping him once on the shoulder. "Good luck, champ."

"Thanks."

"We're all with you, and we're not worried, either. You'll lick him."

"I'll see you, Louie," Eddie said, looking up at him. "Don't worry."

"Who's worrying?"

Louie went out. Doc was hanging his jacket in one of the lockers and Freddie Thomas was hanging Eddie's robe on a hanger over an open locker door. It was a dark blue satin robe with white collar and cuffs and the name Eddie Brown in white letters on the back. He took two white coat sweaters out of the other bag and then he started placing his gauze and tape on the rubbing table.

"Here," Doc said to Eddie, handing him new white woolen socks and the ring shoes and a pair of long, new white laces. "You might as well start on this."

It is a time-killer that some of them use. Eddie took the old laces out of the shoes and then, slowly and carefully, he started a new lace in one shoe. He flattened the lace at each turn, always measuring the two ends. He did a half-dozen turns, and then put the shoe on the bench beside him and started on the other.

The guard opened the door and the commissioner came in, followed by a tall, smiling man whom the commissioner introduced as the lieutenant governor, and by one of the people from the Garden. Eddie stood up when the commissioner introduced the lieutenant governor to him and then to Doc, the smile never leaving the lieutenant governor's face.

"There's a fine crowd out there, Brown," the commissioner said. "So good luck to you."

"Thank you."

"The best of luck to you," the lieutenant governor said, and he was still smiling when they walked out and he nodded to the guard.

"Politicians," Doc said. "Everything that's wrong in this business you can blame on them. Amateurs."

Eddie sat down again and slipped out of his loafers and took off his socks. Freddie Thomas took them and put them in the locker, and Eddie pulled on the new white woolen socks. Then he put on the left ring shoe and swung around on the bench and put that foot up on it and carefully and slowly laced it. When he reached the top he brought the laces around the back and to the front again, certain that they were flat, and then knotted them. Freddie Thomas bent down and cut the laces near the knot with his gauze and tape scissors and then he cut a length of the one-and-a-half-inch tape and handed it to Eddie. Eddie placed the tape around the shoe near the top so it covered the laces and, in the front, the knot, smoothed it so that it was a neat white band and then put on the right shoe and started on that.

Freddie Thomas' brother came in, carrying the pail with a bottle in it, the bottle freshly taped around the neck. He couldn't have been more than twenty-five or twenty-six years old and he smiled and nodded around the room.

"Hello," Eddie said, looking up.

"Hi, Eddie. Doc."

"Make some strips of that tape, Joey," Freddie said to him.

"Where do you want them?"

"Right along the edge of that table. Make some extras, too."

"What are you doing there?" Doc said, looking down at Eddie.

"It's Jay's ring," Eddie said. He had laced the second shoe up to the last pair of eyelets and now he held the ring up to Doc in the palm of his hand. Doc took it and turned it over and looked at it.

"What are you doing with it?"

"I thought I'd just put it on the lace. It won't be in the way. I just thought I'd carry it for luck."

"Never mind that luck stuff," Doc said, still holding the ring. "You know better than that."

"I know. I just thought of it this afternoon in the room, that Jay was with me for all those fights."

"Put it on if you want to," Doc said, handing the ring back to Eddie and walking away. "I don't care what you do with it."

Eddie looked at me and smiled and shrugged. He put one end of the lace through the ring and then crossed the laces and put the ends through the last two eyelets and finished the shoe. Freddie Thomas cut the ends and handed him another length of tape.

When he finished with the tape he stood up and walked up and down, the shoes squeaking a little. Then he did a couple of deep knee bends, letting his heels come up off the floor, the weight forward on his feet to settle them into the shoes.

"What bout's on now?" he said.

"The second bout was just starting when I came in," Freddie's brother said.

"Memphis Kid?"

"Yeah, I saw him climb in."

"Find out how he makes out, I mean, when it's over, will you?"

"Sure."

Now and then we could hear the crowd noise, distant and low. When Freddie's brother finished stripping the tape and sticking the ends to the side of the rubbing table he went out. In about five minutes he came back.

"Memphis won it. A decision."

"Good," Eddie said, still walking. "A good fight?"

"I don't know. I just saw the last round and a half. Some of the crowd was booing for more action."

"Dreadful," Doc said.

"Get Memphis in your story, will you?" Eddie said to me. "He's a great guy."

"Sure, Eddie."

One of the commission deputies came in. He had a sheet of paper in his hand and on his face was the harassed look all subordinates wear at such times. He nodded around the room.

"When you going to tape?" he said to Doc. "It's about time."

"I'll tape right now," Doc said. "Tell one of the other guy's people to come in."

"I have to stay here."

"I'm going down there to watch," Freddie Thomas said. "I'll tell him."

"And you stay right with them until they've got the gloves on in that ring," Doc said. "We'll see you down there."

"Right. Joey'll get some ice for you later."

"He doesn't have to stay there," the deputy said. "Once the tape is on and stamped and initialed he can come out."

"He can stay, too."

"But why?"

"Because I'm protecting my fighter."

"Have it your way," the deputy said, shrugging to me and sitting down on the bench.

Joey moved the tape and gauze to one side and Eddie boosted himself up onto the rubbing table, his feet dangling. A couple of minutes after Freddie had gone, the champion's man came in, tall and dark, nodding and smiling and big-voiced.

"Mr. Eddie Brown. Gentlemen. Gentlemen. Gentlemen."

Since Robinson and Gainford, I was thinking, they all try to play it the same. They've even got it right down to the voice inflection.

Doc started on the right hand, the clean white gauze around the wrist and down around and around the hand and back between the fingers and around the hand. One roll of gauze and a small piece of tape to hold it, the narrow strips, pinched once in the middle, between the fingers, and then he walked away and opened a locker door and reached for one of the two long strips of tape hanging there.

"Wait a minute," the champion's man said, with that big voice.

"Are you hurting?" Doc said, one hand on one of the strips of tape and turning to look at the champion's man.

"Let the gentleman measure it in front of me."

The deputy took a tape measure from his pocket, pulled it out and measured the first strip. He could see that they were both of the same length.

"Two feet," he said. "Exactly."

"You still hurting?" Doc said.

"I just go by the rule," the champion's man said.

"What do you think I go by?"

"All right, fellas," the deputy said.

Eddie shrugged at me and Doc finished that hand with the tape, Eddie opening and closing the hand, and Doc did the other. When he finished with the second he motioned to Eddie and Eddie held his hands out toward the champion's man and turned them, the white bulks on them beautifully done, palms up and palms down.

"All right with you?" the deputy said.

"All right," the champion's man said.

"So," the deputy said. He had a small ink pad and stamp and he stamped the three lines of blue wording across the tape on the back of each hand. Then he took out a ballpoint pen and wrote his initials under the imprint on each hand.

"So I'll see you gentlemen," the champion's man said, affecting a bow, and then he left.

"The SOB," Doc said. "Dreadful. That's amateur stuff. Get your things off."

Eddie slid off the table and, alternating hands, drove one fist into the palm of the other a couple of times. Then he loosened his belt and dropped his slacks. He sat down on the bench, and

Joey pulled the slacks off and hung them in a locker. Then he helped Eddie out of the maroon shirt, and Eddie got out of his underwear and, walking across the room naked except for the ring shoes and socks and the bandaged hands, he hung those up. Then he walked into the toilet.

When he came out he put on the supporter and Doc handed him the white trunks with black and he put those on. Without the cup under them they seemed too loose, and he started to move around the room, first doing deep knee bends, then rotating his arms and shoulders and then shadowboxing. In the silence of the room, disturbed only by an occasional noise from the crowd, you could hear the squeak of the ring shoes and then Eddie's breathing starting to come in rhythm.

Doc stood to one side, never taking his eyes off Eddie, and Freddie's brother went out and then came back with another pail filled with a couple of chunks of ice. He waited for Eddie to move by, and then he carried it into the toilet and I could hear him cracking it against the washbowl. Then he came out and got the ice bag and went back in.

"How are you these days?" the deputy said, coming over to me.

"Fine. You?"

"I don't know," he said, dropping his voice. "He looks good, don't he?"

"Eddie? Yes."

"You think he'll win?"

"Yes."

"Myself, I should be up at Candlewood Lake right now."

"Why?"

"I got a cottage up there. We like to go up weekends, but how you can do it with the Friday night fights? We have to go up Saturdays now. These people that come here, they pay big money for ringside. I don't get it. I've seen too many fights. No fight is worth it."

Eddie came by us now, his face set, his head down, hooking and then hooking again. Then he turned easily and started back, and I could see a little sweat just starting on his back. I looked at my watch and it was 9:46 and I walked over to where Doc stood, his arms folded in front of him, watching Eddie.

"The sweat looks good," I said. "He looks in perfect shape."

"He's never been far off in seven years," Doc said. "When you come to the last step it shouldn't be any steeper than the rest."

"How do you feel yourself?"

"Lousy."

He motioned to Eddie and Eddie stopped and walked over to him, breathing deeply. Doc took a towel off the rubbing table and wiped Eddie's face quickly and then he wiped Eddie's chest and back and arms and, bending down, his legs. He motioned to the rubbing table where Freddie's brother had spread a couple of fresh white towels. Another was folded at the head, and Eddie boosted himself up and lay down on his back. Doc took still another clean towel and placed it over Eddie's chest, and then he got the robe and spread it over Eddie.

"Give me a towel for over my eyes," Eddie said.

He was lying directly under the ceiling light, his eyes shut, and Doc folded another towel and placed it over Eddie's forehead and eyes. Eddie lay there, the robe moving up and down with his breathing.

"How did you feel?" Doc said.

"A little stiff, in the shoulder and thighs. Not stiff, but not loose."

"That's all right," Doc said.

Eddie lay there for five or six minutes, the breathing quieting. Doc had come over and was sitting on the bench next to me.

"What the hell can I tell him?" he said in a low voice, not really as a question but as a statement of fact.

"Nothing."

"In seven years you tell him everything. He's ready. The last thing I'll remind him in the corner is just don't let that other guy back him up. The first round he'll get his distance, then he'll either do it, or he won't. There's nothing I can do about it now."

"That's right. Just remember that yourself."

We heard the door open and the clang of the ring bell and the crowd.

"Last round of the semifinal!" the guard said, sticking his head in and announcing it. "Main event next!"

Eddie sat up, the robe sliding to his legs, and Doc got up. Eddie slid off the table and Doc wiped him again with a towel. Then he helped Eddie out of the trunks and Eddie went into the bathroom.

"You got everything?" Doc said to Freddie's brother. "All my stuff and Freddie's?"

"I got it."

He had on his white coat sweater and Doc went to the locker and put on his and buttoned it. Eddie came out and Freddie's brother handed him his cup and Eddie stepped into it and pulled it up. Then Doc helped him into the trunks and he moved around, swinging his head on that fine neck and rotating his shoulders, until he saw Doc holding the robe and he put his arms back and Doc lifted the robe up onto him and, walking around him, tied it in the front.

"All right! Main event! Eddie Brown!" the guard said, holding the door open, and we could hear the rising expectant mumble of the crowd.

"That's us," the deputy said.

"The best, Eddie," I said as he went by.

"Thanks, Frank," he said, looking at me quickly, his face very serious.

I followed them out and down the aisle behind the cop, the crowd noise high now and the cries for Eddie, and when they passed my seat I took one more look at Doc's back and climbed over the back of the seat. Tom White was sitting on my left.

"Hello," he said. "How are you?"

"Fine. You?"

"All right. I suppose you still like your guy to win."

"That's right."

"I don't."

"I read your piece today."

"I think he'll get licked good."

The crowd was still noisy for Eddie when the champion came into the ring to our left, vaulting the held middle rope with a flourish, his head towel-hooded and his robe flying, then his arms out to the crowd, the noise swelling then for him. One of the deputies was bringing the gloves to Eddie's corner to our right and I saw Doc, leaning on the rope and squinting through those rimless glasses at the other guy. Then he was bending over Eddie, who was on the stool, and then Eddie was standing up and putting his weight down into one glove, as Doc held it, and then the other. Then he sat down for the lacing.

"You see that?" Tom White said. "Look what he's got there on his shoe."

"What are you talking about?"

"A ring. He's got a ring on the lace of his right shoe."

"I know."

"He doesn't even trust that great Doc Carroll with his jewelry while he's in the ring."

"I was there when he put it on. Do you want to know what it's about?"

"Don't tell me. You can have your Doc if you want him. I don't have to buy him."

It will be enough if you knock him out, Eddie, I was thinking, but it will be more if you can pull it off the way Doc said and drop him face to face with Tom White. I know it's impossible, but do it.

"—and a former middleweight champion of the world!" Johnny Addie was announcing.

By the time they were through with the introductions the gloves were on. I saw Freddie Thomas leave the other corner and walk across to Eddie's. Now he was on one knee in front of

Eddie and Eddie had first one foot up and then the other and Freddie was scarring the soles of the shoes with the points of his scissors. Then the lights went out and we stood forever and I watched Eddie standing forever in the semi-darkness while Gladys Goodding played it with that glissade introduction on the organ and Bill Ferrell sang the "Star-Spangled Banner."

"Fifteen rounds for the middleweight championship of the world. In this corner, wearing white trunks with black stripes, from New York City, weighing one-hundred-fifty-nine and three-quarter pounds, Eddie Brown!"

". . . and weighing one-hundred-fifty-eight and a half pounds, the middleweight champion of the world . . ."

The referee was making his little speech for television now, and then they touched gloves and turned and Freddie Thomas slid the robe off Eddie's shoulders as they walked back to the corner and Doc had one leg outside the ropes and one still inside them and you could hardly hear the buzzer above the crowd. Doc was slipping the mouthpiece into Eddie's mouth, saying one last thing, shouting it at Eddie to be heard in the noise, and Eddie's face was stony, looking across at the other guy, and then the bell rang and Doc slapped Eddie on the back and Eddie walked out of that corner.

26

It was all over in one minute and forty-eight seconds.

Eddie walked out slowly, hands low, the gloves poised and rotating slightly, his head down and looking at the other out of the tops of his eyes, and he was beautiful. He never wasted a motion and the champion met him in mid-ring, high on his toes, head-feinting, hand feinting, the feints ignored, and then snapping out the jab once, twice.

The first one Eddie took high on his forehead and the second one he slipped over his right shoulder and, in the same move, he brought his own jab up and in. It reached the champion, perfectly placed, between the eyes, but the champion was moving away, jabbing twice, lithe, still high on his toes, Eddie following him and taking the jabs high, and then, as the champion hooked behind the next jab, Eddie slipped under it and threw his own hook, hard from the low-hand position, to the body.

The champion dropped his right arm across his body and managed to get a piece of it on his elbow. Then, in too close, he reached to tie Eddie up, but Eddie got both hands up inside, high on the champion's chest, and he pushed the champion off.

With this, the crowd noise rose to a quick roar and the champion, now, took his time. He was moving, using the center of the ring. He jabbed twice and, still head-feinting, he faked the move to his left and circled to his right. Eddie made the one step to his own left, and he had the champion in front of him again. The champion faked the move to his left again, feinting the jab, but this time he made the move. For that one part of a moment he had the position on Eddie, but Eddie dropped lower and made the one step to his own right and they were even once more.

I looked at the champion's face and I could see him thinking. Look at this, all of you, I was thinking. See it. Eddie Brown is building beautifully. He is building slowly, perfectly, the firm foundation. Please see this.

The champion put out two jabs, still backing off, the first one short but the second one going in. Eddie stalked him and they exchanged jabs, the champion's snapping out straight, Eddie's coming up and in again. Now the champion was almost in a fencing position, his stance more narrow, with the line of the right foot closer to the line of the left, but suddenly, as Eddie jabbed, the champion stepped to his right with the right foot and threw the right hand over the jab. Eddie turned under it and, as he took the punch back above the ear, he fired his own right return into the body and, as it carried his weight onto the left foot, he came back with everything on a hook to the same place.

This was the moment. Now it came. The punches drove the champion back, and I saw the hurt, bewildered look on his face that they all have in the face of truth, and Eddie threw the overhand right to the head. This was the moment and I heard the roar of the crowd and as suddenly I realized that all the excitement, all the desire so long controlled came out in that right hand, and that Eddie was too far out.

The punch missed. Whether it missed by an eighth of an inch or by slightly more or less does not matter. It missed by Eddie's nine years in it and by Doc's forty-three years and by all of the years all of us have lived. When it missed, it carried all of Eddie's weight to his left foot and now, off balance because, finally and just once, he tried too soon for too much, he started to bring himself back to his right. As he did, the champion, coming off the ropes, that same look on his face, let the right hand go because this was not the place of his choosing or the time, either, and he knew it and he knew of nothing else to do.

The punch hit Eddie while his left foot was off the floor. It hit him on the left temple and he went back on his rump and the back of his head hit the canvas. The crowd was up behind me, with a roar, and he fell right in front of me and of Tom White. He rolled over onto his left side, brought his legs around behind him and raised himself onto his knees, both gloves pressed to the canvas in front of him. He shook his head. He was all right, but he was shaking his head.

The referee was on one knee beside him, his arm dropping. Again Eddie shook his head, snapping it violently. He was all right. He was strong.

". . . four . . . five . . ."

He was getting up now, reaching for the rope just above us. I saw the champion in the neutral corner across the ring, and now Eddie was up and seemed to be searching the ring, the arena in the roar, then shaking his head again. Now the referee was wiping the gloves on his shirt, looking into Eddie's face, and then he stepped back to one side.

In the roar Eddie moved forward, but uncertainly, his hands low again and his head tucked behind the left shoulder, but as the champion moved out to meet him, the right hand cocked, Eddie veered to his own right and started away from him, now strongly but strangely, now searching again. When he did the champion moved around in front of him. Eddie's head was still searching when the champion let the right hand go.

This time Eddie went forward on his face, and I and everyone else knew that it was all over. The referee was kneeling, tolling, and I saw that fine body lying there, writhing, trying to get up, just the very first sweat on it, just the beginning of the quest. There was so much that mind and body could do together, better than all others. Why couldn't it have had its chance?

". . . nine . . . out!"

"I told you," Tom White said, hollering it at me above the cheering and the booing of the crowd. "He's a bum."

Doc was the first one to him, and now the referee was back to him and the doctor was there with Freddie Thomas. They had him sitting up, and now standing up, holding him under the arms. He was trying to shake them off, but they held him, the head still searching, and, when it turned toward me, I saw the stare of a sleep-walker.

"He doesn't even know where he is," Tom White said, above the booing that was stronger now than the cheers for the champion, who was dancing now around the ring, his gloves above his head, his people trying to grab him and pound him.

They walked Eddie to the corner and he sat there a minute, his robe over him, the group around him, the boos still coming from upstairs while Johnny Addie made his announcement and held the champion's hand high for the photographers. Then Freddie Thomas held the middle rope down with one foot and the top rope up with both hands and Doc and the doctor helped Eddie slowly through them. I climbed over the back of my chair and pushed through the crowd and saw Eddie, the robe loosely draped over him, unable to find the first step, stumble. They held him, though, and I pushed behind them through the crowd.

"Hey, Carroll!" someone in the crowd close to them was shouting. "He's a bum! You're both bums!"

27

We stood, almost silently, about two dozen of us, outside the dressing-room door. I saw Louie talking to the uniformed guard and the guard shaking his head, and I saw Frankie and the rest of them from the neighborhood and I scanned their faces and turned away. As I did, Memphis Kid saw me and walked over. He had on that gray suit and a clean white T-shirt under it, and he was carrying his zipper bag.

"Is he all right?" he said and there seemed to me to be even fear in his eyes.

"I don't know. I can't get in right now."

"He was gonna lick him, Mr. Hughes."

"I know."

Memphis dropped his head, and half turned away.

"Are you all right, Memphis?"

He was crying. He took a clean white handkerchief out of his pocket and blew his nose.

"I'm all right."

"Good."

"He was lickin' him, Mr. Hughes."

"He was, Memphis."

"He couldn't lose. That was an accident."

"I know."

"Why do the others always get the luck?"

"I don't know."

"You think he's all right? There was somethin' wrong with him when he got up the first time."

"I think he'll be all right."

"Will you do me a favor?"

"Certainly."

"I can't get in there. I'll wait to hear. When you come out, will you tell me how he is?"

"Sure, Memphis."

"Thank you, Mr. Hughes. I'll wait right over there."

Tom White walked toward me and then stopped and gave me that authoritative, over-the-shoulder motion with his head. I walked over to him.

"The ceiling fell on the plasterer's son," he said. "I told you."

"Yes."

"They're not letting us in?"

"Not yet."

"I'll get in."

He pushed through the crowd around the door. I saw him talking to the guard, and then getting excited, but the guard still stood shielding the door with his body and shaking his head. Then Tom White was pushing back out to me.

"A fine goddamn thing," he said. "I'll fix them. They don't do that to me."

With that the door opened and the doctor came out. He stood on the step, the door slightly ajar behind him, an AP man and a morning paper man and Louie in the front, and three of them trying to look around the doctor and into the room.

"How is he?" someone down front said, and the crowd hushed.

"He'll be all right," the doctor said. "He's still bothered by what I'll call jarred vision. There isn't any exact term for it."

"Any term for what?"

"Jarred vision."

"His eyes are jarred? How do you know his eyes are jarred?"

"I didn't say his eyes are jarred. I said his vision is jarred, and just temporarily."

"What do you mean by that?"

"We don't get this."

"Well, that first punch that hit him, that knocked him down the first time—either that or when his head hit the floor—was the cause. The result is, he's experiencing trouble focusing. Maybe you noticed that when he got up the first time and couldn't regain his direction."

"Is that what was wrong with him?"

"Yes. You very rarely see this, but that's what happened to him. It may be caused by any one or more of three things. The ocular muscles may be out of kilter. The balancing mechanism in his ear may be disturbed. There may be an injury to the brain, cerebral, but I doubt that here."

"Is there any chance he'll be blind?"

"Definitely none."

"Has he got a concussion?"

"Certainly. A slight one. Every fighter who gets knocked out suffers a concussion. He'll be all right."

"But what about his eyes—or the vision?"

"It'll be all right. It'll straighten out."

"How soon?"

"Any time. When he relaxes."

"Is he going to the hospital?"

"No. I think he'll be all right just to go back to his hotel room."

"So let us in, then," Tom White said.

"In a few minutes. Not right now."

"What do you mean, not right now?"

"In a few minutes. All the press will get in."

"What are you doing, giving that Carroll time to come up with an excuse? Send Carroll out here."

"He's with the fighter."

"I don't care who he's with. Send him out here."

"Just be patient," the doctor said. "You'll all get in."

He went back into the room and closed the door and the guard moved back in front of it. The AP man pushed out and past us and ran down the aisle toward ringside.

"A fine goddamn thing," Tom White said, announcing it. "That big phony Carroll. Before the fight they can't get enough publicity. They want you to write about them. Now he doesn't want to talk, but I'll write about him. I'll write plenty."

"Why don't you shut up?" someone said.

It was Frankie, from Eddie's old neighborhood. He was looking right at White.

"What?"

"You make too much noise. Why don't you shut up?"

"Take it easy, Frankie," I said.

"I don't care about this bum," Frankie said. "Who does he think he is, with that stinking column? Just keep your mouth shut around here, mister."

Tom White turned his back on Frankie. He took out a cigarette and lit it.

"You going out to Ebbets Field this weekend?" he said to me.

"No."

"The Braves are in town."

"I know it."

"Sure he's a yella bum," I could hear Frankie saying to someone.

"I'm not going to be stood up out here any longer," Tom White said to me. "For what?"

He walked off. The AP man came back, Ernie Gordon with him. I saw Charley Keener, with Cardone trailing him, hurrying toward us, calling to Gordon, but when he saw me he stopped.

"Too bad about Eddie," he said.

"Yes."

"I didn't think it would be like that. Something must have happened to him."

"Something did."

"What did you think of Vic last Friday?"

"He was all right. You were all right, Vic."

"Thanks," Cardone said, nodding to me.

"It's like I told you. He'll be the next welterweight champion. You want to do that article about him, you let me know. All right?"

"All right."

He took Cardone by one arm and he was trying to get through the crowd to Ernie Gordon when I saw Helen. She was standing at the edge of the crowd, with another woman of about the same age, and she was wearing a long, loose red coat, open, and I could see a black dress under it, and they were both watching the door.

"Helen," I said, when I had walked up to her, "I'm sorry."

She had just turned to look at me when the door opened and the crowd quieted and we saw the doctor come out. The crowd pushed forward.

"Only the press," the doctor said. "Just the newspapermen."

"Show your stubs," the uniformed guard was saying.

"You want to get in, don't you?" I said to Helen.

"Yes, but I don't suppose they'll let me."

"Follow me."

"Will you wait for me?" she said to her friend.

"Certainly," her friend said. "Of course."

We pushed through the crowd, the guard weeding the others out, a photographer, his camera held high, ahead of me, Helen being pushed against my back. When we got to the door I showed my ticket stub and moved aside to let Helen in ahead of me.

"Just the press, lady," the guard said, putting his arm across the door in front of her.

"This is Eddie Brown's wife," I said.

"I'm sorry," the guard said, shaking his head, his arm still there. "Just the press."

"Look. This is Eddie Brown's wife."

"You heard me, Mac. I got my orders. Just the press. I'm sorry."

I turned back to say something to Helen but she had turned and was pushing back out through the crowd. Another photographer was trying to get by me, now, and I turned and almost stumbled over the step and I was in.

Eddie was sitting on the bench, naked and with just a towel across his lap, his head down. Doc was sitting on one side of him and Freddie Thomas was on the other, and when Doc saw me he got up and pushed through them. It was hot in the room.

"How is he?" I said.

"He'll be all right."

Doc looked like he did the night he came back from Jay's funeral.

"How about you?"

"All right. He tried for too much too early."

"I know," I said.

"He keeps doing what he's doing he's got to win it."

"Certainly," I said. "He had the guy stopped all along the line. Then he hit him those two punches in the belly and proved it to him."

"Even that punch that toppled him, that was nothing. The guy threw it out of desperation. He shook that off, but why does that have to happen to his eyes? He couldn't focus. He still can't."

"It has to happen," I said, "because it's the only way you can lose. Don't ask me why you have to lose, but you do."

"I guess we do."

"The shame is that we all lose, Doc, including that champion who right now is being slapped on the back and told again that he's a great champion. For a second there Eddie made him an honest man, but now he'll believe this because the honest winners are so few. Everybody in this place lost tonight, Doc, but they don't know it."

I have just said it all, I was thinking. I—

"What's the use of talking about it?" Doc said. "I want to get back to him."

Doc pushed through and sat down next to Eddie again. The reporters were clustered in front of Eddie, the two in front on their knees, the two photographers taking turns up on the rubbing table and shooting their pictures over the heads of the reporters.

"He still can't focus," Doctor Martin was saying, standing amid the reporters. "We call it past-pointing, but he'll come out of it."

"But he doesn't know where he is," one of the reporters kneeling in front said, looking back over his shoulder at the doctor. It was Ernie Gordon.

"Let me get in there," the doctor said.

The two in front shifted apart and the doctor knelt down between them and directly in front of Eddie.

"Eddie?" he said. "Look at me."

"Huh?" Eddie said.

He raised his head and stared with those blue eyes through the doctor. His hair was wet and so was his face, a red welt beside his left eye, and there was moisture on his body.

"Eddie?" the doctor said. "Who am I?"

It was quiet now in the room, just the flashing of a photographer's bulb.

"Huh?"

"We can't hear in the back, here!" somebody shouted.

"Quiet," somebody else said.

"You know me, Eddie. Who am I?"

"Johnny," Eddie said, staring through the doctor. Then he dropped his head again.

"Johnny?" Ernie Gordon said. "Johnny who?"

"Look at me, Eddie," the doctor said. "Who am I? I'm a doctor. You saw me today. Doctor who?"

"Huh?"

"He wants to stand up," the doctor said. "Let him stand up. He's all right, except for the eyes."

Eddie stood up slowly, Doc and Freddie Thomas supporting him. As he did the towel started slipping from his lap but, still staring ahead, he reached down and caught it.

"Eddie?" the doctor said.

Eddie turned slowly. He held the towel out in his left hand and turned slowly to his left. Freddie Thomas backed away and Eddie, staring, placed the towel carefully against the side of the end locker, as if he were hanging it up, and then let it go. It dropped to the floor, but he didn't see it and he turned back slowly and they helped him to sit down again.

"You see he can't focus," the doctor said, still kneeling. "This happens sometimes. I've seen it once or twice before. That's why he walked the way he did when he got up the first time."

"Who am I, Eddie?" Ernie Gordon, kneeling, was saying. "You know me."

"Huh?"

"Who am I?"

Eddie stared at Ernie Gordon. He stared directly into his face. "Huh?"

"What's my name? You know me."

"Johnny," Eddie said, staring at him.

"Why is he saying 'Johnny'?" someone said.

"Look, Eddie," the doctor said. "Where are you? Do you know where you are?"

"Got to go," Eddie said, starting to get up.

"No, stay there," the doctor said, and Doc and Freddie held Eddie. "Where are you?"

"Got to go."

"Go. Go where? Go where, Eddie?"

"Go? Go to the Garden. Fight."

"You have to go to the Garden, Eddie? Where are you now?"

"Time," Eddie said.

"Time? What time?"

"Time," Eddie said, and then he pointed, staring. He pointed over the heads of the kneeling and standing. He pointed with his right arm, his hand wavering a little. As he did we all turned in the hot, silent room, and looked where he was pointing, high on the opposite wall.

There was no clock on the wall. There was nothing on the wall. The wall was bare.

It was late winter and the wind was blowing off the Palisades and across the Hudson, gusty and raw and cutting through the last light of the day. It was recongealing the gray-brown slush in the gutters and embroidering the dampness to the sidewalk, and I was glad to get inside and out of it.

I walked across the lobby and picked up my mail at the table. Old Jules was sitting on his chair by the elevator.

"Good afternoon, Mr. Hughes," he said, getting up and following me into the elevator. "Gettin' cold out again?"

"Yes, it is, Jules."

I was sorting through the mail, a couple of letters and some bills. Jules closed the gate and then the door.

"A man come to see you this afternoon, Mr. Hughes."

"Oh?"

"Yes, sir, and right now I don't think of his name. He come here only about a half hour ago and he tell me to tell you. I make a mental notation, and right this moment I don't think of his name."

"That's all right, Jules. If he wants me he'll call me or come back again."

"The man, he had one of them odd names."

"What did he look like?"

"Well, he look like a workin' man."

"We're all working men, Jules."

"I mean this man, he look like he work outdoors, like on some building or something, the clothes he wears."

"Oh?"

The elevator had stopped and Jules opened the door. He was starting to slide the gate back.

"Now I think of it," he said, suddenly. "All of a sudden I think of it now. He say his name was Eddie Brown. He say tell Mr. Hughes that Eddie Brown come by to say hello."

"Why, sure," I said. "Eddie Brown."

Jules held the gate back and I got off.

"Jules?"

"Yes, sir?"

"You said he had an odd name?"

"That's right, Mr. Hughes. I remember it seem to me to be one of them odd names, like Jones and Smith and Brown."